MESSAGE FROM PANAMA

By

BRITT VASARHELYI

MESSAGE FROM PANAMA
Copyright © Britt Vasarhelyi 2012

Hanging Moon Press

Published by Hanging Moon Press 2012

Printed in the United States of America
ISBN 978-0-9883985-0-4

For more information, visit
www.DontShootTheWriter.com
Layout by Cheryl Perez, www.yourepublished.com

For Laci, Julie, Charlie, and Cece,

with love and thanks.

You know what you have done.

And to Cat for being there.

PROLOGUE

Death turned its sights on me Tuesday morning. With bougainvillea high-stepping in a hot, salty breeze and the effervescent noises of mankind surrounding me, dying was the last thing on my mind.

There were no white lights or tunnels. My life didn't unfold like a newsreel before my eyes. Death simply seemed determined to claim me.

I was in Panama, on a trip as enigmatic as the country, summoned by my Uncle Henry—literally from the grave. The way things were going, I could ask him about it any second.

CHAPTER 1

My hotel room looked out onto the sweeping mosaic of Panama Bay, its glistening veneer dancing between the colors of water and sky. At one end was a cluster of apartment buildings and hotels, at the opposite, the colonial section of Panama City. Between the two, skyscrapers were strung like fancy jewels in every shape, color, and design. It was an improbable city that sat in the middle of a third-world country, yet gave off the first-world vibes of New York and Miami.

Worthy of a walk to see more.

Behind me lay 9,000 brilliant miles of Pacific Ocean. Ahead, the crown of the Majestic Casino. I'd never gambled in the morning. With an hour to kill before the meeting, it seemed like a good time.

I pointed myself toward the sparkling casino lights, ambled down a few blocks, and entered a crosswalk. $100, I decided, I'd cap my losses at that. I patted my pocket to be sure I had my wallet, took a step forward, and a blinding shock of pain erupted above my left knee. My leg crumpled and I hit the ground, arms sprawled forward.

Before I could move, an SUV shot almost close enough to make my fingers part of the pavement.

There was an ominous rumble and I lifted my head to stare into a pair of huge red lips, coarse strands of yellow hair, a giant whore's face hurtling in my direction.

Death was reaching for me when other hands grabbed my torso and spun me to the side. A devilishly painted bus with the woman's image screamed past in the space I'd just occupied. The monster poured on the gas, puffed smoke in my face, and stormed down the street.

I was still on the ground, vaguely aware of a gathering crowd. My rescuer was on his knees, his heavily slanted eyes bouncing between expressions of horror and disbelief.

Neither of us moved.

"We need to get out of the street," I finally said. I cocked my head at the closest place with chairs, an outdoor café a hundred miles and an acre of stairs away.

"You're right…a minute…I'll get help." The words were in my mother tongue but the voice wavered. The savior was clearly as unnerved as the saved.

He stood up and spoke to the crowd. Two men in shirt-sleeves stepped forward to help all 6'1" of me hobble away. My rescuer followed, carefully brushing the street off his suit.

It took an hour of pain to reach the café, but only two or three minutes in clock-time. I sagged into a chair, fumbled in my pocket, and fished out two twenties from my wallet. The helpers and I exchanged outpourings of *gracias* and my rescuer dismissed them.

Sucking breaths still fueled by adrenalin, we regarded each other. I waved him to a chair.

"Pen Smith." I held out my hand. "Thanks." I inhaled deeply. "A lot."

"Enriqué Soong, glad I could help." By his looks, he was Chinese, by his Spanish, Panamanian. Then there was his excellent English. The long reach, I assumed, of world-class canal-building.

A waitress appeared and uttered something like "Dig me."

"French," I said to Soong, shrugging. "Eight worthless years."

The corners of his mouth turned up. *"Dígame.* She wants our order."

"Brandy," I told the waitress in a pretty good imitation of a gasp. I held up three fingers. "Triple. No ice."

"Café con leche," Soong said, more conventionally.

I surveyed the damage. Ripped trousers, raw skin and lots of dripping red. I snatched a year's worth of napkins from the table and crushed them against the wound. Now that the anesthetic of initial shock was wearing off, my thigh felt like a piece of metal crushed in a burning vise.

Soong pulled out his cell phone and began punching numbers. "Hold on, I'll get the ambulance and police—"

I shook my head. So far, the pain was tolerable. About on par with the time my cousin Val let loose a BB gun on me, thinking it was unloaded. While the doctor picked shot from my butt, I confessed I'd filled the gun with ammunition and forgotten to tell anyone. A BB gun could do a lot of damage in the hands of a maniac like Val and an idiot like me.

"No," I said.

Soong's eyes widened. After a moment, he put down the phone. His index finger beat a quiet tattoo on the table. "All right. You walked away, more or less, and the *Diablo Rojo* is gone."

"The bus?"

Soong nodded. "Red Devils. Deserving of their name, as you saw. Last year, nine people burned to death in a *Diablo Rojo*. But today—" The tapping stopped. He shifted in his chair. "Of course, if another person saw what I did..." His eyebrows rose, disappearing under straight black hair hanging low over his forehead.

I shifted my gaze past him, fixing on an unusually attractive and well-endowed woman at a nearby palm-shaded table. The top of her blouse was unbuttoned and I watched as the breeze blew a flap of wispy material back and forth. Two other tables were occupied, one by a family with several noisy children, another by an elderly man in a *guayabera* shirt reading a newspaper. Behind him, the waitress busied herself underneath a thatched-roof bar. For a moment, I was keenly aware of my surroundings, the air, close and heavy, the waves rolling in, their sound muffled by every big city's hallmark, never-ending traffic. And the backdrop to it all, an ultramodern mall that could have been anywhere.

"Laceration," I finally answered, turning back to Soong. "Inconvenient but no permanent damage."

The way he regarded me said he hadn't made up his mind. Was I out for an innocent walk or was there more to my stroll?

"A bandage will take care of it," I told him. "And the brandy will help."

"You seem to know about these things." This time there was no hiding the question in his voice.

"Iraq." I shrugged. "Patch-ups."

"You were shot. That's why you fell."

It sounded pretty ugly, put like that. I added more napkins and wanted the brandy.

"It's not much of a wound," I said again. "And definitely not worth bothering the police over. They'd keep me tied up all day for no reason."

"No reason?"

"There's no way that bullet was meant for me. I arrived here last night, went to bed, had breakfast in my hotel this morning. You saw the rest."

He regarded me skeptically.

"He was aiming at someone else. Or maybe he fired by mistake."

Soong considered the possibilities.

"Americans have been known to get into trouble here."

"I wouldn't dispute that."

"About a month ago, a woman from Los Angeles was killed. She met two Colombians at a casino and they kidnapped her. For three days, they fed her cocaine and made her withdraw money from the ATMs. When the ATM card dried up, they stabbed her. After she died, they chopped her up, put her remains in a suitcase and set it on fire. People said the dogs smelled it miles away."

From the deep breath he took, I guessed the dogs weren't the only ones.

The waitress materialized with the drinks. I took half the brandy in a swallow and parted with more information. I was from Washington, D.C., I said. A political consultant. Mostly managing the election campaigns of Big Egos looking for Big Jobs. Nothing that would excite anyone in Panama. My little introduction neglected to mention that I was currently out of a job, owing to my most recent candidate's fondness for diddling underage boys. In the Dare, Wisconsin YMCA. Four weeks before the election.

I also told Soong that a local law firm had called me to Panama on family business. I assured him my plans involved no bullets, no Colombians, that I was simply in the country following up on my late uncle's affairs. The only other thing on my radar was to visit a beach or two.

That seemed to settle matters (the eyebrows came down) and we lapsed into silence. Soong spoke first. "All right, amigo, telephone me when you're ready for the beaches and I'll personally make your arrangements."

This time, it was my eyebrows that lifted.

A sheepish smile crossed Soong's face. He handed me a card. "My own firm. Soong and Rivera. Travel agents. Fantastic houses, the best beaches. Other things, too, that might interest you. I hope you'll call me."

I studied the card and promised I would, then asked one of the questions foremost on my mind. How could I thank him for saving my life?

He looked at me and waved his hand. "It was nothing."

"Politeness appreciated," I said. "but we both know otherwise."

"All right then, avoid any more bullets. And narcos. And be careful around casinos." He smiled, but his eyes were serious. "That should take care of it."

"Done," I said, putting out my hand, though dodging narcos and being wary of casinos hardly seemed enough.

We left the table and, without too much trouble, reached the curb, where I tumbled into a taxi. Soong shook my hand through the window. "Call me. Panama has beautiful beaches." The slanted eyes twinkled. "Not to mention beautiful women." He slapped the cab and we took off.

Beautiful women. The image of Maria Ortiz swanned through my mind. Maria, a junior associate at the law firm, had been deputized to be my ride from the airport last night, my escort to today's meeting. I glanced at the time. Forty-five minutes had passed since I left the hotel. Maria was not yet tapping her toe.

A few minutes later, having purchased rudimentary supplies at the lobby shop and explained to the proprietor that the blood and wreckage of my suit were the result of a bad fall, I limped to the haven of my room, peeled off my clothes, and confronted the depressing reality of having been at the wrong end of some unknown villain's gun.

Neither Soong nor I had spoken of it—he might not have known—but a second bullet had slammed into the pavement when I did. The first round had struck me in the thigh. No telling where the other might have lodged if I hadn't fallen.

Fortunately, the wound was a through and through. Unfortunately, that didn't stop the pain. While I cleaned the injury, I gasped and cursed more or less non-stop.

A perfectly good towel gave itself up in the interest of staunching the blood. Another went between my teeth as I applied liberal doses of alcohol, Neosporin, and liquid bandage. When I could breathe again, I slapped on a collage of lobby shop Band-Aids, then wound a couple of handkerchiefs around the wound, and secured them with tape. Makeshift, but satisfactory. Some guys do with less in war.

I cleaned up the gore, rinsed the towels, stuffed my pants into a hotel cleaning bag, and threw that in the trash. I considered whether to postpone the meeting but knew that injuries usually feel worse on the second day. It was probably better to get it over with.

I pulled out fresh clothes and consigned the lobby shop supplies to various pockets. Tentatively, I walked to the door. Later, I'd see a doctor, if needed. For now, I gulped three of the industrial strength pain pills I always pack, made my cautious way back to the lobby, and begged my body not to turn to jelly in front of dozens of strangers.

CHAPTER 2

Punctual to the minute, <u>Rodrigo Fernandez-Chavira</u> swept into the conference room, an entourage bobbing in his wake. I absorbed them like a whale takes in a school of fish, with a single gulp. I was looking for a potential killer. If there was one, he was hidden by the kinetic air of industriousness that sailed in with the group.

<u>Fernandez-Chavira,</u> senior partner of the Fernandez, Chavira, and Villaroel law firm, was the man who resurrected Uncle Henry. Two weeks before, he'd invited me to Panama to discuss "items of interest." Along with his letter were an open-dated first class plane ticket and a handwritten note from my uncle, who'd been dead nearly three months and, by all rights, should have been resting quietly at St. Paul's Cemetery in Alexandria, Virginia.

It turned out my uncle had sunk some roots in Panama. There was a little orchard here I might be interested in. If so, I should enjoy its fruits. The note ran two pages, amazing for a man who'd barely said "Good Morning" when I'd shared a roof with him, even less after I moved out. That accounted for some of the curiosity I had about "items of interest." So did the orchard reference. Was this orchard merely a place where trees grew or was it something else? Uncle Henry had not been a metaphorical man, but I wondered anyway. In the end, I accepted the invitation, not because I was particularly up for puzzles, but because this one had prospects.

And prospects are something I never ignore.

As the group entered, I balanced my leg tenuously and shook hands, making a quick appraisal of my host. His demeanor struck me as cherubic, all dimples, bright cheeks, and conspiratorial smiles. At the same time, he was groomed and dressed like a sophisticate, his dark hair perfectly styled, his nails manicured. I put him somewhere in his fifties, an age he wore with both liveliness and authority. He also spoke highbrow, U.S. educated English.

We exchanged pleasantries, took seats around a conference table, and got down to business.

"Henry Champion was a client of our firm for almost five years," Fernandez-Chavira said. "He was a good friend and a fine man. We were very sorry to lose him."

I saw heads around the table nodding. I nodded back, acknowledging the sentiment.

"For most of that time, as you'd imagine, our work was legal in nature. Employment contracts, real estate matters— that sort of thing. Then about six months ago our relationship changed. Mr. Champion got sick, he knew he was dying, and he asked us to take a more active role in his affairs." Fernandez-Chavira paused. "How much do you know about your uncle's activities in Panama?"

"Nothing," I answered truthfully. Uncle Henry and I had been out of touch for a while and I wouldn't have known he'd died if cousin Val hadn't tracked me down on the campaign trail. Although my uncle had left me his house, life insurance, and a small portfolio, none of those had anything to do with Panama.

"Then we'll take it one step at a time," the lawyer said. He tapped a thin leather folder sitting on the table before him. "The first thing for you to know is that your uncle supervised his interests largely by himself. He had a small office with a secretary—" He nodded toward a woman at the back of the room. "—an accounting firm that handled his bookkeeping—" Another nod to a thin, middle-aged man. "And he kept our firm on retainer for legal work. Occasionally, he hired someone else for a specific purpose."

Inwardly, I sighed. By my count, that was barely enough to run a gas station. Then again, a gas station didn't square with so many people—I counted nine—in the room.

"Since his death, we've been overseeing all the enterprises he had, more or less as temporary business managers. This isn't unheard of but it's a rather unusual arrangement for our firm. Everyone here is currently involved with some aspect of your uncle's concerns."

I glanced around the table. Maria Ortiz, my driver, was one of three women. With big eyes and knockout cheekbones, her face would have been lovely with a smile. Unfortunately, I was still waiting for one. A couple of middle-aged guys I pegged as attorneys, and maybe a youngish bearded fellow. There was a shriveled-up type with a blazing white shirt and unhealthy, almost jaundiced skin. Paper pusher, I figured, as were probably the rest of the people in the room. Still in all, a fairly hefty contingent for Uncle Henry's orchard-cum-gas-station.

Fernandez-Chavira said, "Of course, acting as executor is currently our main interest."

I sat up a little straighter. Executors handle money. Money goes to heirs. Gas station or not and anticipated or not, it looked as though something significant was coming my way.

"In Panama," the lawyer said, "we do things somewhat differently than in the States. That's what we'd like to talk to you about."

"I'm all yours," I answered cheerfully, the pain in my leg suddenly a thing of the past. I could have added, "Just tell me the amount, write me a check, I'm outta here." I actually considered this for a second but decided it would be bad manners. "It sounds interesting," I said instead.

"Good. Then before we begin, let me introduce…" When he finished, I realized I had under-rated the group. All were lawyers except for the accountant, the secretary, and one administrator, a beautifully dressed older woman who liked pearls and smiled at me a lot.

After the introductions, coffee appeared, hot and fragrant.

I drank and complimented the bean.

"It's from my own farm," Fernandez-Chavira said, obviously pleased. "The variety is called 'Renacimiento.' Renaissance in English. Your uncle was also interested in coffee, among other things. And he didn't mention this to you?" Incongruously blue eyes in a thoughtful brown face fixed mine.

"My uncle," I said, "—to be legally correct, also my step-father—and I more or less went our separate ways after I finished college. We really didn't keep up with each other very well. What you've said to me is a revelation." I drank some coffee. "Even if he'd wanted to talk about these things, for the last year I've been buried in work. I spend a lot of time outside Washington. It can be tough to reach me."

"Yes. The elections. Henry told me about them."

He did? As far as I could recall, Uncle Henry never showed a flea's worth of interest in my occupation.

Fernandez-Chavira bent toward me. "You, Penfield Smith," he said, sotto voce, "are an important man in Washington."

I nearly laughed. This was coming from an Uncle Henry I didn't know. "Important is hardly the correct description," I answered wryly. "My life at the moment is—" I searched for the right words. Screwed up? Fucked over? Done in by a sick sonofabitch pedophile? I settled for "complicated."

Fernandez-Chavira made a moue with his mouth and nodded his understanding. Maybe he read the Washington Post. Maybe he saw it on the internet. Kinky sex and politics. Always news.

"To understand our role, you have to first understand your uncle. He was in Panama for just five years, and some of that time he spent traveling. Even so, he accomplished a great deal. His work had an important impact on our country."

My eyes widened. Whatever I expected, it wasn't this.

"You're dubious?"

I shrugged. "Surprised, maybe."

"I understand. Not everyone can make a major impression that quickly." He sipped some coffee, carefully setting the cup in a delicate saucer. "It's not unusual for wealthy people to know about Panama's opportunities, but few of them have good timing—or vision. Luckily, your uncle had both."

This was not unexpected. At home, Uncle Henry had been a businessman, a successful one, although I'd wondered a bit about that when I saw the size of my modest inheritance. Now I understood where the rest of his money had gone.

Fernandez-Chavira leaned back in his chair and drew his hands together, interlacing his fingers. "Henry Champion was, as Americans say so charmingly, a different animal. He came as a guest, he signed our book of visitors, and he spent time getting to know us. You see, Pen, may I call you Pen? And you call me Rodrigo? Yes? All right, Pen, your uncle had the unusual ability to look into the heart of this country and take action. He provided jobs. He rejuvenated businesses. He helped Panamanians realize their dreams. His work was truly exceptional." The lawyer tapped the folder in front of him. "And quite rewarding."

I tilted my head. I looked at the folder.

Things were becoming interesting.

Three hours later, I left the law offices of Fernandez, Chavira et al, declined a ride from the dour-faced Maria, and instead flagged a taxi. I sat back in the seat and connected with it as though it were an anchor. The top of my head was tingling. My hands were shaking. Inside my breast pocket was a piece of heavy vellum paper, in another pocket a set of keys.

I pulled out the paper. Smoothed its already perfect edges. Re-read every line.

I was holding the passport to a new life, to anything I could ever want. Most people dreamed of reading the words before me. I should have been delirious, moonwalking with joy. Instead, I held the paper as though it were my worst enemy.

Someone had shot me.

Now I knew why.

CHAPTER 3

The taxi threaded through traffic toward the *Punta Paitilla* section, where I'd started my day. We passed the casino, then my hotel. A turn brought us to a hill thick with tropical plantings and handsome apartment buildings. The driver slewed the car into a driveway. On the marquee of the building before me was the name: *Condominio El Paraíso del Pacífico*— Pacific Paradise Condominium.

My destination was the penthouse, where a tiny brown wisp of a woman, middle-aged, heavily wrinkled and swathed in crisp, almost ethereal white, greeted me. She was Rosario, the maid in residence, and to all intents and purposes, the majordomo of my new household. Rodrigo had already explained her arrangement—a small suite next to the kitchen, one afternoon and night off, as well as Sundays. In addition to her, there was another domestic, who came in once a week for the heavy stuff, and a yard man who tended the plantings and ponds on the terrace.

Ponds on the terrace. I had smiled.

The sprite bowed slightly, explained that the hotel had already delivered my luggage and she'd unpacked for me. When she asked if I wanted anything and I declined, she retreated, leaving me more or less alone in Uncle Henry's condominium, now mine, as were apparently all the other "fruits" of his extraordinary orchard.

The apartment had an air of city formality about it, antiques mixing well with modern comforts, a nice collection of paintings on the walls, stunning chandeliers, and a superlative view of the Pacific. There were bedrooms aplenty, an office, a library, various other spaces, and after a while I sprinkled mental holy water on it all, pulled off my jacket and tie, and limped to the enormous wrap-around terrace.

I wanted to contemplate ponds—and a few other things.

CHAPTER 4

I chose a chair that had a great view of the bay, lowered myself, and gingerly stretched the injured leg, a pain control posture I'd more or less successfully adopted throughout the day. The hours at Fernandez-Chavira had nevertheless taken their toll, so I gulped a couple of my magic pills and watched the boats go by while I waited for the pain to subside. I had some critical thinking to do—the kind that could save my life. The last thing I wanted was to be distracted by my injury.

As the minutes at the law firm had rolled by and no one tried to throw me out a window or bash me over the head, I'd almost succeeded in persuading myself the shooting was accidental.

Now, the truth was staring me in the face.

$200 million worth of truth. $200 million in an astonishing conglomerate of property, businesses, and currency, all stashed in foundations that answered to no one but an obscure group of people who served as their trustees. I didn't know who these people were and never would. They were Panama's equivalent of Switzerland's gnomes and numbered accounts. But as of today, I had the use of everything in the foundations. I could run the businesses if I wanted to. I could liquidate the entire portfolio and live on the Riviera for the rest of my life. In short, I could do anything I wanted.

Throughout the day, I'd been trying to put it all into a context I could understand. Unfortunately, the process of shifting my brain from thousands to millions hadn't fully kicked in. I'd figured out that if I were to spend all the capital, it would take me forty years to get rid of it at a rate of $5 million per year. That was a new Lamborghini Murcielago, complete Armani wardrobe, apartment in Monaco, and enough change left over to eat caviar and drink champagne at every meal. Plus buying a yacht or two. Every year.

Put another way, I could purchase my own island, populate it with 100 of my best friends, and give each of them enough money to invest and live on for the rest of their lives.

Those were scenarios that were foreign to me but pleasant to consider. There was another scenario that wasn't. $200 million was a sum that could tempt anyone. Could make a person do something beyond the pale. Could make them aim a long gun at me and pull the trigger.

$200 million just might be my death sentence.

I ran down the list of people I'd met at the law firm. Not only were they the prime suspects, for now at least, they were the only suspects. I started with Rodrigo. He had complete knowledge of Uncle Henry's affairs, access to everything, and presumably the most to gain. His culpability seemed laughable on the surface, although anyone could be over-extended, in need of quick cash, all the normal reasons for theft. But a prominent lawyer gunning me down on a public street? I wasn't buying it.

I had the same reservations about the other people I'd met. Delfina, the willowy receptionist, out of the question. Maria Ortiz, while cool to me, hardly seemed the murderous type. I put her attitude down to resentment at being tapped for babysitting duties. Welcome to the world of machismo. Then there were the others: Alberto, a dead ringer for Che Guevara and the maven of Uncle Henry's hotel and resort interests; Bartolomé, who held sway over residential and commercial property and farms; Marcel, the man with the yellow skin; somebody for computers; another somebody for office equipment and furnishings; and, of course, the lovely lady with pearls, the skinny numbers guy, and the secretary. None gave any semblance of being a cold-blooded assassin. Then again, how does a cold-blooded assassin appear? Like most normal people, I had no idea.

I turned my face to the lowering sun and thought: Too many people as familiar with the ways of their country as I was ignorant. Fortunes were stolen and people murdered all the time in the U.S. Obviously it was no different here. After all, Noriega had banked millions and was said to have thrown an annoying priest out of a cruising helicopter. Maybe I should be glad it was only a bullet my almost-assassin chose to use.

A soft cough sounded and I swiveled my head to see Rosario placing a tray on the table at my elbow.

"Señor Henry tell me one time you are liking this drink?"

Beam on ice. He had it right. Another surprise from my seemingly omniscient and more and more mysterious uncle.

An uncle who amassed a fortune in half the time I spent electing second rate people to first rate jobs. The contrast was stark.

Rosario left the bottle and, by the second pouring, I was considering how a person might go about looting the businesses in the foundations—sixty-three in all. The answer to this was simple. He wouldn't. Uncle Henry's supposed genius notwithstanding, not every investment could be as financially enticing as the next one, nor as amenable to theft. Especially, I thought, chewing on a possibility, if certain managers had set up certain foundations to be plundered.

That triggered a previous train of thought. On the surface, it seemed like a concoction of Hollywood for an entire law firm to collude in ridding itself of a client. So, all right, maybe not the entire firm. Perhaps one or two bad eggs. After all, Rodrigo's large and elegant offices spoke to the firm's solvency, the employees' general well-being, the dependability of Uncle Henry's choice. And Uncle Henry, always the good businessman, would have made sure of that before any contract was signed.

On the other hand, I knew better than to rely on appearances. My world was politics, where a person's exterior means everything, even if the inside is stinking rotten.

I had cut my teeth on the first unwritten rule of politics: Assume Nothing. If I could become the beneficiary of $200 million dollars overnight, an entire law firm certainly could be pickpockets and would-be executioners.

I would do well to remember that.

I stopped musing long enough to eat something, learn that the alarm system was broken, and ask Rosario to order the installation of a new one. I also instructed her to call a locksmith to replace the locks right away.

Then I adjourned to the living room, opened my laptop, pulled out my cell phone, and set to work. I disposed of a few emails, mostly routine, one from a New York Times reporter who was doing a wrap-up piece on Congressman Lawrence's "indiscretion." No thanks, I wrote him back. Lawrence had been indiscreet but that didn't mean I would be. The reporter would write his story about Lawrence's nasty bit of recreation without me.

That done, I was ready to call my cousin Val, real name Valentine, a moniker he detested. He was my all-time best friend, go-to guy, and, yesterday, chauffeur. We'd been on the way to Dulles Airport when he quizzed me about Panama.

"It seems like a strange place for a trip," he'd said. "Especially without a woman." I laughed. Every place was strange to Val unless a member of the opposite sex was with him. "Why not go to Cayman or Vail or someplace fun?" he asked.

There was a gleam in his eyes and the beginning bite of envy in his voice.

"A mention by somebody," I answered vaguely. For some unknown reason, I was reluctant to explain. If it came to anything, then I'd clue him in. "I need a vacation," I told him, "and it sounds different. If I don't like it, I'll go somewhere else."

"Lucky you, able to pop away like that." Val's own job was Deputy Managing Partner of a large Washington accounting firm, heavy on financial benefits but crap for independence. Val spent his days tallying other people's money and his nights frittering away his own on women, a succession sporting the inevitable, expensive, sparkling gifts my favorite cousin inexplicably showered on them. Despite the ample rewards that supported his lifestyle, the job remained his biggest grievance. "You don't have to be in an office all day," he groused. "Really, Pen, it's not *fair*."

"The election is over," I pointed out. "At least for me."

A theatrical sigh rose into the air. "Games," Val said, and downshifted for emphasis.

Allowing for temperamental differences, Val and I were alike in many ways. Both in our mid-thirties, we'd each inherited the gray eyes and ruddy complexion of the male Smiths in our family, though I was dark and he was fair. It never occurred to me to worry about losing my hair, while Val supported a dozen drug companies trying to keep the blond fluff he had left. I topped him by an inch and ten pounds, but at a muscular six feet he was no pushover. We competed in the usual sports. I was more the outdoor explorer but we each liked women—a lot—and sometimes, exasperatingly for me because I didn't give baubles, the same ones.

"Console yourself," I added mildly, "you don't work seven days a week most of the year before an election. Or have the job insecurity I do. You also don't have to kiss bloody ass every time you turn around."

He waved my comment away. "Games," he said again, "not a real job." And there the conversation stuck, as it usually did, in between the corporate man, who hated it but would likely never change, and myself, his antithesis, begrudged for having what was hardly a better deal but would always be one in his eyes. By mutual agreement, we changed the subject.

"When you decide to come back, shoot me an e-mail, I'll pick you up," Val said, as we drew up before the massive slanted windows at Dulles Departures.

"Right."

"Let me know if you find yourself in trouble down there in the jungle."

"I doubt I'll make it to the jungle and I think the politically correct term these days is 'rainforest.'" I grabbed my laptop and suitcase. "By the way, Val, don't forget—"

"Covered," he said. He patted the dashboard of my biggest indulgence, a vintage Jaguar XKE convertible. Robin's egg blue. Original rag top. Mint condition. Val had been in covet mode since I first roared it into my driveway. He was taking care of the car while I was gone.

"Have a good time," Val said.

"Right," I responded and with that, I had turned my back on my favorite cousin and favorite toy and begun my adventure.

I put away my laptop, topped up the Beam, and dialed the familiar number. On the third ring he picked up and immediately launched into a breezy, self-absorbed monologue.

I listened for a moment and, when he took a breath, jumped into the gap.

"Val, listen, I've bumped up against—" Something fucking unbelievable, I started to say, but for some reason settled for "an unexpected situation down here."

"A woman?" he asked. Of course, that would be his first thought.

"No, but things are complicated and I need someone I can trust."

"I've got your back," he said. "Always."

"Good," I answered, "That's exactly what I wanted to hear." After that, it was several minutes before he absorbed what I was saying and in the middle of it, the doorbell rang, and I had to put the phone down and promise to call him back.

"Pen," he panted, "you can't go now. For God's sake, $200 million dollars." I chuckled and promised not to be long, then opened the door to find a man holding an over-sized toolbox. He was thin to the point of ouch.

"Buenos noches, Señor," he said, and after that I was lost in a deluge of Spanish.

"Uhm," I answered in the universal language of confusion. I pointed to the door and jiggled the knob.

Behind me came Rosario's voice, alternately instructing and chiding. She vigorously led the locksmith away to her domain.

I returned to the phone.

Rather than calming down, Val had ratcheted up a notch. He told me he'd made a plane reservation for the next day.

"Great," I said, "but what I need you for is long-term, Val, not a quick trip. You'll need to be on site to sort out all the accounts and get the financial end of this thing pulled together. I'm guessing it'll take a good chunk of time, six months maybe, probably more like a year. Then there'll be the regular management of it."

Val was silent while he evaluated the shock to his cozy little ecosystem. How many times have you said you wanted my life, I thought, my *games*. Now you've got your chance. Let's see what you make of it.

"Take whatever time you need to exit gracefully," I told him. "But when you get here, I want you completely on your game."

"I really—listen, Pen, you know I'd like to help you out. Holy Jesus, $200 million."

"We're not talking employment here," I said. "You'll be an owner. Maybe Uncle Henry managed this by himself with some lawyers and bookkeepers helping him, but I can't. The whole thing needs evaluation, support, and an organization. I'm starting with you."

Val's hesitation disappeared. He'd orchestrate his departure, start working on a replacement, and be down for a short visit as soon as possible. Not tomorrow. Probably Sunday. There'd be a bit of back and forth for a period as all the details were worked out with the firm, but that wouldn't undermine his commitment to the new venture. I could count on him.

While we spoke, I debated whether to tell him about the shooting. I knew the inner Val would be desperately unhappy if he opted out of this new opportunity. I considered that I was doing him a favor by not giving him an excuse to beg off. He would learn the situation here on the ground soon enough, and, if he wanted to go back, the next plane out probably had an open seat. I went back and forth on it for a while, but, eventually came to a decision. For better or worse, Val Smith would be in Panama Sunday night.

The man in the hall had finished up.

Feeling slightly more secure, I limped to the large master bathroom, ultra-modern in design and kitted out for maximum comfort. I was momentarily surprised there were no faucet handles visible. Then I remembered a friend's house at the beach where we spent two delightful days hopping in and out of the Jacuzzi and other interesting spots that had no handles.

I unbound my leg and took a good look. Not too bad, considering. I redressed it with my new supplies.

"SHOWER ON," I said. I listened for the response of flowing water.

Nothing happened.

Shit, I had to teach the damn thing.

I found the control panel. My friend had shown me how her system worked; this one looked the same. There were only a few commands—JACUZZI ON, TOILET FLUSH, SINK ON, etc. The big deal was programming my voice so the contraption would recognize me. After a few tweaks, I tried the shower again.

The water flowed, I turned it scorching hot, and felt the tension in my muscles slacken. I soaped all the strategic places, reached outside the shower for a sip of bourbon, and thought idly about the remote Miss Ortiz. Maybe she was aloof with everyone. Or—a depressing thought—just with men. Even more depressing, maybe just with me.

I toweled off and went in search of clothes, put away neatly in the adjoining master bedroom. Jesus, I thought, as I entered. The space was enormous made even more so by balconies on three sides. I'd feel like a sitting duck in here. I chose another, smaller, bedroom. The size suited me for now as did its manageable balcony. I also gave stars to a sturdy yet maneuverable chest which I used to barricade the door.

It wasn't a day I wanted to reprise, yet as I climbed into bed and tried to relax in my self-made prison, I had to smile ruefully at the karma of the situation. Inherit a fortune, nearly lose your life. Sounded about right if you believed in retributive justice.

I didn't. Uncle Henry's legacy was stunning but I had no illusions about giving myself up for it. This was not the same as climbing a mountain or parachuting or any of the sports that I found exhilarating. If there was sport involved it was on the other end of the gun. Not a comforting feeling.

I mulled that over for a few seconds and finally slid into a disquieting slumber, where orchards sported grenades for fruit and brown-skinned girls stalked toward me on legs like the trunks of trees. I sat in the path of a *Diablo Rojo*, knowing that something terrible was going to happen, and being completely powerless to stop it.

CHAPTER 5

My driver was there, behind the wheel of exactly what I'd hoped for, a small, slightly battered car with dark windows. Not quite a beater, but close. He already had the door open and was meshing the gears as I dived into the seat.

"Real James Bond stuff," he said with a shit-eating grin on his face.

"Yeah, I heard he was in town making movies. I figured we could ease into his slipstream."

Soong swung the little car hard around a corner. He concentrated on driving as we wound up a succession of streets. I tried to keep a wary eye to our rear. Cops 'n Robbers, James Bond. If it weren't so serious, I'd have been laughing.

"I don't see anyone trailing us," he said. "You?"

I hesitated. "There's a silver SUV a block back. Hard to say with this traffic when he joined us. And I can't tell if it's the same one as yesterday."

"That one had tinted windows and a decal on the windshield," Soong said. "Blue and yellow, I think."

We both watched the SUV for a minute.

Suddenly, Soong turned into a street big enough for only one lane, darted into a driveway, and slammed to a halt. Ten seconds later, the SUV, sleek and silver, zoomed past us.

Acting as though this were something he did every day, Soong nonchalantly backed up, smiled at a woman walking her dog, and turned into the street.

"Hold on," I said, "this is one-way. We're heading in the wrong direction."

Soong shook his head.

"You mean we were going the wrong way back there and the SUV followed us?"

"I'm afraid so."

My outlook for the day suddenly turned to shit.

"If you still think the bullet wasn't meant for you," Soong pronounced grimly, "now might be a good time to reconsider."

I went through the unwelcome mental exercise of accepting what just happened and sketched out for Enriqué— somewhere along the line we'd graduated to first names—my activities after he and I parted yesterday. As I had in my brief phone call to him the night before, I left out the exact dimensions of Uncle Henry's "surprise" and glossed over my nighttime security arrangements. It was his security prowess that was important now. The back of his business card had provided the entrée with the simple line: "Protective Driving and Other Security Services Available."

"So, people at the law firm could be behind the attack on you. Bad. Very bad."

"Yeah, seems like the only logical conclusion." I deliberated. "Whatever he was, my uncle was no fool; neither is Rodrigo. That makes me think we're probably dealing with only one or two people at the firm, maybe some folks who have a fiddle going and are trying to protect it."

"Fiddle?"

"Fraud of some sort. Anything from submitting expenses that don't exist to looting an entire enterprise."

"It's hard to imagine someone attempting murder for cheating on his expense report," Enriqué said sensibly.

I thought about that for a moment. There had actually been that kind of case in Maryland not too long ago.

"Whatever it is, they may have covered it up for years, or they might have started when Uncle Henry became sick. Then along comes the new beneficiary—me—and suddenly people are asking questions, making sure things are in order, and the crook starts worrying about being discovered. I can understand that."

Enriqué executed a quick series of turns.

"What's curious is the timing of the attack. It was before I visited Rodrigo's office. Someone had to know what I looked like and the only person I'd met at that point was a junior associate at the firm, a woman. She picked me up from the airport."

I mulled that over. Tried to think of Maria as an armed assassin bristling with weaponry. Didn't realize I was grinning until Enriqué asked, "Attractive, this woman?"

"Mmm," I said. "Smart, too. Bit of an attitude."

My driver smirked. "The worst kind."

"On that we totally agree."

Enriqué looked thoughtful. "I don't suppose your uncle carried pictures of you?" he asked.

"If he did, it's doubtful he'd pass them around the law firm, if that's what you mean." I tried to remember what I saw in the condominium yesterday. Unfortunately, a haze of pain had inhibited in-depth sight-seeing. "There were a couple of family pictures in the condo. Too many faces to be helpful. Ah, damn, on his desk, a newspaper clipping from one of my campaigns." I recalled that I'd been surprised at seeing it but couldn't remember if the article had included a picture. Probably.

We both absorbed this information. I wondered again why Uncle Henry had troubled to learn so much information about me. It was one of many things I was puzzled about, not the least of them why he'd left me his fortune in the first place.

"Presumably, only one or two people had access?" Enriqué asked in a hopeful tone.

"Rodrigo for sure. He gave me the keys." I exhaled a deep sigh, realizing what I was up against. "Uncle Henry might have thrown wild parties for hundreds, for all I know. Then of course there's the internet…."

"You have pictures there?" Even in the Facebook era, Enriqué seemed surprised.

"From work," I said. I knew it wouldn't take much to find them. Well before the scandal broke, the press had crawled through the campaign, and produced (without my say-so) not one but two lengthy stories about me: "The Razor-Sharp Strategist Behind the Candidate" and "When Smith Calls a Shot, Lawrence Plays It." Smith had been annoyed (but secretly flattered) by the articles. Lawrence, on the other hand, was white-hot furious at Smith. Both stories included excellent quality pictures, which Lawrence could barely stomach since his own candids always left a lot to be desired.

Except, I assumed, in the Dare, Wisconsin YMCA.

I was giving more thought to the pictures when I glanced in the rear-view mirror. "Christ." I looked again. "I don't believe it."

Enriqué spotted the SUV an instant later and immediately executed a series of loops that should have been enough to discourage anyone, but ominously didn't.

There was no question of stopping and accosting the bastard. I already knew he was dangerous and probably armed. Although Enriqué and I together would outnumber him, a gun would even the odds, if not tilt them in his favor. On top of that, he didn't seem to have any qualms about using it in public.

Enriqué stepped on the gas, threaded through traffic, skewed around corners, zoomed up one-way streets in the wrong direction, and generally tried everything except having a helicopter dive in and carry us away. Finally, we slid into a rush-hour packed street, and merged into heavy traffic, seeking safety in numbers.

We drove by a big brash casino, scores of shops, coconut palms, and banks. Horns blared. The hot morning sun pumped its energy over the scene. Brown-skinned men in colorful shirts cat-walked through traffic selling food, dolls, lottery tickets, the fare of the day. *Diablos Rojos* threatened other peoples lives. I took a deep breath and looked around.

"He's here," I said to Enriqué with disgust. "About six cars back." I balled my fists. Who was this guy, anyway? Superman?

We slowed to a crawl, something ahead of us holding up traffic. Enriqué swore, *mierda* sounding a lot like the French *merde*, which I knew as the good old English all-purpose declarative: "shit." I looked ahead and saw a group of people down the block, a bubbling sea of red t-shirts and white signs.

"SUNTRACS labor union," Enriqué said. "Very violent. The members are mostly socialists, communists, and *Chavistas*. And a lot of students, of course."

Enriqué saw a space and wiggled the car ahead a few more feet, pulling abreast of an unfinished building. "*Mierda,*" he said again. I followed his gaze. A man stood about ten storeys up, holding a glass door panel. As we watched, he moved toward the edge of the floor, pulling the glass along with him.

A collective noise poured from the crowd, shouts and foot stamping, a pulsating, throbbing chant that was growing in intensity by the second. I looked up again at the man. One hand pumped the air. The other rocked the glass back and forth in time to the crowd. The man had a look on his face…

"Enriqué," I said urgently, "one way or the other, we need to get the hell out of here."

Suddenly, the man jerked his hands away and threw his arms up in a V. There was a dazzling flash of sunlight as the door momentarily hung in the air. An instant later, it met the sidewalk in a brilliant explosion that sent deadly shards of glass in all directions. I looked up and saw more men, more glass headed our way. I wondered how long before they got around to tools, metal fittings, anything that might drive a hole in the top of our car.

Enriqué found an opening and squirted through, out-maneuvering the car ahead of us. Simultaneously, the police arrived with sirens, lights and full riot gear. In a minute, they'd roped off the road, stalling everyone behind us. I blinked a few times and realized we were the last car in front of the police barricade. We were still moving, but, six cars back, the SUV didn't stand a chance.

Another few minutes and we broke through the last of the demonstration and came out on *Avenida Balboa*, heading swiftly away.

"Thanks," I said gruffly. "I appreciate your getting us out of that mess back there."

Enriqué waved the comment away. "I'll pick you up this afternoon," he said through tight lips. "I'll work on a plan and have recommendations ready for you then. In the meantime, if you need to go anywhere, call me and I'll have a man drive you, or I'll come myself."

I nodded, my mind running in different directions. Cat and mouse games had never appealed to me, especially not the deadly variety. I'd had enough of those in Iraq. Based on what had already happened, this one had the potential to be just as lethal as any I'd encountered before. That meant I needed some fast adjustments to my security, which Enriqué would formulate. Beefing it up was a given. Turning tail and running back to the States wasn't. That being the case, I supposed I could find another apartment or stay in a hotel. But, for that to be effective, the law firm would have to come to me instead of the other way around. And that wouldn't guarantee my safety. The lawyers, in all likelihood, would be followed. One might even be my adversary.

I thought about money, specifically about making a deal. A million dollars, say, to make it all go away. The problem with that was how to get the proposition in front of the bad guy without knowing who he was. I could wait until he was chasing me again and leave a note for him to collect, although to do that, I'd be exposed, or Enriqué would be, and, at the end of the day, who knew if he'd pick up the note or not. Still, a million dollars for my life. Sounded pretty good to me, even if the modus operandi might be a little sophomoric.

My final option—which admittedly should have been my first one—was the police. I wondered how they'd react if I went to them now, if they'd try to help me or if they'd dismiss me out of hand as some crazy gringo who foolishly hadn't called them yesterday. Probably the latter. It was the truth, after all.

We arrived at Fernandez-Chavira while I was still chewing on the possibilities. I thanked Enriqué for delivering my molecules safely and arranged our rendezvous for later in the day. Then, I packed up my indecision into a tidy bundle and consigned it to the back of my brain.

I'd thought long enough about death. Now it was time to think about money.

CHAPTER 6

My mood slowly improved. I poured some coffee, sat in the temporary office the firm had provided, and started on a series of briefings Rodrigo had set up. I'd never been a businessman and hadn't the slightest knowledge of how to run a company, so the briefings gave me an insight into the way the enterprises were structured, the kind of personnel who staffed them, and the resources they had at their command. I was still in the "pinch me and see if it's real" stage, but I was absorbing information.

I also found myself curiously comfortable at the firm. I looked over my shoulder every hour or so but more from a developing habit than from actual fear. Whether or not someone from the firm was involved, it seemed unlikely anyone would attack me on the premises. Occasionally, my mind wandered and I thought again about the police—or lack of them. My ace in the hole was that I didn't have to stay in Panama. If the heat got too intense, I could catch a plane home and leave the estate in Rodrigo's care. It might not be a permanent solution but it would at least get me out of the bulls-eye.

I toyed with that thought for a minute and came up with an unpleasant possibility. What if there were a link back to something in DC? If all this stemmed from an unknown adversary in the political world? A person I'd wronged—or my candidate had. The parent of a child diddled by Lawrence, for instance.

No, I decided, a parent was illogical. But, the idea of someone at home, specifically someone in politics—that could use some more thought.

Shortly after lunch, we had an "episode." The conference room was in use so Bartolomé and I were in the library finishing up his briefing. Maria had just walked in to retrieve a book. She was on the ladder, reaching for the top shelf.

Suddenly, the ground beneath my feet shuddered. I looked up to see Maria starting back down the ladder, her foot poised between steps. There was a second, larger tremor, her foot slipped, and she lost her grip. I darted the few steps to the ladder and the perfect shape of Maria Ortiz tumbled straight into my arms.

I turned a big smile on her and held her for a moment while the earthquake played itself out.

"You can put me down now," she said, her voice somewhere between cool and relieved. She stood and straightened her skirt. "I suppose I should thank you," she said.

I shrugged.

"Well…thank you. I could've been hurt if you hadn't caught me." She smiled—a bit. Maybe that was as far as her mouth would stretch. Maybe she had a psychological fear of good-naturedness. I refused to think she simply didn't find yours truly appealing enough to favor with a full-blown smile.

Hope springs eternal and all that.

CHAPTER 7

Enriqué came for me in the late afternoon. We drove to his office where I was introduced to Ignacio, my new driver, and Bruno, whose name and bulk both correctly said bodyguard. I declined a bulletproof car, which felt excessive, but promised to reconsider if there were any more silver SUV sightings. Ditto a bulletproof vest. Enriqué and I discussed the idea of a payoff and decided to hold off on it. First of all, while my stalker, as I now thought of him, had demonstrated he could get close to me, there was no certainty we could get close to him. Then there was the question of whether a payoff would just prime the pump and result in demands for more money. What was missing was a good understanding of the man's motivation. If we could get a grip on that, we could go a long way toward mapping out a strategy.

Overall, however, I felt pretty good about the new arrangement. Ignacio was trained in special defensive driving techniques. Bruno came with all sorts of combat experience. Both carried guns and attitude. A good start.

The news was less pleasing when I reached the apartment. The security system had not been installed. A Trump project had sucked dry all the alarm companies in town. Apologies from the companies. Someone would be free on Thursday.

I had sent Ignacio and Bruno on an errand and while I was waiting for their return, I poured a glass of Beam and worked on the computer, answering emails, sending notes to contacts, basically staying in the political loop. Given the size of my inheritance, I wouldn't be returning to the political world, at least as an operative, but that didn't stop me from wanting to be in the know. Also, I was curious about Lawrence. Except in the Wisconsin papers, the scandal had died down after his arraignment. The next blip of interest would come when he resigned from Congress. The political powers-that-be were pulling those strings, and I guessed they'd have Lawrence dancing out the door any day now.

After an hour or so of political immersion, Rosario announced that the men had returned with packages, which I asked to be put in the bedroom. A few minutes later, I followed them. I opened the doors to my small terrace, stepped outside into the darkness, and inhaled the aroma of the city. It was pungent at night, heavy, complexly aromatic. Like a woman. I smiled ruefully. If wishes were women. Not tonight, in any event.

I returned to the bedroom and examined the results of the errand-running. Three bags meant Ignacio had been successful all around.

I opened the smallest bag and pulled out the carabiners, oblong-shaped steel rings used in mountain-climbing. The second bag contained ropes, enough to safely reach the ground.

I secured the ropes through the carabiner, fastened it to the porch's iron railing, and made two double loop knots which I judged would provide enough staying power at the top. Then I wrapped the rope in a heavy plastic garbage bag and placed it snugly against the side of the terrace next to a large potted fern. I grabbed another garbage bag and wrapped it around the exposed rope on the railing. After a moment's thought, I walked into the bedroom and returned with the third bag. It went next to the fern as well.

It was as much as I could take care of then; the only thing that remained was to check it all by daylight. I locked both the porch and hall doors, made sure the bureau was in place, took a final swig of bourbon, and brushed my teeth. I told myself that I had definitely made things safer. Then I climbed into bed and spent the rest of the night not believing it.

CHAPTER 8

Ignacio and Bruno came for me in a faded red SUV that felt chopped off in the back but was comfortable enough inside. We swooped up and down roads. Pulled in at FedEx to pick up some paperwork Joy, my secretary, had sent me. Stopped at a computer store to buy a printer for the apartment. All very efficient, fast and, most important, totally without incident.

The rest of the day went about as the previous one had, minus the earthquake. Alberto/Che Guevara gave me a briefing on the hotels in the portfolio. They ranged from small specialty hostelries in Panama City to a few run-of-the-mill motels in smaller cities, to a couple of waterside inns on the Caribbean side. One was pet-friendly and included a grooming salon, another offered special wine-tasting seminars and cooking classes. The hotel I'd stayed in my first night was the largest and most elegant of the group. I reflected that the accommodations had been more than comfortable, a junior suite with a great view, but definitely not the best such a hotel could offer. I smiled to myself. Rodrigo, or maybe Alberto, had been frugal with my money. I approved.

At the end of the day, Rodrigo and I left together in his car. I dismissed Bruno and Ignacio, preferring to keep the shooting and my security arrangements private for the time being. Rodrigo had his own driver, who looked burly enough to protect both of us, and I spent a moment wondering if perhaps this was the norm, not the exception, in Panama City.

We started off at the tony Bristol Hotel, where we had a drink. The dark green walls and mahogany fittings of the bar provided a clubby atmosphere for Rodrigo's mostly entertaining reminiscences about Uncle Henry. Then, we adjourned to a Panama City landmark, the *Siete Mares* (Seven Seas) Restaurant on *Calle Guatemala* in the *Cangrejo* district. *Cangrego*, Rodrigo said, was at one time the center of Panama's Jewish community. A large exterior head sculpture of Albert Einstein and a street named *Via de los Combatientes del Gheto de Varsovia* were remnants of that.

At Rodrigo's recommendation, we sat on the mezzanine and ate *Langosta de Monseñor Laboa*, a caviar-topped crustacean named for the celebrated Papal Nuncio, whose intervention two decades earlier had helped coax strongman Noriega out of hiding and into an American jail. It was truly an ecumenical evening.

After dinner, we smoked Cuban cigars, drank excellent cognac, and spoke about politics, the latest upheavals in the world, and the enormous expansion of Panama City, fueled by people everywhere with money and the desire to protect it. Rodrigo ordered coffee and I used the moment to mention that Val was joining me on Sunday. A cousin and CPA. Perhaps Uncle Henry mentioned him?

No, Rodrigo replied, but how fortunate to have a financial man in the family. It could only help my understanding of what must seem a complicated and overwhelming enterprise.

If only you knew, I thought. And saw again the silver SUV, the monstrous bus, and a shrouded gunman out there somewhere, possibly planning another attack. I found myself wondering if the bastard would try to murder me tonight. Wondering if he shot well in the dark, if he'd be lying in wait when we pulled up to the condominium. Or maybe he'd try to pick me off as we exited the restaurant.

I shook off the feeling. There hadn't been anyone in the Fernandez-Chavira lobby when Rodrigo and I left. No one to ask where we were going. No one to spy on us. Whoever the shooter was, he wasn't omniscient, nor omnipotent. I reckoned the chances of him finding me tonight were negligible.

As we left the restaurant, Rodrigo's big car pulled up. "We'll go first to the *Paraíso,* then home," he said to the driver. I hesitated a moment. "I think I'll take in some nightlife instead. A casino, maybe a nightclub."

Rodrigo raised his eyebrows in a slight question mark. In a country where prostitution is legal, Panama City is known for its "gentlemen's clubs."

I smiled. "I was thinking of jazz."

Rodrigo was full of recommendations. For a casino, the *"Via Veneto."* Good tables, good drinks, good entertainment. Then *"Scena"* or *"Indigo"* in the old town for music. Panama

City was all about jazz. Any cabdriver would know. He looked at me. And after that?

"Umm." There could be an "after that," but I hadn't made up my mind yet.

"*Le Palace*," he said, his eyes a memory. "Beautiful girls, Parisian-style striptease. Exceptional."

I wrote down the suggestions while Rodrigo's driver piloted us to the lively *Calle Cincuenta y Cinco* and the *Via Veneto Casino*. I bid goodbye to Rodrigo, who'd declined to accompany me, made my way through a clutch of people coming and going, and a moment later was having a bourbon and considering craps versus roulette versus blackjack, usually my preferred game. Not a novice gambler but a cautious one, I finally decided on the wheel to start. After twenty minutes, I moved on to craps and from there to blackjack.

At the last table there was a surprise. Alberto/Che Guevara, sitting next to an attractive woman with a nice-sized diamond on her finger.

"Room at this table?" I asked. Alberto stood up, shook my hand, and introduced me to the woman, his fiancée, Felicia. The dealer seated me and play resumed.

I didn't think one way or the other about Alberto being at the casino. He was young and presumably earned plenty of money. The casinos made their living off men like him. I glanced at his pile of chips. Respectable, about the size of mine. The difference was mine grew over the next hour and his got smaller.

I was about to call it quits when Alberto motioned a tuxedoed man over and whispered something in his ear. A quick glance showed the lawyer out of chips. Whatever the man answered—my guess, a denial of credit—Alberto didn't like it. While he was occupied, I stood up, collected my winnings, and waved generally in his direction. A moment later, he and Felicia walked over to me as I was cashing out. "I know another casino over on *Avenida Peru*. Better drinks and good entertainment," Alberto said. "Why don't you join us?"

I hesitated.

He clapped me on the shoulder. "Wait a minute. I forgot my briefcase." He walked over to bag check.

I turned to Felicia. "I'm really not up for more gambling tonight. Tell Alberto I appreciate the invitation but I'll see him tomorrow at the office."

She put her hand out to shake mine, and I thought I saw a flicker of worry cross her eyes. I was no expert on gambling problems but being refused credit at a casino could obviously be a symptom. So could a worried fiancée.

I thought about that for a moment. Could it also be what was behind the attack on me? From what I'd seen of Alberto so far, I didn't put him down as someone who'd take a pot shot on a busy street. Something about him seemed too light-hearted for such serious business. Still, it certainly wouldn't be the first time gambling debts had been settled at the point of a gun.

I stood in front of the casino running it over in my mind. I could keep the "what ifs" going all night if I let myself. Better to put them aside and get on with what I was going to do next. Rodrigo's recommendations were a possibility, but *El Cangrejo* appealed to me. It was busy, loud, and lively, and lots of people were enjoying themselves. Perhaps I'd find something interesting here. I looked to the right. A crowded intersection half a block away, with restaurants on both sides of the street. To the other side, not as much activity, but a neon sign for what looked like a club. You never know. Often, the lesser known places have the best music. I aimed in that direction, crossed one street, passed a small hotel, and paused next to a darkened parking lot to light a cigar I'd picked up at dinner.

I bent my head to the flame.

There was an almost imperceptible shift in the atmosphere.

I straightened up and started to turn around when a great whack to the side of my head stopped me cold. In a tumble of limbs, I crashed to the sidewalk, disoriented and unprepared for another attack. It came anyway.

I heard voices, the sounds of running, someone screaming.

Oh holy shit.

Not again.

"You need an ambulance." It must have been Enriqué, going on about ambulances and casinos and such. Hadn't I already told him? I tried to speak and gobbledygook came out. Then, my eyes cleared, my ears stopped ringing, and I focused on two faces hovering over me, both wide-eyed.

"Alberto," I said. "What the hell?"

"Someone hit you," he answered. "Twice."

I raised my head carefully. It hurt. "Do you know who?"

Alberto shook his head. "Felicia screamed and that spooked him. He ran off through the lot."

"Jesus," I said softly to myself. For a minute, I wondered if Alberto had actually been the assailant, then dismissed the thought as being foolish. If he had been, wouldn't he have finished me off? Plus, there was the fiancée. She hardly looked like the mugging type.

"It was a *ladrón*," Felicia said. "People have to be very careful on the street, especially foreigners. These thieves hide everywhere."

"Especially near casinos," Alberto said, helping me up. "They know a lot of money is being carried and people have been drinking so they aren't on guard. It didn't look like the guy had a lot of time to rob you but you might want to check, just in case."

I did. "Everything's there," I said, and staggered a little.

"You'd better let us get you home," Felicia said. "Alberto's car is here in the lot."

"Thanks," I said, rubbing the back of my head as I climbed in. Two lumps had already formed but no blood came back on my hand. Good. I'd had enough blood for a while.

Whether I'd been right or wrong about Alberto's gambling, there was no question he'd helped me when he had the chance. That made two people I now wanted to thank properly. I idly wondered how many more there'd be.

I arrived back at the *Paraíso* and immediately applied ice to the lumps on my head. After a few minutes, I nixed that treatment, put the cubes in a glass and poured Beam over them. I dumped out some aspirin as a chaser and began to feel a pleasurable numbness beginning at my neck and traveling up.

The pain nearly gone and replaced by fatigue, I retreated to my fortress room, ropes safely stored on the terrace, chest in front of the door. I clambered into bed, gingerly turned on my good side, and, whether from exhaustion, fear, or whatever other emotions I was experiencing, fell deeply asleep.

Little did I know, the next morning all hell would break loose.

CHAPTER 9

There's something about elevators that makes whatever kind of headache you have worse. Mine was the pounding all over variety. I felt like crap when I got on, I felt like double crap when I got off. Anger about last night wasn't helping the pain either.

Over to the side, I saw Maria deep in conversation with Federico, both with tight faces and down-turned mouths. An uncharacteristically ashen-faced Rodrigo appeared in the hall and beckoned the three of us into his office.

We trooped in. No one met my eyes.

"There's a problem, Pen," Rodrigo said heavily. "The authorities are already investigating. I'm certain they will resolve the matter very soon."

The formal tone was disconcerting and, despite the usual cool blast from the air conditioning, I noticed that Rodrigo, in otherwise impeccable blue shirtsleeves and Italian blue and yellow silk tie, seemed a trifle…damp.

"Ah," I said as evenly as possible. "A problem."

Out of the corner of my eye, I saw Bartolomé dourly staring at the rug. It appeared to be the tenor of the day.

I waited.

"There's been a break-in," Rodrigo finally divulged, hands in pockets, the cherubic face somewhere between dismay and anger. "Someone compromised our computer security. Our technical experts said they moved funds, deleted records. There have been...losses."

"Obviously this involves me," I said, not in the least surprised that the fiddle had shown itself. A glance around the room and a quick body count revealed eight plus me. The fiddler had absconded.

"The police think perhaps..." Rodrigo could go no further.

"They've put the finger on Marcel," Alberto volunteered in Chicago-style colloquial English, barely able to suppress his glee. Rodrigo looked murderously at Alberto and the young lawyer's face remolded itself into a respectful, doleful mask.

Despite the news and my generally bad mood, I smiled inwardly. Alberto, I decided, was the perfect anti-authoritarian personality cast into a doctrinaire existence. He didn't resent it the way Val did; in fact, I thought he was enjoying himself.

As for Marcel, my mind needed a little jogging. I finally came up with the sallow looking guy who seemed partial to blinding white shirts.

"Marcel has been with this firm for twenty-two years," Rodrigo said. "I entrusted him with some of my most delicate matters. It's impossible. Impossible."

Although I vaguely remembered, I asked anyway. "Tell me again, which one of the foundations does Marcel handle?"

"*La Fundación de Chucherías,*" Rodrigo replied. " 'Odds and Ends,' it means in English. Henry named it. Well, he named them all. They amused him, the names."

"What's in it?"

Rodrigo took a deep breath and let it out. "Cantinas, independent petrol stations, some shops with discounted clothing, some electronics. Also places to buy sandwiches, beer, sundries. We call those mini-supers."

To be expected. Quick turnover. Lots of cash—probably few of the businesses took credit cards. Highly skimmable. And no doubt extremely simple to hide.

"How much?"

Rodrigo shook his head. "We're waiting for the auditors to say exactly…but….in your accounts alone—"

Deep, unhappy sigh.

"Possibly several…maybe more…possibly five…" He sighed again. "Millions."

A few days ago, that would have been breathtaking. "All right," I said deliberately, "the police are investigating, your computer people are on it, the auditors are here. There's nothing else we can do right now. Let's get back to work."

Rodrigo's eyes widened. "Pen," he protested, astonished. "Your assets, Henry's work…the thief gone. How can you trust us?"

Simple, I said to myself, it's only money. The shooting, the attack last night, that was the last of it. I no longer had to look over my shoulder, had no reason to fear another bullet or conk on the head. I would gladly have traded more than a few *Chucherías* for that.

To Rodrigo I merely smiled. "We'll see about rounding up the horses and getting them back in the barn," I said. "For now, let's take good care of the ones still inside."

The rest of the day was a bust. The police were underfoot and the auditors were stern-faced and shook their heads a lot. The computer guys were the only ones with a reasonably bright outlook. They loved puzzles, lived for great ones like this, and generally whistled their way through the firm's misfortune.

After lunch, the auditors huddled with Rodrigo, whose increasingly gray complexion contrasted poorly with his attire. Not only was the loss substantial, the firm was liable for it all. Good news for me but lousy for Rodrigo, as the insurers would be sticklers for proof of every penny. Since Marcel had trashed the computer files, the firm would also be on the hook for the not-insignificant amount of time and expense required to reconstruct them. "And, even then," said Rodrigo cheerlessly, "who knows how much of the documentation the insurance companies will accept?"

The computer experts were only too happy to start solving their part of the conundrum. The insurers, on the other hand, were pressing the police to immediately investigate everyone and everything. Facing such a large potential payout—close to $5 million for me, plus whatever the firm's other losses were—it made sense. If they were able to somehow demonstrate collusion with Rodrigo (a confidence whispered by Alberto in an incautious moment), the case would enter a different realm and the likelihood of anyone being reimbursed might easily be lost in a perpetual legal tangle.

Still, for me, the bad news barely outweighed the good. Knowing there was no more reason for anyone to attack me made everything else almost irrelevant.

Faced with working out a compromise among the steely-eyed insurers, disapproving auditors, happy-as-a-lark computer geeks, and the impatient police, Rodrigo might have been excused any number of things, including screaming mania. I misjudged his moxie, though, as he calmly took me aside and offered what reassurance he could.

I listened with half an ear, while my mind wandered to Val. I silently thanked the gods that I'd asked him to come to Panama. Even before the Marcel affair, Val had a job and a half waiting for him. Now, I needed to split him in two—one Val to help search for the missing money and the other to tear apart the books of the remaining foundations and make sure no more surprises were in store.

That led my mind to a different Smith cousin, Thomas, a tenacious trial lawyer in Washington. If anyone was able to sniff out malfeasance, it was Thomas. I also veered off into thinking about my older cousin, Stanley Smith, one of many vice-presidents at a large but currently struggling conglomerate. Before I knew it, I was sorting through a long roster of kin, tapping this one for X job and that one for Y, a farce, as I myself had barely gotten to the point of knowing about A and B.

I came out of my reverie to hear Rodrigo wrapping up. Long years of service, he was saying, invaluable guidance, very difficult to believe his old colleague had betrayed the firm. I shook my head a lot, drew my eyebrows together, and tried to seem as down in the dumps as everyone else.

Three days ago, I had no real money to speak of. Two days ago, my pocketbook had swelled to an unbelievable sum. Cut to today and the balance sheet was reduced by five very big ones. I rolled that number through my gray cells, hoping to conjure some sense of outrage. The synapses sat on the sideline, stubbornly uncooperative. No matter how I chose to look at it, the amount had been a small one to pay for my life.

When Rodrigo left to rejoin the fray, I breathed a sigh of relief. Being cloaked in a false air of dejection was definitely wearing out my newly minted good mood.

CHAPTER 10

Hours passed. Rodrigo worked out an arrangement allowing the computer guys to start looking for the money, the auditors went back to tut-tutting over the firm's bookkeeping, the insurance people withdrew for the time being but left a pall over the entire office, and the police began pursuing Marcel in earnest.

I received another briefing, this time from Reynaldo Somebody, a thickset man with a voice that hummed like a refrigerator.

When we finished, the office was mostly empty. The mystery of my assailant solved, I was ready to explore more nightlife. Delfina, freshening her make-up and making signs of leaving for the day, looked like a prospect for a pleasant evening. I give up that idea when a tall, slender man dressed in Armani exited the elevator and perched possessively on the corner of her desk.

I called Enriqué instead. He was up for a drink or two and suggested an area called the Amador Causeway, which turned out to be a beautiful palm-lined peninsula consisting of three small islands with posh hotels and a marina.

As Ignacio obligingly drove us on a wickedly crooked route to Amador, I had plenty of time to fill Enriqué in.

"Great," he said enthusiastically, then caught himself. "Not the robbery—"

"No."

"But identifying the gunman…"

"Ye-es," I said, then laughed at my equivocation. "I just hope he's not hiding behind one of these palm trees."

"You think he's still in Panama City?"

"Not really. Would you hang around waiting to be caught with a big chunk of stolen change?"

"Definitely not."

"My bet is he's sitting on a beach somewhere with a cold rum drink in his hand."

"Or Paris," Enriqué said. "A sidewalk cafe. A priceless bottle of wine."

"A beautiful woman."

We both looked out the window for a minute. I took in the spectacular view from the peninsula, the huge sun, heavy strawberry clouds tinged with gold, the deep blue of the bay. At the horizon, I saw islands. I pointed toward the largest one. "What's that?"

"*Isla Taboga,*" Enriqué said. "The Isle of Flowers. Old, founded somewhere in the 1500s. Like everything else around here, sacked by Henry Morgan."

I raised my eyebrows. *"The* Henry Morgan? The pirate?"

"One and the same," Enriqué said. "Spanish treasure from all over South America came to Panama for shipment back to the mother country. Morgan, being the opportunist he

was, made his fortune off it. *Taboga* was one of his pit stops."
Enriqué flicked a piece of lint off his trousers. "It's also the
place Gauguin came to paint before going to Tahiti."

"Gauguin." I sucked in the fresh sea air and turned to
Enriqué. "Let's make a deal. Tonight there isn't a Marcel on
the loose. There isn't any stolen money. There weren't any
bullets and I never fell down. I met you at a cafe and we had
coffee together. Now we're having some drinks."

Enriqué nodded. "Sounds good to me," he said. "Except
you left out the women." He raised his eyebrows and cracked a
smile.

"A momentary oversight," I said. "Definitely the
women."

Enriqué directed us to the terrace of "The Wine Bar." It
was a pleasant, popular spot with a good mix of locals and
gringos. For a while, we enjoyed the humanity that swirled
around us and several people who stopped at our table to visit.
We soon learned that mingling with the crowd was a small
group whose yachts were tied up at the marina.

"Do you sail?" a tanned, blonde girl with muscles asked
me. "I don't like boats," I said honestly. The blonde's smile
turned down. "Hey, I do like boat people, though." She
laughed but her heart wasn't in it. Soon she excused herself
and found some authentic mariners to mingle with. Enriqué,
putting the moves on another boat-type—deep tan, casual
shift, deck shoes—rolled his eyes.

"Aw, I was about to ask you both aboard," Enriqué's girl said, gesturing in the direction of the moored boats. "We're having a party."

"You go ahead," I told Enriqué. "Have a good time."

"You're sure?"

I was and he was hoping I'd say so. "If you're not here when I leave, I'll send Ignacio back," I told him.

"Okay, then," he answered. The girl's eyes sent out happy lights and Enriqué's arm curled around her waist as they left.

I ordered another drink and put my mental feet up.

I didn't think about it often, but in this setting, it was probably inevitable that I would. Ever since the accident—I'd always called it "The Murder," although the courts never did—I've been incapable of setting foot on a boat. When my father and mother were alive, I loved being on the water. But that ended the day a motorboat piloted by a drunk teenager plowed into my parents' beloved "Skidaway," a forty-foot ketch which absorbed much of their earnings and energy—and a full tank of gas the morning it happened.

Both boats exploded. The teenager tumbled overboard seconds before impact. Typical of havoc-wreaking drunks, he came through unscathed. Two local boaters caught the whole thing on video and the media shamelessly replayed it for a week. I watched it endlessly at Val's house, before his mother caught us and made me hand over the tape.

I was supposed to be with my parents on the water that morning. In that odd way in which fate can intervene in a seemingly mundane way and turn your life around forever, I had a cold and they'd made me stay home. The first I knew anything was wrong was when Uncle Henry and his wife, Aunt Cam, roared in like an out-of-control wave and sent the babysitter skittering with a curt command and a fistful of money. Aunt Cam attacked my drawers and closet with a vengeance, Uncle Henry held my hand and told me to be brave. Within minutes, I was swept from my home, completely and forever. I was eight years old.

"I am Gina. I can sit down?" a voice asked charmingly. I glanced up and saw a squeezably attractive *Panameña* next to my table. I looked at her just tight enough dress and heart-shaped face. "Absolutely."

Before long, she'd knocked back three Margaritas and a double order of mini-empañadas, as she animatedly told me about her work. "I am gambler *aprendiz*," she said, smiling. "I am learning to take other people's money."

Well, there was a variation on a theme. Nimble fingers could definitely be used in a variety of ways. I contemplated one of them and then was hit with an unwelcome realization. As entertaining as Gina was, nothing was tugging on me to underwrite another round of drinks. Constantly being on the go meant most of my romances were superficial. While I liked a good-time girl as much as the next man, being only a couple of weeks off the campaign, I realized I was momentarily full up with that kind of relationship. To go past the two-drink mark tonight, there had to be depths to explore.

I was relieved when some people I'd met earlier stopped back by the table and we chatted for a few minutes more, exchanging phone numbers and email addresses in the casual way you do at a bar. Gina spotted a group she knew and, after unsuccessfully pulling me in their direction, good-naturedly concluded that they offered more opportunity than I did.

Later, I met a seventyish German yacht broker and his artist wife, a still-glorious blond in her late fifties. "There was this time in Fiji…" she said and I was sucked in for story after delightful story. Somewhere in the hour that passed, I found myself examining her closely. If my own mother had lived, she would have been about this woman's age. She and my father might conceivably have been on the same kind of trip, even visiting the same port. Thinking about "'what if" usually made me melancholy but, oddly enough, this time it didn't. My parents loved sailing. In a way, it was fitting they'd died on the water. I wondered about asking the Germans whether they'd rather perish on their boat or be killed more mundanely, say, in a car accident. I didn't ask because I felt certain I already knew their answer.

When we split up, I glanced at my watch and saw it was almost midnight. I thought about staying longer but knew there were emails to check and correspondence from Joy to deal with. More opportunities to meet pretty girls would have to wait for another day. I said goodnight to "The Wine Bar," the sailors, and those who were learning to take other people's money, and walked out the door.

As though sensing my thoughts, Ignacio and Bruno had the car gliding in front of me almost before I reached the end of the walkway.

CHAPTER 11

I entered the apartment, went straight to the computer and was surprised to find an almost empty Inbox and a short note from Joy. Nothing going on. Leaving early. Talk to you tomorrow.

Okay then. May as well spend a half hour in the Jacuzzi. I poked my head in the kitchen for some ice and grabbed the Beam.

"TUB CLOSE." The mechanism clicked. "TUB FILL."

Within seconds, there was steam on the mirror and condensation on my glass. Perfect.

I relaxed into the water, feeling knots unwind, and peered at the bullet wound. Red but not infected. The head throbbed but the bourbon was helping. Life could be worse. I could be $195 million poorer, for instance.

I sipped my drink and my thoughts returned to Marcel. I wasn't aware of all the nuances, but I was convinced the shooting and plunder of the *Fundación de Chuchería* were related. Perhaps Marcel thought being shot would discourage me, that I might turn around and race home, leaving him time to clean up his mess. Maybe he simply needed an extra day to complete his embezzlement.

I realized I might never know the cause behind his actions. The only thing I could say for sure was that Marcel must have wanted or needed the money badly to be willing to kill for it.

My mind took another turn. As long as I was toying with the "whys and wherefores" of this mess, what if Marcel *hadn't* left Panama with the money? What if he wasn't finished with me? Marcel was now publicly linked with the theft. Did he think I would connect him to the shooting, too?

I'd met plenty of opportunistic and twisted individuals in my lifetime. Politics is a magnet for people who have misplaced their souls. But I'd never known anyone outside of war who'd taken a gun and aimed it at me with the intent of ending my life. There was no way to know what was in Marcel's thoughts. Realistically, no way to determine if his exposure as a thief meant I was any safer today than I was yesterday when he held a gun in his hand.

Suddenly, the water seemed cold. I stepped out of the bath, grabbed a towel, and walked into my room. There was no ignoring it. I was thoroughly unprepared to consider the situation from the perspective of the criminal mind. Give me the self-absorbed brains of politicians any time. I could dissect that kind of thinking. But this—I was no further along than I had been an hour ago. Some brain cells had been sacrificed on the altar of the unknowable, that was all.

I reached for a pair of briefs, and heard a sound in the hall. Someone was coming toward me. And fast. Not Rosario's birdlike tap-tap walk. Someone with a heavy tread.

I lunged for the door to the terrace, threw it open, and scrambled for the bags. Pulled the equipment out and quickly knotted the ropes under my left thigh and over my right shoulder. I pulled in deep gulping breaths of air and grabbed the other bag, my fingers fumbling with its opening. There were more footsteps and an ominous dragging, rolling sound.

Almost at my door.

The bag came apart, I hurled the contents into the room, and only a second later slung myself over the railing, spinning into a combination of abseil and free fall, bouncing, scraping my bare feet, legs, back—all of me—against the wall as I played out the rope. *Too fast* my brain cautioned and my hands and feet obeyed the warning. I slowed, even as objects zinged down around me.

Then, there was a huge thump.

"Goddammed shit, Pen, I'll fuck your hide for this!"

It took a moment to register. Then, I laughed with relief, lungs functioning again, heartbeat pulling back from Olympic pace, slowing the rate of the fall with arms and legs both, and gaping at the sight three stories up and not believing it.

"Val, you sonofabitch," I shouted back, partly to him and partly to an aghast woman behind the window where my left foot rested. "You unbelievable, sight for sore eyes, fabulous sonofabitch. Haul me the hell up!"

If moving furniture in the middle of the night hadn't made Rosario think twice about me, the sight of marbles littering the floor and Val holding his head with one hand, my

Beam in the other, should have done it. And if that didn't, there were the small, lightly bleeding scrapes on my bare feet, legs and hands—my torso and groin were now modestly covered—not to mention new leaking from the bullet wound. Eyebrow-raising as those were, I was sure it was the rope still around my body, plus our uncontrollable bursts of hilarity, that were causing her to rapidly back out into the hall, fervently murmuring, and clutching the medallion at her neck.

Val saved the situation with a talent I'd never known he had.

"*Señor Pen es un escalador de montañas. Él está practicando para una ascensión del Volcán Barú.*"

I stare at him with the mother of all Gump faces.

"You're going to climb a local volcano. You've been practicing."

"You speak Spanish," I said. "Since when?"

"About the same time you learned French, for all the good it's done you."

I laughed. He was right.

Flimsy as it sounded, the story about practicing for mountain climbing seemed to get through to Rosario. She halted in the doorway and re-surveyed the scene. She apparently decided I was a lost cause and turned her attention to Val, fussing over his bruises and escorting him to Uncle Henry's enormous bedroom, the only spot she apparently considered suitable for his recuperation. After sticking a few Band-Aids on my scratches—without assistance—I padded behind with Val's suitcase, which had a stuck wheel and made an altogether too familiar rolling, dragging sound as I pulled it.

"Enjoy the room for the moment," I told Val amicably, "but it's mine. My stuff in the closets—" I opened them and pointed at the proof. "My stuff in the bathroom." I waved my hand in its general direction. To anyone but Val, that might have sounded churlish, but in our youth, it was always Val who staked out the top bunk, Val who grabbed the newly restrung tennis racket, Val who was first in the ice cream line. Val, now reclining on the bed, head propped up on pillows organized by Rosario, merely grinned.

"So, explain yourself," I said, matching his expression. I settled in a chair, scattering a few leftover red droplets on the floor.

"Nothing to it," he answered. "We have a go-getter who's been pushing against his harness. Everyone knew it was just a matter of time before he made partner. This seemed as good a moment as any. The The firm will be fine. I'll go back and forth for a couple months, and everyone will come down to visit us and drink Margaritas on the beach."

"So why didn't you call and let me know? I thought you were coming Sunday." I studied my various scrapes and bruises and wondered how many more I might accumulate before this little adventure was over.

"Oh, I decided to sort of surprise you," Val said. "I mean the whole thing is so Hollywood anyway. Here you are, answering some kind of summons from the grave..." He warbled the last few words.

"Don't do that spooky thing with your voice," I interrupted. "I never liked that, not even at Halloween."

"Anyway, you gave me the address and Rosie was—"

"Rosie? *Rosie?*"

"Yeah, Rosie answered the house phone. You were taking a bath or something."

"There's a house phone? Nobody told me there was a house phone."

"Next time, study Spanish," Val said, enjoying himself. "Ask Rosie about it. I think it's in the kitchen. I told her I was your *primo*—that means cousin—and when I came up she'd checked on you and heard cute little bubbling sounds from the bathroom. That's when she told me to make myself at home while she fixed me a Coke. I was just bringing my luggage up the hall when you erupted."

"Make yourself at home," I spluttered. House phone. Rosie, my foot.

"The marbles got you," I said. "Admit it."

"Old trick," Val answered loftily.

"Your trick," I pointed out.

"That, too."

We were both silent for a moment.

"Why did you do...all that?" he asked.

"*Primo,*" I said, "let me fill you in."

One thing about inheriting a fortune in a foreign country, you have absolutely no desire to run around screaming about it at the top of your lungs. My sole confidante so far had been Enriqué and I'd shared only enough to gain his confidence and support. To Val, I told everything—the shooting, the theft, last night's assault, the lot.

"Holy shit," he said.

"Yeah."

"So this…Marcel?"

I nodded.

"He's some ordinary middle-aged guy who one day just decides to rob the cookie jar?"

"Seems like it."

"But why would he want to shoot you?"

"To prevent me from making an appearance. From being exposed. All the normal reasons you'd wanted to gun someone down." As though I knew what those were.

Val shook his head. "Uh-uh," he said, his face creased in disagreement. "Embezzlers aren't murderers. They're stealthy and they understand numbers. But most of them wouldn't have the nerve to shoot a gun period, much less in a public place. I've seen embezzlers up close. I know."

It wasn't what I wanted to hear. "So if Marcel didn't shoot me, who the shit did?" I flicked my finger to brush a speck off my T-shirt and realized with annoyance that somewhere along the line I'd transferred smears of blood to it.

"Look for a person with something to gain." Val said sensibly, sounding like a cop in a TV show. "Maybe there's someone you haven't thought of."

I'd thought of everybody a dozen times over, I started to say. Instead, I yanked the t-shirt over my head, balled it up and pitched it into the closet. I stalked across the room to the bureau where Rosario had stashed my clothes, and searched roughly in a drawer for something to wear that didn't have blood on it.

I caught my reflection and Val's in the mirror over the bureau and saw that our matched set of gray eyes were not duplicates in feelings. Mine were narrowed, angry, Val's half-lidded and clearly dismayed.

"So?" I asked, calming down, "since you have all the answers, how about giving me one?"

He didn't respond at first, just sat there with his accountant's mind clicking away. "All right, it sounds like we have two problems," he finally said. "First, we need to make sure the rest of the foundations are protected. That's the easy one. Numbers are numbers, no matter what the language. So, don't worry, I can do that. But, this other shit, Pen—" He rubbed his hand over his forehead. "It isn't a matter of not wanting to help. If I were a policeman or a soldier..."

"Hold on, Val." I stopped him before he could get into it. "I'm not expecting you to be a bodyguard. I've already got one of those and it's only my stupidity that he wasn't around last night when I got whacked over the head. I need you to keep us protected on paper. That's a big enough job as it is, especially since we have no idea what the rest of the financials look like. Believe me, if you do that, I can handle the rest." I looked at him and grinned, trying to lift our spirits. "Hell, I've outrun the bad guy so far. Who's to say he won't just give up?"

Val mumbled something I didn't catch and I glanced back in the drawer. I pulled out an ancient "Sting—Nothing Like the Sun Tour" t-shirt. My other hand found another shirt, a noisy but cheerful red, white and blue affair from the last campaign. Sting dropped to the floor as my hands tensed around the campaign shirt. I held it up.

"What the—?" I saw Val's eyes grow wide and his mouth even wider. The shirt fell jaggedly open, huge white and red letters which had once spelled "Lawrence" dancing disjointedly in the air. The unfortunate eagle above had been sectioned into tail feathers, feet, arrows, and beak.

"Jesus," Val said, his eyes riveted in my direction.

My mouth was too dry to speak but I swallowed hard and looked again at the shirt.

Someone had repeatedly slashed it from collar to hem.

CHAPTER 12

Val bucked off the bed to see the butchered item up close. I dropped it in his hands, shook my head, and went to the kitchen for fresh glasses and ice. I grabbed the bourbon from my room, poured liberally for us both, and took a gulp. My hands were shaking in anger.

"Who had access?" Val asked. "It can't be Rosie."

"No." I slammed my fist furiously onto the chest. "This is some morally bankrupt sonofabitch."

We both were silent, contemplating such a person.

"My luggage was in the hotel Monday until their people brought it over here," I finally said. "Suppose Marcel managed to get access to my room somehow? Suppose he was trying to scare me into leaving. Then this would still go back to him."

Val frowned.

"Somebody had most of the morning and probably a good part of the fucking afternoon to screw around with my clothes. Until I'm proven wrong, my money's on Marcel. There's nothing else that makes sense."

Val nodded, conceding the argument or maybe deciding it wasn't the best time to pursue it. "Who knows?" he said wearily. "We need to give it some thought and work on it again tomorrow. Listen, I'm sorry, but I'm bushed. You're probably done in, too."

That didn't begin to cover it. All the days had been long here. Except for last night, I'd had very little sleep. So far, tonight didn't look promising.

"Val," I said. "Look at it this way. If it wasn't Marcel, there's still someone out there trying to kill me. Hell, it's like open season on Pen Smith. Ladies and gentlemen, step right up, rob him, shoot him, hit him over the head, you win the prize."

Val just shook his head and stirred the ice in his drink.

My eyes followed the ice and a cold understanding settled in my mind. I looked at my cousin. It hadn't occurred to him yet.

"There's another problem," I told him, knowing my voice sounded as dull as the cubes Val was swirling. "Marcel is the thief, everyone accepts that. But if the thief isn't the shooter, that means the prize isn't the money."

Val looked at me quizzically.

"Val, if it's not the money, what the hell else are they after?"

Having Val with me swelled the ranks of the good guys and helped cover the local geography. The condominium's sprawl argued for another pair of good ears, Rosario being at the far end of the floor. The new locks were a positive and the alarm system—finally installed—was a plus, but I still wasn't taking anything for granted.

For tonight, Val—against his mild protests—was ensconced in another bedroom further down the hall. I was in my fortress. The marbles had been re-gathered and placed in a new bag. Ditto the rope. Both were back on the terrace behind the fern, which came through the escapade serenely undamaged.

I pulled the chest in front of my door as usual, having warned Val of this recent eccentricity, and sometime later heard a heavy scraping noise coming from the direction of his room. I smiled a bit, somehow certain that Val wasn't a target, but glad, nonetheless, that he was taking his own safety seriously.

After I got into bed, I reran the evening. Val thought I should tell Rodrigo everything that had happened. I agreed in principle, but doubted if Rodrigo was in any shape to absorb another blow. As to Val, despite the moral and physical support of having him on the scene, there was no security at all to be derived from our conversation. I went back and forth between my take on things and Val's, one moment understanding why Marcel would want to scare me shitless and dispose of me, the next hearing Val's reasonably spoken words: "Embezzlers aren't murderers."

Even with Val's appearance, the mutilation of the t-shirt took center stage in my mind. I put it in the category of the SUV, deliberately menacing, the shooter showing me how close he could get. Even though the cutting was probably done in the hotel room and not in the condominium, it still felt very, very close. And despite the fact that the shirt had been cut before the embezzlement was discovered and Marcel presumably had blown town by now, the mutilation still had the desired effect. I went to bed as I had the previous nights, with my nerves jangled and my brain unwillingly engaged.

If I ever found the bastard who was doing this, I wanted first crack at him for ruining my sleep.

CHAPTER 13

Val accompanied me to Rodrigo's, courtesy of Ignacio and Bruno in an old blue Hyundai that did all the tricks without protest. Val kept an eye out for silver SUVs, I watched for guns sticking out of flower pots.

At the office, the dispirited atmosphere was not lost on Val. He greeted Rodrigo with the right balance of tact and concern, met the remaining cast of characters, and homed in on the computer specialists and auditors.

Val was born to be a CPA. There was something about his intuitive sense of numbers that allowed him to zero in on key issues in an uncanny way. People sensed this and entrusted their financial secrets to him the way others might share confidences with their priests. I was glad to see that by eleven o'clock Val had carved out a niche for himself and had folders piled up and people waiting to tell him things.

For obvious reasons, he and I agreed he should concentrate on La *Fundación de Chucherías*. I, meantime, would continue learning the business end of the portfolio. The result was a dragging morning for me. Alberto gave a second presentation, this one on resorts. The subject matter alone should have made for an interesting report, but it was a long way from Alberto's first briefing two days ago. His delivery then had been energetic and effervescing with optimism. Not today.

I wanted to tell him things would be fine and not to take the theft quite so seriously. Yesterday, I might have been able to say that. But today, as Alberto inhaled the depressed air of the firm and expelled it in my direction, I was again preoccupied with the murderous intent of Marcel. Palm-studded views of the coastline and occupancy figures were all wasted on me.

The second foundation that day included new technologies and small businesses poised for major growth. Its name was *La Fundación de hoy y del mañana* ("Of the Here and Hereafter"). I smiled with raw amusement and wondered if Uncle Henry could possibly have imagined how apt that name would be.

Maria was the presenter. She was cool and professional, and gave me a decent smile. Millimeters wider than the last time. A definite mood-lifter.

Afterwards, I chatted with Val, who ogled Maria as she walked by. "Careful," I said. "Barbed wire."

"Doesn't seem like it." His eyes were locked on her retreating figure and his face had a lazy smile I'd seen before. I shook my head.

"I'm leaving," I told him. "Going to *Paraíso*, hanging out all afternoon. Don't call me."

Val lifted a hand and I left to speak with Rodrigo. On the way back, I poked my head in Alberto's office, giving him a thumbs up. It was one in the afternoon and I was blowing the joint. I felt like a kid playing hooky.

Rosario was surprised to see me but whipped up a delicious cold seafood salad on the spot. I ate it, checked all the locks, then changed into swimming trunks and a t-shirt, and went out to the terrace. In addition to the charming ponds and abundant vegetation, there was a lap pool. I thought about using it, then changed my mind. The leg was improving but I didn't want to do anything that might slow it down. I opted instead for a chaise and promptly fell asleep under a thatched umbrella. I might have stayed that way indefinitely had my phone not jolted me awake.

"Pen Smith," I answered.

"Hello, Pen," a woman's voice said, "My name is Robyn Butler. I was a friend of your uncle."

Ms. Butler was calling from *Montañas del Cielo*, a mountain community about two hours west of Panama City. She'd be there for the next week and wondered if I'd like to visit. There was a guest house at my disposal. She also had a few private items Uncle Henry left with her to give me.

"Private items?"

"Yes, some things he wanted to make sure you received when you came to Panama."

"You were a business associate of Uncle Henry's?"

"No," she said. "I was a friend." Her voice caught. "A very good friend."

I thought about that for a moment. Was this woman saying that she and Uncle Henry were lovers? The notion of my uncle having a romantic life was a surprise. He'd been married when I first went to live with him. His wife died when I was fifteen and I had no particular memory of him with other women. That probably meant nothing because I was a teenager by then and mostly preoccupied with my own love life. The idea of Uncle Henry and this Butler woman shouldn't strike me as odd. He certainly had been young enough to be attractive to the other sex.

After putting that to rest, I took only a minute to consider Ms. Butler's invitation. I was finished with the initial briefings, the experts were preoccupied chasing the thief, and, above all, I was in need of a change of scenery. Meeting Uncle Henry's girlfriend might even be fun.

"Would tomorrow be too soon?" I asked.

Tomorrow would be fine, she said, and gave me directions. We agreed on a one or two-night visit and disconnected.

I phoned Enriqué and alerted him to the change of plans. While I waited for Val to make an appearance, more of Rosario's good cooking came my way, followed by packing a bag and sending a few emails. Finally, Val appeared.

I was expecting him to be somber, reflecting the events of the day. Instead, one look and I knew it was bad. It was the whistling and grinning at the same time that gave him away. I sighed and watched him do a little soft shoe.

God. It might be even worse than I expected.

"Long day," I commented, as I steered Val to the terrace and we sat, facing the moon-bathed ocean. The tide was out so we looked mostly on mud. Silvery mud at least.

"Well, tell me, what did you find out?" I glanced over at him and saw a smile creeping across his face. I knew his next words would not be about the theft.

"Sweet little Maria," he said, stretching out his legs and putting his hands behind his head. "Quite a firecracker."

"A professional assessment?" I asked. I was stunned, but trying for all I was worth not to show it. "Have you bought her jewelry yet?"

"That, cousin, shows the blackness in your heart."

"Not at all. Your love life is of paramount importance to me. It just happens to rank a little below securing my own life-expectancy, which, by the way, seems to be teetering on the edge. Not to mention a big pile of money that's gone missing."

Val pretended to be mildly chastened. "Hey, I was on that," he said defensively. "Most of the day. And not fruitlessly. But…" Long, satisfied sigh. "Man must have his exercise."

"I hope you got it chasing her around a desk."

His grin broadened.

I tried not to be small-minded. After all, I'd had an opportunity for "exercise" with Gina the gambler and hadn't pursued it. As for Maria, I wondered if my annoyance stemmed from having seen her first or from failing abysmally to get anywhere with her. I told myself it didn't matter. Having been scorched a time or two, I generally avoided business dalliances. Val, of course, had every kind of relationship by the dozens and always seemed to emerge unscathed. I was convinced the baubles had something to do with it. "Love 'em and leave 'em—but leave 'em with something" would have been a fitting motto for Val. I sighed inwardly. I'd been through this before, when both Val and I had our eyes on the same woman. Val, more often than not, came out on top, and wasn't above saying so.

"There's a lot more to Maria than sex," he informed me.

"Pretty," I said neutrally.

"Of course, but she has an interesting family, too. Father's American, mother Panamanian. Second wife. He was in charge of security for the Canal."

"Uhm," I answered. The security business was interesting but I refused to contribute to the conversation.

"She grew up with a foot in both countries. A whole family back in the States. Law degree and a Masters in civil jurisprudence from the University of Florida."

"Educated in the States," I murmured. That leant further credence to my theory that she'd bridled at the role of being my personal babysitter. In America, she probably could have sued for discrimination.

"Let's save any more details on Maria for later," I suggested, switching to my conversation with Robyn Butler.

Val listened. "Great," he said after a minute. "Maybe she can help point us in the right direction."

"Does that mean," I asked, "that the compass is currently spinning out of control."

"Actually not," Val said, to my surprise. "Rodrigo travels in rarefied company. I'm telling you, Pen, you could hear the sounds of screws being applied all over town. It looks to me like these banks might not be quite as impenetrable as everyone's been telling us, at least if you know the right people."

"Rodrigo's calling in his debts?"

"I think so. About five o'clock, there was a big stir, the auditors were all excited, started talking to the computer wizards. Somebody heard a rumor. Then a little later, Rodrigo comes along, calm as can be, and drops a big one."

Val must have read my face. "Hey, I didn't call because I didn't want to get your hopes up. There's still a lot of work being done to find this guy and I know you've been having a rough time these past few days. I was hoping to have a little more information before I filled you in."

I sighed. "Let's face it, Val, at this point any information is more information to me."

Val stood up to pour himself a drink. "Okay, there's possible bank activity. Apparently, HMSC had some big numbers run through the afternoon before Marcel went missing. The money was in and out, one of those instantaneous deals. Rodrigo's trying to get the routing information for the outbound transaction. Probably not going to happen but at least we know where the money started.

"Also, the police have Marcel traced on a flight that left here yesterday noon for *Bogotá*. Despite the problems with the drug traffickers, who annoy the hell out of everybody, by the way, the Colombian government is very friendly with the Panamanian government. That's good for us because both police forces are out looking for this guy. Marcel apparently told Alberto he has relatives in *Bogotá*, so that's where they're starting.

"Now, on the down side, we're a day behind on this, so he's got a good jump on us. As if this weren't enough, Colombia is one incredibly porous place. It borders five other countries and two frigging oceans, and it has all kinds of jungles and mountains. I mean if Marcel wants to go, he'll go."

I pondered these good news/bad news developments.

"But," Val said, "here's where Rodrigo's pressure comes in. If we can find the accounts where he actually stashed the money, as opposed to washing it, well, maybe we'll get lucky and have the bankers on our side. All sub rosa, of course. And assuming the loot is still in Panama."

"Oh, right, assuming that…"

"Rodrigo thinks it is," Val said firmly. "Why would Marcel experiment with Lichtenstein or Switzerland or some other place where he probably doesn't know the system? Plus, this guy has always been a nickel and dime kind of lawyer. Rodrigo talks about him having done important things for the firm, but I think he's just blowing smoke. What I hear from everyone else is that this is a mousy kind of guy pretty much being thrown the bones of their legal work. I mean, look which foundation they gave him—the dollar stores, for God's sake, cantinas and gas stations, little 7-11 type businesses. Nothing that takes imagination or vision. It was just his luck these businesses pull in a lot of cash."

"It makes sense," I said. "Sometimes, I think about lawyers and expect them all to be F. Lee Bailey. Obviously that's crazy, which is why so many end up in politics. Couldn't pull their weight with clients, so what better thing than to try to run the country? In this case, Marcel couldn't hack the real work, so he turned to another way of making money."

Val, whose interest in politics, even peripherally, bordered on the non-existent, put his head back, gazed at the sky and exhaled contentedly. "So," he said, "all we have to do is work on locating those accounts and once we've found 'em, sit tight. When Marcel tries to access the money—bang, we've got him."

"I don't know about the sitting tight part," I said. "Let's find Marcel *and* the loot. We all have a big stake in how this comes out. We need to push on both fronts."

"Agreed," Val said. "I was talking mostly about what I can do to help locate the accounts." He coughed. "And speaking of our interests, I've also been giving some thought…in the odd moment or so…to how we might actually organize…for lack of a better word…the ownership of this thing."

My eyebrows rose involuntarily. Val backpedaled fast.

"Not what you're thinking, Pen. You're the beneficiary, I know that, but I've more or less burned my bridges and you did say—"

I put my hand up to stop him. "You're absolutely right. I said you would be an owner, and you will be. But I've got to find out precisely what we're dealing with first or I may not be around to be part of your plan."

Val focused on his feet. "You know, it's not a plan, not after one day. Just a few thoughts. And I hate having to put it like this, but it's also because of this threat and the shooting and the mugging that I think we need to put some guidelines down on paper." He looked up. "Sorry, that was a shitass thing to say."

"No." My turn to apologize. Val had rightly judged the hazard facing me and the problems it posed for him. He had, after all, made a huge leap of faith.

"Okay," I said, "why don't you pull a salary for the next six months? Double what you were getting back home."

That produced a smile.

"Add some expenses, whatever's necessary, just make it work. Get it on the computer and printed tonight. I'll sign it. Then do some kind of statement that has to do with ownership. A memo of understanding, that kind of thing. Call Thomas. Run it by him. Or ask him to do it. Take it to Rodrigo tomorrow. There's probably some kind of document to fill out here but at least it'll get things started."

"Done," Val said, "and thanks for that."

"I also wonder if we shouldn't get Thomas down here to look at the legal side of things. I was thinking about it earlier today. There's no way we can make any major changes until you've gone over the books and somebody we trust, preferably Thomas, has a chance to get a grip on the legal side. Even with that, there's nothing to stop him from writing up some serious agreements that will protect everybody." I sighed and looked at the silver mud. "Just in case the next shot hits…"

"Pen!"

"… the other leg," I said.

We sat quietly for a while, drinking Beam, enjoying the breeze, the rustle of exotic plants, and the gentle murmur of water flowing into the ponds. Eventually I stood up, made my way through the landscaping down the terrace, walked back, then down and back a second time, feeling all the injuries but also the bourbon. Val, knowing me, waited quietly until it came out.

It wasn't that I expected Marcel to be nabbed particularly soon. So far we had two countries involved; there might easily be others. Despite Rodrigo's connections, we were still dealing with a fiercely protective banking sector. Things like that were complicated and took time to resolve. I fully appreciated that we might be in for a lengthy wait on the money. That would be fine as long as I was still around when we found it. But, in a way, this was old pie. There was something else nagging me. Something I hadn't been able to talk about with anyone else. I struggled to explain it to Val in a way that wouldn't sound positively ludicrous.

"Look, Val," I said, "think about it like this: Here I am a normal guy with a job. Sometimes boring, sometimes exciting. I meet interesting people, I do a lot of socializing, do some other cool things, too, but it's more or less mainstream, a job most people can understand.

"One day, I wake up, I'm rich beyond my dreams. I have not one, but sixty-three companies, all wrapped up in a bunch of arcane foundations in a foreign country. I've gone from a life I was completely at home with to something that could be on the Moon for all I understand of it."

"It's early days yet," Val said sensibly. "Things will sort themselves out. We'll get Marcel. It'll all settle down."

"I wasn't thinking about Marcel so much as this whole enterprise. I still don't have the slightest clue about this beneficiary business But I have a penthouse. I can spend all the money I want. I can go anywhere, do virtually anything, it's as close to heaven as you can get. It sounds like there are no restraints, no obligations. Nothing."

I paced some more. I felt Val's eyes following me.

"In reality, I don't own any of it. Not this apartment, not the businesses, not the cash in the banks. It's all an illusion. We were talking ownership a minute ago. I know what you were getting at but it rams home the fact that I literally don't have a dollar more than I had when I left Washington on Sunday. But I can use it all. And spend it all. And I could probably take every last dime and live on the Riviera for the rest of my life—legally."

"Sounds pretty good to me," Val said.

"Right, but there's a catch. I never thought I'd say something this bizarre, but the thing that worries me most is that nobody expects me to acknowledge one single penny. And something even scarier—the word taxes has never been mentioned. In fact, it's almost as though everyone is carefully avoiding it. I may not have known about these Panamanian foundations, Val, but I know that Panama is a tax haven. And I know what our government does to people who use one."

A tug began at the corner of Val's mouth.

"Smile all you want," I said, "but if you think almost getting killed and being embezzled aren't enough to keep a person awake at night, just try taxes on for size. When I do sleep, you know what my dreams are about? Not lying on a gorgeous beach with beautiful girls. No. Men in blue suits. Guys with short haircuts and calculators. They carry huge briefcases and have the letters IRS stenciled on their pockets and they're the meanest looking SOBs you've ever seen."

Val did his best not to laugh.

"But you and I both know those are only dreams," he said soothingly, as though he'd reassured hundreds of clients, which he probably had.

"Dreams or not, those barbarians are taking me away in handcuffs and, I'll tell you, Val, my psyche doesn't like it one little bit."

Val turned serious. "Look, give me a few days to work through the theft and get a grip on what that means, then I'll call Thomas and between us we'll figure this out. In the meantime, the IRS isn't after you. So stop dwelling on it."

"Huh."

"I mean it. They probably figure you're still playing with Lawrence."

"Well, that's comforting," I said. "I really want folks thinking I'm hanging out with a pedophile."

"My advice is to start focusing on women." Val's standard, no matter what the problem.

"Right," I said, not very hopefully. "Then at least, if I don't sleep, it'll be for a good reason."

"Attaboy," said Val, grinning. "Contemplate exercise and you'll be a new man."

My skin burned at the thought. Easy for him to say after exercise with Maria.

The bastard.

We both went indoors, Val prepared the paperwork and I signed it. Afterwards, I thought about a comment Val made. Something along the lines of: "When Marcel tries to access the money—bang, we've got him."

Now, in the privacy of my own room, the words came back to me. Finding Marcel's accounts and waiting for him to dip into them might be a good strategy for recovering the money. But giving Marcel free rein to move about and take another swipe at me was definitely not part of the deal. Despite the plane ticket, no one had convincingly proved the guy was in Colombia and Val's insistence that embezzlers don't make good murderers had failed to sway me.

I made a decision. It had been a possibility in the back of my mind since the shooting. Now, it was time to become a reality.

My final act of the night was to phone a friend, a man whom one did not call lightly.

Marcel had been playing me long enough. It was time to see about turning the tables.

CHAPTER 14

Friday morning, I went down to the lobby with Val to watch for Bruno and Ignacio. For the first time, I was concerned about my cousin. I suggested he move to a hotel.

Val shrugged off my unease. "If Marcel's the guy, he's gone. And if it's someone else in the firm, by now they realize there's no point in killing either of us. What would it accomplish?"

I started to answer, then stopped. He had a point.

"Besides, Enriqué will take care of my transportation, Bruno will prevent any bashes over the head, and the guards here seem competent—"

We both glanced at the two bulky men lounging behind the reception desk. Competent is not the word I would have chosen at that particular moment. Well-fed and half-asleep maybe.

I was saved the necessity of a rejoinder as a black SUV pulled up and Val and I jumped in. The comforting bulk of Bruno and the skilled driving of Ignacio were reassuring. In no time, and especially, no time worrying, we were delivered to Fernandez-Chavira, Villaroel and Marroquin.

The scene that greeted us was different from the past two days. People seemed more relaxed. Some were smiling. I wondered if the happy faces were reflecting genuine good news or if they were simply projecting cheerfulness in the face of calamity.

The question was answered seconds later by a clearly buoyed Rodrigo. The police had a credible informant, he announced, and were at that moment conducting searches in two *Bogotá* neighborhoods. "It's only a function of time," he said. "The Colombian police are efficient." His blue eyes glittered. "Once Marcel is in custody, it won't be long before the location of the money becomes clear."

I was surprised at how quickly Marcel, the faithful company servant who couldn't possibly have committed a crime, had become Marcel, a traitorous thief. Even though I was convinced he was the one who shot me, I still winced at thoughts of how he might be made pliant. At the same time, I recognized this part of the world had a different set of rules, tougher than I'd ever played by, and ones I couldn't have influenced if I tried. What would go on between Marcel and his captors, I was sure, would never reach my ears. It might have been base of me but I asked no questions. All I needed or wanted to know had been conveyed by the cold sparkle of Rodrigo's eyes.

CHAPTER 15

After dispensing with the subject of Marcel, I told Rodrigo about my trip, then took off with Ignacio and Bruno. Leaving the city was a relief. Over the last several days, I'd become increasingly curious about the Panama that existed beyond its modern, thriving capital. Money had insulated me from the moment I'd arrived, providing the kind of barrier against real life that I supposed most rich people enjoy. Not only was I not accustomed to the barrier, it had begun to chafe. I wanted to put my hand on the country's pulse and feel it beating.

As we moved through the city, the buildings on our route became older, the populace less well dressed. People relentlessly dodged in and out of traffic hawking their wares. Street-side markets popped up on every corner. We passed large government buildings in Spanish-colonial style and pristine lawns studded with royal palms. A university appeared and with it protest signs I couldn't wholly decipher but, certain things being universal, understood anyway. Capitalists are pigs. The revolution is good. *Yanqui* go home.

After that came the slums. Nothing special there. Sadly, slums are slums, and I'd yet to see a city without them.

As we went further, dense tropical foliage appeared. I'd read somewhere that Panama City has an actual rainforest within its boundaries. With enormous trees towering over us and exotic plants pressing against the road, this looked close enough. A few moments of intense greenery later and we found ourselves on the "Bridge of the Americas," an edifice that effectively spanned two continents and towered over the Canal. All too soon, both it and the greatest man-made waterway in the world were solidly behind us, and we were entering what Panamanians called "The Interior."

Panama runs in an East-West direction, the only nation in the Western Hemisphere to do so. Shaped like a thin, twisted snake, it has one country-long road, the "Pan-American Highway." This thoroughfare flows uninterruptedly from Alaska to Chile, except for the southernmost part of Panama next to Colombia—the infamous *Darien Gap*. With impenetrable jungle and rampant lawlessness, the *Gap* was considered one of the most dangerous spots in the world.

As Ignacio sped us westward on the well-paved Pan-American, I looked out the window and saw slices of towns, all similarly scruffy the way roadside communities usually are. In between, small cement houses dotted the road. No matter how humble, most had well-manicured topiary in the front yard, an oddity that I found charming.

After a while, I consulted the map and figured we were about an hour from our destination. A few hills and a few minutes later, we passed the town of *St. Fabiano*, a pleasant little hamlet distinguished by a pretty central square with an equally pretty church. Ignacio turned us in the direction of the mountains, and we began our ascent to *Montañas del Cielo*.

The new road was an unpleasant surprise. Barely wide enough for one car, its foundation was rubble and its surface was pockmarked with holes. We climbed grades that had increasingly precipitous drop-offs, flirted with the edge of the road, said our prayers. More than once the SUV lost traction, entered a skid, and began grinding to regain its footing. I looked out the window and wondered how soon one of our wheels would slip and we'd hurtle into nothingness. I'd jump out, I decided, if that happened. It had to be a better alternative than plummeting down the side of a canyon and winding up in a flaming coffin.

To his credit, Ignacio held us steady as we cautiously wound around a series of particularly steep bends. His hands were clenched with the effort of holding the steering wheel straight. His face was wet with perspiration.

We slid around one bend, then another. "Stop!" I yelled, and simultaneously Ignacio slammed on the brakes. The car shimmied and, for one god-awful moment, fishtailed, before stopping only millimeters short of an enormous pile of trees, rocks, mud, and ruptured pavement—a huge mountain slide that obliterated the road and spilled into the valley.

Ignacio, Bruno and I all sat dazedly for a moment, then Bruno and I climbed out of the car to help Ignacio back up and begin the arduous process of turning around. Eventually, we had the SUV swung back in the direction we came from. I pulled out my cell to call Robyn Butler and give her the bad news.

Before I could punch in her number, the phone rang.

"I'm glad I've caught you," she said. "There's been a landslide on the road."

"We're at it," I answered, "about to head back down. We're probably fifteen minutes or so from San Fabiano."

"Perfect," she said. "There's a helicopter here in the *Montanas*. The pilot's taking some people to Panama City and he'll drop me off on the way at a beach resort called *Boca del Mar*. It's not far from *San Fabiano*. I've already reserved two cabanas. We can start with lunch and a visit to the beach and you can decide how long you'd like to stay."

"Sounds great."

"It should take you under an hour," she said. "The helicopter's not leaving until almost then so you'll arrive a few minutes before I do. Grab yourself a seat on the terrace and have a Margarita. They make the best ones in the world."

Fifty minutes later, I saw the sign for *Boca del Mar* and we snaked through the colorful beach town of *Las Naranjas* to the resort. Ignacio pulled in and we drove around a circular drive that ringed a giant banyan tree. Bruno and I walked up some steps and came to a huge thatched, open-sided room that seemed to serve as lobby, reception, reading area, bar, and dining room all in one. I had been expecting a typical modern resort behemoth by the sea. What I saw was a pleasant surprise.

While Ignacio looked after the car, I reconnoitered for a few minutes, wandering down to a secluded pool and over to a small, lush garden. Fronting it all was a magnificent beach with high rollers coming in on a rising tide. Half a dozen surfers were out in the water; a few more taking breaks on the sand. I made my way to the bar and ordered. " I'll have a Margarita if you can put some bourbon in there," I said. The bartender looked mystified. "Okay, Margarita on the rocks." I sighed. When in Rome and all that.

I took my drink to the terrace, waved Bruno over to the bar, and found a comfortable table under more thatching. I looked again at the gardens and saw cabanas peeking through the heavy vegetation. Each one fronted on the beach but seemed private enough. Time to claim mine.

I finished my Margarita and returned to the bar. "Another one," I told the bartender. "I'll be back to get it in a minute."

I headed toward the car, but Ignacio was already approaching reception with my bag. "I'll be fine here by myself," I told Bruno. "You can come back to check on me if you like but it's not necessary. Go find yourselves a comfortable place to stay and have something to eat. I'll call if I need you." I peeled off five twenties and handed them over.

Ignacio protested. "No, es mucho, mucho."

"Keep it," I told them. "You never know when you might need some cash." They stared at me the same way the bartender had.

A few minutes later, I surveyed one of the cabanas Robyn had reserved. Lots of louvered doors, ceiling fans, tile on the floor, a cathedral ceiling made of what looked like teak. All very tropical. Very nice. And nobody hiding in the closet. I stowed my gear and headed for the bar and the waiting

Margarita. Then it was back to the terrace, where I plopped down again and checked my watch. It had been a little more than an hour since Robyn phoned. I took a sip of my drink and began listening for the distinctive sounds of a helicopter.

Moments later, I heard noise and saw a speck in the sky off to my left. The speck grew larger and I surveyed the beach for the likeliest spot to set down. The chopper would stir up one hell of a sandstorm when it landed and the wind was briskly blowing in my direction. Any closer than fifty yards and the resort would look like Saudi Arabia.

I watched as the speck grew into a decipherable shape and bore down on the beach about a football field away. Suddenly, without warning, the rhythmic heartbeat of the copter spasmed and the machine went into a sickening, lop-sided spin, a giant, sick bird, flailing at the air and losing altitude every second. As I leapt off the terrace and began sprinting, the copter wheeled uncontrollably, its blades aiming for the ground. "No!" I screamed as the nose plowed furiously into the sand, tail disintegrating, deadly metal shards shooting out everywhere. A gigantic rush of sand came toward me.

Some of the surfers saw the crash and were sprinting for the downed chopper. I raced as fast as the sand would let me, trying to clear my eyes as I headed into the sandstorm, my pace quickened by ominous black smoke coming from what was left of the helicopter. I looked back for a second at the men following me. There would be enough of us to help, if we could just get there in time.

I poured it on for the last twenty-five yards, despite being nearly blinded by the sand. I could see two people outside the copter but, as I got closer, I spied another on the ground, unmoving, half buried by debris. A man in a flayed suit was trying to dig him out. A third man, large and fleshy, was dazed and staggering. Shattered pieces of the copter were everywhere. There was no sign of anyone who might be Robyn.

The staggering man shouted at me. "There's a woman inside! She can't get out!" Then he grabbed his side and fell to his knees.

The gas fumes hit me just as I was reaching the wreck. The helicopter had fallen almost at a right angle, with its skids pointing at eleven o'clock and what was left of the nose and passenger side rammed deep in the sand at a 45 degree angle. The guy who was moving the debris off the prone man hurried over. "Nothing to be done for him, poor bastard. Maybe we'll have more luck with her." He cocked his head toward the intact portion of the copter, dropped to his haunches and began trying to dig out the passenger door with his hands. "We opened the pilot's door on the other side but she's wedged in pretty tight between the seat and the floor back here," he said. "We tried to pull her out but she screamed that her foot is caught. We have to get this door open."

I dropped to my knees and joined in the digging. "The pilot?" I asked. My fellow digger inclined his head toward the man on his knees. "It's a miracle he made it." He kept digging. "I'm Bill Atherton. Down here on business, mostly."

"Pen Smith," I answered. "Ditto."

By then, the surfers had arrived and we organized an effort to save the woman—Robyn—from the wreck. The smoke had thickened and the gas fumes were nearly overpowering. Two of the surfers joined us in the digging. We were trying to carve out enough space to expose the passenger side and, more particularly, the door, but it was hard going because of the needle-like metal shards that had buried themselves in the sand. In addition to the rest of our problems, we had to dig down and then under the copter until we reached the handle or the door fell open.

After a while, a small part of the window was exposed, but at an awkward angle. I craned my neck and looked through the opening, trying unsuccessfully to make out a shape. I put my ear to the glass. Ominously, no sounds issued from the cabin. I dug faster, wrapping my shirt around my hands for protection. Another of the surfers came over and asked what he could do. "How about you and your buddies get those two back to the resort? One needs help pretty bad." I nodded at the pilot and the man who was prone on the sand, still partially covered with detritus. "If this thing explodes, we all need to be scarce."

"Sure," the man said. "No problem." He motioned the remaining surfers over. They combined forces to remove the debris on the unmoving man. Quickly, they lifted both men and headed down the beach toward *Boca del Mar*.

I grabbed a piece of jagged metal we'd thrown aside and ruthlessly hacked off my trousers above the knee. Then I slit each pant leg lengthwise and handed everyone a piece. I tied my own around my nose and mouth, the others following my lead. It helped, but the fumes were getting stronger by the second and every other breath ended up in a cough.

"Hey!" someone shouted. "We've got the handle."

That kicked us into double-time. We dug furiously, still trying to avoid the embedded metal but occasionally feeling a slice of pain as we hit a piece. As soon enough of the door was exposed, I slid a few feet under the copter, grabbed the handle and pulled, sending a light shower of sand down on my face, enough to momentarily blind me.

The other men were still digging. "Oh, Jesus," Atherton said, pulling his hands up. He held them in front of us. They were dripping with gasoline.

"Put your hands back down in that shit," I said to the diggers. "Get your fingers as close to this bird as they'll go. Then, on the count of three, push up and back as hard as you can. Got it?"

Their faces showed fear but their hands buried themselves in the sand. I turned over on my back and bent my legs, feet on the fuselage.

"All right, one, two—"

At three, we all pushed. There was a jolt as the copter rocked back about a foot. I caught my breath, praying that we wouldn't all go up in flames. "Hold it there," I yelled, as the door fell open and swung a few inches. "Not enough!" I hollered.

I held the space open with my arms, fighting the sand, and turning my body sideward to try to force myself into the tiny space. "Robyn, can you hear me?" I wedged my foot in between the door and the jamb and my hand touched something soft—and alive. "Keep digging!" I called to the men. "I can feel her!"

I pulled against the door, trying to widen it. Through the slit, I could finally make out a dark shape covered by sand and debris. Beyond her, where a seat should have been, there was nothing but more sand. A head jerked up between a long, bent scrap of metal and what looked like part of a seat. I saw a shock of black hair, a pale face streaked with blood, and one huge sapphire blue eye.

"Give me your hand. I'll pull you out."

The eye opened wide with fright.

The men were digging like crazy and the door opened another inch, then another, and sometime after that I pushed myself into the space, forced as much junk off Robyn as possible, and reached my arms around her. "We've got to go before the fuel tank blows. I'll pull as hard as I can. It'll probably hurt like hell but your leg should be able slide out from this angle." I heard a whimper. I lifted her under her arms, wrapping my fingers tight.

"We've got fire out here!" a voice bellowed. "You gotta get out—NOW!" A second voice, abnormally high pitched, suddenly pierced the cacophony of noise. "Run!" the voice screamed, panic soaking the words. "Everybody run!!"

"We're coming out," I shouted. "Pull my legs!" I felt hands grasp my ankles, a tug, then a harder one and we both slid out, free, collapsing into each other and onto the sand. *"Go, go, go!"* I screamed at the man who pulled us out. I lifted Robyn with both arms and stumbled forward. My arms and legs were feeling the stress of fighting the chopper, my thigh was burning from pain, Robyn was dead-weight. There was too much soft sand to cover. I tried to go faster and felt it sucking at my feet.

I thought frantically, then stopped and turned abruptly toward the ocean.

"Robyn, can you hear me? I'm taking us to the water, then I'll swim us down to the resort. If the thing explodes, we'll go under for a few seconds to avoid the debris, then I'll get you right back up." I didn't say the rubble was likely to be coated with fuel and burning as it rained down on us.

A second later, we were in the water. The beach was at a slant and the breakers were much smaller than they were in front of the resort. I pushed us out, then turned parallel to the shore and began swimming, holding Robyn in the crook of my arm. It was hard going but not nearly as much as trying to race in the sand, and someone was smiling on us because the undertow was running in our direction.

I heard and felt the explosion simultaneously. The force of it pushed us underwater and Robyn panicked, one arm flailing away at my face and a leg weakly jabbing me in the groin. As gently as I could, I brought her to the surface, both of us sputtering water. There were fragments of the helicopter all around, smelling of gas and fire. Robyn began thrashing, and her arm hit a fiery piece of junk. She screamed, her body jerking in pain. "We're going under again to get clear of this crap," I told her. "Take a big breath, don't fight me and we'll be on the surface again in less than a minute. I promise you." A whimper. "Whatever you do, don't try to stop me. Okay, here we go. Deep breath. Now."

I pulled us down again, looping my arms to hold Robyn by the shoulders. I swam forward, letting the tide help us, and when I felt Robyn begin to squirm, popped us up to the surface. I looked around and realized the debris was following us. "Once more," I said to Robyn's terrified face. "Big breath. Go!"

The third time was easier. By then, Robyn knew I'd get us back to the surface and stayed still until it became clear by small pinches on my arms that she was running out of air. I took us up. We'd cleared the wreckage. "Everything's okay," I told Robyn, coughing. "We've made it."

I pulled her carefully through the water and we were halfway to the resort when I heard a noise coming from the beach. I looked over and saw people standing there, clapping and cheering. Two muscled men were swimming toward us fast. More surfers. They reached us and gently lifted a nearly comatose Robyn from my arms and rushed her toward land. Once there, two others laced their arms to form a chair. Robyn was lowered and the men took off. I watched for a minute, feeling my exhaustion as I slowly waded out of the water.

"Need some help, man?" someone on the beach asked. I shook my head. "No, thanks, I'm good." A couple of others patted me on the shoulder. One guy gave the thumbs up sign. I doubled over unexpectedly and spit out black water. Somebody thumped me on the back and I brought up some more. Eventually, everyone turned toward the resort. Breathing deeply, occasionally coughing and spitting more black, I let my legs go at their own pace. With every step, I wondered if Robyn would make it.

CHAPTER 16

When I finally reached the resort, it became nothing more than a pit stop for dry clothes, a fresh bandage for the leg, and a phone call to Ignacio. Robyn and the others had already been taken to the nearest hospital, forty minutes away, in the opposite direction from Panama City. While I waited for Ignacio and Bruno, the bartender pressed a fresh Margarita in my hand and people clapped me on the back. A couple of Americans and a Brit sprinkled their comments with the word "hero." I tried to smile and make nice, when all I wanted was for my bodyguard and driver to show up.

As soon as they appeared, I dove into the car and we rocketed toward the city of Santiago, reaching the hospital in what must have been record time. Once there, I sat in a tiny waiting area until someone took me to Robyn's room. When her gurney was finally rolled in, she was asleep, not a bad thing to be when you've got a patch over one eye, a wad of gauze for a head, and splints on your arm and leg. Then there were the tubes. Despite all that, I couldn't help but notice the soft curve of her cheek and the pearl-like quality of her skin. Surpising, I thought, to have come through an ordeal like that and maintain any looks at all.

"You are the husband?" a man in a white coat asked me in pretty good English. Embroidered on his coat was *Julio Arauz, Medico.*

I stood up and shook hands. "No, just a friend, Dr. Arauz. I was with her after the helicopter went down."

"Ah, you are the American who saved her."

"A lot of people helped," I said. "Is she all right?"

"Yes, yes. She'll be fine. She has a mild concussion, some lacerations on her scalp—not very deep—a hematoma next to her eye. Her ankle is sprained, and she has a broken arm. That's why we had to operate. To put in a metal plate, you understand."

I nodded.

"She's lucky," Dr. Arauz said. "She'll need to rest for a few days, but she can probably go home tomorrow." The doctor sighed. "Unfortunately, another passenger was not so fortunate."

I thought back to the scene and the man who wasn't moving. I hadn't paid him much attention except to tell the surfers to get him back to the resort.

"It was a terrible crash," I said. "How are the others?"

The doctor shook his head. "The pilot is being treated here. He has a head wound, several broken ribs, and some internal bleeding. He's been able to say there was a mechanical problem but not much more. Another passenger sustained almost no wounds at all and he confirms the pilot's story." That would be Atherton, I thought.

"He's with the police at the moment, but I believe he plans to return to Panama City," the doctor said. "Eventually, they'll want to talk to Miss Butler. In the meantime, you can speak with her when she wakes up. Not too long, though. She needs to sleep."

Dr. Arauz left and I moved toward the woman in the bed. She was pale but breathing regularly. The arm in the cast was folded on her stomach, the other one lay beside her. I looked at her hand. Her fingers were straight and long, her nails painted a deep ruby hue. She was younger than I'd expected. Close to my own age.

I sat down and watched her for a while, then suddenly her lashes blinked and I saw a spark of life in her good eye.

"How are you?" I asked.

She tried to smile.

"Stupid of me," I said. "How about: 'Can I get you anything? Water, Margarita, a new helicopter?'"

I could tell she was trying to laugh but it was hurting her. "Don't," I said. "I promise, no more wisecracks. It's just that I feel pretty useless."

"You saved my life." Her voice was husky, soft.

"Yeah, but that's over. I need something new to do."

This time she did laugh. It came out like a dog's bark.

"Seriously, can I buy you some clothes, toiletries, that kind of thing? Call your husband or boyfriend, someone at your house?"

The good blue eye tracked me as I moved from one side of the bed to the other. Hospitals made me nervous so I tended to walk around a lot.

"My parents are on vacation in Europe. I'll tell them when they get back. There's nobody else to notify except my housekeeper," she answered thickly. "Her number is—" She paused. "Well, that's silly, I can't remember it." She thought a moment. "Anyway it's in my purse. If you'll just take a look—"

"*Was* in your purse," I said. "Nothing could have survived that explosion."

She gave me a cute, lopsided kind of smile. "I had the purse underneath my jacket, looped around my neck and under my arm. I always wear it like that when I travel. Such a bitch if it gets lost." Her good eye crinkled. "Didn't you feel it when you grabbed me?"

I thought back and shook my head. "I was a little distracted at the time. Or maybe I did and thought it was part of your outfit." I smiled back at her. "Women's clothes are always a mystery to me."

"Mine don't usually have lumps," she said and the eye danced.

I opened an empty cabinet, then a bureau. I found the purse in the top drawer.

"There's an address book that's probably soaked. If you can, go down to the Cs and find the number for Carmencita. She speaks English. Maybe it would be better if you explain to her. My mouth isn't working too well."

"Yes ma'am," I said, gently thumbing the wet pages. I was surprised they weren't just sodden goop. After a minute, I found the number and punched it in, then explained to the housekeeper what had happened. "Lots of *Dios Mios*," I told Robyn, as I hung up.

"The clothes and toiletries are probably a good idea, if you don't mind," she said with an effort. Sleeping pills kicking in again.

"I'm on it," I answered.

"Size six for clothes." Robyn looked at me, a slight flush on her cheeks. "Underwear...well...34C for the bra and four for panties. Then toothbrush, that kind of thing, please."

I scribbled it down with only the barest thought as to how intimate this woman and I had suddenly become. After all, she was Uncle Henry's "very good friend." That put her in a different category.

"Go to sleep. I'll get these and give them to the nurse. Tomorrow, I'll be here to take you to the resort. Since you can't get up the mountain for a while, the cabana looks like the perfect place to recuperate."

The eye drooped and I walked toward the door.

"How are the others?"

I told her what I knew.

Robyn closed her eye on a whimper. It was accompanied by a fat tear that glided down her face.

I waited a moment, then went to her bedside. I put my hand over hers. "You need anything, have them call me." I scribbled my number on a piece of paper and stuck it on the table next to the bed.

"A knight in shining armor," she murmured. "How lucky am I?" She gently squeezed my hand and then let go. She'd fallen asleep.

I headed for the door and turned back to look at her.

Intriguing.

I wanted to see what lay underneath the bandages.

OH my!

They kept Robyn an extra day, which gave me plenty of time to shop, confer with the doctor, and locate a private duty nurse. I poked my head in, let her know she had clothes and toiletries, and asked if she needed anything else. "Just sleep," she said, and promptly closed her eyes.

When I entered the hospital room the next afternoon, I was struck by the change in her appearance. She was sitting in a chair, most of the dressings off her head, wearing the airy white blouse and tan pants I'd bought her. Her ankle was wrapped, her arm in a soft cast and sling. She looked comfortable enough, except for a swollen and very blackened eye, which was already turning an ugly shade of purple. Although her hair in the helicopter had hung more or less straight to about chin level, it was now standing up and out in floppy black spikes, pulled away from a smattering of stitches criss-crossing her scalp.

"Love what you've done with your hair," I said with a grin, before my inner angel could stop me. Amazing what you felt you could say to someone you'd met in a helicopter crash. Instinctively, I had also known Robyn had a good sense of humor. Her kooky, one-sided smile shared the joke with me.

"Tomorrow I can shampoo it," she said. "Until then, I'm just your average punk rocker."

"It's becoming but why don't we dye it blue? Then it would match your eye."

"Or purple? That would match the other eye."

We grinned at each other.

"Are you ready to blow this place?"

Her good foot wiggled at me. "I guess I can get by without shoes."

"Ma'am, I just happen to have a pair." I pulled some slippers out of a bag behind my back. "Forgot to give them to the nurse."

"Comfy," Robyn said, her feet transformed into giant pink appendages with rabbits' ears.

"I thought the bunnies were a nice touch. But I didn't know your size," I said apologetically, "so I just guessed."

"What are they, a sixteen?"

"Of course not, they're a ten." Robyn pushed her lips out in a pretend pout. "Hey, they're smaller than what I wear."

"You really don't know much about women's clothes, do you?"

"I think I did pretty well with everything else," I said, stung that my efforts weren't being appreciated.

"Yes, the red hooker panties are especially nice."

"The choices were limited. Also, they looked good to me. Of course, I had to use a bit of imagination to make sure I picked the right ones."

"You didn't!"

"I'm not saying I enjoyed it." I smirked. "It was a chore."

"Men!" Robyn narrowed her eyebrows.

"We can't help it. It comes out of our pores."

"Uhm," she said, looking straight at me. "You, Mr. Pen, are a tease."

I looked right back at her. "You'd better believe it," I said.

Two hours later, we were sitting on her cabana's terrace having a drink, a diluted Margarita for her and some miraculously found bourbon for me. We chatted mostly about inconsequential things—the weather, the accommodations, the ocean. "I don't know when I'll feel like swimming again," she said with a sigh. "All that horrible stuff on fire around us. And I know I'll never get near another helicopter."

"Not surprising you feel that way." I tilted my chair and looked at the orange-tinged sky, pondering metal beasts plunging to the ground.

"When the engine first sputtered, my heart stopped beating— I didn't think I could be more scared than that. Then I looked down—" She began to shake. I reached over and covered her hand with mine. "I just knew the door was going to open and I'd fall out and the helicopter would fall on top of me. I'm sure I was screaming, everyone was, except maybe Andreas." She turned her good eye on me and the terror was still there. Memory. Such a double-edged sword.

I sipped my drink and gently ran my fingers over her hand. Her skin had a compelling softness. "I was in choppers a lot during the war. It wasn't my favorite method of transport but I didn't have any problems with it. Of course, none of those birds ever dropped out of the sky like yours did." I thought a moment. "You might not believe it but the safest aircraft ever built is a copter. The Bell Jet Ranger."

"You'll never convince me." The skin was tight around her mouth. A full, beautifully shaped mouth, I noted.

"No, I guess not." I hadn't meant to make her uncomfortable. Some people work out their fears by talking, others don't.

I decided to change the subject. "So, tell me how you met Uncle Henry."

Her good eye sparkled, and, for the first time, I was struck by how lovely she was. Lovely despite the damage from the wreck and the spikes in her hair. Lovely in a chic woman meets girl-next-door kind of way. I liked what I saw.

"You still call him Uncle Henry," she said. "That's cute."

"Well, I went to live with him when I was a kid, after my parents died in a sailing accident. Even after he adopted me, I always thought of him as my uncle."

"So he was your step-father. I didn't know that. You never visited him here in Panama?" she said.

"I didn't know he was here. I knew he traveled a lot but I never knew where. He surfaced occasionally in D.C. and he'd call. Sometimes, if I was in town, we'd get together. Obviously, we weren't particularly close." I took a pull on my drink. "How about you? How long did you know him?"

"Long enough to appreciate what a wonderful person he was." The eye and the smile colluded in remembered affection. There was a touch of sadness, too, I thought.

"Yeah, he seems to have struck other folks that way, too. Very different from the man I knew—or thought I knew."

"Sometimes, it's hard being yourself around family."

"I guess so. People said he took after my grandfather. He was a quirky genius, an inventor, and a businessman, too. His inventions are in factories around the world. Uncle Henry modernized the business after Granddad died."

"What about the rest of your family?"

"Granddad's will split his company between my three uncles and my mother. Mom sold out to Uncle Henry as soon as she realized she could buy a bigger boat, throw more interesting parties, and send me to all the right schools." I smiled. "The schools were boring but the parties were fun, even for a kid. On the other side of the family, I have two aunts. Fifteen cousins altogether."

"Nice sized family," Robyn said.

"How about you? You don't look Panamanian. Blue eye and all." I thought about it for a second. Rodrigo also had blue eyes and he was obviously Panamanian. Again, the interesting by-products of a mixing bowl society.

"I'm not really. I was born in the Canal Zone. My dad was a physicist who worked for the Canal Authority. My family stayed on after the Canal reverted to Panama." She sipped her drink. "Lots of Americans have settled here and you've probably figured out that English is the country's second language. It's a nice place to live."

"And then Uncle Henry crossed your path."

"At a charity reception about five years ago," Robyn said. "He was giving and I was taking so it worked out perfectly. Later on, he invested in my business."

"That would be…?"

"Fashion. When I met Henry, I had dreams of opening my own house. The reception that first night was to honor up-and-comers in the arts. I was lucky. I received one of the prizes. Henry and I got to know each other and a year later, he became my partner."

"Hmm," I said. I couldn't picture the stern, businesslike Uncle Henry I knew playing with lace and beads and watching a bunch of naked models. Actually, that part I could see. Of course, he might just have been besotted with Robyn.

"He was—you were—?" For some reason, it seemed important to clarify the relationship.

Robyn smiled gently. "Yes and yes."

Although I'd asked the question and expected the answer, I was uncomfortable with it. I especially hate it, I decided, when a dead, ex-uncle is giving me competition—even if I haven't decided whether I want to be in the running.

"How about some dinner?" I said, switching subjects.

"Okay," she yawned. "Sorry, it's all that medicine they've been giving me."

I was alarmed. "I thought you weren't taking that anymore?"

"Oh, don't worry, they don't give you anything strong in Panama. Except the morphine, of course."

I nodded. "Sure, in the hospital you'd need that."

"I have some here, too."

"What?"

"That's the way it works. They pretty much go from Ibuprofen and a few other not very helpful medicines to morphine. It has something to do with their fear of the drug trade taking over everything in between."

"Je-sus," I muttered. "What have you taken today?"

"Don't worry. A couple of Tramacets—they're nothing—and some aspirin. I might dip into the morphine when you leave."

"In that case, I might not leave."

In the almost-darkness, I saw her lips turn upward. "You're not only a tease, you're a nanny. What else are you, Pen Smith?"

For some silly reason, it pleased me that she wanted to know.

The rest of the night passed easily. Bruno came by once or twice to check on me. Robyn and I talked about nothing much and tucked into mountains of seafood and acres of lime pie, which seemed ubiquitous to Panama.

After dinner, Robyn was showing signs of growing weary, so I retrieved her crutches, walked her to the bathroom, and waited while she changed into one of the intimate items I'd bought her. "Not Saks quality, but sturdy and serviceable," I pronounced with a grin as she came out. She gaped at me and tried to keep the skimpy purple and black teddy covered with a towel. It was hard to do with one arm in a sling. I took in a big, satisfied breath. "You know, I could get used to this cross-gender shopping."

"You've obviously lived a depraved life," Robyn said acidly. "Most women do not wear clothes with slits in—in— the wrong places."

"For someone who survived a helicopter crash, you're not very adventurous."

"If I want adventure like this, I'll rent a porno movie."

"Look, I apologize. What you're wearing was the most conservative thing I could find."

"I don't believe you. I think you're a pervert."

"Now, now, Miss Robyn, I've actually seen a pervert up close and I can tell you I'm nothing like that." Just the thought made me uncomfortable.

"Fun and games are over," I said, a tad regretfully. "Time to get in bed."

She made no sign of wanting to move.

I saw the problem. "Okay, I'll help you over so you can sit on the side of the bed and then I'll turn around so you can drop the towel and get under the covers. Deal?"

The blue eye looked skeptical.

"Cross my heart I won't peek." I walked her to the bed, feeling her soft, rounded shape against me as the clumsy towel pulled away from her side. Suddenly, I was sorry the evening was ending.

"All right, you can turn around now."

"Well, thank goodness that's over," I said.

"Worm."

I picked up the phone and called out to the lobby for the nurse to come to the room.

"This worm would now like to see the morphine," I said.

"I don't trust you."

"I just established my trustworthiness. And this time I'm the one who doesn't trust you. I fully intend to make sure the nurse knows how much you've had to drink."

"You'd think I'm a baby, the way you're treating me."

"No," I said softly, "no baby." The words escaped from my mouth before I could stop them.

"Oh, all right, you've got me with that sappy stuff. It's in the bedside table. Little white pills."

Just then, the nurse arrived and I explained about the morphine. The nurse clucked, took the pills, and put them in her handbag. Robyn pouted.

"Remember, I'm next door. Anytime you need me," I said, planting a chaste kiss on her cheek. She looked vaguely surprised.

"What? You thought I'd ravish you or something?"

Robyn turned the lop-sided grin on me, sleepily.

"Well, you could've tried."

"Tomorrow, my lamb," I said, "is another day."

I got up early the next morning, ordered breakfast for two and walked next door. I knocked and sat down on the terrace to wait, listening to the songs of the birds, the chirps of geckos, and the deep-throated a cappella of the ocean.

A few minutes later Robyn appeared.

I poured her some coffee and told her how nice she looked. She sipped from her cup and smiled.

The swollen eye had opened a little. Her hair fell in a shiny black helmet that curled inward a couple of inches below her ears. Her cheeks had color to them and her mouth was delectable in something shimmery and tasty looking. Cover-up had been skillfully applied to the black and purple circle around her eye.

"About the trifles Uncle Henry left for me," I said. "Any chance you had them tucked away in that purse?"

I wasn't particularly hopeful but a moment later I was looking at a small box and a sheaf of papers. I took the top off the box and slowly removed its contents, laying them on the table. I didn't know what I'd expected. What I had were more puzzles from Uncle Henry.

"Do you know anything about these?" I asked with a sigh, holding up four keys.

Robyn munched toast and shook her head.

I sipped coffee and examined the next items, two snapshots, remarkably dry for having been in the ocean. The first was of my mother and father, caught in a moment of radiance on the deck of the doomed *"Skidaway."* The second, a picture of five men posing for the camera and laughing.

I showed that one to Robyn. "No idea," she said. "Except—" She scrutinized the photo. "I've never seen any of them before but, a wild guess, they could be Henry's poker group. He spent a lot of time in a town named *Boquete*. He called it his poker retreat,"

At last, an intersection of something I knew about Uncle Henry and something known in Panama as well.

The final item in the box fit with Robyn's theory: a playing card, the King of Hearts, with a hole through the head. I tapped it against the table. "At home, around his poker friends, Uncle Henry was known as 'The Killer.'"

We both spent a moment contemplating that.

"There's one more thing," Robyn said. She handed me some papers. "It's only a fax. When I decided to come down here on the helicopter, I mistakenly left the original at home. Thank God. I had Carmencita fax a copy here this morning."

"It looks like a deed," I said, flipping through the pages.

"Do you want me to translate for you?"

I handed it to Robyn. "Maybe just hit the high spots."

"All right." She read for a minute. "Yes, it's a deed. Let me see—it's for a coffee farm in that town I mentioned, *Boquete*. Altogether, it consists of 95 hectares." She did some quick math. "About 250 acres, probably planted in a mix of both coffee and oranges—they do that there—and most of it would be mountainous."

"Right."

She flipped through several more pages. "It all seems to be in order. Lots of official stamps everywhere—the Panamanians love to stamp things. The more times the better. There's one other interesting thing. It has a lovely name. *Sophie de las Estrellas.*" She looked over at me. "That means 'Sophie of the Stars.'"

I felt the moisture on my face before I even realized I was crying.

"My mother's name," I explained, after pulling myself together. I fingered the papers, let out a noisy breath and stood up. I'd been blindsided—again. How much longer would Uncle Henry's little surprises go on? Every day brought a new piece of raw meat to digest.

"Uncle Henry is playing with me," I said.

"What do you mean?" Robyn asked.

"I mean all this crap. Just when I think I'm clean, more shit comes along." I reached over and picked up the handful of keys. "These crazy things in the box. A farm with my mother's name on it. From the letter he sent me about his quote orchard unquote to this, nothing's been straightforward." I thought about the fact that even Robyn bore my uncle's imprint, then caught myself. For God's sake, I barely knew the woman. Okay, maybe that wasn't entirely true. I knew her a little bit. And I liked that bit. I could like more bits, given half a chance.

"I'm sorry." She shrugged. "Maybe—"

I flipped my hand in annoyance. "Not your problem."

Bad move. The sapphire eyes turned frosty. She gave me a smile like you'd give the substitute postman.

I sighed. Never flip off a woman. Never.

I knew that.

I really did.

CHAPTER 17

I made peace with Robyn. Her feelings for Uncle Henry were obviously still raw, so I put myself on a leash. Who was killing who in the world was okay. Griping about Uncle Henry was not. Our work provided plenty to chat about, and my new status, of course. Uncle Henry crept in here and there but I resisted the urge to comment, except in general terms. Overall, we seemed to have lots to say to each other, although sometimes it was enough to simply sit and watch the ocean together.

We took most of our meals on one or the other of our terraces. Twice, we went to the resort's dining room and ate to the sounds of reggae music, the squawks of toucans, and the jabber of parrots. It was a surprisingly pleasant interlude, and, if I hadn't known there'd been a helicopter crash, it would have been the last thought on my mind.

On the first day at *Boca del Mar*, I'd accepted that I was attracted to Robyn. On the second, I wondered what I was going to do about it. Her relationship with Uncle Henry posed a problem, seemingly for both of us. She was desirable, he'd been her lover, now I wanted that status. An unusual triangle, but a triangle nonetheless. After thinking about it almost nonstop, on the evening of the second day, I received a phone call that sent my mind in an entirely different direction. The next morning, I was off on a mission, piloted by Ignacio and protected by Bruno.

It took us about two hours to reach our destination, a restaurant that sat up on a slight hill facing the ocean, thatched roof ruffling in the breeze. To one side there were spreading trees and wattled gray Brahman cattle. On the other, a bright green rice field.

It was mid-day but the restaurant was large and surprisingly cool. I looked around and saw the costume of the day was swimsuits and Ts. My clothes consisted of a blue polo shirt and khakis. I felt over-dressed.

After I sat down, I put my newly acquired Spanish vocabulary to work and ordered a *cerveza*. When the waitress burbled back at me, I heard two recognizable words: *"Panama"* and *"Balboa."* In a display of mixed-up sentiment for the nation that seemed to want me both rich and dead, I ordered a *"Panama."*

Seconds later, the beer and menu arrived, both in Spanish. I eyed the menu suspiciously.

"Maybe I can help you with that."

I rose. "Sax."

"Pen."

We smiled and shook hands.

"You picked a tough spot for the other side," I said as we sat. "Anybody follow me in?"

"Would we still be here if they had?"

I laughed. "Dumb question." Sax's eyes were unobtrusively but relentlessly examining every person in the room, lingering on Bruno.

"Bodyguard," I said.

"Looks it. No subtlety."

I chuckled. I'd seen Sax only once since the war, though we'd talked by phone a few times, three nights ago being the most recent. He'd let his eyebrows go a little wild, his hair was longer and pulled back into a neat black ponytail, and he had an immaculately kept goatee. Otherwise, he looked pretty much the way he always had, his clothes all black and Italian, his superb physical condition projecting a leanness and height he didn't actually have. His only striking defect was the absence of the two middle fingers on his left hand. Sometimes I'd seen him wear a glove; today, he was au naturel.

"You're lookin' good," he said. "Especially for a guy who oughta be dead."

"Trying to avoid that," I pointed out.

"Unh," he said and lit a cigarette. "You were lucky to find me, another two days I'd have been in Budapest."

"Work?" I asked.

"Nope. Visiting a woman. Met her here doing some white water."

I remembered that rafting was one of Sax's interests. Big rafting. He'd probably been on one of Panama's Class IV rivers, the kind Olympians use for training.

"Enough small talk. Your boy's not in *Bogatá*," he said. "That was bullshit they handed you."

I raised my eyebrows. I'd spoken to Rodrigo before I left and the word was that Marcel still was in *Bogotá*. If Sax was correct, he'd done some fast work to demolish a fiction supposedly believed by the police forces of two countries. As an international security consultant, he made his living off this kind of intelligence. Experience told me to believe him.

"So he's hiding in some other Colombian city?"

"Hell, no." Sax flagged down a waitress and took his time ordering more beer and lunch. "Who fed you that crap?"

I explained about Rodrigo.

Sax snorted.

"I can tell you this much," I said. "I watched while he was talking and he believed it." I remembered the coldness in the blue eyes. "His money is on the police to find Marcel."

"The Colombian security forces," Sax said, "are right now trying to find a cache of explosives FARC has squirreled away somewhere near *Nieva* in central Colombia. They're pretty serious about it. FARC blew up a police station two days ago and bombed a bus yesterday. All the police forces are on high alert."

"FARC being...?"

"*Fuerzas Armadas Revolucionarias de Colombia.* Homegrown Marxist thugs."

"Oh," I said, "That FARC." I vaguely remembered a group that kidnapped a woman running for President of Colombia. The Colombian army rescued her and her fellow prisoners from the jungle in a daring, theatrical escapade.

"FARC is the single most important conduit for drugs in this part of the world," Sax continued. "Farmers grow it, drug chiefs, sometimes with FARC's help, refine it, then FARC ships it. They make plenty of money from their capitalist exploits. They also go in for wholesale kidnapping. Very lucrative sideline."

"So the police have their hands full."

"Always. But the Colombian leaders are tough. The last President took a lot of steam out of FARC and the current one's hanging tight. Still, the group's a Hydra. Cut off a head and five more appear. They've got Venezuela stirring the pot and Russia, Hamas, and Iran are the latest ingredients. Even China's in there somewhere. I wouldn't want the job of dealing with it, that's for damn sure."

I listened intently. There was a reason for this background. My former Army comrade wasn't the kind of person who wasted information or time.

Sax drank his beer, pulled out a piece of paper, and unfolded it. It was a satellite map, with pencil notations of cities, rivers, and other items of importance. Most of it was green jungle or filmy white clouds.

"This little black line right here," Sax said, drawing his finger across the paper, "that's the border between Panama and Colombia.

"Now down here is where FARC is generally strongest, in the Southern and middle part of Colombia. But they also have a strong presence in *Choco* Province, which runs along the Panama border. When things get hot, they cross the border for some R&R, or massacre a village of Panamanians or, you never can tell with them, maybe they just go shopping."

"Shopping?"

"Their style. Clean out a village's food supplies, shoot all the livestock and haul away what they can. People live to tell about it but pretty soon the village winds up deserted. There's a whole string of these little ghost hamlets. Makes your spine go cold to see them."

"And this has what to do with Marcel."

"I'm getting there. Now, some of these FARC folks—especially the 57th Front—they're big on paramilitary organization—are particularly enterprising. Transportation and kidnapping aren't enough so they've started their own coca farms and underground processing plants. Managing pretty well, by all reports. Want to guess where they're doing it?"

I was beginning to dislike the direction the conversation was taking.

"OK," I said reluctantly, "I'll bite."

Sax put his finger down on an area of the map that was totally swathed in green. I had a bad feeling. It was on the other side of the line from the familiar names of *Bogatá*, *Cartagena*, and the infamous *Medellín*.

"The *Darien* jungle," he said. "Not a nice place."

He sketched the outline of a long, skinny oval paralleling the border on the Panama side.

"Affectionately known as Camp Coca," Sax said.

"And this," he announced quietly, slowly sliding his finger to an almost invisible speck just north of the oval and next to a town called *Yaviza*, "is where to find Marcel. *Piña Abajo*, a tiny, pathetically poor village, constantly beaten down by narcos, *contrabandistas* and other assorted hoodlums. They'd starve to death if it weren't for so many *bandidos* hiding out there and paying them to keep quiet." He shrugged. "Life in the middle of the *Darien.*"

We both took a break to receive plates of seafood. Sax pulled on his beer and continued.

"It's possible Marcel might leave *Piña Abajo* and go someplace where the security forces could find him. Or, he might lay down a dozen false trails. Eventually, he'll try to access his accounts. Somebody that slippery, though, I'll bet he has plenty of accounts to play with. When you come down to it, who has any idea what the hell he'll do? All I know is that he's reported to be in *Piña Abajo* now. In a week…" The restless eyes fixed on me. "He could be anywhere."

"You think we should go in and get him," I said.

"Well, I always did like a challenge." Sax crossed one immaculately trousered leg over the other. "It wouldn't be cheap, though."

I looked at him and thought about what had brought me to this place and time. A week ago, life meant Washington, DC, politics, family, a busy life, a decent one. A few bumps in the road, but satisfactory.

Uncle Henry, my surprise benefactor, changed all that. Time had sped up here. Events were happening one on top of the other. It was overwhelming, this new life. I felt like a sponge dipped in water, left out to dry, only to be dropped in again.

The *Darien* would be a soaking for sure.

Sax looked calmly at the ceiling.

"So, tell me," I said, "how do we do this?"

CHAPTER 18

I returned to the resort in a thoughtful mood and walked in on Robyn having her nails done. While the decorating finished up, I adjourned to the terrace, my mind turning over the conversation with Sax. The trip sounded like a smart idea. As long as no one got shot or stabbed, it might even fall into the category of a great adventure. I had no doubt the *Darien* was a tough place. But so was the Mideast. At least here there were no sandstorms or IEDs, and, if we nabbed Marcel, I'd go back to Panama City with the prize.

I looked up to see Robyn standing near the door, on her crutches. She moved toward me and sat down.

"You look terrific," I said.

She smiled back at me, full wattage.

"Any news on the road?"

"All bad." Robyn sighed. "Just when they almost had it cleared, there were two more slides." Her mouth twisted. "So stupid. If they'd just built it right the first time…"

No road meant Robin was stuck, which was not a good thing. The next day, I had to return to Panama City, and it was starting to look like there was no choice but to take her with me. I debated with myself for a moment. If we were going to travel together, she deserved to know the risks. "I have something to tell you," I finally said and gave her the story, the shooting, the mugging, and the rest.

About thirty seconds into it, Robyn's mouth gaped open and an "Oh my God" escaped her lips. When I finished, her eyebrows were pulled together and she was chewing on her bottom lip. "And I thought my experience was bad," she said.

"It was. They both have been." I put my hand on hers. "We're the walking wounded. And there's more to come."

She looked at me, not moving a muscle.

"Day after tomorrow, I'm going to the *Darien*. To find Marcel."

"You're doing what?" Her face said I'd lost my mind. "I thought you said the police were after him?"

"The police have their game plan. I can hardly tell them they're looking in the wrong direction. I know Sax is credible but the police would probably just listen politely and then keep on doing what they're doing."

Robyn wasn't ready to give up. For the next fifteen minutes, we argued about it, one *Darien* horror story following the next. Finally, I called a halt and switched the subject.

"More important is the question of what we can do about you since I'll be gone."

She shrugged. "I'm sure the nurse can take care of me. And eventually they'll fix the road enough for me to get back to the *Montanas*. Don't worry, I'll manage."

"What about friends in Panama City you could stay with?"

"Like this?" She waved her bad hand and foot. "I think not. Besides, I have an apartment there."

That was good news. "And someone to take care of you? Housekeeper, maid?"

"No. Carmencita travels back and forth with me." She thought for a minute. "I can find another temporary nurse."

"And if you don't, what then?"

"It won't be a problem," she said.

I considered it. "Listen, this will be easier all around if you come to Uncle Henry's. Rosario can look after you. Then I won't be worrying while I'm trekking through the unconquerable *Darien*." I smiled a little bit, just to let her know that having her there might be pleasurable, too.

"I can't do that," she said.

"Sure you can."

"It's a nice offer…" She twisted a lock of shiny black hair around her index finger. "I have things at my apartment I need."

"We'll pick them up."

She caught her bottom lip with her teeth.

"Come on, how bad can it be? My cousin, Val, is there. Women love him. He'll keep you entertained."

"All right," she said, letting go of the hair. "But only for a day or two, until they fix the road, then I really have to get back. I took some sketches up with me and I need to get to work on them."

"Carmencita can fax them to you," I said sensibly.

"Umm." Biting her lip again. "I suppose so."

"Look, do whatever you like, as long as you're mobile when you go back up there. The last thing you need is to fall and break something else and be stuck in the mountains."

She sighed. "Okay." She allowed just a hint of the lop-sided smile.

For some reason, I felt my heart do a little flip.

The next day, we set out for Panama City.

We did some basic housekeeping in the morning. Went by Robyn's apartment to pick up clothes, then grabbed a bite of lunch, accompanied by light conversation. I learned more about Robyn and I liked what I was hearing. I flattered myself it was a two-way street.

Once we were at the apartment, Robyn decided to take a nap. I made for the terrace with my laptop and a guilty conscience for not having touched base with Joy. Fortunately, all was quiet on the Washington front, so I disposed of some correspondence, consulted a thing or two on the internet, and, when I finally looked up, Robyn appeared in the doorway, dazzling in an ultra skinny pencil skirt, an eye-popping scarlet silk blouse, and a brilliant slash of lipstick to match.

I swallowed. Jesus. And I had to work tonight.

"Hi there," she said.

Make nice, Pen. You can't just throw her to the floor and have your way with her. Remember, women expect subtlety.

"Are you all right?" she asked.

"Just…thinking," I said. I looked at my watch. Fifteen minutes before Sax would arrive. What could we do for a quarter of an hour? Legally.

"Do you have a date?" I asked. "You're all dressed up."

"No, no date. I just felt like celebrating." She sat down in a chair next to me. "I think I'm finally over the shock of the crash. I was a little numb there for a while. I kept thinking I was this close—"

She held her thumb and forefinger up.

"—to being killed. But now, I'm feeling everything, like every little nerve is sparking inside me. Really, I'm so alive, I'm tingling."

I grinned at her and watched the tingle. Watched the smile that started at the top of her head and didn't stop until her toes. Listened to the words that glistened as they spilled from those red, red lips. I sat back and let myself be dusted with Robyn's joy and exuberance, and when I had to part from her, I regretted Sax, regretted the *Darien*, most of all, regretted myself for giving a damn about Marcel and a few million dollars.

CHAPTER 19

Sax arrived at six ready to do business. Val joined us. Overall, he was taking the whole thing better than I expected, trying his best to suppress his misgivings, and trailing along silently as we went into Uncle Henry's suite and shut the door. Val wasn't alone in having qualms. Now that I'd had a day to think about it, I was half wondering about the plan myself.

"This is what you want to do?" Sax asked presciently.

"Well," I said, "I've always wanted to do a jungle trek. This seems as good a time as any. Also, since apparently everyone else is looking for Marcel in the wrong place, I think it makes sense to grab the little son of a bitch before he runs again."

"Okay," Sax said, satisfied. If I'd expressed complete enthusiasm, he'd have been worried. To him, a little skepticism meant your brain was engaged, not just your gut.

"First, you need to strip," he said, "so I can get you into the right clothes for the jungle. The first part of the trip will be by bus, but we'll have a long walk in what the environmentalists so charmingly call the rainforest. Like they call some ferocious wild pig trying to gore you a 'protected' species or a pathetic little hut 'native housing.' To me, the jungle is the jungle and it had better be the same to you. If you start thinking of it as a rainforest, you may never make it out."

Val looked at the no-nonsense ex-Ranger and began nervously rubbing the top of his head.

He must be upset, I realized, to endanger his remaining fluff. "It'll be all right," I reassured him. "Nothing worth losing your hair over. Besides, I've already made my will and you figure prominently in it."

Val, transparent as usual, hovered between concern and pleasure.

"That's better," I laughed, and he had the decency to look at least moderately shamed.

While I undressed, Sax pulled out packages from a bag he'd brought and emptied them on the bed. "First rule," he announced, "No underwear. No jock straps, no briefs, no exceptions. This time of year, there'll be heavy rains. We'll also be crossing some rivers and creeks. Most of the time, you'll be wet and your clothes have to be loose or you'll get a case of jock rot you'll never forget. The exception is this—" He flipped a pack of condoms my way. "To keep out the nasty parasites."

Val's face was a sight to behold. "Parasites up your dick," he said. "Shit."

"You can try the rubbers on tomorrow," Sax said, with what passed for a grin, "but let's see how these do now." He handed me a pair of khakis with knee and leg patches and elasticized hems.

"They're fine," I said, zipping up.

"Money goes under the right patch," Sax pointed just above my ankle. "U.S. dollars. Take enough to lubricate the way and buy us out of a jam but not so much somebody gets ideas about turning things into a kidnapping. Five hundred for you, five hundred for me should do it. The payroll's in the account?"

I nodded yes. I'd put it there on my way back to the condo.

"Fine, I've given instructions. Just in case."

Val interjected. "Exactly which 'just in case' would this be?"

"It's nothing." Sax said. "A precaution. Your boy slips on a banana peel and can't get to the bank, I still have bills to pay."

"Ah," Val said unhappily, "that kind."

Sax continued. "The patch on the other leg covers a waterproof map. Hand-drawn. This part of the *Darien* hasn't been mapped."

If Val didn't faint now, I decided, he never would.

"Now, look under the waistband—carefully."

I fiddled with nearly invisible Velcro and brought out some tight-fitting zip-lock baggies and other items.

Val peered over my shoulder. "I'll be damned." He picked up two flat metal objects embedded in thin plastic.

"Scalpels." Sax said. "Razor sharp. You don't want to mess with them."

"I'll take your word. What's this?" Val held a long, looped strand of wire.

"Snare," Sax answered matter-of-factly.

I looked at the rest. Safety pins, needle and thread, water-proof matches, salve, rubber bands. I fingered a piece of netting with strings at each corner.

"Fishnet," Sax said. "The *Indios* have something similar to catch shrimp in the rivers. For fish, you can also use a sharpened stick."

Val looked at me. I had an image of myself conquering the jungle one fish at a time.

The last article was a mini-switchblade. Almost flat and close to weightless.

"Impressive. Do I really need it all?"

"Oh, this is just for starters," Sax said happily.

He handed me a sturdy beige shirt with a Ralph Lauren label and a wealth of pockets. I put it on, rolled up the sleeves.

"You look like an explorer," Val said, "for GQ."

I caught my reflection in the mirror. "Maybe when I've worn out my newest career as a bounty hunter, I'll consider modeling."

"Unh," Sax grunted. "You need Italian clothes for that."

"I didn't know Ralph was into survival gear," Val commented.

"We cheated a little," Sax said. "Give me the shirt for a minute."

I pulled it off and handed it to him. He lifted one corner of the label and tugged. Underneath was a tiny folded piece of paper.

"Escape map—again, subject to the same qualifications as before. Ralph's labels are a good size for it. We owe a lot of these gimmicks to the backpackers, the guys who trek around the world. Amazing what they come up with."

I thought so, too.

"OK, put the shirt back on and pat it down."

"Maybe some things in the hem," I said. "And the cuffs." I messed with them for a second. "What do we have here?" I held up three plastic strips covering tightly packed rows of tablets. "Suicide pills?"

"Z pack antibiotic and sulfa. Chloroquine in the third strip. Take one now. Should've started a week ago but…"

"Chloroquine?" Val asked. "As in…?"

"Anti-malarial," Sax answered. To me: "The water puros are in a strip behind the buttons. On the other side are filters made to look like fabric liner."

I surveyed my chest. Now that I knew I could see the slight pucker.

Sax reached over and plucked at one of my buttons, popped a thin piece of plastic, and palmed a compass about a quarter of the size of a dime. I peered at the tiny object. "Which button conceals the magnifying glass?"

"All the services use them now," Sax said. "You'll get used to it."

I played with the compass for a moment, reinserted it, and closed the button.

"You have two changes of clothes. Wet, which you'll remove at night and hang out to dry, unless it's raining. The other set is for sleeping. Plus your standard camos for the jungle.

"Wait a minute," I said. "I thought the idea was to take a bus ride and hike a few hours to *Piña Abajo*. Then, assuming we get lucky, we nab Marcel, hike a few more hours, and basically get the hell back here. I mean that was the plan, wasn't it? Where do pajamas and an entire pharmacy come in?"

"Don't you remember anything from Iraq?" Sax asked with disgust.

"As little as possible," I said, grinning. "That's why I have you."

"So pretend you're a Boy Scout," Sax scowled. "Be Prepared. We don't know we'll get Marcel the first day. Might be two or three." He returned to the shirt.

"There's extra wire running down the other side of the front where the filters are. Fishing lures and all-purpose line. Collar has a wire saw sewn in like a stiffener. Underneath the collar is your mossie head net. Cuffs have parachute cord, sutures, some other things."

Now that I knew I was wearing half of Ace Hardware, I took off both shirt and pants and laid them carefully on the bed. I grabbed my pants and pulled them on.

Val was wide-eyed. "Unbelievable," he said to Sax. "Where do you keep the grenades?"

"No grenades this trip," Sax responded. "These are only basic survival items in case we get separated from our regular gear." He grinned, enjoying himself. "We keep the daisy cutters in the rucksacks."

"Ha, ha," said Val, mirthlessly. No doubt screaming with laughter inside.

Sax came back to me: "There's a tactical vest in the sack, if you want to use it. You'll remember some of it from Iraq— that is if your eyes were open. Jungle adaptations are different, of course. This is a stripped down version. It has your usual paraphernalia, GPS, water bag, ammo pockets. Leech straps for your pants."

Sax was fiddling with something else. I looked at the machete that had materialized in his hand. I wasn't particularly good in the kitchen and sometimes nicked myself shaving. "Is there one a little smaller?" I asked.

Sax gave me a look of utter contempt. "The little ones are for babies in their bassinets," he said, and showed me how the tool nestled in a leather-lined sheath attached to the back of the rucksack.

"Handy," I said.

The machete was followed by rations, gloves and quantities of DEET. "You do know this can cause cancer?" I said.

"Tell the mosquitoes about it. And it's your choice. You want to get Hemorrhagic Dengue Fever and bleed out? Encephalitis? West Nile? Not to mention Malaria and Yellow Fever. Hey, be my guest. The symptoms won't show up until we're back and you definitely won't die before you get a chance to ask Marcel about the money." He paused. "Now spending it might be something different."

I muttered because it was expected of me and looked at what was left on the bed. Sulfa powder. Boots. 12 feet of coiled nylon rope. Poncho. Gloves. Socks. Except that it was made by companies for militias, small countries, and private security contractors, it was all right out of the Army Field Manual.

"Cover your feet with the powder," Sax said, "and as much of your body as you can. Foot infections are nothing you want in the jungle. Worse than snakebite, poisonous frogs, jaguar attacks, the lot.

"On a good note, I think you'll find this rucksack is lighter than what we toted in the Gulf. Lot of improvements there. Ditto the boots. The tent's a special design by a fellow I know. Weighs under twenty ounces wet and converts to a hammock. There's an insect net, of course. Luminous strips for the back of your hat. Water bag, carabiners—"

"And do I have a gun or is someone teaching me how to use blow darts?"

Val gurgled. With laughter or anxiety I wasn't sure.

"We won't get weapons until just before we reach *Yaviza*. Can't arouse any suspicion heading there. Machetes are no problem because everybody carries one. After we leave the town of *Chepo*, we'll be stopped by the cops regularly, so you need to be prepared. Remember, the police and security forces are the equivalent of the military in Panama. They'll copy down everything, even the serial numbers of our money. They might look through the rucksacks. Change that—they will look through them. Then, they'll do it all over again at the next stop, and the next, the whole way to *Yaviza*."

"Sounds like overkill," Val said.

"They have to weed out the bad guys any way they can." Sax shrugged. "Otherwise, they'd be overwhelmed. In the Plug, five kinds of people travel." He ticked them off on his hand. "Locals. Narco guerrilla terrorists. Some general criminal types—mostly grifters, whores, other lowlifes. And birdwatchers, if you can believe it. Then, finally, folks like us who are nutty enough to want to tell our kids we braved the *Darien*. We need to make sure they don't have any confusion about which group we fit into."

"The Plug is a euphemism for the *Darien*?" Val asked.

"Yeah," Sax answered. "Being so hard to cross, it's supposed to stop the drugs coming from Colombia." He took a deep breath reeking with skepticism. "Like anything could."

"Now, you," he said, turning to me, "have to stick to your story. Don't deviate, no matter what."

"No problem. I'm just a dunderhead who wants to explore the famous *Darien* Gap before I head back to the States."

Sax nodded approval. "I'm going to watch out for you but you have to do what I tell you. Don't forget, a man has only one friend in the *Darien*—the guy who gets him out of there alive."

I knew that drill. SOP for the military. Still, it made me wonder how on earth, in the span of five days, I'd gone from my cozy life in Washington, D.C. to something ominously called "The Plug."

Sax, on a roll now, reached down to the bottom of the rucksack and pulled out a well-used "Yankees" baseball cap. "Everyone down here loves the Yanks. You'll fit right in."

For the first time, Val managed a genuine smile. Another Yanks fan. Out of loyalty, I was still stuck on the hapless Nats. Nonetheless, I tried on the cap.

"Now," said Sax, "the last item." From a plastic bag on the bed he pulled out several small green and red spiny fruits.

"How about getting us some sharp knives and spoons," he said to Val. "And three bowls."

Momentarily, Val arrived from the kitchen with his fetch-its.

"We'll go in the bathroom for this," Sax said.

Using Uncle Henry's marble counter, Sax neatly chopped each fruit in two. He palmed a spiny piece and began scooping little red seeds into a bowl.

"Here, you do this." He turned to Val and handed him the cut red fruit and spoon. "Actually, you're gonna get some of this on you so you'd better take off that nice looking shirt. Brioni, isn't it?"

Val preened.

"I guess the pants don't matter but you might want to get rid of them, too."

Val's glow receded just a bit.

For the second time, I removed my clothes.

Sax reached in the bag and produced a piece of wood, six inches long with a knobbed end. He handed it to me with another bowl.

"When he has a few more seeds, switch bowls with him and use this knob to crush them."

While Val and I worked on the red fruit, Sax cut out the clear gelatinous flesh of the green fruit and dumped it in the final bowl.

"Okay," I said, after the third red fruit, "the seeds are mashed. Now what?"

"Dump them in my bowl. Stir it up real good."

I followed instructions and soon had a sticky, clear, red substance coating my spoon.

"Start putting this muck all over yourself, especially your face. Work it into the skin evenly. When he's finished, Val, do his backside."

"What is it?" I asked, as I began spreading the mixture. "Sun protection?"

"Not exactly," Sax answered. "This clear gel is called *Jagua*. The red one is *Achiote*. When the *Jagua* is exposed to air it turns a blue black color. The *Indios*, especially women, use it for insect control and body paint. You'll see women who are painted with it up to the top of their lips, like a mask. Sometimes, they create patterns like lace down over the boobs.

"The other goop, as you know, is red. Combine the two you get brown. It's hard to gauge the exact color you'll wind up being. It's based in part on your natural skin coloring and partly on the interaction of the two plants. The red works faster. The *Jagua* takes a few hours. By morning, believe me, you'll look different. There's no way Marcel should recognize you."

"Not permanent, I hope."

"No. It's only good for a couple weeks. And you can remove it anytime with chlorine and water. But, stay away from anything wet tonight. You can shower in the morning, but no scrubbing.

"Oh, I almost forgot…" Sax fished a jar from his pocket. "Usually, this fruit combination works just fine but in case you want to, say, tone it down a little or even it out, you can use some of this.

"Just…" He hesitated. "Well, you have it if you need it."

I looked at the jar. "'Max Factor Pan-cake Makeup?' You can't be serious?"

"Go through the rest after I leave, memorize the maps," Sax said rather hurriedly. "I have to meet a guy to square away some things tonight." He made for the door, Val following out of politeness. "By the way," he called from the hall, "don't shave in the morning—we need you rough. I'll be here at five. The bus leaves at six so we'll have time to go over the plan. See you then, pal."

Yeah, right, I thought, holding the Max Factor and looking in the mirror.

See who?

While Val rubbed goop on my back, I examined my face in the mirror. It had already turned light pink.

"What do you think?" I asked.

"You've lost your mind, you're headed for a loony bin, and I'm going to inherit all your money right away."

I turned a little to see what the rest of me looked like.

"Stand straight while I finish this," Val said. "By the way, how do you plan to disguise the eyes?"

"Hmm," I answered, seeing two gray orbs staring back at me. Sax's gear hadn't included any colored contacts. "Sunglasses, I guess."

"At night?"

"I'll have to cogitate on that."

"Well, while you're cogitating, you're beginning to look like a lobster. This dye works fast as hell."

"You heard Sax. The other one will kick in soon." It'd better, I thought. I'd be damned if I'd parade in the Panama version of war paint. And there was no way that Max Factor crap was getting anywhere near me.

The application finished, Val returned to the bedroom and examined the equipment, then came back to the bathroom.

"I hope to hell you know what you're doing," he said, shaking his head.

"Maybe, maybe not," I answered. "But this much I can tell you. We're not getting any closer to Marcel sitting here in Panama City. I'm sick of looking over my shoulder and wondering when somebody's going to take another crack at me. I can turn around right now, head for Washington, and admit I got my butt kicked, or I can try to get this jerk Marcel off my back."

Val sighed.

"Besides," I said, "Sax has spent a lot of time in Panama and knows the natives cold. The *Darien* is practically his back yard." I spoke with an assurance I didn't quite feel. Sax said he knew the *Darien*. But he also said we'd be relying on other folks to guide us. In terms of items I'd carry tomorrow, trust would definitely be one of the biggies.

I looked at the maps. Our route was a simple one. There was a highway of sorts from Panama City to the town called *Yaviza*, tantalizingly dubbed "The End of the Road." As Sax said, lots of people went there: locals, a few tourists, *bandidos*, and the inevitable kids of all ages who want bragging rights.

Fools, I thought. Like me.

The place where Marcel was reputed to be—*Piña Abajo* ("Upside-Down Pineapple" in English) was a patch of intimidating jungle away from *Yaviza*. At some time in its past, Sax had explained, the canopy trees of the original rain forest were cut, probably for logging or to clear space for farming. Unfortunately for farmers, a virgin rain forest makes for poor cultivation. After a season or two, the soil gives out, and the farmer moves on to another location, repeating the devastation.

At the original site, the jungle encroaches and the result is what's called a "secondary forest," a tangled mass of weedy roots that can reach a mile, leaves the size of a car, ferns even bigger, and vines that will wrap themselves completely around you, given half a chance and an hour or two. That—not the pristine canopied rainforest—was the type of jungle we'd be crossing. It'll be daunting, Sax had said. Inhospitable. We might pass a hut or two, but basically we'd be in the wilderness until we arrived at our destination. I hoped like hell he was right about it being deserted. The map said it was also only thirty ominous miles from the Colombian border.

For the next hour, I inspected my kit. I memorized the maps, especially the escape route, which had penciled in paths and waterways, all next to *Yaviza*, not *Piña Abajo*. "So you can erase them if it looks like the map might fall into the wrong hands," Sax had said. "Of course, you could eat it, too. Safer that way."

The whole thing seemed preposterous for what amounted to no more than a hike in the woods.

A compass the size of a button?

A saw encircling my collar?

Eating my map?

What the hell. Let Sax have his fun. I'd see a unique part of Panama, visit a jungle for the first time in my life, and get a break from the strain of everything I'd encountered so far. If nothing else, I'd get some outdoor activity, a chance to exercise my skills. And if a little risk came along with it, well, who was I to complain? As far as the danger, it was Sax's nature to see villains around every corner, part of what made him such an invaluable partner.

At the most, the bastard Marcel would be dealt with. At the very least, it would make a good story for the cocktail circuit back home.

Throughout my repacking, Val and I talked about what he'd do while I was gone. Finding the missing money was the most critical task, but also important was persuading Thomas to join us as soon as possible and keeping people at the law firm generally placated about my absence. A new and more enjoyable task for Val was to look after Robyn and, if possible, deter her from leaving until I got back. Val's eyes lit up at the prospect but became more subdued at the single word all men hate to hear. "Taken," I said firmly.

The next day, Val would tell Rodrigo I'd unexpectedly gone back to the States on unfinished election business.

Enriqué and Bruno would get the same story. I'd asked them to collect me at eight in the morning. Instead, they would find Val and the news that I'd already caught my plane.

"Don't count on hearing from me until I get back," I said. "Despite all that preparation with Sax, I'm still hoping it's a short trip—one day if we're lucky. In the meantime, watch yourself. If we get Marcel back here, we'll at least have some answers, but there's still an outside chance another person was working with him. If you're nervous—"

Val hooted.

"—move to a hotel, shoot back to the States, have Rosario find a nurse for Robyn and move her over to her apartment, whatever it takes to feel comfortable. Nobody's expecting you to be a hero."

"Look who's talking," Val said.

"You haven't been attacked. Your options are a little broader than mine."

Val shook his head as though emerging from a bad dream. "If I'd known what we were getting involved with..."

"Believe me," I answered, "I can see myself sitting in D.C. in my new Thomas Pink suit right this minute, while some smart lawyer figures all this out. No two ways about it."

"You can still do it," Val said, eyeing me.

He was right. I thought about my life back home. About the next elections. The Sunday TV shows I'd secretly hoped to appear on. Thought about all the perks of being a political princeling, even one tainted by Lawrence.

"Nah," I said. "This is way more fun."

CHAPTER 20

By the time Val and I finished, it was after eight. He left for dinner with Maria and I joined Robyn in the library.

She looked me up and down and gave me the lopsided smile. "Are you sick or did you overstay the tanning bed?"

"I'm going to the *Darien* incognito. This is my disguise." I sat down on the sofa next to her.

"I'll give you that. You do look different."

I stretched out my legs and saw that my feet were a deep crimson. "Supposedly, this will turn deep brown by tomorrow morning. It's a mixture of fruit the Indians in the jungle use."

"I don't guess there's anything that will change your mind?"

"No," I said bluntly. "I want Marcel." Robyn made a disapproving noise under her breath. I turned to the side so I faced her. "There's something you could do that would make the trip a whole lot more pleasant."

"Oh?" She cocked her head

I leaned over and brushed her lips with mine.

"I see. Like the boys going off to war."

"Something like that." I kissed her again, tilting her face up to meet mine. She sighed and laid her head back against the cushion. I followed her, tracing a fingertip down her cheek, all smooth and delicate.

"Mmm," she said, in a voice that was somewhere the other side of honey. I brushed back her hair and looked at three small crisscrossed lines of black thread that lay beneath them. Tenderly, I kissed each one.

"They're awful," she said.

"They're behind your bangs."

"Still..."

"The doctor said they'll barely show when they've healed."

Robyn was silent then, maybe because I covered her mouth with mine. I put my hands on her shoulders and looked in her eyes, huge and deep and very blue. Eyes that could kill you, if you weren't careful.

I felt her tremble as I let one hand drift down the perfect slope of her jawline to her incredible scarlet lips. I gently passed my thumb over them, and lingered. "Maybe I should make a habit of going off to war," I said.

She reached up and guided my thumb between her lips, nibbling it like a soft, baby animal.

God, I thought, and buried my face in her throat, licking the tiny throbbing point at its center. She fumbled at my buttons, pulled open my shirt, and gripped my chest, her fingers urgent, kneading. A tremor went through my body. I took her head in my hands and plunged my tongue deep in her mouth, thrusting it in and out until she gasped.

"Oh, my God," she exhaled. I opened her blouse and floated my hand along the top of her breasts, caressing the silkiness that's found solely on a woman—and then only a special one. Her breathing caught and, with my other hand, I reached under her blouse in the back, found her spine, and slowly glided my fingers down, underneath her skirt, underneath her panties. I cupped her ass and pulled her tight into me. My knee slipped between hers and I stroked her thigh, slowly working my hand higher. A moan escaped one of us—maybe both.

"All these clothes," I mumbled. "We can do better than this."

She looked at me, eyes shining.

I put both arms around her and lifted her up. "Let's check out Uncle Henry's bedroom."

Robyn stiffened. Her fingers, stroking my shoulder, paused.

I was intensely aware of the rise and fall of soft breasts, of hair gliding across my cheek, of small feathery breaths which sighed past my ear. I stifled a groan as I gently lowered her back to the sofa.

We looked at each other. Henry and I were very good friends, her eyes telegraphed. Too good for this.

I crouched in front of her and brushed a satiny lock of hair back behind one ear, then let my hand travel down her neck to the hollow of her throat. I wanted to enfold her in my arms again, to replay the last few moments. To make things come out a different way.

Would it have mattered if I hadn't mentioned Uncle Henry? He probably would have come into the picture anyway. Robyn was having a hard time, that was obvious. But, she wasn't alone. I was an old-fashioned kind of guy, a territorial type. Despite the fact that I'd known Robyn for only three days, I didn't like her relationship with Uncle Henry worth a damn. Now, I had even more reason to dislike it.

That didn't stop me from kissing her ear, kissing her face, saturating myself with the taste of her lips. Then I was on the sofa again, grabbing her hips, shuddering. I closed my eyes for a second, trying to restrain myself.

Robyn gently disengaged my arms and quietly slid over on the couch to straighten her clothes. "He was very dear to me," she finally said. "Very special."

I took a deep breath and blew it out. "He's a ghost, Robyn. We need to accept that. Both of us."

The sapphire eyes saddened. I took her good hand, turning it over and lightly tracing her fingers. I held it gently, as though any pressure would make her draw away.

"Maybe..." She swallowed and didn't go on.

I tightened my grip on her hand and looked deep into her eyes. "He's gone," I said. "Gone forever."

"I know. I just, I just..." She pulled her hand away, shook the helmet of black hair and squared her shoulders. "Hand me my crutches, please."

"Robyn," I said, stalling for time, "we can still—"

"No, I don't think so." She smiled faintly and drove home the ultimate disappointment of the evening. "I think I should go to my apartment."

"Low blow," I said. "Plus, there's no one to take care of you there."

"I'll call someone. It'll be all right." Her eyes were sad. She picked up the crutches and left the room.

I put my head in my hands and rubbed my face angrily. After a minute or two, I went looking for Rosario to call a cab and help Robyn pack her clothes.

She was quick about it. She'd called a temporary agency and found a nurse who could start right away. Great. That removed my last argument for her to stay. There being nothing else I could do, I grabbed her bag and we headed for the taxi. Minutes later, I escorted her to her apartment. Neither of us had spoken a word since leaving the penthouse.

I put my hands on her shoulders and brushed my lips across hers. "I'll be back in a few days. Let's see how things are then."

She smiled in a small way and kissed my cheek.

"Shit," I said to myself. "Shit and shit and shit."

CHAPTER 21

After a restless night trying unsuccessfully not to think about Robyn, I met Sax the next morning. By then, I was oak tree brown but, thank God, without the aid of Max Factor. Sax looked me over and rumbled his approval. He handed me a pair of cheap shades.

"Keep those on, day and night, except for the jungle," he said. "When we get to *Piña Abajo*, add the cap and keep the brim down."

I donned the glasses and took on the role of Pen Smith, Secret Agent, Panama. Sax completed the role with a white Panama hat and an unlit cigar in his mouth. Classic.

We made our way to the bus terminal along with the other early risers. Our bus to *Yaviza* was not non-stop. For reasons unclear to me, we were getting off at *Meteti*, a town half-way there.

"We're meeting somebody," Sax said without elaboration as we settled ourselves in a *Diablo Rojo* painted screaming turquoise with wavy yellow and hot purple stripes down one side and a mural of the Last Supper on the other. On top of the bus were three large white globes, purpose unknown;

around the front were multi-colored fairy lights, which sprang to life whenever the driver felt like it.

"Interesting—the painted windshield," I commented, looking at the portrait of a reclining, almost-naked woman which stretched the length of the glass and covered ninety-five percent of the available space.

"There's a thin strip that's clear," Sax answered. "See it? Between the girl's legs. Keeps the bus driver motivated when there's a shortage of scenery. Most of the trip is pretty boring."

You could've fooled me. The bus was blaring salsa music so loud you could hear it back at the condominium. Inside, it was deafening. Having arrived early, we were sitting in choice seats, firmly anchored to the floor and with most of the upholstery stuffed back in the rips. There were no suspicious wet spots to avoid.

In front of us sat an Indian family. Two men and two women with long black hair, Asiatic features, and embroidered, brightly colored tent dresses. "*Ngöbe-Buglé* tribe," Sax said. "Clothes are a tip-off." One woman held a toddler, the other a baby.

The rest of the passengers included three teenage boys with unusually impassive faces ("small-time dealers," Sax pronounced), a pair of young lovebirds (no explanation needed), an older pair of shoppers clutching as many filled-to-the-brim plastic bags as they could squeeze in the seat, and a mother with a little boy who sneezed and coughed most of the trip.

"Uhm," said Sax, "glad that kid is sitting downwind."

"Not a good time to catch a cold."

"Or meningitis," Sax said. "There's an epidemic here."

He looked at me. "Oh, you didn't know?"

The bus started and I opened our window the extra millimeter it would allow.

"Any meningitis pills in there?" I asked, looking at Sax's pack.

"Viral," Sax said. "Pills don't help."

Shit, I thought. Now I could add deadly disease and possible brain damage to my fun time in Panama. I deliberately ignored Sax as we wound out of the city, picked up people at a suburb called *San Miguelito*, and then *Tocumen* Airport, where I briefly considered escape and throwing myself at Robyn's feet in total abasement. After that, the bus stopped for anyone standing by the side of the road, a good 40 or 50 people by the time we reached *Chepo*, the next significant town. There we had our first encounter with the National Police, who, as Sax had said, looked for all the world like uniformed military.

It took some minutes for everyone to be glared at, inspected, and, in our case, told off for being fools, which Sax dutifully translated. True to his warning, the police asked a lot of questions, wrote down our answers, and recorded the serial numbers of the moderate sums we carried in our pockets. They inspected our backpacks, fingered our sparkling med kits, and raised their eyebrows at our brand new, relatively small machetes. They missed the big money, little saw, and the other goodies we carried in our clothes.

"Hmm. Now, they're making bets on what parts of our bodies we'll chop off," Sax whispered, all the while grinning broadly like the dimwit he was pretending to be.

As Sax had coached me, I responded to any and all questions with the same answer. I wanted to explore the *Darien* Gap. It had been a lifelong dream of mine. I planned to see the bird-watching paradise of *Cana* and the famous "Holy Ghost Gold Mine."

Yes, I knew it would take days to reach our destination. I knew there were narcos, terrorists, deadly serpents, and impenetrable jungle standing in my way. Not to mention wild pigs as big as elephants, jaguars, scorpions, and para-military groups. I could have told them it was all nothing compared to a woman's scorn, but instead I meekly nodded. I understood the risks. I inanely said I just wanted to be part of the magnificent wilderness.

Sax told his story, a subtle variant of mine featuring a cousin who had traveled across the rainforest on a motorcycle and lived to tell about it. Sax didn't want to do anything that challenging. But, the honor of his family was at stake. After all, if his cousin could do it…

The Panamanians understood honor and we were given a pass to continue.

We returned to the bus to find the other passengers busily eating ice cream, chips, fruit, whatever they had bought in *Chepo* or previously squirreled away in their bags. It was not unexpected, but definitely a piss-off, to find our good seats appropriated by others. This time, we sat over the wheel, a torment impossible to describe. There were several additions to our group and the bus was considerably noisier, hotter, and fuller as we left. One new passenger was a future meal for some other passenger, a chicken which pecked up and down the aisle and periodically squirted under a seat to evade the grasp of the sneezing kid.

The stops became more frequent. Periodically, we saw police in camouflage fatigues lining the road. M-16s were now prominently displayed, along with sidearms. Mostly, the men simply stood and watched us pass. Hard, brown faces. Unsmiling.

Between *Chepo* and *Aguas-Frias,* no more than twenty kilometers, we were hauled out of the bus twice, once into a police station that closely resembled a sand-bagged military outpost, complete with camo covering and heavy armaments.

"Typical hardware," Sax commented, giving me the lowdown on the weapons. "Beretta 70/90 assault machine guns with clip."

"Mmm," I said. That was serious ordnance for a police station. But then, sandbags weren't your usual building material either.

As before, we were not alone in being examined. Everyone was grilled. Equal opportunity interrogation, Sax called it. With our U.S. passports, I figured we were getting a little more opportunity than most of the others.

On top of it all, *Aguas-Frias* marked a change in the road. Sax had not prepared me, nor had the map, nor especially the lying internet, which had falsely shown a shining yellow strip extending well beyond our present location.

Everything, including legend, pointed to *Yaviza* as the "End of the Road," when in actuality it was this ignominious spot. Without warning, we left a pot-holed, but marginally paved tarmac for a plunge into rough dirt tracks, camouflaged mud bogs, and ruts deep enough to swallow a cow.

Most of the time, we alternated a painful jarring ride with sudden complete immobility, followed by all passengers, male and female alike (babies, toddlers, and sneezer under arms), giving the bus the old heave-ho to free it from whatever swamp the driver had blundered into. The entire bus load was soon covered in mud up to our knees, with grime coating the rest of our bodies. When those delightful activities got old, Sax joked that we could always count on a police grilling to spice things up.

After six hours on a conveyance named in exquisite perfection for the cruelties it imposed on its passengers, the *Diablo Rojo* drew up at *Meteti*. Everyone poured out the door, causing a minor log jam. The chicken, I noticed, used the occasion to scurry away from its owner and make a beeline for safety in some nearby woods. I grinned. Finally the authoritative answer to why the chicken crossed the road.

The fun didn't last long. It had been sweltering in the bus. There was a moment's respite outside, then we were escorted to the spare, oven-like police station to again undergo the third degree. We accepted a particularly stern warning about all the dangers of the *Darien,* then walked out of the station where several converted pickup trucks with wooden bench seats and canvas tops waited beneath drooping palms. People were already throwing their children and belongings inside the first vehicle and following them through the opening.

"*Chivas,*" Sax said.

I looked around for the inevitable cantina. "Do they even have that stuff here?"

"The trucks. *Chivas*. That's the fucking name." It was Sax's turn for eye-rolling. He pointed to the third in line. "That one there is ours."

"It looks full," I said.

"Full on a *chiva* is when people are hanging off the tires," Sax answered. "Like in India. Besides, when I said this is ours, I mean *ours*."

I climbed through the hole, given an arm up by a stern-faced man at the opening.

"Thanks," I said automatically.

"No problem," he answered with a heavy accent. I moved toward an empty spot up near the driver, Sax behind me. The truck jerked once, I braced for balance, and the *chiva* took off like a shot, thumping me onto the bench—hard.

"We don't want any more company," Sax said, by way of explanation.

Introductions followed, the kind that let everyone know where we stood.

"This is Pen," Sax said in Spanish. He pointed to the next man, dark and expressionless. "Raoul."

After him was Miguel (short, stocky, lots of facial hair), then Carlos (preoccupied, but managing a nod) and so on through the whole group. Six including the driver. No last names mentioned. That way, under "provocation" (Sax's term), we would not be able to rat out the others.

Rat out the others?

"Try to memorize their names and faces before we get to *Yaviza*," Sax said in a low voice. "Your life may depend on it."

"Aren't you being a little melodramatic?"

"It's the *Darien*," was all he would say.

Despite its discomfort, the earlier part of the trip had been colorful, with no hint of darker moments ahead. Now, as I faced six tough-looking, uncompromising men, I knew this would be more than the mild adventure I'd been anticipating.

I looked at my compatriots, as Sax had instructed, committing them to memory. Once, I asked Sax to refresh a name. Every now and then, he'd have an exchange with someone in Spanish. Sometimes he passed it on to me in English.

"Fernando says a *Diablo Rojo* turned over on its side in the mud yesterday. Took five hours and a whole village to drag the damn thing out…"

I thought about our bus trip, the innumerable times we'd done the old heave-ho. That was bad enough. But five hours at one spot?

Again. "Last week the rains washed away some guy's house. Carlos had him pegged for a drug dealer. Right, Carlos?"

Carlos, who seemed given to nods, laid one on us.

"So money begins showing up on shore and the whole town races out and starts scooping up the *dinero* and jumping in boats so they can catch the bills that are floating downstream. Nobody'll rent the *trafficante* a fuckin' boat so he runs around mad as hell. Meanwhile, the townspeople are raking it in with crab nets, fish nets, digging through the mangroves with their hands. The police are standing there laughing their heads off…"

Everybody in the *chiva* cracked up over that one.

We calmed down. More quiet conversation in Spanish. One long animated discussion at the other end of the truck. Sax clued me in. "Guillermo has an uncle who lives in *Yaviza*. Got an ear lopped off in a machete fight. Guy who cut him came to apologize the next day and brought a peace offering. Bottle of *Seco*—that's local booze distilled from sugar cane— and the ear in a burial box. Nice box, Guillermo says. Pink satin lining and everything…"

As the stories continued, the men broke out cigarettes, drinks and empanadas. Guillermo passed me a Coke and a couple of the pastries.

I continued examining my companions. They were young, late teens to mid-thirties, with semi-bald Rubén, the driver, evidently the oldest. Their clothes were mostly Ts and jeans. All were in superlative condition, not an over-developed bodybuilder among them, only men with sleek, toned muscles. Their personalities were different but each one carried an air of authority, even as we bumped and swerved and jiggled and bounced through mile after awful mile of road. I decided these men were either police, ex-military, or narco-hunters, described by Sax as the toughest of them all. Some were probably all three.

While the trip by *Diablo Rojo* had seen on and off showers, the *chiva's* nonstop windshield wipers were already foretelling the rest of the journey. The vehicle had four-wheel drive, big mud-churning tires, and off-road suspension, but, if

not for some bulldozers excavating along our way, we'd
probably have been mired for hours. Periodically, when the
rain poured down and the mud made things virtually
impassable, a dozer pulled up with a load of gravel, dumped it
around if not on us, and gave us a nudge over to the next
patch of unnavigable muck.

"Your money at work," Sax said, and I regarded him
thoughtfully. The bulldozers, while apparently working on
some existing project, did seem opportunistically positioned.

"Nice job," I murmured.

Except to provide names and a few minutes of
translation, Sax didn't speak much after the preliminaries. I was
left to consider our "guides," there to help us get through the
jungle, latch onto Marcel, and find our way back to *Yaviza* and
Panama City. I wondered why it needed eight of us to do this,
and wondered even more when the *chiva* pulled over to the
side of the road and two more men climbed aboard.

The short one was clearly a man of rank. His skin was
medium-toned and he had a lot of hair—jet black mustache
and brows, salt and pepper pelt on his arms, curly steel capping
his head. He was powerfully built with a square-jawed face and
body to match but with soft brown eyes and a surprisingly
gentle mouth. Something about him said he would always
manage to look at ease, no matter how grim his message or
task might be.

The man with him was tall and thin with loose joints,
which made him seem less muscular than he was. His face was
high in the forehead, long in the jaw, and sporting a huge
smile. The other men were brown. This man was lights out

black and without blemish. "Hello, mon," he said in a true Caribbean accent.

I saw that both newcomers were armed. The others, I took it for granted, also had weapons tucked away.

Sax did the honors and introduced the older Panamanian as Hector, the gangly black man as Felipe.

We nodded and spoke fractionally to each other. Hector stretched out his legs.

After a moment's silence, I cleared my throat and asked a question in Hector's direction.

"What's all this about?"

"What do you think it is about, Señor Pen?" Hector answered amiably, his eyes taking me in.

"No, no," I said. "I asked you first."

Hector looked at me, his face proclaiming all the goodwill in the world.

"You are looking for a thief, no?"

"Yes," I said. "A man who ran off with a great deal of money that doesn't belong to him."

"We also are looking for someone who took large sums that were not his."

"Judging by your presence, I'd have to guess we're after the same guy."

"That may be."

"And I assume you learned of my interest in this person through my good friend, Sax, here?"

"My understanding is that you asked him to determine the whereabouts of this *ladrón*, this thief. And, when he asked questions, certain people became very interested. It just so happens that your information and our information made…I don't know…let's call it a package."

"And how is that?" I asked. I looked around the *chiva*. There were now ten of us. "I'm searching for an ordinary thief, not Goldfinger."

Hector's mouth creased in an almost-smile. He said slowly, "Ah, but do you know that?"

"It never occurred to me," I answered. "I'm not exactly the James Bond type."

Felipe laughed, Sax grinned, and those who could understand English seemed amused. Some quick translation and soon everyone was in on the joke. I peevishly thought I might want to take back the comment. I did after all drive a flashy Jaguar, spend a lot of time in dangerous small aircraft during campaigns, and I was (grudgingly) becoming accustomed to being the target of violence. I had to admit I didn't give women diamonds, but my cousin did. And—I'd almost forgotten—I was filthy rich.

While I was pondering my new status, Hector gazed at me, leaned his head to one side, pursed his lips, and began speaking of serious things.

In retrospect, the story, pieced together from facts, calculations, and the glue of assumption, was simple enough.

Marcel, whom Rodrigo, Val and the rest of us had regarded as an effective, though amateur thief, was no neophyte at all. While we had been looking to find my purloined *dinero* and put paid to the potshots, the Panamanian Security Forces had their eyes on bigger game.

Marcel, known to them by the pseudonym Angel, was, I learned to my complete astonishment, one of the illicit drug industry's primary "bankers." Although it was hard to believe at first, his job was to receive enormous amounts of drug money from *Fuerzas Armadas Revolucionarias de Colombia* (FARC) and redistribute it, washing the proceeds through one legitimate business and investment after the other. Daily, this "amateur" managed tens of millions of dollars, and more, which he continually moved around the globe with agility and stealth.

His job at the law firm and longevity there had given him exceptional cover for his activities. When my foundation and its abundant cash flow dropped in his lap, he saw the perfect vehicle to launder even larger quantities of receipts. At times, Hector said, my bankbook had probably bulged with incredible sums, only to have them whisked away to other accounts, and then others still.

Hector posited that Marcel had been performing this "service" for many years, but, because he probably kept meticulous separate books for the law firm's auditors, there was nothing pointing to a crime. It was only when Uncle Henry died and I was about to appear on the scene that Marcel would have begun to fear exposure from the far more rigorous audits that usually accompanied a change of beneficiary.

Hector's people had managed to unearth another reason why Marcel should be afraid, a vastly more important reason. Instead of moving the lucre rapidly, Hector's people believed Marcel had started delaying the transactions. That in itself would not have been a problem as long as the money was collecting interest, and the interest and capital were eventually laundered together. The difficulty came when Marcel succumbed to a common weakness of criminals. Not satisfied with what FARC paid him, the interest started disappearing into his pockets.

"This kind of betrayal is the gravest sin in the narco underworld," Hector said. "Marcel knew its discovery would prompt an immediate bullet in the head. Or possibly something far worse." According to Hector, Marcel had avoided detection thus far because of his superior laundering expertise. Presumably, during most of his tenure at Fernandez-Chavira, FARC had asked no probing questions. But information channels were humming, said Hector, and all that seemed about to change.

Back at the firm and faced with imminent preparations for my arrival, Marcel, the supposition went, had uncharacteristically panicked and hurriedly removed the drug deposits from my accounts. In his haste, he had scooped up my money as well and started the process that would eventually connect all the elusive dots. By the time he realized his mistake, it was too late to correct and he fled.

On the other side of the information chain, the Panamanian Security Forces had been accumulating intelligence for almost two years about the man they knew only as Ángel. Investigators had tracked large sums of money through the pipeline to FARC and from there to FARC's launderers. Occasionally, they were able to follow the funds further, though not reliably and not to their final destinations. For their tracking, they relied on a network of informers, some embedded in FARC, some in the Colombian drug gangs themselves, others in various parts of the *Darien*, through which much of the money passed.

The security forces knew a great deal about Ángel but not his real identity. When Sax began asking questions about Marcel, things clicked into place. "In effect," said Hector, "Sax closed the loop."

This put the security team one step away from the kill. As I shortly learned, it was a very big step.

While Hector spoke, I listened, nodded, and occasionally asked a question. Hector, in turn, skillfully but gently interrogated me.

Gradually, I told my story. I explained the shooting and the assault near the casino. The precautions I took, the suspicion I had of virtually everyone, and the unexpected interest I'd developed for a trip into the *Darien*. I needed a break, the lure of the "End of the Road" was powerful, and I didn't want someone else to apprehend Marcel; by now, I was itching to confront the bastard and retrieve what was rightfully mine.

The fact that this escapade would land me even peripherally inside one of the most tenacious and vicious drug wars on the planet had, of course, never entered my mind.

CHAPTER 22

"So now," I said without rancor, "You'll go to *Piña Abajo* and extract Marcel/Ángel and I'll return to Panama City, probably with no hope of ever seeing my money again. The good news, I suppose, is that you'll have removed a big fish from the pond."

"Oh yes," Hector said, "a big fish indeed."

I wasn't finished. "There's one thing that puzzles me. Why am I here when we could have talked about all this in Panama City?" I looked at Hector and shook my head. "I haven't given you any more information than you already had and you've given me quite a lot that wasn't necessary. Not to mention, you've chosen a rather unusual venue to tell me all this."

Hector crossed his feet and put his hands behind his head, brown eyes calm.

"You might see your money yet," he said, "but there is one slight problem."

The part about the money was a surprise but the problem wasn't.

Hector was studying me, not as though he hadn't made up his mind but as though he was wondering how to harness me without my feeling corralled.

"I could appeal to you on several grounds," he said, "and you might accept my proposition. But, when I was younger, I was a businessman and I appreciate the value of a contract. So, now, I propose a contract to you." His face was easy, no wrinkling of his mouth, no narrowing of his eyes. In an odd way, a very peaceful countenance. Probably a useful quality in his line of work.

I was intrigued.

"Ordinarily, yes, we would have met with you in Panama City. What information we wanted we would have asked for. We would not have told you much. Decidedly, we would have discouraged you from visiting the *Darien*. You have been in the military. You understand about chains of command, foreign citizens, persons who are non-combatants, all of that.

"Well, in this war, we have only one army and that is FARC. Panama has no army, we have only policemen, our security forces, and SENAFRONT, our National Frontier Service. These counterterrorism forces are the front line in this war.

"Sometimes, unfortunately, we have a hole in these systems." He lifted his hands, palms out. "What organization doesn't?"

"And this particular hole...?"

Hector sat back and folded his hands in his lap. Despite the bumping and thumping of the *chiva*, he looked like a man at complete rest.

"We know the man you call Marcel from his transfers of money and information from our informers. We can describe his actions and trace some of his transactions. Here and there we get lucky and have even followed his movements in real time on the internet. But…" Hector smiled wryly. "We do not know what Marcel looks like."

It took me a moment to understand. "Surely there are photographs…?"

Hector shook his head. "We have used every source, our own services, Interpol, DAS, the Colombian government's *Departamento Administrativo de Seguridad,* your FBI, the CIA, but no one has an accurate picture of this man. Oh, yes, there are official dossiers, but they're all missing the required Panamanian documents. Normally, he would have a driver's license, a *cédula*—our identity card—possibly a passport. No record of any of these exists. It's as though he never existed except for his trails on the internet and in person at Fernandez-Chavira, Villaroel and Marroquin, where of course, he no longer is. Our sources know only that he is reliably reported to be in *Piña Abajo* and even that may be incorrect."

"Why there?" I asked.

"You have put your finger on the right question. The answer, I believe, is that he is afraid. But the more interesting question is why? He does not know we are close to him. Only a handful of people are aware of this. Also, he would never imagine the police would look for Marcel, the embezzling lawyer, in such a place. As far as we can tell, there is nothing to connect him with *Piña Abajo.*"

"So what does this mean?"

"We are convinced it is not us but FARC he fears. Perhaps he was not so careful in his transactions as he thought. Perhaps they were examining his movements more closely than he knew. They might have had their own informant who reported on Ángel's, shall we say, extracurricular activities.

"If it is FARC he is afraid of, the selection of *Piña Abajo* would be sensible. *Yaviza* is heavily patrolled; FARC does not openly operate there. *Piña Abajo* is nearby and is often used by fugitives of one type or another to hide from the authorities or from rivals in the underworld. This gives Marcel a measure of protection. He seeks to confuse everyone. He lays down tracks to Colombia, to this city, to that one, and undoubtedly there will be more leading in other directions very soon.

"A man who can move and hide so much money, this is a man of unique talents. If it had not been for you, for your friend, we might never have found him. As it is, we may have only this small window of time before he disappears forever.

"So now we come to the crux of the matter. We believe we know where Ángel is. We have the resources to remove him. But, we have no way to identify him. This is what only a person at Fernandez-Chavira or Pen Smith can do. And, of that group, it is Pen Smith who has the most serious stake in the game."

Hector looked at me expectantly and added, "It goes without saying, your money would then be returned to you."

I thought a moment, less about the money than the logistics. "If he's changed his appearance, I might not be able to identify him. I only saw him a couple of times." I gazed at my own deep brown arms.

"It's a risk we run," Hector answered. "Certainly, he can't have undergone and recuperated from significant plastic surgery in only three days. That leaves him few options—some sort of basic disguise, changing facial hair or altering his hair style or color. Is there any special feature Marcel has that he can't cover up or change? I'm thinking perhaps of a tattoo, a limp, or unusual ear shape, that sort of characteristic."

I thought for a moment.

"There's one thing," I said, again looking at my arms. "Marcel is jaundiced," I said. "Seriously."

"Ah," Hector sighed. His eyes crinkled. "In this case, *Piña Abajo* makes even more sense. A place where no one will think of looking for Marcel, a lawyer/thief, where his jaundice will not be circulated to every policeman. Also, a place where he can hide and use his considerable talents to direct everyone to misleading destinations."

"The money he used to buy the ticket to *Bogotá*…"

"Purchased on an account opened eighteen months ago using a false name and address. He has already disposed of it. There will be a dozen more he can use…and perhaps a dozen after that. This, after all, is what he did so well for FARC."

I let it rest a moment before saying any more. I had committed to the project in its infancy two days ago. Many of the original elements were still there. The legendary "End of the Road." The deep jungle. The excitement of being present when Marcel was captured. Of course, I had anticipated the unprepossessing Marcel I'd seen at Fernandez-Chavira, not a person operating in concert with FARC. But I also hadn't expected a squad of highly trained commandos to back me up.

All told, it seemed as though the balance was still tilting in my favor.

A glance around the *chiva* at the other men confirmed what I already knew. For them this was a day's work. What they trained for. What they did. The same was true of Hector, his calm and pleasant face notwithstanding. But for me, the trip, the excitement, even the danger represented freedom. In its own way, this was every bit as much a part of my new life as sitting in Rodrigo's office and digesting the facts and figures of the sixty-three businesses that had made me rich.

I looked at Hector, then at Sax. It was my turn to nod. "This week I inherited a considerable fortune. Just met a gorgeous woman. I can go anywhere I want. Do anything that strikes my fancy. The world is my oyster, as they say. Why on earth would I want to put all that at risk?" I smiled.

Hector's face remained impassive but Sax's mouth began turning up.

I had come to the *Darien* for adventure. Well, I was about to get it.

"There's no way on earth I would turn this down," I said. "Hector, you've got yourself a deal."

CHAPTER 23

The rest of the trip was given over to being briefed. We were to arrive in *Yaviza* shortly, be quietly escorted past police headquarters, and, in the early darkness, separate to eat and take up accommodations where they had been arranged. We would reassemble at the rendezvous place in staggered pairs over a half hour's time. Five or six hours later, we'd be in *Piña Abajo*. With luck we could spot Marcel quickly and be back in *Yaviza* by tomorrow night, having accomplished our purpose. If not, we'd station ourselves in the jungle until we saw him or determined he'd flown the coop. We went over the details and I had a look at the small armaments store that had been traveling in hip pockets, at waistbands and ankles, and just about anywhere else you could hide a gun or knife. The collection was impressive, a minimum of one gun per man and knives of every size and type.

Felipe reached inside his pack and passed over a Sig Sauer P226. My eyebrows went up as I took it. A second one went to Sax. I glanced over at him. The Navy Seals used the P226. Sax and I had been honored by the choice of weapon.

"There'll be rifles at a place on our route," Hector said. "We'll pick them up there."

The munitions duly inspected, all the hardware silently disappeared back where it had come from. The jostling and bouncing slowly diminished, along with most of the rain, and about an hour later, the *chiva* rolled into *Yaviza*.

Hector jumped out and disappeared into the bunker-like police checkpoint. He had done this four other times on the trip from *Meteti* and each time we'd been waved through without disembarking. This was obviously the pass we most needed to receive and it came a few minutes later with Hector sounding the all-clear. He double-checked us on directions to the rendezvous point and, in the hot and lowering dusk, we quietly scattered.

Sax and I walked together past the bars lining the road, barefoot whores strolling the sidewalks, and menacing groups of thug-like kids who would be at home on the streets of Washington.

In this setting, ten men exiting a *chiva* would elicit a yawn.

"This was Noriega's hometown," Sax said off-handedly as we passed a church, looking and sounding for all the world like a disco nightclub. "He never outgrew it." Two men appeared in the church doorway with a third man between them. Unceremoniously, they threw the guy to the ground and retreated inside. "Brotherly love, *Yaviza* style," Sax commented. "Probably reneged on his donation."

Further on, a shoving match generated some bored attention from a mostly listless crowd. "Small time," Sax said. "They'll get to the real entertainment later."

A few minutes after leaving the *chiva*, we deposited our packs in a hotel for whom the words modest and marginally clean were mere hopes. We returned to the streets looking for a meal. Sax wore a faded blue kerchief around his neck, the Panama hat on his head. I sported my shades and intentionally gawked like a tourist.

"Watch how you walk," Sax cautioned. "Stay away from anyone who looks wasted. The men all have machetes and, about this time of night, they usually wind up swinging them. It's a long way to the hospital if something important gets whacked off."

I watched how I walked.

The cantinas were doing a rousing business, the music cranked up. Arguments, drunks passed out in the road, questionable services being negotiated, and in at least one instance, consummated—all took place in the public's face. A cockfight had drawn a crowd and a little girl was selling the onlookers food. "Iguana," Sax said, wrinkling his nose.

We took in more sights. A block from the hotel, a short, stocky man, an *Indio*, was in front of a brothel doing a brisk trade in something poured from a large plastic jug.

"Local hooch. Fermented monkey stomach," Sax told me. "Good cheap drunk."

We walked on. Another *Indio* was in business. His attire consisted of shorts, a multi-strand necklace of brightly colored beads, and a large black tattoo covering his naked torso. "The tattoo is made with plain *Jagua* juice," Sax explained. "The checkerboard pattern means he's a shaman, a medicine man."

"Ask him what he's selling," I said.

Sax and the *Indio* spoke for a moment. The man reached in his bag and brought out several bottles.

I reached over and took one. "What's this for?"

Sax asked, the man answered, Sax translated. "Snake bite. Fer-de-lance. Usually fatal."

The *Indio* kept talking.

"He says the base is *Seco*. He puts leaves from a special plant in it and lets them dissolve."

More talking.

"He guarantees it will work if you drink it right after you've been bitten and take enough of it."

"How much is enough?"

"He says if you fall down dead, you needed more."

The shaman laughed heartily. A doctor with a sense of humor.

I grinned at him in the spirit of things. "What about the square bottle?"

This time, the conversation was lengthy and animated.

"I don't know, Pen," Sax said, scratching his jaw. "I'm thinking maybe we ought to have some of this."

The *Indio* nodded vigorously.

"Uh huh. What does it do?"

"He says it's a wonder potion. Cures skin diseases, sickness from poisonous frogs, aches and pains, cancer…"

"Gotta have some of that," I agreed.

"You haven't heard the good part yet." Sax wiggled his amazing eyebrows. "Monster woodies." He held his hands apart at least a foot. The *Indio's* head went up and down.

Robyn chose that moment to jump into my mind.

"Mmm," I said to distract myself, "I wonder if he sells much."

Sax and the shaman had a short exchange, both glancing at the busy bordello down the street.

"Sales are booming."

"Tell him we'll think about it."

The *Indio* spoke up again and talked excitedly to Sax. He jabbed the air repeatedly, held the third bottle for me to see, and then made a circle with his arms.

Sax's eyes widened and he pulled his head back. "The last bottle is *Ayahuasca*," he said. "I can tell you that we don't want it and I don't think he would sell it to us anyway."

"Why not? Something he won't sell sounds like something we'd want."

"I had it once." Sax frowned. "Believe me, you don't use it casually. The shamans use it to induce trances, see into the body, find diseases, that kind of thing. It's a take-no-prisoners hallucinogen." Sax glanced over at our new friend. "They conduct vision quests with it. You know, where you go to meet the spirits. To be absolutely safe, you have to be with the shaman the whole time you're under the influence."

"You, of course, took it for medicinal purposes…"

"Hell no, I used it to get high." Pause. "There are better ways of doing that." Pause. "Also, it tastes like bat shit."

We said goodbye to the doctor and walked on, minus the bat shit.

On both sides of the street, I saw heavily armed police. Sax said they were there for the truly bad guys, who fortunately had yet to make an appearance. The whores, machete-wielding drunks, and small-time crooks were part of *Yaviza*'s ever-present background. As far as the law was concerned, they didn't exist unless there was a murder and the police had to deal with the inconvenience.

We walked some more, turned a corner, and I heard a loud eruption of voices behind us, then something connected with my back and I staggered forward a step. Spinning from the shock, I turned around and caught a fist on the side of my face. My reflexes kicked in automatically and I landed one square in the other guy's stomach. He doubled over with a grunt. The other man with him swayed menacingly but dropped the club he'd hit me with.

"Drunks," Sax said. "They were swinging at each other and got you instead."

"Do I give a shit how it happened?" My fists were balled up. I took a step toward the guy who thought he was Fred Flintstone. Sax grabbed my arm and yanked me back. I looked at the wooden club lying on the ground. "That damn thing nearly knocked me out." I felt a welt growing between my shoulder blades and another one on my face. "Fucking bastard could have killed me." The fucking bastard was doing his best to look like he'd just happened along, never seen the club before, nor his friend, who'd progressed to vomiting on what passed for a sidewalk.

I was spoiling for a fight and Sax knew it. He had my arm in a lock and was slowly pulling me away. I lunged back and the man on the ground, who was trying to get up, thought better of it. "I ought to beat the crap out of you," I shouted to his frightened face. Sax tightened the lock and dragged me several yards. "Remember why we're here," he said. "Any minute now the buddies of those guys will show up. The last thing we need is to lose you to a street fight."

I allowed him to persuade me but grabbed my arm away as he relaxed his hold. "Fucker might have loosened a damn tooth, and I'll have a frigging black eye, too."

"Trophies," Sax said. "Besides, you can always cover up with the Max-Factor."

I looked at him murderously out of the one eye that seemed to be working. I fingered my bruises and was pissed off a second time. Pain, it seemed, was to be my companion on our trek through the jungle. I fished out two of my magic pills and gulped them down dry.

Yaviza, I thought. The fuckers could have it.

Around the corner, we found ourselves a rundown cantina where the only thing fresh looking was a drawing of a nude blond in exquisite detail covering an entire wall. I looked at her for a minute and suggested to Sax that we get a table facing in her direction.

I checked out the rest of the customers: a drunk snoring away in a corner, a surly-looking thickset man in shirtsleeves whose eyes were focused on the door, and a smattering of heavily gold-chained men, whom I guessed were not stay-at-home family-type guys. There were some women, too, but none I had a hankering to get up close and personal with. There were also kids, mostly small boys looking for a coin or a bill or an unguarded pocket. Loud rap music, Spanish style, was unrelenting. The bar was heavily lined with people, including one man who openly wore both a pistol and a bulletproof vest.

"Town councilman," Sax said, motioning at the guy. "He's famous for it." I felt my heart skip a few beats and add some extra ones.

Sax bought us beer and held his up in a toast. "Welcome," he said, "to the End of the Road."

CHAPTER 24

Sax and I left our hotel at 4:30 a.m., about an hour and a half before dawn, when even the drunks had gone to bed and the whorehouses had shut down. Hector had divided us into pairs exiting the town five minutes apart. A minute or two of walking in the most absolute blackness I have ever known and we reached an abandoned hut gone to ruin and mercilessly picked over for anything useful. A few badly splintered poles and some beaten-to-death palm fronds remained. In the middle of this waste, a large clump of banana trees had grown up. It was there, behind the tall, wide shields of the leaves, that we assembled.

No one talked. No one shuffled, spit, or farted. There was a well-used path to *Piña Abajo* not fifty yards away, and there was no way to know who might be using it. Advertising our presence was not part of the plan.

The men ahead of me began moving. When it was my turn, I saw that we were sliding into the jungle through a slit in a nearly impenetrable wall of vegetation. Two of Hector's compatriots in the town—Hector's spies, Sax called them— had hacked out a path sixty to seventy yards long, and tacked up luminescent markers that guided our way around fallen trees and other major obstacles. The minor obstacles were left to us to navigate.

At the end of the path was a small clearing, which contained several wooden boxes. We immediately lifted the tops and brought out rifles, ropes, prepackaged food, a roll of wire, a hemp rescue ladder, and what looked like a deflated air mattress, which would be useful for ferrying items across a river. My eyes widened with every new item.

We spent the next few minutes examining the weapons and loading them. We also took a last look through our kits, and reviewed essential elements of the plan. Several members of the group were tasked with carrying the contents of the boxes. Some of their rucksacks already jutted out at odd angles and I was willing to bet there were other interesting toys as yet unseen. I smiled to myself. "Saxitis" had probably infiltrated the entire group. Or perhaps it was the other way around.

Even before we arrived at the clearing, I had begun to seriously appreciate the difficulty of traveling the jungle. I began perspiring the moment we entered, my sweat mixing with a light mist that was virtually unnoticeable on the outside but now squatted over me like an oppressive layer of humidity. Although the big impediments were either removed or skirted around, there were still plenty of small, taxing hazards. Roots were a particular problem, as they crisscrossed the ground everywhere. Some were as thick as a medium tree trunk, and the smaller ones had a nasty habit of hiding themselves under foliage and what groundcover there was. Their companions in crime were the vines that grew at crazy angles virtually all over the place.

What particularly surprised me was the early-onset fatigue I felt. While I might not have been as ripped as my compatriots, I was in good shape, able to climb mountains with the best of them. Sax told me jungle fatigue was not unusual. The heat was draining, and the terrain stretched muscles to the limit.

When I'd first heard that *Piña Abajo* was less than two miles away but would take us six or seven hours to get there, I'd laughed. Then, Hector told me the story of a trekker who'd spent five days going from *Yaviza* to a small hamlet three miles away. We were one up on the man, Hector said. Most of our guys had undergone specialized warfare training in the *Darien*.

"Give me a desert," I said, and Hector had the decency to laugh.

Hints of light were filtering through the trees when we started moving again. Raoul verified our position with his compass and GPS. Carlos and José took the first shift as point men. Their job was to look for game trails that we could exploit, and machete-chop a path through the unrelenting gnarl of vegetation that stood in our way. It was exhausting work, and we rotated men frequently.

Shortly into the trip, the ground became meaner, with sucking mud, immovable boulders, and ground vines so thick they couldn't be hacked and had to be scrambled over. We alternately fought and cajoled nature. The rocky cliffs were like home to me, but I slid down the waterlogged gullies like everyone else. The worst of it was the rain, ever-present, eroding the ground, making river crossings nightmares of shapes without definition. Once I found myself chest deep in water, clinging to triple-threat rocks—slimy, jagged and moving. Sax, standing on a wobbling rock in mid-current himself, reached out and pulled me from a foothold that was sliding away under my boots.

The plants were another story altogether—towering, dense, and capable of administering stinging bitch-slaps. Sax told me about a man who fell against a vicious black palm and came away screaming, with hundreds of two-inch long spiny thorns embedded in his back. I kept a close eye out for black palms after that.

Periodically, the rain ended and the mosquitoes arrived in squadrons, led by wing-commanders with jaws like a raptor's. The mossie head net was indispensable. I pulled out the Deet frequently.

The background to all this was a cacophony of sounds— the music of birds, chattering of monkeys, bleats from what Hector said were wild boars, and an occasional ominous roar. Panther, Felipe offered, and I quickened my step a bit.

About halfway through the trip, we came on a deep gorge that bottomed out onto a treacherous white water river. It was one of those no good option kind of deals. A detour was the most logical course, but a serious mountain stood smack in our faces. There was no way of telling how long it would take to circumnavigate it; for sure, we wouldn't get to *Piña Abajo* today, or maybe even tomorrow.

A second possibility was to rappel down the intimidating face of the gorge, and take our chances with what was obviously a very dangerous river. No one seemed to think that was a great idea either.

That left us two choices: we either roped our way across or we tried to reach the other path between *Yaviza* and *Piña Abajo*. Since by now we had no good idea where that lay in respect to our location, the alternatives quickly dwindled to one.

As soon as the decision had been reached, Miguel reached into a bag he'd been carrying and pulled out the components of a line thrower rocket with a folding grappling hook. I walked over and watched as he fit the pieces together. "Nice," I told him.

"I built it myself," he said. "You ever use one of these?"

"Just the hook part. Climbing mountains."

"I remember Sax telling us that during our first meeting," he said. "Hector thought anyone who climbed mountains could cross the jungle."

I raised my eyebrows. "Let's hope he's right."

Miguel swiftly assembled the contraption, wrapped one end of the rope around a sturdy tree, and fired. On the first attempt, the hook went true, disappearing into a giant clot of vegetation on the other side. "Now, we pray," Miguel said as he, Felipe and Benjamin pulled the rope taut around the tree. For a moment, it caught, but, as the men applied more strength, it hiccupped and went slack.

"*Mierda,*" Felipe said, but Miguel gave a knowing smile, played out a little more line, gave it a shake, and the men planted their feet again and pulled until their faces turned red and veins stood out on their arms. Against all their strength, the line held. Smiles broke out all around. Benjamin fashioned an anchor knot and secured the rope to the tree.

Carlos quickly stepped forward, holding a hastily assembled rappel seat. I had used rappel seats many times. An easily assembled web of ropes that encircles the waist and is pulled tight through the legs, its basic purpose is to center and support your body weight. An indispensable part of every mountaineer's kit, it was obviously equally important to our current challenge.

Carlos threaded our other long rope—this one doubled-over on itself—through the rappel seat and tied it off. Once on the opposite side, this rope would be used as a pulley to ferry over our gear. There was a brisk wind so the second rope would be anchored about six feet from the first one, making sure we wouldn't wind up entangled in the equipment.

Carlos put on his rappel seat and lay face up on the ground, parallel with the rope and beneath it, his feet pointing toward us, his head at the edge of the gorge. He wrapped his legs around the rope and clipped his seat to it, using a carabiner. Fernando attached Carlos' rucksack the same way and gave him a shove off into the air. Carlos began pulling himself forward in a smooth, steady motion that ended a few moments later on the other bank.

While Carlos was crossing, the rest of us made our own seats and prepared our rifles, removing the ammo and securing it in our packs. After that, the rifles, rucksacks, and the rest of our gear were clipped to the pulley.

There was no particular order to the crossing and about half the group had already arrived on the other side when I stepped up and fastened myself to the line. At some point, patchy fog had moved in, partially shrouding the ravine. I grabbed the rope, launched into the air, and merged with a light, frothy cloud of mist. Like the others, I pulled myself hand-over-hand, swaying with the wind, moving steadily. By the time I reached midpoint, the fog had closed in, and there was an ethereal quality to my surroundings. Almost enjoying myself, I pulled methodically, but not quickly, satisfied to move at a steady pace. I couldn't see it but I felt and heard the river foaming beneath me, and, in that soft cocoon fashioned by the elements, I forgot for a moment that I was soaked with sweat and grime and on the hunt for a would-be murderer.

I was in this state of other-worldliness when I felt a shiver come through the rope. A bird, I told myself. Finding a new perch. Just stopping by.

I could wish.

My heart pounding, I lifted my head up.

Barely ten feet behind me, the rope was unraveling.

My first thought was the hauling line. If the air had been calm, I might have reached it. But the wind was solidly, hopelessly against me. And, the bad news didn't stop there. If I screamed, I wouldn't be heard over the sounds of the river. If I waved, no one would see me for the fog.

That left nothing to do except try to outrace the unfurling strings.

My body was ahead of my mind, already pulling in great gulps of air and using every muscle to put as much distance from the break as I could. My hand-over-hand movements became explosive, eating up the line. I was beginning to think I could make it—

It began to rain.

Heavy, splashing rain that immediately slickened the rope and soaked my clothes. I fought down the urge to scream, clutched my hands tighter, and tried to keep moving. I was, I realized sickeningly, becoming a sodden, dead weight.

While I was reckoning with this news, there was an ominous jolt on the line.

Then another.

God and I were having a conversation when the rope split and catapulted me forward with a force that sucked the air out of my lungs. I barely had time to register the canyonside racing toward me before I smashed hard, one shoulder taking the brunt of the collision, leaving me in shattering pain.

I bounced off and came at the cliff again, this time my back absorbing the ferocious impact. My hands clenched in a spasm, my boots grabbed for the surface, and I spun around and sailed away again. One more blow like that, I knew, would be the end of me. Instead, instinct took over and my knees bent coming at the rock, cushioning the impact. I inhaled a big gulp of air and absorbed the next blow the same way. After that, the kinetics of the fall worked themselves out and finally I was able to still myself. I hung there, my face against the face of the gorge, fighting shock, just holding on until someone arrived to haul me up.

The cavalry came a moment later in the form of the rope ladder, guided down the rock by Felipe's long arms and legs. When he got a few paces above me, he walked himself down and around to my side, then calmly reached out and snaked one arm around my torso, pulling me toward him. I watched, numbed, as he threaded two carabiners through the rappel seat and firmly secured me to the ladder. He gave me a big grin, then, his arm still gripping me, yanked twice on the rope to signal we were ready. The other men pulled and we slowly moved up. When we neared the top, strong arms hauled me over the edge and dragged me a safe distance away. I started to stand but thought better of it, and for long moments, lay on my back, my mind still somewhere out in the ether, my body collapsed on itself. Sax told me later they had to pry the rope out of my hands.

After the gear had been moved from one side to the other, the equipment line was inspected for flaws, then used to get the rest of the group across. I finally sat up and allowed my injuries—scrapes and bruises mostly, a gash or two across my arms, and a couple of cracked ribs—to be tended, while everyone had a gander at my rope.

One of the first things a mountaineer learns is that ropes are incredibly safe, to the point that breakage is statistically negligible. Those that do break have almost always been pulled against a sharp rock, something ten of us could swear hadn't happened here. In the end, we all shook our heads. It was a mystery we couldn't solve. The rope was a statistic. I was a statistic. As frustrating as it was, we'd just have to leave things that way and get on with the business of finding Marcel.

Our new route took us through much the same kind of punishing ground as before. Despite my magic pills, I slowed us down. The bullet wound having bounced against the gorge a time or two, my leg was a witches brew of pain, and, although I tried to walk normally, I pretty much defaulted to a limp. I took more pills, Raoul cut a walking sick for me, and Sax tried to help by offering to carry my rucksack. I compromised and let him take my rifle. While it wasn't heavy, it banged into my side with every step, hitting a spot that had been especially battered. I concentrated on putting one foot forward, and then another one. I hated to admit it, but all the assaults on my body were beginning to take their toll.

On top of that, I was thirsty as hell. Sax had already explained this was commonplace in the jungle, caused by heavy sweating from the heat and closeness of the atmosphere. Since there's a practical limit to how much liquid a person can carry and still have the strength to cover the terrain, we spent a necessary chunk of our time looking for water, in particular that collected inside bamboo. Fortunately, bamboo is plentiful. Unfortunately, bamboo in the jungle grows to enormous sizes. A stand of it is extremely hard to walk through, can cover a dauntingly large area, and generally has to be circumnavigated. Bottom line: we were always hoping to find bamboo, just not too much.

We trudged out the clock. One river looked like the next. One gorge. One mile-long root system, one implacable wall of trees and bushes and slick, slithering vines. Then, Benjamin, who was in front of me, stopped, turned his head and put a finger to his lips. I passed the signal to Sax and in short order our entire column had fallen still. From up ahead came faint sounds and a fleeting trace of odors that could only have come from food being cooked.

I was tired from walking, from the rope failure, from the heat and humidity. I was beat up, shot up and fed up. I looked at Sax. He wiggled his eyebrows optimistically. I looked at my watch. Six hours. Six long, hard, grueling hours.

Another signal came down the line and we all sat quietly, on fallen trees, boulders, small patches of dirt. I wound up on a muddy nest of vines. It really didn't make any difference by then. I wasn't sure I could get much dirtier or more miserable than I already was.

Fifteen minutes went by, then a half hour. I was just getting used to being off my feet when word came down that we'd reached our destination. *Piña Abajo* was dead ahead.

Grins broke out all around. We fell back a comfortable distance, found a suitable section of terrain, and cleared a space big enough for an encampment. Most of us sat on the ground, more comfortably this time, quietly talking, pulling out rations, recovering from the journey. I knew that any minute Sax would be telling me to clean up, pull on my fresh trekking outfit, and get ready for the next act in this *Darien* play. I groaned at the thought of it. There didn't seem to be a square inch on my body that wasn't hurting, and, temperamentally, I wasn't too keen either. None of that mattered. I could groan all I liked, but this was the climax of our trip, the reason we were all here. What I did now and how convincing I could be might very well make a difference in whether we captured Marcel or not. I took in a deep breath and coughed it out in pain. Fuck it. I was here because of Marcel. I was in pain because of Marcel. I had nearly died because of Marcel. There was no way on earth I was going to blow this opportunity. If Marcel was in *Piña Abajo*, we were going to nail the bastard.

CHAPTER 25

Freshly clothed, Sax, Felipe and I stood behind a thin stand of bamboo, eyeing *Piña Abajo* from about fifty feet away. At its outskirts on the left-hand side, there was a large grove of banana and orange trees interspersed with rangy coconut palms. On one side of the trees was a bright green field. "Rice," Felipe said. On the other was a tract of golden pineapples.

Closer in sat a large rectangular thatched building, which Felipe identified as a market and community center. Twenty or thirty huts on stilts ringed this "downtown" area. There were no streets, only dirt walkways. Calling *Piña Abajo* a town was probably giving more credit than was due.

The main feature of this hamlet was a large pool fed by a vigorous and breathtaking waterfall. Unfortunately for *Piña Abajo*, beauty didn't translate into currency. While the town had fresh drinking water, a place to bathe, and a productive fishing hole, the pool drained by means of an underground stream which surfaced at some unknown spot far away. This deprived *Piña Abajo* of one of the most important assets any town in the jungle can have—a navigable waterway.

As I had seen on Sax's satellite map of the *Darien*, roads were almost non-existent, which meant that accessible rivers were the lifeblood of every community. Without one, a hamlet like *Piña Abajo* had no viable way to engage in meaningful commerce, forcing it to live mostly on its own meager resources. It didn't take much to see that the town was barely holding on. Its people were known to get a little help from fugitives and drug runners looking to go to ground, but often those accommodations were achieved at the end of a gun, with minimal dollars changing hands. It was a sad existence at best.

While we took a minute to examine the town, I adjusted my Yankees baseball cap and hung a camera Sax had supplied from my belt. I looked over at my compatriot, whose clothes were somewhat different from mine on the outside but identical in the treasures they concealed. Once again, we looked like trekkers out to experience the wonders of the *Darien*. Felipe had also donned another identity, that of a semi-bored guide who had probably been paid too much to beg off the job.

All went as planned in the beginning. We entered the village just before noon, Sax and I staring wide-eyed at everything. After the obligatory picture-taking, Felipe guided us to the market, which also served as school, cantina, chicken coop, and café. We sat at the single plastic outdoor table under a sagging thatched roof.

Felipe ordered lunch for us—rice, beans, fish, and orange juice that was served in a coconut hull. Plantains appeared unbidden but were delicious.

"Eat, but stretch it out," Sax said. "We may be here awhile." I ate a few slow bites and soon realized I was genuinely hungry. When our plates were empty, we had a second order of orange juice, waited awhile, then ordered more beans, rice, and plantains.

The chickens apparently liked us since they congregated under the table and clucked throughout the meal. People, but not Marcel, ambled up and placed carry-out orders, mostly for skinny-looking empanadas. Several admired the chickens. They all inspected us and, as most Panamanians do, politely said hello. We returned the greetings, Felipe answering questions about his "guests," and we took more pictures with the locals. Some people smiled a lot, some nervously shied away. I had my sunglasses on although it was a cloudy day with more rain threatening. I was sure I looked exactly like the idiot I was pretending to be.

Just as I was thinking I couldn't consume another grain of rice, face a fifth serving of orange juice, or photograph another coconut palm, I saw a familiar profile out of the corner of my eye. The sallow skin registered immediately and even the down-turned brim of his white Panama hat couldn't keep me from recognizing him. Almost not believing our good luck, I hissed under my breath to Sax and Felipe, "He's here. The two men walking toward us. It's the guy on the left."

Felipe smiled, waited a moment, then stood up languorously, looking around like a man satisfied with his meal but needing a place for part of it to exit. The Caribbean lilt issued from under his breath: "Yellow skin, white shirt, white hat. You sure, mon?"

I nodded.

"Any idea who dat odur guy be?"

"No," I said. Marcel's companion was squat with pocked skin and *Tonton Macoute* sunglasses. He bore an unnerving resemblance to Noriega and moved with the finesse of a cement truck.

Felipe walked toward Marcel, every loose-jointed bone in action. His long fingers held a cigarette. He began whistling a reggae tune.

"Ey mon," Felipe said to the *Tonton Macoute* man, putting on the full Creole. "Weh di batruum, deh?"

Initiating the conversation was the signal for our guys, who burst from the jungle at a dead run. Marcel instinctively swiveled to look over his shoulder and I watched *Tonton* reach in his pocket and bring out a huge black object. As Marcel turned back, his mouth wide in unuttered speech, I saw the deadly black gun come up, the man's finger contract on the trigger, and then, as I opened my mouth to shout a warning, Marcel's head blew apart. There was a slow motion shower of brain, bone, and blood, then the pieces submitted to gravity and settled down on the earth around the collapsed and nearly headless body.

The gun shifted to Felipe and I was back in real time. "No!" I screamed, running toward Felipe, as bloody pulp spotted my field of vision like thick red rain.

The man was pumping out bullets in all directions as he raced for the protection of the jungle, two of our men sprinting after him. I threw myself on the ground next to Felipe, who was leaking blood from a jagged hole in his stomach and another on his left arm. Sax was there the next second, ripping open his rucksack and yanking out his med kit. He found some gauze pads and pressed them against the stomach catastrophe. Immediately, they were soaked red. I took on the arm, which had a long, ugly, deep gash. Somewhere behind me, children were wailing.

I dived into my med kit, found something for a tourniquet, then ripped the sutures and needle from my shirt. Sax, his eyes not moving from the gushing wound in Felipe's stomach, nodded toward his rucksack and said, "Use as few pads as you can. I'm going to need them over here. Also, get the guidebook. It has a compartment with morphine."

The book yielded up its painkiller. I grabbed a syringe and plunged it into Felipe's shoulder.

"That's a good dose. He'll be out in a minute," Sax said. "Felipe!" He shouted over the other man's moans. "We've given you some morphine. We're going to sew up your arm and bind your stomach. Then we'll get you back to Panama City. Understand?"

Felipe's face was a bloodless shade of gray and his lips almost blue but he managed a sound and a second later the morphine grabbed him and his muscles relaxed.

I unpacked the threaded needle, looked up and saw Hector speaking on a sat-phone. He strode over to us, took one look at Felipe and barked something into the phone. "Helicopter," he said to us and swiftly walked back to talk to his men.

"I need some help here," I shouted in their general direction and Miguel broke into a run. We worked in tandem, I with the needle, Miguel pushing together the terrifyingly bloody mess that I prayed would once again be a wholly functioning arm.

I took a deep breath, thrust the needle into the skin, and pulled the suture through, expecting it to grip. Instead, it trailed out, dragging slimy pieces of gore. I choked down bile and tried again, my fingers wet and slippery. For the second time, the shredded skin and blood let the suture slip. Miguel pushed harder, I took a deep breath and plunged the suture into healthy skin further away from the damage. I felt resistance and the suture held. Then another.

"I'm going to kill him," I said to Sax at one point, pulling the needle through a particularly gruesome piece of flesh. "Either that or he'll never forgive me for the God-awful hash I'm making of his arm."

"You won't kill him and he'll be grateful," Sax replied, packing more pads into the stomach wound, his arm dripping red up to the elbow. "You're almost finished. It's the blood that's making it look worse than it is. This is the one we have to worry about. Looks like the bullet went more to the side than the middle. He might catch a break if we can get him back in time."

I understood. Once learned, never forgotten: Belly wounds are a bitch.

Sax was right about the arm. Miguel and I redoubled our efforts and soon the last suture was through and tied off. Both of us immediately went to help Sax with the bigger problem.

Between us, we applied more pads, tried our best to staunch the blood, and tightly bound Felipe with bandages that were soaked through almost as fast as we put them there. I held Felipe while Sax pulled off his vest and wrapped it around Felipe's torso to hold everything together. Hector was still on the phone, maybe with the guys who'd followed the shooter, maybe the copter. After a minute, he put the phone in his pocket and walked back over to us, looking at Felipe.

Sax shook his head and glanced at Hector. "It all depends on when that bird gets here," he said, without being asked. He turned to Miguel. "We need more things we can wrap around him." Miguel went in his own rucksack and came up with an extra shirt. After that, he went to the others, returning with a small pile that he put on the ground. I added my vest.

Miguel and I raised Felipe up and Sax began wrapping him with the new clothes, Felipe gasping a time or two through the morphine. I heard Hector bark out orders.

"Shit for the town," Sax said.

"What does it mean?"

"Loosely translated, Hector says there's someone here who knows about Marcel and the guy who shot him. He's telling the guys to tear apart the fucking town to find them."

"Jesus," I said, "there's nothing here to tear apart. What's he going to do, set fire to their huts?"

"That's what you get for fucking with the devil," Sax said.

Hector came back over. After what happened to Robyn, I would have been happy never to see another chopper, much less ride on one. But Hector had other ideas. "I need my men here," he said. "We have to learn everything we can about

Àngel and his time in *Piña Abajo*. His computer will be here. If we're lucky, some paperwork, too. There's only one man on the helicopter. You both have to go with Felipe."

While I was absorbing that good news/bad news information—after all the chopper would save me another six or so hours in the jungle, not to be sneered at—the helicopter came into hearing distance.

"Showtime," Sax said, and I watched the copter until it was hovering over us, fairly certain they would send down a litter. A rope ladder came down instead.

Sax sprinted for it, scrambled up and drew it in so the litter could be dropped. Hector braced himself and steadied it as Miguel and I lifted Felipe and strapped him in. There was no hydraulic hoist; Sax was hauling up the litter by hand. As soon as they'd pulled Felipe into the hold, the ladder shot back down and I threw myself up it as fast as I could. I hauled myself though the door and looked over at Felipe.

Still breathing.

Good man.

No thanks to that bastard Marcel.

At the airport, we handed off the barely-alive Felipe to a medical team, then Sax and I shared a cab ride into the city.

At one point, Sax spoke viciously. "No one said he had a fucking minder."

"No one knew," I answered, unwilling to assign blame. As far as I was concerned, it was no one's fault, not Felipe's, not ours, not even Hector's. For my own role, I was satisfied

Marcel had not recognized me. Ditto the other man. I'd never set eyes on him before.

"Goddam royal fuck-up," Sax said. I understood. Like it or not, Sax had brought Hector to the game and Sax wasn't one for screw-ups. But neither, I thought, was Hector. The problem was the whole thing didn't make sense. Marcel had been the goose with the golden egg. Why kill him?

"We know Marcel was a little weasel. He cheated me, Fernandez-Chavira, he even cheated FARC. Maybe the other guy wasn't his minder. He could have been a partner."

"What did Marcel...Ángel...whatever the creep's name was—why did he need a partner? He was doing all the work."

"True," I said. "But what would FARC be doing hiding Marcel out there and then killing him? Unless...ah, shit...they already know where the money is."

"If they'd gotten that information, you can bet Marcel would already have been feeding the frogs," Sax said. "No, I think this is your classic screw-up. The minder was FARC. Sent to pull Marcel in. He was keeping Marcel low in *Piña Abajo* for a few days until the misdirection worked, then he would have hauled that piece of shit back to wherever his fellow cretins are, somewhere near the border or just over it. Marcel would have talked there, I can guarandamntee you."

"So...?" I didn't get it.

"Unless they find the motherfucker, we'll never know for sure," Sax said, "but I'd guess the minder was trigger-happy for some reason. Maybe he got a tip from an informant in *Yaviza*. Maybe that *Indio* with the batshit. Some whore paid to check out the *extranjeros*. Might be anybody. There are more eyes and ears in the *Darien* than there are in New York City."

"So he panicked."

"Well, it wouldn't be the first time somebody did. There he was in this one-horse town, out-manned, out-gunned. I think we'll learn if we ever catch up to the sonofabitch that he didn't plan on killing Marcel. In fact—" Sax poked a finger at my chest and pulled his lips into an almost frightening parody of a grin. "—the bosses may not be too happy with Marcel's minder if he makes it back to them. He could be in for some rough sledding."

"I like that version of events," I said. "For one thing, I thought Hector had his act together."

"He did. That's what makes it so fucking shitty. But FARC is the most tenacious terrorist group in the Americas. They're that way for a reason. They play big time. It's hard as hell to outfox them. Even when you're as good as Hector."

"There are a hundred maybes in this," I said wearily. "I don't care what the reason is. I'm not in the blame game. And as far as I'm concerned, I'd rather have a dead Marcel who's taken my money and escaped with it than a live Marcel using me for potshots."

"Well, yeah, there is that," Sax admitted.

"So let's call it a day on the who's at fault business. Right now, Marcel is dead and Felipe wounded. Got to hope Felipe pulls through."

Sax nodded and fell silent. After a while we spoke a little more. Sax's apartment was a good forty-five minutes further on, so I offered him one of Rosario's meals and a bed in the condominium. He appreciated it, he said, but declined.

I understood. There are some kinds of fatigue that are best coped with alone.

For me, there was no alone; Val came to greet me the moment I set foot in the hall.

I saw myself reflected in his shocked eyes. "Christ you look terrible what in God's name happened do you need a doctor you're covered in blood!"

Val gets that way sometimes.

I looked at myself in a mirror and saw a dirty brown face covered with cuts and bruises, shirt and pants splotched red, and weary eyes staring back, one of them verifiably black. How the guards downstairs ever recognized me I couldn't imagine. If our roles had been reversed, I would have hauled my filthy ass off to jail.

"No doctor, I'm okay." I tried to calm him, even while my ribs felt as though a knife was slicing through them. "It's mostly someone else's blood, not mine. I'm just tired as hell and hurting, not dying. Listen, do me a favor and bring some Clorox to my bathroom, would you? I'm ready to get this shit off my skin—at least the parts I can touch." I headed for the bathroom, unbuttoning as I went and shivering in the air-conditioning. "And some bourbon. I'll tell you all about it while I clean up."

"Sure." Val expelled a semi-relieved puff of air. "You definitely…?"

"Yeah, yeah, I'm fine, really Val."

He turned away, stopped himself, hemmed and hawed for a minute, then finally spoke. "Look, Pen, I know it's a bad time…"

I stopped and half turned, which drove the pain in deeper.

"Well…Maria's here."

I resumed walking and made a weak gesture of dismissal. "I don't care," I threw over my shoulder, "as long as she's not expecting to get in the shower with me." The next minute my brain registered what I'd said. Holy crap. I was more exhausted than I'd thought.

"Actually, that's not all."

I looked at him. I was not in the mood for any more surprises.

"Robyn's here, too."

"Robyn? My Robyn?" Why would Robyn be here with Val and Maria?

"It's a long story," Val said, "but apparently they were in the same school in the Canal Zone years ago and they've been in touch here and there since they graduated. So, today, when Robyn called you—"

"Robyn called me?" I was tickled pink, if it were possible under all that brown.

"Yeah, so when Maria heard me say Robyn, she asked if it was Robyn Butler, and you know how women are, the next thing I knew, Robyn was here on the terrace and she and Maria have been chatting away like long lost friends. A lot of it about you, by the way." Val, I thought, looked uncharacteristically envious.

Since Robyn and Maria were here, I told Val I'd fill him in later and be out as soon as I was presentable. The next half-hour was devoted to serious showering and painfully attacking the mixture of *Jagua* and *Achiote*. I felt like a dishpan must after a good scouring but wound up looking more or less like a human being with all parts intact, if black and blue, scraped, scratched, swollen, and broken. A long list of adjectives to show for my day in the jungle.

It had taken most of the strength I had just to get cleaned up, but the prospect of seeing Robyn propelled me toward the terrace and made me put a good face on things. I replenished my drink, opened the door, and went out. Val, Robyn and Maria all turned toward me, one immensely relieved at my physical improvement, another with a smiling mouth but eyes aghast, the final one lukewarm. Well, two out of three wasn't too bad.

Val and Robyn were generally aware of how I'd spent my weekend. I wasn't sure what Maria might have picked up, but both Val and Robyn had agreed not to talk about the trip. I decided a climbing accident would cover all bases. And it wasn't far off the mark, after all.

I sat in a chair and waited to see if there would be questions.

Val obliged. "So, how was your trip?" he said, his eyes rolling around in some bizarre rendition of concern.

"Helluva mountain climb," I answered.

"Looks it. Want to see a doctor for any of those, uhm, scratches?"

"Nothing important," I said, aware of Robyn's all-too-seeing eyes.

"What about Marcel?" I asked, pushing the horrible image of his death from my mind. "Progress?"

Val shook his head. "Still hiding out in Colombia, I guess. I haven't seen Rodrigo since yesterday afternoon when he dropped off something for us. Hold on a minute."

He opened the door, went in, and came back holding two tantaluses of ornately carved wood. Each bore a heavily cut crystal decanter. Around the necks of both decanters hung silver medallions, one reading "Val" and the other "Pen."

"I'll be damned," I said, lifting mine and feeling the weight. I got a breathtaking jab in the ribs for my effort. "This is something," I said. What prompted it?"

"He wanted to say thank you. For being understanding about the theft and not firing him, I'd guess."

"Nice," I said, replacing the decanter. "So, from now on, we each have our own bottle. I'd better not catch you dipping into mine."

Val smiled.

I felt my muscles slackening into a kind of rubberiness and decided if I planned to get inside under my own power, I'd better do it now. I stood up and announced I had some things to take care of.

"See you later." Val lifted a hand.

I motioned to Robyn. "Let's go," I said, and, to her credit, she rose and followed me without any fuss. And without crutches, I noted.

I opened the door. "Oh, by the way," I commented as I stepped into the living room. I winked at Val with my good eye. "Beautiful bracelet, Maria."

Val blanched and Maria turned pink. I laughed inside, which was the only place I could laugh without doubling over. With everything else a wreck, at least my good humor was still intact.

Robyn didn't say anything as I guided her along the hallway. She didn't say anything when we entered Uncle Henry's bedroom. Didn't say anything as I enfolded her in my arms, my mouth finding hers, my hands tracing the delicate skin of her face, her neck.

She said something when I pulled off my clothes and stood before her, battered, shot, veritably flogged, a mess of a human being.

"Oh, my God." Her eyes welled with tears. Her hands gently guided me to the big bed, pushed me under the covers, then she silently removed her own clothes and slid in next to me. Her soft hands stroked my cheek, her head lowered itself to my chest. I felt the wetness on her face.

"Sleep now," she said. She kissed me sweetly and moved her body closer to mine, enfolding me in a tender, protective shroud.

I closed my eyes. I didn't care about Uncle Henry, didn't care about any past he and Robyn shared. I did care that she was beside me now. The last thing I was aware of before drifting off was Robyn's whisper. "So this is what happens when I let you out to play on your own." It was said part laughing, part crying and was music to my ears.

I woke up once in the middle of the night, felt a warm breathing pillow enveloping me, and went back to sleep.

CHAPTER 26

The next morning, there were two notes on the door. One from Robyn: "Try not to injure anything else before I get there. Call you later." Another from Val dated last night: "Felipe in guarded condition, per Sax."

"Guarded condition" was hospital-speak for hanging in there. Something to be thankful for anyway.

My own injuries were no fun. At this rate, I thought, gulping down the morning's ration of medicine, I'd be a magic pill addict before too much longer.

When I made it to the breakfast table, Rosario hovered. *"Montañas,"* I said, trying to explain away the visible bumps and bruises. Val obviously filled in some specious details, as she clucked, *Dios mioed* a couple of times, and fussed over me.

"I wasn't sure you were going to show up for breakfast," I said, grabbing some toast. "Thought you might have stayed with Maria."

"Other way around. We stayed here. She's putting herself together right now."

"Umm," I mumbled around a mouthful of bacon.

"I made you a hero," Val said. "You rescued somebody and saved their life."

"Must you overdo everything?" I shook my head, then realized I *had* helped save someone's life. Whether he would stay saved was an open question.

After a few minutes, I told Val the story, which had him wide-eyed and horrified. I left out some of the worst details, such as how a head looks when it explodes. We were eating, after all.

"It's a big mess," I summed up. "Our only hope seems to be the guy who ran away. Sax calls him the minder. Probably for FARC." I took a swallow of coffee and asked Rosario to refill my cup. "Hector promised to keep us in the loop but who knows when that might be. Tomorrow. Never. Anything in between."

Val nodded a couple of times. Was it my imagination or was he not particularly disturbed by the story's end? Perhaps a few million dollars here, a few million there had become nothing to sneeze at. On the other hand, I had never known Val to disdain a lowly penny. I looked at him and detected smugness.

"Okay, what's going on?" I asked through a forkful of egg. "There's something you know that I don't."

Val grinned. "All is not lost, cousin, Val may just ride to the rescue." A look of concern crossed his face. "Well, that and something else."

"Don't tell me this is one of those good news, bad news scenarios." I said. "Please, I'm all paid up in the bad news column."

"Fine, I'll take the positive first," Val said, as we both stood up from the table. We went to the terrace, where I intended to loll all day, preferably with Robyn.

Val dived into his briefcase. "Let's start here," he said, pulling out a sheaf of papers.

For the next fifteen minutes, Val traced a lengthy series of transactions for me. The central fact I already knew: Marcel had been moving gigantic amounts of money around, not just emptying my account but dealing with some truly staggering sums. It all made sense now, Val said, in light of what I'd told him over breakfast.

If I read Val's information correctly, the real news for me was how much time Marcel must have spent shifting funds and what that might mean to us in terms of recovering the money. So much activity, said Val, was tough to undertake without slipping up somewhere. Too many quick and dirty transactions could leave trails and, though Marcel had made elaborate efforts to conceal his activities, Val and the computer guys had a few tricks of their own. After days of frustration, they'd begun stripping away the layers of his defenses.

No one at the law firm knew exactly what they were looking at, but there were some pretty astute guesses. Everyone was still astounded by the sheer amounts of money. The only sensible explanation was drugs and nobody wanted to say that aloud.

While the others still pored over the data in its raw form, Val had done some extra homework of his own. Possibly, just possibly, he'd located several of Marcel's hidden accounts.

I looked at him in awe.

"I'll be damned. You figured it out."

"Child's play," he said, not meaning it for a second.

"You are good, Val, you are outrageously good."

Val's chest expanded an inch or two.

"Actually, I'm not finished by a long shot. I've found pointers to some of the accounts, now I need to firm them up. Then comes figuring out how to get into them."

"Give me a minute to digest this," I said, thinking about Hector. Over beer in the *Yaviza* cantina, Sax had more or less explained how we'd come by our partners for the *Darien* trek. What he'd had to say mostly echoed what I'd picked up in the *chiva*. The only additional information had been his account of the way he and Hector had met.

In a nutshell, my call to Sax had prompted him to contact an acquaintance in the Panamanian security forces. Within hours, two policeman knocked on Sax's door and escorted him to a meeting where I was the topic du jour. Several people, including Hector, attended. The link between my problem and Hector's had been sketched out. A deal was struck, basically the same one I agreed to in the *chiva*. "I took these guys seriously from the get go," Sax told me. "There was no bullshit."

The night before our trip, Sax learned more details of the plan and met the other men who accompanied us to *Yaviza* and *Piña Abajo*. Based on the two encounters, Sax considered Hector a power to be reckoned with. But who Hector actually was and precisely what organization he represented Sax never learned.

That made me consider whether or not we were going to share Val's information. I thought Hector might have resources that could help us crack the accounts, but I was also nervous about how much authority he had. Could he confiscate funds, for example? If Val traced the rainbow and found a not-quite-full pot at the end of it, would Hector take the whole thing and cut us out? I didn't think so, based on our previous conversation, but there was no way to guarantee it. One thing I did know for sure, before doing any sharing, I wanted Val to determine exactly what belonged to us and what belonged to everyone else. I was satisfied with who "us" was. About others, I preferred to reserve final judgment.

"I have something else to show you," Val said, interrupting my train of thought. He had a small smile on his face.

"This isn't the bad news, I gather?"

Val shook his head and handed me two pieces of paper. I looked from one to the other. "I'll be damned again," I said. "What a day for surprises."

"We're not finished yet," Val told me soberly.

"Well, let's keep this one to ourselves. Now, you've got me sufficiently primed, so on with the bad news."

"You don't know how much I hate to tell you this, Pen." He pulled another stack of papers from the briefcase. "This is the same information I showed you a few minutes ago but it's sorted differently." He handed me the pages. "Look at the headings."

My eyes followed his finger across the top row.

"First column—date. This column—log-in time," he said. "And this is the log-out. Between them are activity points. They don't tell us what was being done on the computer; they just tell us the computer was being used."

I looked where his finger was pointing, then lifted my head and stared at him in disbelief.

"Are you positive?"

He nodded, his expression deepening.

My heart sank.

"But, if it's true...how?"

"I don't know," Val said. "But there's no mistake."

"Maybe it was someone else using the terminal."

Val shook his head. "I already checked. You need a password. That was the first item the computer geniuses had to figure out."

I stared at the paper, following the lines that showed Marcel at his computer, no doubt doing what he did most days, moving money around the world.

The printout was for Monday morning.

Monday morning, I had been shot.

The conclusion was inescapable.

Marcel was not the one who shot me.

I was bewildered. If not Marcel, who? And why? The old questions raised their heads again. And again I had no answers.

There was a man out there with a gun, who shot me, attacked me on the street, tried to scare me with a knifed t-shirt and a silver SUV. I'd been concentrating on the "why" and assuming all this activity was because somebody—handily Marcel—wanted my money. Maybe I needed to reorder my thoughts. Maybe I was not the actual target, except as I was related to Uncle Henry. Was it possible he'd unknowingly pissed someone off? Someone who bore a dreadful grudge?

I wrangled with the concept, and, at some point, Val stood up and went inside. I was still sitting on the terrace when he poked his head out. "Maria," he said, gesturing in the direction of the front door. "We're off."

"See you later," I said.

"Look, why don't you call Robyn, we'll grill some steaks tonight?"

I nodded okay, my mind still on who might have been slighted enough by my uncle to attempt murder. Of course, it was an empty exercise. I had no way of knowing who had been in his address book, nor what insult, real or imagined, might have occurred.

About noon, Robyn called. "How is what's left of you?"

"Passable. All of this is making an alcoholic out of me." I looked at my pre-lunch Beam.

"Feel like a visitor?" she asked.

"That depends on how spry you are," I answered, suddenly perking up.

"Don't worry about me, take a look at yourself."

"All assembled parts fit and ready for service, ma'am." Some parts readier than others.

"I was thinking more of a quiet visit than a ten-mile hike," she said. "Why don't we relax and see what the day brings."

"Bring your bathing suit." I paused. "On second thought, don't."

Robyn laughed. "Should I stop and get some sandwiches?"

"Rosario will fix something. Just bring the delectable you."

I found Rosario and informed her about lunch. I didn't mention clothes or lack of them, but I did give her the rest of the afternoon off.

Robyn and I started with an alfresco lunch, which we gobbled up right to the last morsel of the ubiquitous Panamanian lime pie. After Rosario cleared the plates and said goodbye, we moved on to the real delicacies. Robyn excused herself and reappeared on the terrace in a black bikini. I slipped on a pair of swim trunks.

"Mmm," I said, pulling her close. I gave her a long, deep kiss and drew her down the terrace and around the corner, just off Uncle Henry's—now my—bedroom. There was a hedge with a wrought iron door in it. I held out a hand to Robyn and took a deep breath. "Ever been here before?" I asked lightly, hoping she would lie if necessary.

She stepped through the door and her gasp said it was her first time in this miniature Garden of Eden. There were walls of flowers and ferns, palm trees with vivid red stems, rambunctious climbing plants mixing with formally potted orange trees, a fan-shaped banana tree. The air was lightly aromatic.

Sitting on the floor of the terrace and surrounded by flowers was a free-form rock Jacuzzi.

"Unbelievable," Robyn said, her eyes sparkling. "Bougainvilleas, ginger lilies—"

She took a deep breath through her nose. "Gardenias. And some jasmine. It's—it's exquisite."

It was. We sat on a bench, held hands and, listened to the muffled sounds of the city. There was a bar under the eaves and I got up to check the offerings. Champagne, *Veuve Clicquot*. I poured a glass for Robyn.

"It's just too hedonistic for words," Robyn said. "I'm getting in."

"Not like that, you aren't." I grinned at her.

She tossed her head and lowered herself into the water, favoring her ankle.

"I warned you," I said, following her in.

She looked at me with her lop-sided smile and stood before one of the jets so it hit her between the shoulders.

"Just try to get me here," she said, moving slightly to the side so the jet shot out toward me.

"Hmm," I said, considering my strategy. I wanted to be careful around the jets in case one of them hit an injury—but some things might be worth the pain. I ducked under the water and grabbed Robyn's legs, drawing her down with me.

We surfaced, laughing through our sputters. A long way from our last dip in the water.

I put my arms around her. "You're going to lose," I said. "Actually, you're going to win. And so am I. But, first, something's got to give."

"Uh oh," she giggled.

"It's not what you think," I said, and pulled off my trunks in one fast movement.

There was a quick intake of breath from Robyn. I moved in, caressing her thigh, rubbing myself up against it. My fingers found her bikini bottoms and I slipped my hand in at her pelvis. My finger slid in further.

"Stop," she said, "you're—"

"Yes?" I pulled on the bikini and felt it slowly slip down, over her hips, down to her knees, then I didn't care where it went.

I unhooked the top of the suit and threw it into the froth of the tub. The combination of bubbles, warmth, and the proximity of Robyn intoxicated me. I pulled her closer and felt the exquisiteness of her skin, her slickness, the unstoppable onslaught of desire that forced me inside her, to be received by a clench of muscles that left me momentarily unable to breathe.

She was straddling me now, rocking against me, her breasts hard and soft at the same time.

"I have an idea," she said, gasping. As difficult as it was, I paused.

"Come over here," she said, pushing us near the steps, where there were jets at all levels. Robyn pushed me some more and suddenly I felt a shot of water on my butt.

"What??"

Robyn hooked her leg on mine and spun us around. The Jacuzzi jet spewed forth its energy exactly on the point where the two of us were joined.

"Oh, God." I gripped her and felt myself explode, then a second later, felt a second explosion from Robyn.

My muscles were contorted, then slack, but Robyn was lost in the sensation. Her back arched, she twisted her torso against me, her nails stopped just short of making scratches to rival the jungle, then after a moment she was reduced to an occasional quiver and then she and I both collapsed on the steps, half in, half out of the water. We stayed that way for a few minutes.

"I may never be normal again," Robyn said, her head nestled below my chin. I pushed a lock of hair behind her ear.

"That's the whole idea."

"Yes, but I have to be able to walk."

I chuckled. "You will. If not, I'll carry you."

She sighed and moved her head to my shoulder. Her hand skittered around and found her glass. She took a big swallow. "That's the real way to drink champagne," she said, offering it to me.

"I can see the ad now. *'Veuve Clicquot,* lip smacking good.'"

She did that lop-sided thing with her mouth.

"Uhm," I said, "I like that." I traced the outline of her lips. Then I lowered my head and began kissing sensitive places.

"Oh, shit," I said, abruptly sitting upright, water sliding off me. "I nearly forgot. I agreed we'd grill a steak with Val and Maria tonight." I looked for my watch, then remembered it was inside.

Robyn looked as unhappy as I felt.

"I'll call and cancel. We'll do it another time."

"No," she said. "It'll be fun and then we can have even more fun after they've left."

That didn't make the grade.

"And there's always the shower now." A wicked little grin made lots of promises.

God, I liked this woman.

I kissed the top of her nose.

She laughed delightedly and we went to get dressed and grill steaks and, somewhere in there, get clean—or something.

CHAPTER 27

Monday morning found me waiting for Rodrigo to finish an appointment. After he did, I said, "I'd like to talk to you, but somewhere private, and out of the office."

For a second he was taken aback, probably as much by my battered face as my request, but then he led the way to the elevator. As we descended, he commented on a family wedding he'd attended over the weekend. I thanked him for the decanter. We both avoided any serious discussion.

Moments later we sat in a lightly populated café, coffee before us. Rodrigo looked at me, deep concern on his face.

"I'll explain the cuts and bruises in a minute," I said. He nodded, fixing me with unsettled eyes. "But first, Val tells me the computer guys are beginning to get somewhere."

"I hope so," Rodrigo answered. "I can't honestly say what they've found. It's all very complicated, as Val probably explained. Marcel made so many transactions and the amounts were so large that there's only one thing capable of producing that much money." He shook his head. "Today, I'm meeting with the authorities for drug investigations. It won't be pleasant."

"I imagine not," I said. "But there's something happening that might make you feel a little better." There was no reason not to share Val's most recent news, so I explained about the possible discovery of some of the accounts.

The blue eyes instantly topped up with energy. He asked me a battery of questions and to all of them I pled ignorance and referred him to Val. He stood up to leave, find Val, pull the answers out of him.

"Not yet," I said, "there's more." And then I told him the story of my weekend. Rodrigo reacted much as Val had, incredulous at times, aghast at others, and shaking with fury at the degree of Marcel's betrayal.

"He deserved what he got," Rodrigo said vehemently, the cherubic face receding before a mask of angry contempt. "He's caused everyone anguish. I wish he were here to give us the information on the bank accounts, but if it had to be this way, my only regret is that he suffered so little."

"I'm not entirely sure of that," I said. "If the guy who killed him really was a FARC minder, that means FARC probably knew Marcel was stealing from them, too. I imagine Marcel spent a couple of sleepless nights in that little village contemplating his future. Or lack of one."

"Maybe so, maybe so," Rodrigo said. "Well, it's done, thanks to you and the mysterious Hector. Now we have to look to your ingenious cousin for the next step."

Rodrigo again began to leave the table and once more I motioned him back down.

"I've only told you about my weekend," I said, "but the story actually goes back to the first day I met you."

Finally, I unburdened myself.

Throughout it all, Rodrigo sat transfixed. And then when I broached the theory that Uncle Henry might, without knowing it, have precipitated the attacks, he reacted.

"Impossible! Your uncle was one of the most decent men I've ever known."

"You notice I said 'without knowing it.' This is just one possibility."

"It's a possibility you can put aside," he said firmly.

"Actually," I said, "I've had some other thoughts, too. First of all, I'm not sure it was intended for me to die. If the gunman had been serious about it, he'd have gone for the upper body. Someone who aims for the torso and gets the thigh—hell, if he's that bad, he could easily have hit another person and missed me entirely. But I don't think that's what was going on. I think this guy knew exactly what he was doing. If he'd wanted to send a bullet into some place vital, I'm convinced he could have done it." I thought for a second. "Same with the assault."

"I'll leave that kind of assessment to you," Rodrigo said. "My expertise isn't in marksmanship—or beating people up."

I shrugged. "I've also wondered if both the shooting and the mugging weren't real attempts. Just messages maybe, or sport."

"Sport!" Rodrigo was disgusted.

"Never know. If I had to make a choice right now, I'd say these things have all been intended to send me racing back home."

"And what would the purpose of that have been? Since we know it wasn't Marcel who shot you."

"Marcel might have a partner," I said. I'd been avoiding the thought ever since Val's revelation. It was time to consider it.

Rodrigo's forehead creased. "That would mean," he said slowly, "there's someone else in the firm, an accomplice."

"Maybe." I shrugged.

We were both quiet for a long moment.

"If he's there to find, I'll find him," Rodrigo said eventually. "When I do he'll wish his end was as easy as Marcel's was."

I felt the menace behind the words. "No police for now," I said. "They'll just tell me to leave Panama. I'd rather leave on my terms than some thug's."

"The police are probably considering an accomplice already," said Rodrigo. "But I agree, there's no need for us to throw fuel on the fire. Perhaps when word filters back about Marcel's 'difficulties' at the end, this other person, if there is one, might decide to be more cooperative. That would solve a lot of problems."

I nodded.

"The main object, Pen, is for you to be protected. If going back to the States will be the safest thing, I think that's what you should do. You obviously want to be involved in managing the companies. I've always believed that would be the best solution for your inheritance. But not at the expense of your life."

"I won't be foolhardy," I said. "I have a driver and a bodyguard and the only time something has happened to me since the first day, I stupidly gave them the night off. Let's see if you can find someone else in the firm who could have been acting with Marcel. I'll take good care of myself in the meantime, then we'll put our heads together again."

Rodrigo agreed and, that settled, we returned to the office. Rodrigo sought out Val to learn more about the accounts and I called Sax. There was, I learned, news from Hector. No sign of the minder as yet, but they'd found the man in the village who'd hidden Marcel and his murderer. The man was terrified but talking. Unfortunately, he knew nothing except that the killer was *híbrido feo*. An ugly bastard.

Hector was disgusted.

Sax was disgusted.

Perfect mirrors for my own feelings.

CHAPTER 28

Bowing to Rodrigo's wishes, there was an addition to my security team, Guillermo, a big, broad man who preferred to be called Billy. His job was to rotate with Bruno and stay with me wherever I went, upping my protection to 24/7. When I was at Fernandez-Chavira, whoever was on duty hung out in the reception area, getting an eyeful of Delfina. When I was home, they swapped stories with the guards in the lobby and kept an eye on people coming and going. Billy had been trained by the U.S. Drug Enforcement Agency (DEA) for a job with a special unit of Panama's *Policia Nationale.* After five years, Enriqué had hired him away to become one of the anchors of his fledgling security division.

Tanked up with so much protective muscle, it almost seemed a shame we had no more encounters with guns, silver SUVs, or two by fours to the head.

By six o'clock most days, Robyn and I were at the condominium for a drink, dinner, and whatever else the evening brought. Since Val was usually at Maria's, we didn't go out much, preferring to enjoy ourselves at home. Slowly, my injuries healed, and Robyn's as well. On Thursday, much to my disappointment, Robyn left for a fashion show in *Sao Paulo*.

Determined to put the extra time to good use, I delved deeper into the foundations. The awe I'd felt in the first few days had given way to a serious appreciation for the businesses. Simultaneously, a picture was emerging of my future. I'd be spending some serious money, no doubt about that, but I would also pay close attention to what produced the money. I started thinking of myself as the keeper of the orchard, a role that pleased me.

For five days, I brought work home to study. On the sixth, Robyn was back. To celebrate, we went out.

Every time I'd been with Robyn, she'd had a slightly different look. Tonight was uptown, all slithery in a low cut black dress with on-fire red stiletto heels and that devastating slash of scarlet lipstick against her pearl white skin.

"Yum," I said, "I'll have some of that."

The girl next door surfaced long enough to giggle. "You're not bad yourself."

I fluffed my feathers a bit, pleased that she appreciated my attempt at sartorial sophistication, with a soft blue shirt, white linen pants and a navy slouch jacket. All right, so maybe I looked like I'd stepped from the pages of a Ralph Lauren catalogue but actually it was Armani and another Italian designer whose name I kept forgetting. Even Val would approve of my wardrobe.

After we were done complimenting each other, we sat down to some seriously good food, a little Caribbean, a little Chinese, some Peruvian in there and a tender-as-Robyn's-tush

Argentinean steak. Cocooned by mellow music, the evening was laid back, the conversation mostly about Robyn's show. At one point, she said "You know, I almost feel as though we're an old married couple."

"Disabuse yourself of that notion," I said sternly. "We're about to perform activities married couples only dream about."

"I dream about them, too," she said, giving me the lopsided smile.

I smiled back. I didn't tell her that my dreams the past week had been about nothing else.

"We've only known each other a couple of weeks but it's all so…easy."

"Nothing like a helicopter crash to speed along a relationship," I said. "Especially when it includes shopping for panties on the first date."

"If you can call those red things panties. I call them a G-string, without the G."

"Just conserving resources," I said. "I believe in going green. Speaking of which—" I pulled out some money and handed it to the waiter. "Let's go."

Needless to say, the rest of the evening was peachy, except that Robyn had to leave just when it was really getting fun. "I have an early start tomorrow," she said. "I need to be in *Cerro Azul* at eight to meet with a buyer who's visiting there."

"*Cerro Azul* being…?"

"About an hour away on the other side of Panama City. In the mountains."

"You could stay here and let me take you." I tried to look my most appealing.

"My assistant and another designer are going with me. We'll be there for two days, then to *Bogotá* for another four." She rumpled her mouth and gave me a pretend sad look as she began pulling on clothes.

"Good God, woman, do you travel all the time?" I sat up, not quite resigned to the fate of more nights alone in the big bed.

"It's the season," Robyn said. "And we're especially busy this year. But, I'll be back on Sunday." Her sapphire eyes glowed and she looked coyly at me. "Will you be up for some non-married activity then?"

"Baby," I said, grabbing her before she could cover anything else. "I am always up for non-married activity." I planted a big kiss on her cleavage, then gently moved her bra back to expose a nipple. I took it between my lips and slid my tongue around it, then gently nibbled with my teeth. Robyn gasped. My hand found her lower back and began rubbing, slowly, languorously, in circles, moving further and further down. Robyn was standing very still, doing her best to resist. My other hand slipped into the front of her panties.

"Unfair," she said. "If you keep this up, I'll wind up going to my meeting naked."

"Uhm," I murmured, guiding her back to the bed. "Then, I'll definitely have to go along."

There was no more ridiculous talk of going home for the night.

CHAPTER 29

Wednesday started off slow, then went to crazy. Ignacio and Bruno picked me up. Billy had just come off the night shift and was getting some sleep.

One place Bruno did not like to go was Dunkin' Donuts, which was in a dead-end shopping center he considered dangerous. The client has certain prerogatives, however, and as much as Bruno complained, I kept us all in the sugary treats. Today was no different except that confectioners' sugar sprinkled me twice on particularly sharp turns. When I arrived at Fernandez-Chavira, I was sure I looked like the sugar plum fairy had dusted me. Unfortunately, Ignacio fared worse. Coffee went up his nose and down his shirt. Some landed in his hair. He followed me into Fernandez-Chavira to clean himself up before returning to the car. Bruno sat in the lobby as usual, casting his eye over everything and everyone.

By now, I was beginning to get a clearer picture of how a corporate organization might be structured to handle the businesses. Over coffee, I discussed it with Rodrigo, listened to his suggestions, and eventually went to the conference room to consolidate my notes.

There was a shrill sound outside that broke my concentration, followed by a clamor. Delfina threw open the door and pulled me out. I heard the word Ignacio, Delfina pushed me into the elevator, and Bruno jumped in behind me.

The first thing I noticed outside was the clutch of people. Then details came into focus. A man and a woman were on their knees next to my car. The woman was blowing into Ignacio's mouth. The man was pressing his chest in a non-stop rhythm. They had evidently been at it for some time as the man's face was red from the effort and every now and then he had to remove one hand to wipe the sweat off his brow.

I walked over to them and stooped down. Ignacio was blue and turning bluer by the second. The man and woman looked at each other. The CPR wasn't working but it was obvious one wouldn't stop before the other one did. Bruno spoke to the man, presumably to ask if he could take over. The man shook his head "no." I watched and felt helpless.

The problem was solved by the arrival of the police and an ambulance. The ambulance men looked grim as they took Ignacio away; I noticed there was no further attempt at resuscitation. One of the officers, a sergeant by his stripes, began to ask questions, while another policeman took photographs. A rather large, older woman in an expensive pink suit clutched at her heart with one hand and the sergeant with the other.

"*Esta el corazon, el corazon,*" she said.

His heart, his heart.

A second woman stepped forward and began talking in a low, quavering voice. I had no idea what she was saying but, whatever it was, the policeman seemed interested. He crossed his arms and looked intently at the woman. I turned to Delfina and asked her to translate.

"The lady is telling him that her car was parked next to yours. She was waiting for her daughter to come out of the building and she was bored so she watched Ignacio clean the car. She says he put down his rag and bottle and went to open the back door. He grabbed the handle and pulled his hand away in pain. His eyes grew very wide and his face became extremely red and he clutched at his throat. His eyes rolled up in his head and he fell down. He had some kind of spasm and then he didn't move after that."

Delfina paused as the woman became quiet. We all watched the policeman direct his attention to the door handle. He squatted down and looked underneath it for a long moment, then stood up, walked over to the lady in the pink suit, and asked her a question. Immediately, she dived in her purse and brought out a make-up mirror. The sergeant took the mirror back with him to the car, dropped into a crouch, and held the mirror under the right rear door handle. He repeated his investigation of the other three handles, dismissing the front doors with cursory looks. Finally, he stood up, shook his head and passed a hand over his forehead. Whatever he'd seen, I was willing to bet money a) it didn't belong there and b) it had caused Ignacio's death.

Things moved quickly after that. Bruno spoke briefly with the policeman, obviously laying claim to the car and reluctantly pointing me out. Another policeman strung yellow tape around what was now obviously a crime scene. Everyone was asked to remain in the immediate vicinity. They wanted to interview us, particularly Delfina, who'd directed Ignacio to the bathroom to clean up his spilled coffee, and, of course, me. I was in hot water now and knew it. With Ignacio dead, there was no way I could avoid telling the police everything that had happened since I arrived. It wasn't something I looked forward to.

Delfina told the police we'd be upstairs and smartly volunteered the conference room if the police needed it. They gave us no trouble about leaving and we silently entered the elevator, along with Bruno and some other Fernandez-Chavira people. Bruno, for all his toughness, looked sorrowful and could barely meet my eye.

"It will be very sad for Ignacio's family," Delfina said after a moment. "They won't be able to bury him tomorrow."

"Is it normal to have the funeral that soon?" The only people I knew who interred their dead the next day were Jews. I'd been told this was a matter of respect for the departed. Perhaps Panamanians were the same way.

"Absolutely, it's necessary," Delfina said, "otherwise they smell."

Ah. No embalming. Not a pleasant thought. I took a breath. "I imagine they'll keep Ignacio, you know…refrigerated for a while. Until they do their tests."

"But the family…" Delfina said quietly and I understood what she meant. No burial, no tradition, no finality, an additional torment inflicted on his loved ones.

"What do you think, Señor Pen, was it something on the handle that made Ignacio die?"

"It certainly looks like it," I answered grimly.

Delfina turned her bewildered face toward me. "Who would want to do that kind of terrible thing? Ignacio seemed like such a nice man."

I nodded, my intestines contracting.

"I've never known anyone who was murdered," Delfina said softly.

I took her arm. "Neither have I."

Bruno called Enriqué and delivered the bad news. I followed him on the phone. There was really nothing to say. It was my fault Ignacio was killed—mine and Marcel's for shooting me. Mine and the firm's for luring me to Panama. Mine and Uncle Henry's for giving me the bloody $200 million to begin with.

"Ignacio had a wife and four children," Enriqué said, his voice reflecting bewilderment at what had happened. I offered to help them with expenses, and more. Not enough, I knew. Never enough for losing a loved one.

"It had to be poison on the handle," I said. "The way the policeman looked after he examined the passenger doors. But, what kind of poison could kill a man so fast?" Like everyone else, I knew about arsenic and cyanide, and had heard of some other poisons, but I'd never expected to encounter them.

"The *Indios* have lethal poisons that kill quickly," Enriqué answered dully. "We study them in school. The Golden Poison Dart Frog is used by the *Emberas* in the *Darien* Province. The poison of one frog is enough to kill ten to twenty men."

Even over the phone, I could tell Enriqué sensed my disbelief.

"It's true," he said. "It's the deadliest poison in the world. The *Emberas* use it on blow darts to bring down game. The animals die almost immediately. The *Indios* are very skilled at cutting out the meat where the dart entered the body. The rest is safe to eat."

I shook my head. A sense of otherworldliness was beginning to envelope me. A normal afternoon had morphed into one with lethal poison and a murder for real, with all the horror I now knew murder brought. The horror was compounded by knowing the murder was meant to be mine.

There wasn't any question of resuming work. I still had the police interview ahead of me, as did Delfina and Bruno. I paced the halls, drinking coffee until the sergeant and another policeman came upstairs and called me into the conference room.

The best I can say about the interview is that it was an unpleasant experience. There was a lot of disgust that I'd failed to report the previous attacks. Not once but twice, they said, *two* crimes. And now someone was dead. They looked at me as if I were an imbecile. Clearly they wished I'd just go home. On the other hand, there was a $200 million nugget sitting in Panama, a nugget they obviously didn't want to lose to Grand Cayman, Lichtenstein, or some other tax haven.

We can't protect you from a madman, they said.

I understand that.

It wouldn't be a good idea for any more Panamanians to get killed.

Tell that to the madman, I answered. And, speaking of him, what about the handle?

The laboratory will analyze the car.

You already know it's poison.

How do you know that? Now they were interested.

It's pretty obvious. Ignacio touched the handle and died. You looked at the handle and suddenly the place became a crime scene.

Stay in touch, they said.

As long as I'm alive, I'll do it.

They didn't look optimistic.

I grabbed a cab and headed for the apartment with Bruno. There was no conversation. I stared out the window, caught somewhere between sadness and anger, determination and uncertainty. It was a kind of purgatory, where one step forward was also one step back, and truth was still around the corner and behind the next hill. Ignacio, poor devil, had already found his truth. I hoped I wouldn't have to go through what he did to find mine.

CHAPTER 30

I spent what was left of the afternoon drinking Beam and wondering for the hundredth time what I could have done to prevent Ignacio's death. I was also giving serious consideration to Marcel's possible collaborator in the law firm. The only window of opportunity for applying the poison was when Ignacio was in the bathroom cleaning up the spilt coffee. That pointed the finger directly at someone in the office. The police obviously knew that from their questioning. It seemed to me they had plenty to work with and, if we were all lucky, they'd find the bastard within a couple of days.

While I was turning this over in my mind, Val arrived.

"How did your interview with the cops go?" I called out from the terrace.

He grabbed a drink from his decanter, folded himself into a chair next to me, and loosened his tie.

"Shouldn't have been a big deal," I said. "You haven't failed to report an attempted murder or anything."

"No, I'm the straight arrow in the family. Anyone tries to kill me, you'd better believe I'd let the police know."

"Val, you do realize the poison was on *two* handles, don't you?"

Val blanched.

"I think it's time for you to pack your bags and hop a plane home."

"If you come, too," Val said.

"Probably not. Not until I see this through. Now that the police are involved, I think things will move a lot quicker. Remember, they didn't know anything about the shooting or the bash on the head. They've just come into all this."

"You're a stupid bastard—you know that?" Val said. "What's with this non-reporting thing anyway? I can see— almost—the shooting. I mean, that came out of the clear blue and made no sense at the time. But the second attack. You knew by then they were after you. Shit, I'd have called the police that second."

"Yeah? And said what? Somebody shot at me but I didn't know they were really aiming at me. Someone conked me on the head next to a dark parking lot after I'd just left a casino? Alberto said it—that area is thick with robbers just waiting to grab a fat wallet. Anyway, all that's irrelevant. I want you on a plane as soon as we can book you a seat. Tomorrow morning, if possible."

"I'm not going. If you stay, so do I."

"This isn't a tennis match, Val. We're not trying to one-up each other by scoring points for courage. We're on the same side." I blew out a breath through my nostrils. Sometimes it was a pain in the ass dealing with my cousin.

"There are two objectives here. The first is to stay alive. The second is to keep the money. The money—the companies—need managing, they need a corporate structure.

If I have to dump them for a while and run, I will—but not yet. You, on the other hand—"

"I'm not going."

I threw up my hands. "Stupid sonofabitch. Fine, get yourself killed."

"We'll take precautions."

"I took them or hadn't you noticed? That was a security-trained driver who got killed today."

"We'll take more precautions."

"Asshole."

"What about Enriqué? He probably wants to bail."

"No, the exact opposite. He's committed."

"Well, there's another question. What else can he provide or do we seriously need to consider a different company?"

I gave up. "He can provide pretty much everything. He has his own people and he can tap into other outfits that are more specialized, too."

"He needs a list of the basics," Val said.

"Did it on the phone with him already," I answered wearily. "Bulletproof car, sweep it for poisons, bombs, deadly gas, whatever the clever boys can think of. Office checks every morning before people get there. As many armed bodyguards as we want, including ones for you. Extras in the lobby. Plus whatever else Enriqué's people recommend. Enough precautions for you?"

Val smiled. "I think we're in business again."

"Tell me the real reason you want to stay, Val. This is a horror story."

"Pen, I'm an accountant. I cut my teeth on money. This is the biggest honey pot I've ever seen or ever will see. I want to help you organize the companies. I want to get my hands around the finances. I want to find the stolen money. I can't do any of that back home. If it means taking a little risk, hell, why not? Besides, I think the big threat is behind us. As you pointed out, the police are involved now."

"You'd better hope the big threat is behind us," I said. "And any little threats, too." So far, there had been a shooting, a mugging, and poison. I figured there were about a hundred other ways to go about killing someone. I didn't want to find out what those hundred might be. Hell, I didn't want to find out what even one would be. With that thought to chew on, I went to bed and hoped I'd actually wake up the next morning.

CHAPTER 31

Thursday, I had a dilemma. Robyn's trip to *Bogotá* had been cancelled and she was returning to Panama City in the morning. That posed a serious problem that I chewed on most of the day. While I wanted her with me, jeopardizing her safety was out of the question. The decision wasn't one I relished, but I couldn't see an alternative to keeping her at a distance until the police caught the murderer. Not wanting to spoil her trip, I'd refrained from telling her about Ignacio. Friday morning, I could postpone it no longer. I called her and shared the bad news.

"That poor man," she said. "To die that way."

"Gruesome."

"And it could have been you."

"Should have been me."

There was silence on the phone. "I'm not sure I'll be able to sleep tonight," she finally said.

I massaged my temple, hoping to cut off the beginning of a headache. "I share the feeling. Listen, can you work from your mountain house for a while? Just until the police catch this bastard? I'd feel better if you were as far away as possible."

Exasperatingly, Robyn would do no such thing. No one would hurt her, why should they? Ignacio's murder was a mistake, he wasn't the target. Sadly, I was, and needed all the support I could get.

"You can support me from afar," I said. "I'll still get the message."

Silence again. "I'll think about it." The agreement was grudging.

"I love you," I said, to my total surprise.

For the third time, there was dead silence. I didn't know if there was a lopsided smile on the other end of the phone or an "Oh God, what a jerk he is" look on her face. I didn't care. I had said it. Maybe it was my proximity to imminent death that pushed it out of me, kind of like a deathbed declaration. Or maybe it was just because I felt good saying it. Didn't know, didn't care.

"I love you," I told her again, proving to myself that the first time hadn't been an accident.

"Gosh, I guess I should answer or something," she said.

"No, there's no requirement to balance out the conversation."

She paused a moment. "Well, that's good, because I have a real hard time with the 'L' word."

Don't we all? "No problem," I said. "I understand."

"It doesn't mean we still can't see each other."

Right, sure, while trying to avoid a cold-blooded killer with poison, 2x4s, bullets, and God knows what else in his arsenal. I was just trying to see if there was anything I could salvage from the conversation when Robyn spoke up again.

"Oh, what the hell," she said. "I guess I can make an exception this time."

Had I heard right? I took a deep breath before I spoke again. "Dear Robyn," I said. "I'll take all the exceptions I can get."

Robyn and I finally worked things out in between lots of verbal silliness that attended our pronouncements of love. She agreed not to be in my vicinity but refused to leave Panama City. Her apartment building had guards, ditto for her workshop. She'd only been seen once in public with me, except for the time at the beach. What reason was there for her to leave town?

I didn't like it but eventually I gave in. I would, however, provide her a bodyguard. That produced a fit of giggles that nonetheless eventually resulted in the new employee showing up on her doorstep the next morning. "You would give me a goliath named Rocky," she said later. "I'll bet his real name is Juan or something."

"A goliath is what we want, love, whatever his name is."

She took it all pretty well, considering. We'd talk on the phone, of course, and if the police hadn't made an arrest in a week or so, we'd go somewhere outside Panama and have a short vacation. It was a plan that gave us something to look forward to and made the burden of being separated a little lighter.

"Think of me," she said, as we concluded the conversation.

"A lot. All the time. Every minute."

"Ah, that's what I like to hear." She laughed. "Think of the hot tub, too."

Oh, Jeez. Like I didn't already have enough reminders of what I was missing.

CHAPTER 32

The days began to take on a new shape. I went into the office earlier and stayed later, often for meetings with Rodrigo. Val and I spent lots of time going over finances and management and discussing who else in our family might be suitable for our emerging umbrella corporation. Thomas, our lawyer cousin, was at the top of the list, so we made tentative plans to get him down as soon as his schedule allowed. We also found the names of several well-known corporate consultants and flew two of them in for interviews. In short, we acted like the beginning of a management team and we put in the kind of hours that a serious effort requires.

I also spent some time with the police. At one point I went with them to the Majestic Casino to re-enact my first morning's walk, and to the parking lot where I'd been hit over the head. Neither place looked ominous and I had a hard time believing I'd sustained serious bodily injury at either.

Although the police weren't particularly keen on discussing the case, I managed to pry a few items out of them. They had sourced the poison to the Golden Dart Frog that originated in the *Darien,* just as Enriqué had speculated. Unfortunately, there wasn't a lot they could do to trace the person who bought it. Most of the *Embera* knew how to extract the substance, meaning there would be hundreds of people who could have provided it. Making things even more difficult, not all the *Embera* lived in villages. Some simply had huts strung along a river and made haphazard contact with the rest of the world only when they visited *Yaviza* to buy supplies or sell boatloads of plantains. Of course, the police told me, their counterparts in *Yaviza* would question people, but *Yaviza* being *Yaviza* it was unlikely they would unearth anything.

The bottom line: the police didn't want to tell me, avoided it for as long as they could, but it was pretty obvious anyway; the murderer was nowhere in sight. That cast a pall on my days, and put me in a blue funk. My only solution was to work harder, which I did.

During this period, my nights were shorter because I spent so much more time at the office, and longer because I missed Robyn. At the same time, Val was almost exclusively at Maria's. One night they joined me for dinner and I was surprised at how much Maria had warmed up to me. The influence of Robyn, no doubt.

The rest of the time I spent alone, except when Val had some work he wanted to discuss after-hours.

Such an occasion occurred toward the end of my self-imposed seven-day exile from Robyn. I'd found it especially hard to concentrate at the office that day and the night was feeling longer than most. I was rummaging through the bookshelves for something to read when I heard the sound of the alarm being turned off. Almost immediately, I heard Val's voice.

He was filled with bonhomie and in a chatty mood. I was glad of the company, especially since it was good-humored. We talked about family, women (Maria, of course, and a passing mention or two of Robyn), a big tennis match one of our friends back home was playing in. Desultory, easy talk. Best bud kind of talk.

After a while, Val looked at me out of the corner of his eye. "Got a surprise for you."

"Great," I said, casting a wary glance at him. "I remember the last time you had a surprise."

"Naw, you're going to like this one way better."

"Give."

Val was all grins. "I found an account."

My eyebrows went up. "No shit!"

"Yep, sitting right here in a bank not four blocks from Fernandez-Chavira."

"Tell me."

Val sketched the details. The account was held under the dummy name of Gilberto Aguilar of David, Panama. It was opened almost two years ago, so we knew Marcel had been running the scam at least that long. The account held almost $2 million, not quite half of what had been stolen from me. I was very pleased with my cousin, almost as pleased as he was with himself. If Val hadn't already earned his place in the organization, he damned sure had now. In spades.

My good mood carried through the next day and, when Alberto suggested that he, Val and I visit a casino and catch a jazz feature, I was up for it. Since he'd saved me from a savage beating, my opinion of Alberto had been nothing but positive. I'd put aside my concern that he might be a compulsive gambler when I registered the quality of work he was turning out for me, the long hours he was putting in on my projects, and his cheerful, laid back attitude—hardly hallmarks of someone with a destructive gambling habit.

As it turned out, Alberto and I hit the casino on our own since Maria had a migraine and Val wanted to stay with her. Alberto had some luck at blackjack. I broke even. The jazz was Latin, hot and inventive, played by a trio from Brazil. It was good to get out and I actually spent a moment or two thinking of something other than business and murder.

Bruno, Jesús, the new driver, and I dropped off Alberto at his apartment, then headed for the *Paraíso*. Bruno went in with me, surveyed the lobby, and settled himself near the guards' desk. Billy would be arriving shortly for the night shift and I would see Bruno again the next morning.

I boarded the elevator, arrived at the apartment, and entered to muted darkness. Val was at Maria's and Rosario was gone, taking her weekly afternoon and evening off.

I walked to the living room, flipping on lights as I went, and poured a nightcap from my new decanter. I leaned back, took a drink, and opened my laptop.

At the moment there was someone who needed attention. Since I'd come to Panama, my secretary, Joy, had been mostly out of the loop. Not only had I left Washington with a hundred small strings hanging and expected her to tie them all up, I'd also come to a decision that would seriously affect her future.

For almost a decade, Joy and I had been bound by politics. Now, the question was whether our professional relationship would stretch to include the new direction my life was taking. The next elections were just around the corner, it was sign-up time in the world of political consultants, and Joy deserved to know where she stood. I needed to make her a proper offer, one with enough come hither that she'd be willing to join me in Panama. For a moment I considered the phrasing of the message, then prepared to write.

With dull surprise, I realized the letters on the laptop were fuzzy.

I ran my hand across my eyes. The room began to tilt. So did my stomach.

Get to the bathroom, I told myself. *Fast.*

My legs decided against it. The computer and I bounced to the floor, my face buried in the keyboard. I sucked in a great breath and blew it out, spritzing the keys. The keys jumped up, swirling like raging bees, pushing me down. They covered the ceiling. They ate up the chair. They began chanting. My head rolled across the floor. My mouth opened. The bees poured in. Hundreds, then thousands. They pulled back my jaws. The Queen's swollen body passed through my lips, over my tongue, undulated down my throat, slid into the cocoon of my lungs. I uttered a dying cry. The chanting grew louder. Over it, I heard a terrible shrieking and keening and wailing. I heard sobbing. I heard screams.

It was the keys.

The insects.

No. God.

It was ME.

But I was already dead.

CHAPTER 33

Something prodded my shoulder.

"Get up."

A voice. Piercing.

"Help," I whispered into the keys. "Need…to…breathe," I said through a convulsive shudder.

"Lift your head," the Voice commanded.

"But the bees…"

"There are no bees."

"No…bees?"

Hands grabbed me by the arm and tore me from the laptop. The keys stuck to my face, driving themselves deep into my skin. I clawed blindly at my cheeks, nose, ears.

The keys grew tentacles and buried themselves in my flesh.

I dug them out and rivulets of blood spilled to the floor, where the bees bathed in the splashes.

The Voice ordered me to get up.

What was up?

I watched the tomato red liquid drip onto the bees. Beautiful.

The order came again. The hands yanked me to a crouch and I crab-walked-crawled-sprawled backward. Where were the bees? I had to open my mouth. I had to have air. But the bees...what if...? "I can't...I can't..." I whispered through clenched teeth.

Suddenly, I vomited and the Voice erupted with shrill squeaky noises. I drew a breath but the air wouldn't come. The vomit was racing toward me. I threw myself backward to get away from it.

The squeaks stopped and I was in another place, this one all smooth and cool.

The hands helped me stand up and the Voice spoke. "Walk to the chair." I walked. The hands pushed me down and I saw the bees and I screamed and the hands put something in my mouth to keep the bees away.

The Voice was speaking to me. I was dizzy again and I tried to answer but my mouth was full and I couldn't breathe and inside I screamed and screamed and screamed.

CHAPTER 34

I awoke to blackness. There was a presence next to my body, something grasping my hands, a peculiar feeling under my neck.

And the Voice. "Listen to me. If you move you die. Any movement will blow you away. Believe me. Move and you die."

I heard a click and my gut twisted.

The Voice spoke again.

"Listen to me. If you move you die. Any movement will blow you away. Believe me. Move and you die."

Another click. Something hard sliding under my chin. A door closing.

Silence.

"Listen to me…"

I listened.

"Believe me…"

I believed.

I listened and believed for what felt like an eternity.

When the initial terror had quieted enough to think, I allowed myself to take inventory. I started with what was covering my eyes, a blindfold made of rough material. It was tight and unpleasant, but nothing compared to the way the rest of my body felt. Every one of my old injuries had reawakened. The gunshot wound, my back, my head, the bumps and bruises from the *Darien*, they all began screaming for attention. They got it.

Given the message from the Voice, moving wasn't high on my agenda, which was good since I was bound tight to a chair. The word helpless occurred to me. Then I decided that might be too positive an assessment.

Breathing seemed to be my biggest problem. My lungs and sternum were sluggish, and I was afraid to take big, movement-producing gulps of air through my mouth. Instead, I opened my nostrils, inhaled, and an electrifying pain shot through the middle of my face. Somewhere along the line, someone had probably broken my nose.

All of that was bad enough but there was more. I was shivering from the cold. The last time I looked, shivering counted as movement, which meant I was already on the way to being dead. I tasted vomit in my mouth, felt bile rising, and choked it down. The Voice spoke again. "If you move, you die."

Shit, I already felt like death. There was something strangely awful about my face, as though the skin had been dipped in boiling liquid and then peeled off.

A nightmarish review of my bindings didn't improve the picture. Chest, arms, legs, all immobilized. Something was wedged between my knees, my hands secured around it. My right thumb was twisted away from the fingers. I licked the inside of my mouth and my tongue found particles of cloth, possibly from a gag that had been removed after my nose was broken. A concession to breathing, I supposed.

Finally, my head and neck were bent over, and a hard object—a rod of some kind—propped up my chin. I thought, but couldn't tell, that whatever was below it was also fastened to my body.

My mind raced through the possibilities, none good. Somehow poisoning, mugging and a bullet in the thigh were beginning to seem pretty tame. I put my mind to the task, discarding various options until I came to the only one that seemed to fit. Something that would kill me if I moved. That would blow me away.

I went coldly still, hardly daring to breathe, hardly able to.

A bomb.

Jesus. A bomb.

Dynamite or plastique or whatever maniacs used now. It was attached to me somewhere. A trip wire. The plunger holding up my head. Some new device I never even heard of. Blow your body away. BLOW your body away.

I held my breath for a moment and listened to the Voice. Not blow up your body. Blow it fucking away. A distinction without a difference? I listened again through my terror. Maybe not.

The thing wedged between my knees didn't feel like explosives. For dynamite, too thin, too hard, not wide. For plastique, there was no need for any bulk at all.

It felt like a shaft, narrow but sturdy. And the object beneath my chin didn't feel like a plunger. It was vertical, not horizontal, and seemed to be a cylinder.

I thought, trying to tune out the numbing, repetitive message of the Voice.

What would be a cylinder?

How far from my knees to my chin?

And then my brain stopped.

I felt the hairs stand up on my neck.

It wasn't explosives. It was a gun—a rifle or shotgun secured between my knees, the barrel propping up my head, the trigger waiting for the slightest motion from my thumb. As effective as a bomb. But not as savage. No, this was more refined, more sophisticated.

More malevolent.

Now, I understood about my hands, my thumb.

I attacked the conclusion, trying to rip holes in it. Bomb. Gun. What difference did it make? But I knew that answer. A bomb would tear me apart. I would die instantly, as my parents had, blown into a thousand infinitesimal pieces. But gunshots to the head were different. I had heard the horror stories of attempted suicides gone bad. I understood why police officers ate their guns if they wanted to put an end to things. If they wanted to be sure they didn't end up with half a head blown off and the other half pitifully clinging to life. I felt a moan start deep in my body. The barrel was fastened to my chin, not my throat. If the gun went off, I would definitely die. But it would be a slow and horrific death.

I had moved past shock and was sliding into terror. Next would come panic, and that would be my undoing. Somehow, I had to remain calm, discipline my body to remain absolutely still.

Easier said than done. The air was getting colder. The shivering had intensified. My shoulders were beginning to shake for real. That made me think about all the other distractions I couldn't manage. The backfire of a car. A sudden sneeze. A clap of thunder coming out of nowhere. And about a hundred more.

Monks in the Himalayas learned to turn off discomfort, ignore their environments, raise and lower their body temperatures. At that moment, I would have given anything to be a monk.

Even though I'd never reach that level of restraint, I knew discipline was the key to surviving long enough for someone to find me. I was already holding myself as rigid as I could, now I had to find something that would sustain me through the madness, something that would tap into my body's reservoir of courage and control. I needed something strong to hold on to. I needed rocks. DON'T PANIC was a monster rock. DON'T GIVE IN was another. BE DISCIPLINED. DON'T PANIC. DON'T GIVE IN. I made the words into a mantra, tried to fuse them into an impenetrable, hard-as-rock life jacket. BE DISCIPLINED. Above all SURVIVE. I repeated the words silently, weaving my courage rock by rock.

My heart slowed, my brain began to think past the horror, I willed the cold down to a chill, made the shakes loosen their hold. Refused even to consider that the Voice might return. Finally, I achieved an acceptable level of calm, sat with my muscles as loose as I could make them, and began trying to figure out what in the hell had happened to me.

The last thing I remembered was sitting down to write Joy an email. Sometime between then and now, I'd undergone enough trauma for the old injuries to surface and new ones to emerge. Those were the facts, as far as I knew them. After that came assumptions.

It stood to reason I was out for a good while in order for the Voice to truss me up this way. I remembered none of that, which meant I'd either been unconscious, or I was suffering from amnesia. I racked my brain but couldn't conjure up an image of the person who'd done this to me. While I supposed he could be some crazed half-pint, it seemed more likely it was a big sonofabitch who'd hauled me into the chair and inflicted the damage.

As to the "where" question, it was supposition, but I thought I could come close on that. I felt confined, not in some oppressive place like a closet, but in an area where I was loosely surrounded. At the least, I was in someplace cold, and, from the way the recording slightly reverberated, possibly tiled. I thought I might be in a bathroom, maybe a shower.

Considerate, my murdering friend, sticking me in a place where my blown-out brains could simply be sluiced down the drain, not leaving any slop.

And slop was what I would be if I couldn't stop the suddenly renewed shivering and the overdue protests of muscles kept in a single position past their tolerance. As if those weren't enough, I felt tremors in my legs where the edge of the seat bit into my thighs; I worried about my thumb, which had become numb and therefore doubly dangerous; and I could feel my neck muscles straining to maintain my head at its awkward angle without going into a spasm.

On top of it all and maddening beyond belief, I was getting sleepy. I became desperately afraid I would either yawn or twitch myself into death or go from one kind of sleep to the kind from which I couldn't be roused.

My biggest problem, though, was breathing. For some reason, filling my lungs felt like sucking air from water. My tendency, obviously, was to take big gulps, but every time I did, I felt the gun barrel push harder against my chin.

I tried to create a breathing strategy. Breath in…out. Short…shallow…slow. Breathe through the water. Find the oxygen. Keep the lungs alive.

I silently spoke to myself, repeating my mantras, trying to tune out the bloody, fucking, never-ending words of the Voice.

My mind was beginning to wander. The Voice was monotonous. The cold had returned with a vengeance. I was getting sleepier. It would all end the moment my eyes closed.

Except…

What if…?

I rolled the idea through my mind.

It was all I had.

In a minute I would know the answer to at least one question.

I took the deepest breath I thought was safe and spoke like a ventriloquist, so I wouldn't move my chin

"SHOWER ON."

Nothing happened. Maybe the Voice was too loud, I was too soft.

"SHOWER ON."

Again, nothing.

Inwardly, I sagged. I had been wrong. It had been a false hope. Worse than no hope at all.

Shit, I told myself, you give up too easily. Quit the goddammed whining and try once more before fucking embracing fucking defeat.

Okay, I thought, here fucking goes.

I waited for the tiny lull between the end of the Voice's message and the beginning of the next loop. I had to time it just right. My resisting lungs forced more air, I pushed out the words again, this time speaking in as close to a normal voice as I could.

Into my desperation came a faint answering rumble in the pipes.

Almost unable to believe it, I braced for the onslaught of the water. The temperature was set for a normal shower so I knew there would be no shock from cold water. But bodies instinctively respond to external stimulus, anticipated or not. Ignoring that programming could be fatal. So I gave it all I had, willing myself into absolute stillness, letting the water find me, feeling its cloak of warmth, almost sobbing as it soothed my cramped muscles and began shutting out the deadly, shivering cold.

After a long time in the water, another idea quietly crept into my mind.

Some rifles and shotguns had to be kept dry. Wooden models, especially. Water could seep through to the firing mechanism, to other nooks and crannies that could freeze up if too moist.

Most important, to the ammo. As everyone with half a brain knows, wet ammo won't fire.

The piece between my legs felt like wood. My senses told me it was wood. And because I wanted to believe it and I had no other options, I began to treat it as wood.

I turned my attention to the gun barrel. Could feel through the haze of pain exactly where the barrel met my skin. As the water cascaded onto my head, I pictured a single stream slithering down my cheek, gliding an inch further, dripping around the bulb of my chin. I saw a tiny, infinitesimal hint of wetness seep into the equally miniscule crack between my skin and the hole in the barrel. My brain watched as a micro-drop collected at the rim, as another micro-drop joined it and then another and another. And then, slowly, something almost distinguishable as water reached the lip of the rim and the first atoms of liquid slid into the barrel and down toward the vulnerable entrails of the gun.

I didn't know for sure if I could render the gun incapable of firing. I just knew that I had a possibility, my only possibility, and if I had the ability to stay alive until someone came home, maybe I could make it.

I also realized much depended on *when* someone came. That was beyond my control. But for the first time, discipline and hard thought had given me a weapon against the Voice. A weapon that might prolong my life until someone discovered me.

I no longer struggled to stay awake. I no longer listened to the Voice. I concentrated everything I had on the water. After some long moments of abominable cowardice, I used the slipperiness of the liquid to slide my chin a fraction of a fraction of a millimeter to one side. My chin was fastened so tightly to the barrel, I wasn't sure I could do it. And I was so terrified I practically stopped breathing what little air I was getting. But when I moved my chin the width of an ant's antennae, the gun barrel didn't move with me. It took a moment to endure the relief, regain my courage, then I repeated the process and slid my chin another virtually immeasurable distance. All I needed was a Lilliputian space, a dot, an opening for the micro-drop of water to squeeze in. And then another and another and...

The minutes ticked by. The ant antennas mounted up. I was cold again and spent some of my carefully orchestrated breath ordering SHOWER HOT ONE DEGREE, then a little later, repeating it. I tried to inhale and exhale even more shallowly and imperceptibly, conserving as much movement and strength as possible. I forced the tiny motions of my chin again and again, each time certain it would be the moment the gun would slide with me and force my wedged-in thumb the deadly distance it needed to send me to the hereafter.

The trickle of water continued its uninterrupted slide down my cheeks, at some point mixing with tears which came unbidden and detested. At least, I consoled myself, they made a contribution. I prayed they were flooding the tiny opening between the muzzle of the gun and my skin.

If I had created the hole.

If the liquid could find the hole.

I prayed that both were true. I prayed there would be enough water to wreak mayhem.

I prayed more than I had ever prayed in my life.

And, eventually, an angel heard my prayers and came to save me.

CHAPTER 35

Rosario stood in the doorway and screamed. A small, quiet scream befitting a small, quiet woman. At first, I wasn't even sure I heard her.

"SHOWER OFF."

Through the background noise of the Voice came something else.

"Señor Pen?"

"Stop!" I came as close to shouting as I could, caught off-guard between jubilation and fear. "Don't come any closer, the gun could go off." I tried to project calm but my voice was still that of a ventriloquist, enough to scare the bejesus out of anyone.

My appearance wouldn't be helping either.

There was a small sob.

"Rosario," I said, "Call the police. Tell them what you see." Mentally, I gulped, realizing that things were about to get vastly more complicated. "Explain that they can't touch me. No matter what. You understand? *If they touch me I could die.*"

Her acknowledgment, in trembling, barely understandable English accompanied by another sob, told me just how bad it looked on the other side of things.

I couldn't think about that.

"SHOWER ON."

I counted silently to one hundred, breathing very slowly.

"Rosario?"

Nothing.

More counting.

"Rosario?"

"The police is coming," she answered, her voice wavering.

"SHOWER OFF," I said, sounding to myself like a bird trying to warble for the first time.

"You want I stay here with you, Señor Pen?"

I debated. "No," I ventriloquized. "Go back and wait for the police. When they come, speak to the Comandante. Make him understand. *They…cannot…touch…me, Rosario.* If they touch me I will die."

"I understand, Señor Pen." Her voice was tremulous, like mine.

Luckily, hers would recover. I prayed that mine would. Forcing my throat to remain almost immobile, at the same time pushing out enough air to speak, strained my muscles with every word. Not to mention the gun barrel that was wedded to my neck. I was afraid of provoking spasms and terrified I'd lose the ability to communicate.

Even so, there was something else that had to be done.

"Rosario, on the desk… a brown book. In front, the name of a man. S…A…X. Sax. He is an expert in guns. Call the number. Tell Sax to come. He must come. *Now.*"

'Si," she said. "Sax." She said the name over and over again until she disappeared from hearing range.

The police would be efficient at investigating, but actually freeing me was another matter. The language barrier alone could kill. I needed Sax to bridge that gap and I needed his experience. His apartment was across town and then some. Where he kept his girlfriends I didn't know. I tried not to think about that and went back to the discipline that had kept me alive so far.

"SHOWER ON."

Short. Shallow. Slow. Concentrate. Calm.

Don't panic.

Survive.

When the police arrived, they did so with less noise than I anticipated.

"SHOWER OFF."

Rosario said something in Spanish. A deep rumble answered her.

The rumble directed itself to me and I heard some words of English over the recording of the Voice.

The policeman who possessed the rumble said he was very, very sorry for my situation. This was a despicable act. He would like to free me but the woman had made it clear this was not my wish.

Yes, I told him in abbreviated form. Listen to the tape. Movement would kill me. I believed my thumb was wedged next to the trigger. *Anything* could make the gun go off.

The policeman said he understood. But he would like to approach me to better examine the situation. He would stay outside the glass unless I permitted him to go in.

First, he said, his associate would turn off the recording. He did not want me to be alarmed when this happened.

Thank you, God, I said, for sending someone who not only speaks English but who can *think*.

A second or two later the Voice stopped and I heard the normal sounds of people whose clothes rustled and feet shifted, who murmured things to each other. I became uneasy. I couldn't see these new sounds. I felt the loss of the Voice, its rhythm, its predictability, the words that spoke only to me. It had been horrible at first, irritating towards the middle, a cloak at the end. Not comforting but familiar.

"I…I miss," I said, feeling a fool, "I miss…Voice."

"Yes," said the policeman. "This can happen with captives who have been held for many hours or days. It is known as The Stockholm Syndrome."

Of course, I thought, remembering, and felt marginally better. My opinion of the police had gone up, too. This was an intelligent, trained man, one who would act cautiously before he did anything.

It cost me an effort but I asked anyway. "Name…?"

"Sergeant Raphael Caldera," he said. "I have two men with me, Corporal José Medina and Corporal Salvatore Finnegan."

Salvatore Finnegan? My spirits lifted a miniscule amount.

"I am near you now, looking through the glass," Sgt. Caldera said. "Do you want me to explain what I see?"

Did I ever. "Es," I rasped, my vocal chords deteriorating by the word.

"You are blindfolded with some dark material held in place by tape and this tape is wound around your head. In the U.S., this is called duct tape, I believe. Very durable. Water resistant. It seems your mouth was also taped at some time. The skin there is very red." He stopped and murmured to someone in Spanish before he resumed. "Your nose...I cannot explain it well...it is swollen, there is blood."

"Es," I said.

"Yes, you have had many hours, I think, to contemplate this. Your nose may be broken. You also have many cuts on your face. You understand?"

"Es."

I heard some movement and his next words came from a different direction.

"There are also some, how do I say it? Articles? Yes, articles in your nose, possibly pieces of bone. They are difficult to see. I think you can't breathe through them?"

"No." More a sigh than an actual word.

Sgt. Caldera took what sounded like a deep breath.

"You realize that you are bound to a rifle?"

"Es."

"The muzzle is pushing your chin."

"Es."

"The gun extends below your knees."

"My ans?" I barely whispered.

The Sergeant exhaled. "The person who did this terrible thing to you—" He sounded both sad and disgusted. "Your hands are fixed to the mechanism. Something white covers part of them. I cannot tell from here but it must be that, inside this white material, your hands are bound to the trigger. Not at this moment, but soon we will have to get inside to see exactly how they are secured.

"Señor Smith," he said, "it is remarkable you have survived this at all. But the time to save you—"

I had to speak now or I would have no energy left to make myself understood. My voice came faintly and things suddenly got quiet in the room as everyone strained to hear me.

"Deres…"

Sgt. Caldera gently interrupted. "I am very sorry but I cannot understand you. I must open the shower door. I promise no one will go in. Not even myself."

I started to nod, realized with horror what I had nearly done and struggled to produce something that to my ear sounded disappointingly like "Eh." I swallowed gingerly.

"Man…te help…essprt…" I stopped, dismayed I could no longer form the letter X. I hoped Sgt. Caldera could understand at least the important part of what I was saying. I tried one more time. "Knows guns…friend help…me."

I could not have forced one more sound from my throat if God Almighty had commanded me on the spot. I took more shallow breaths and knew they hadn't understood me. I despaired. I was losing it. Not just my voice. My ability to hold myself together. My body would move from exhaustion before Sax arrived. The gun would go off. They would wash me down the drain.

I was so close.

I would try again.

I took a breath, readied my throat muscles, but before I could say anything, I heard someone else.

My angel was speaking up for me. Her soft little voice was strong and determined. I heard her say Sax. I heard her say *amigo, experto, pistola*. The rest was a blur of Spanish.

Sgt. Caldera was silent for a moment before he said, *"El doctor es pronto y ambulancia."* And my angel said *"Sí, bueno. Necessario."*

A doctor might not be a bad idea. At least they hadn't called a priest.

If only Sax would come.

Sgt. Caldera spoke again, this time to me.

"I understand about your friend. Señora Paloma-Bandera has explained."

Rosario. My angel. I'd never known her last name.

"A doctor and ambulance also have been summoned and will be here any minute. If your friend doesn't arrive soon, Señor Smith, very, very soon, I fear there will be no choice. I believe you could die. I think we should give your friend another five minutes, no more. Even that is generous. After that, assuming the doctor is here, I will have to try to free you. You can be assured that I will do everything in my power to save your life."

Inside I nodded. Outside I was silent. I felt sure Sgt. Caldera understood my feelings. As a policeman, he knew what it was to place your trust in someone familiar. But he was also right about the timing. Sax might be just around the corner. He might be miles away. A doctor was coming. He would have instruments. Maybe it wouldn't be as hard as I thought. And if the gun did go off, there was always the hope that I would die immediately. With luck there would be no suffering. Only the torment of these past hours and the terror of the final minutes. There were worse fates, I knew.

Sad, but at the time I just couldn't think of them.

As soon as I'd made my rather disjointed peace with what I assumed was my fate, Sax nearly broke down the door trying to get in. The doctor entered almost immediately afterwards and I could hear Sgt. Caldera briefing both of them, Sax in English for my benefit, then the doctor in Spanish.

The Voice had been even more diabolical than I imagined. It was not only my chest, knees and head that were secured to the rifle but everything else, too. My hands, in particular, had come in for special attention, fastened both with tape and plaster. From chin down, the rifle and I had become one.

When Sax and Sgt. Caldera finally entered the shower with the doctor, the room fell completely silent. A quiet, tense discussion in Spanish followed. I tried to listen but understood nothing. I thought: I can't do this anymore. I can't stop the trembling. I can't keep my focus. There were too many people. Too many distractions.

As I had so many times in the hours before, I teetered on the brink, then pulled back. I wasn't alone anymore. These people were trained; they would know how to release me. I also wasn't the kind of person to surrender within crawling distance of the goal line.

One way or another, dragging myself across was the only option.

It might have been fifteen minutes later, maybe less. But when I heard his voice, even in Spanish, I knew Sax had it worked out. There was a flurry of conversation, some murmurs of agreement, and finally Sgt. Caldera began issuing commands. The doctor spoke rapidly, presumably on a cellphone, and Sax sounded almost cheerful. "We've figured the way out of this Pen. Now, when I give you the signal, you're going to make yourself totally still. There won't be an atom in your body that moves."

What did he think I'd been doing all these hours? Playing volleyball?

"Somethin' new," I managed to say.

I heard Sax chuckle. I was glad I could provide humorous material. I was glad I could provide *any* material.

Someone new entered the room and there was a lot of agitated talk.

"Okay, Pen," Sax said, "here's the deal. The doctor will stick a bunch of needles in your arms, around your knees, in your chin and your neck. Your muscles will instinctively want to tighten. You have to avoid that as much as you can. Don't tense, don't move. It's hard to keep a lid on both but try your best."

"Hnh," I said.

"It'll pay you to cooperate. If the doc is feeling particularly perverse, he may jab you in a couple other places that would really hurt."

I started to chuckle, caught myself in time.

"After a few minutes, you're going to experience a sort of paralysis around the areas where the shots go in. That doesn't mean you don't still have to keep from moving. It just means you have a little help. Make a noise, anything, just so I know you've got it."

"Sas..." I heard him moving away. "Robyn...Take care..."

He stopped. "Hell no," he said, sounding surprised. "You'll take care of her yourself."

I heard a chuckle.

"Erg," I said.

"You're in for one hell of a shock," Sax said. "You get outta here, you're gonna look like a million bucks. You won't be able to fight off the women. Those needles, my friend, are filled with fuckin' Botox."

Once I'd absorbed a mother lode of the paralysis drug, the doctor, Julio Alvarado-Navarro, began snipping away the duct tape that bound my head to the barrel. He wouldn't take off the blindfold, he told me, as any abrupt change might be disconcerting. A lousy excuse for keeping the horror hidden but I agreed with him. Like a kid avoiding looking at his arm while getting a shot, I had no desire to see what was happening in the real world.

The doctor's movements were delicate and sure. Because of the Botox not a muscle quivered, which he dryly said made me one of his better patients.

Sax, meanwhile, concentrated on my hands. He kept up a running explanation of what he was learning so I had the opportunity to be appalled, dispirited, and ultimately infuriated right along with him. I figured his real motive in yakking away was simply to keep me awake.

When I was first told my hands were encased in plaster of paris, my reaction had been a thrill of hope. I remembered from school days that the stuff breaks down in water, a commodity certainly not lacking throughout the night.

Cautiously optimistic, I bleated out enough recognizable words to ask if the plaster had softened at all. Sax gave me the bad news. The plaster had been shellacked. The surface had shed the hours of drenching water like the tiles that lined the shower.

Sax also explained in depressing detail exactly how my hands were secured. Some of it I had guessed already; other parts I dreaded hearing. The trigger of the gun was facing me. My fingers, all except my right thumb, were taped to the barrel. From above the wrists to just below the knuckles, a plaster cuff was keeping the gun rigidly in place. The right thumb had been left free. Angled into the trigger guard and prevented by the cuff from sliding out, it was still loose enough to set the whole thing off.

To remove the thumb from the guard, it was necessary to remove the plaster. To remove the plaster, it had to be sawed. To saw it was to send me to the grave.

It was a simple formula, really.

Having gotten nowhere with the hands, Sax turned his attention to the stock extending below my knees. "Always a chance someone did some custom work on this we can exploit," he said. Even to my hopeful ears that sounded improbable and when his observations came back to me couched in phrases like "if," "if only," and "otherwise," we both knew what language was being spoken. There was no way of avoiding it. As the Voice had said and I'd believed all along, movement was my biggest enemy. The fact that I hadn't already set off the trigger was a source of amazement for us all.

The same was true of my battle with fatigue. Fear had kept me going through the night but by morning the adrenalin had dissipated. I was doing my best to stay awake, Sax, the doctor, and Sgt. Caldera were trying their damndest to free me, but underlying the atmosphere of intense effort there was a new concern. The properties of exhaustion weren't elastic enough to keep me going much longer—and we all knew it.

We also decided to ignore it. Dr. Navarro kept quietly snipping away, Sax talked and asked questions, making sure I didn't nod off, and I did my part by continuing to stay alive and not shooting anyone in the process.

There was another element to this drama. Sgt. Caldera was poised to take my head in his hands when it was released from the tape. It was a critical job requiring a precisely timed, flawlessly executed changeover. Anything less and my head would slump, destabilize the gun barrel, and, more likely than not, push my thumb against the trigger. If that happened, I might not be the only one in the path of a bullet.

I was aware of various parts of the plan but not all of it. I didn't learn until later that the gun was a semi-automatic assault rifle capable of blowing big holes in walls. Sgt. Caldera, on the other hand, had taken one look and immediately realized the full extent of what could happen. The police had prepared all areas within range, evacuating the floor below and shutting off access to the building. Plywood had been brought in to cover the windows and, with Rosario's help, bedding was gathered to drape over the all-glass shower.

If the gun went off, Sax quietly explained to the doctor, it wouldn't much matter where it was aimed. I took silent issue with this on the grounds of self-preservation, but grudgingly agreed on principle. In an open space, a bullet can penetrate glass and make only a small hole. But a gun discharged in an enclosure this confined would shatter the walls by concussion. There was nothing that could be done about it; we were up against the laws of physics.

Our collective hope was for the shower to be made of safety glass. Unfortunately, there was no way of proving it short of shots being fired. To make matters worse, safety glass not infrequently fails. Hitler had been known to fire a pistol at the bulletproof glass in his armored Mercedes-Benz. He was not the last dictator to do so.

The bottom line for all of us—if we survived the bullets, we could be killed by flying glass. I assumed (correctly) that the others were already covered with Kevlar vests and pants and soon would be wearing full-face helmets. I mostly had what nature had given me and very light clothes on top. The bedding was thin, no comforters or duvets in this tropical

climate. It might provide some slight protection against
erupting glass—emphasis on slight.

As I considered this, Sgt. Caldera's men finished draping
the sheets over the shower, producing a small change in the
acoustics. From that moment on, it would be more difficult to
make myself heard, putting additional stress on already
traumatized throat muscles. Talking might verify my
wakefulness but it could also launch a cough, a gasp, even a
spasm. I had worried about it all night, each time I spoke.
Now, with the water off and my mouth growing dry, it was an
even greater hazard. Fortunately, with all the people in the
room and the air-conditioning turned off at my request, the
temperature had risen enough that shaking was no longer an
issue.

Along with the change in acoustics came an acceleration
in tempo. I felt my heartbeat speed up again and a new fear
creep in. I'd been petrified for hours. I'd believed I would die.
But my fate had been mine to determine. Now that it
depended on others, I was overwhelmed with dread that they
would fail. I thought this must be what passengers felt on a
plane, knowing it was going to crash, desperately praying for
their pilot to save them. It was a penetrating, sick fright where
I thought longingly about the escape of madness, or the solace
of a Zen-like trance where I would simply retreat from any
awareness of my body and its actions. Deliberately, I walked
the path between being hyper-alert, which seemed to prompt
trembling, and a calmness that could lead to inattention and
loss of control. Eventually I entered into an armistice of sorts.
A professorial type might say that I came out on the other side

of myself. I knew only that as much as anyone could be, I felt prepared for whatever would happen.

I was not nearly so at ease about the lives of the three brave men who had chosen to share my nightmare. Every snip put the doctor at deadly risk. When Sgt. Caldera took my head in his hands, he would place himself directly in the line of fire. And what of Sax, my friend? His task would be the most pivotal. I did not take the commitment of these men lightly. Whenever I died, this day or another, I would owe them to my last.

As the final piece of tape was severed, the plan went into action. The handoff to Sgt. Caldera was perfect. "Now, the soap," Dr. Navarro said quietly and I could feel a dribble of warm liquid playing over my chin and down my neck.

"On the count of three," Sax said, and in what could have been my last seconds of life, my mind went to the astronauts who also live by a countdown and think of being blasted into space.

"Three."

Everything happened so fast, it was over before I could comprehend it. The water had not stopped the gun. There *had* been a lethal barrage of bullets. They would have blown my head off.

But Sgt. Caldera had wrenched my head one way, in the same instant Sax had thrust the gun barrel in the opposite direction, my thumb had pushed the trigger—and the bullets had spent their fearful lives on the glass and the opposite wall and the nerves of every one of us.

Amazingly, nobody suffered serious injury. Some of the safety glass had done a credible job, other parts hadn't. Even so, most of the shower had simply disintegrated into granules and the few truly lethal airborne daggers had thankfully embedded themselves in walls, cabinets, doors, everywhere but in living flesh.

Considering the potential, damage was minimal. The shower was destroyed and fourteen chilling holes appeared in the opposite wall near the ceiling. But the short hall through which Sax and the policeman helped me walk me was untouched, as was Uncle Henry's bedroom, where I was gently laid on the bed.

The real damage was inside us all. Rosario, my angel, would never forget the first moment of seeing the thing that had been me in the shower. Sax, Sgt. Caldera and Dr. Navarro would probably have sweaty nightmares in which their own heads were blown off, or they watched me die, or they were caught in some other incendiary illusion.

I had seen soldiers permanently changed by events far less traumatic than this; I knew I would carry the aftermath for my lifetime. It might become an unbearable burden, a protective scar nominally covering the wound but in reality barely concealing a septic, festering memory. Or, if I were fortunate, it would be an experience hated for the act but accepted for the opportunity to reach into my soul as I probably never would have done otherwise. Now that I had come through the experience mostly intact, I hoped my reaction would be the latter. In an odd way, of the five of us, I believed I would have the least troubled sleep of all.

CHAPTER 36

On examination, my nose was severely bruised, but not broken, and the doctor decided he could treat it without transferring me to a hospital. The immediate problem was to clear the nostrils of whatever was blocking them. Before Dr. Navarro began, Sgt. Caldera joined us in the bedroom with a police photographer, who took photos of my torn face and distorted nose from all angles. It was from him I learned my final sufferings had been filmed. Yes, he said proudly, I caught everything. From the first moment of the doctor's snipping, to the gun being pushed aside to Sgt. Caldera and your friend carrying you away. He would put the footage on a CD, he said. Many people in the police department would view it. There was a lot to be learned from this event.

It was such a small thing compared to what I had just been through, yet the prospect of having total strangers view my most vulnerable moments was distressing. I hoped the police would treat the video with confidentiality. Above all, that it would not make its way to the internet or The Washington Post. On the other hand, I reminded myself, I was hardly a recognizable persona in any medium. For most of the time, my eyes had been shrouded and my face looked like it had just emerged from a Cuisinart. An unplanned but surely effective disguise.

The time had come to perform the salvage operation on my nose. With a long pair of pincers, Dr. Navarro went slowly into my right nostril, unleashing a small red stream that trickled to my lip. "It can't be helped," he said apologetically. "There's a wound from this object being forced in and it will be aggravated coming out."

The small additional pain caused by removing the object was nothing compared to my amazement at seeing it. The "thing" that had kept me from breathing, the "thing" that had made me think my nose was broken was a simple key from a computer. A piece of plastic about ten millimeters square. An "I" covered in blood.

We all looked at this improbable item.

Sax went to the living room and examined my laptop lying on the floor. It was in a sorry state, he reported. The lid was split in half and the screen cracked. The police wouldn't let him touch it but he could see enough to know that two keys were missing.

"We'll take the other one out now," said Dr. Navarro, shaking his head and breathing deeply as though he still couldn't believe what he was seeing.

"Are you ready?" he asked.

I nodded as much as the drug would let me. They had been big shots, the doctor had explained, to achieve the temporary paralytic effect. Not a middle-aged lady's normal look-at-me dose.

"Can't wait to see what in hell this one is," Sax muttered, looking on in disbelief.

It became obvious to me at just that moment. "I already know," I said slowly, feeling defeated, resolute, and goddamn angry all at the same time.

The whole room turned to me. Even the police videographer was still.

"It's a D," I said. "D…I. Die without the E."

It was.

Sax found me some pajama bottoms and a T-shirt, pushed everyone out of the room, and forced my again shivering limbs into the clothes. Rosario returned with a blanket, and, at my request, also brought me the best narcotic in the house, a welcome glass of bourbon, which the doctor would probably have prohibited had he known. I put it up to my lips, started to drink, and something about the familiar motion made me stop.

I'd had plenty of time to think about it in the shower. I'd come home, poured a drink from my new decanter, taken a good, long swig, then put the computer on my lap so I could write Joy.

And plunged into a world of torture and would-be murder.

Slowly, I lowered the glass and looked at Sax. "Sgt. Caldera," I said. "Let's get him in here again."

The tantalus was taken away, open bottles of whiskey and other liquids were carted off, and the police did some more of that forensic alchemy you see on TV. Rosario found an unopened bottle of my preferred beverage, presented it to Sgt. Caldera for inspection, and handed me a glass of bourbon I could drink. It was eight a.m. and I didn't care. As Val might say: Man must have his nourishment—or, in this case, pain relief.

In the middle of it all, Val himself arrived. His normal perkiness after spending a night with the girl of his dreams was nowhere in evidence, evidently dampened by the gauntlet of police outside.

He asked all the normal questions and I gave him all the abnormal answers. He looked in what was left of the shower, saw the rifle bagged on the floor, the wads of tape and pieces of plaster in other bags. He saw the CD player through more plastic, the fourteen holes in the wall.

He returned to the bedroom a very grave man indeed.

Just as things were looking up for me, they took a nose-dive for Val. I wasn't surprised he was on the list of people to be questioned, but when he was escorted to police headquarters, I hoped it was merely a formality. I had forgotten too soon my own interrogation by the Panama City police and that there are no formalities when it comes to crime in Panama.

Three hours went by in which I alternated moments of dozing and "chats" with the Comandante, a stern-faced man of senior rank who asked questions like: "Why someone did this to you?" (don't know, wish I did) "Why are you coming to

Panama?" (my uncle asked me to) "Where is this uncle now?" (he's dead) "Who killed him?" (a disease—leukemia), and more of the same. My favorite was: "Are you a *traficante de drogas?*" (Sure, couldn't you tell from the stuff up my nose? I longed to say it, but didn't.)

The Comandante asked if I remembered the Voice from before the time I woke up, sitting in the chair blindfolded. No, I replied. I had no memory of anything after reaching for the computer. My first conscious exposure to the Voice was when it spoke in my ear, saying the same words the CD then played over and over again. If I moved I would die. Straightforward enough. Oh, and the voice sounded like a combination of a man, a woman and a duck. Speaking from inside a grizzly bear.

Rodrigo appeared, prompting conversations conducted in staccato Spanish and bristling with words like *"Su Superior"* and *"El Presidente."* The kind of words that seemed to have an important, if reluctantly received, effect.

Val, Rodrigo informed me, the blue eyes never leaving the Comandante's face, would be returned in a few minutes. The police had also finished with me. I could stay here or go back to the States as long as I remained accessible by phone. Getting as far away as possible sounded like the best idea of the day, and I said so. Everyone agreed with me.

As we were talking, the doctor returned with various injections, pills, and ministrations. It turned out that Sax had not been quite on the money when he mentioned Botox. The doctor had actually shot me with a neuromuscular blocking agent that derived from the rainforest and had a much shorter half-life than Botox. I moved several muscles that had been injected and could tell the medicine was already beginning to wear off. It was a sad irony, I thought, that a jungle poison had taken Ignacio's life, while a jungle drug had given me mine.

My injuries were another story. The swelling of my hands and feet would go down in a day or two. The face, of course, was another story. The cuts would have to heal and they would take some time. It was a possibility plastic surgery would be needed—nothing scary, dermabrasion or chemical peeling if there was much scarring and there was a good possibility there wouldn't be much scarring at all. I was incredibly lucky, the doctor said, the horror of what could have happened showing transparently in his eyes. Yes, I nodded, again thanking this kind and brave man.

At one point, Sax came to me and imparted information.

"They've taken Enriqué, Bruno, and Billy for questioning. I've told them how Enriqué saved your life. I don't know how much good it will do. They'll start on the folks at the law firm next. Rodrigo knows it. He's prepared."

Yes, I thought in sympathy, it would be a rough day for a lot of people. Even if I could protest, there was nothing I could do to change the process. Like nature following a healing course, the police would carry out the investigation in their own way. The best I could do was ask Sax to keep an eye on the interrogations and let me know when Enriqué and his people were in the clear; meanwhile, I took comfort in knowing that of all those unfortunate enough to have been in recent contact with me, Robyn at least was safely out of harm's way.

Ultimately, I tuned everybody out. Like Louis the XIV, I drifted into unconsciousness in the midst of a roomful of people. The Sun King had been surrounded with courtiers, sycophants, in-fighters, and confidantes. I was encircled by family, friends, and protectors. Undoubtedly, I thought as I fell asleep, I had the better part of the deal.

CHAPTER 37

When I awoke a few hours later, Rosario was sitting in a chair at the end of the bed like a tiny white-clad elf.

She smoothed the sheets, offered me water, looked carefully at my face.

"Rosario," I said and slipped my big, puffed-up hand under her child-sized fingers. But for her I never would have survived. Unlike others who might have taken one look at the apparition in the shower and fled, Rosario had not panicked. She had shown the kind of fortitude that may not always be on display but that percolates to the top in times of need. Thank God she percolated for me.

I let her hand slide off mine and smiled at her. After a moment of embarrassment, she reached into the top of her blouse and brought out the small medallion that always dangled around her neck.

"*La Medalla de la Santisima Virgin Maria,*" she said, showing it to me, her tiny face a beatific reflection of the image on the medal. "I pray to *Santisima Virgin Maria* for your life, Señor Pen. And she hear me. God have sent her to save you." She kissed the medallion, her face showing all the wonder of the true believer.

I smiled at her indulgently. I wouldn't dispute that God had a hand in saving my life; I had certainly begged Him enough. But as far as who got the credit—with sincerest apologies to Mary, Mother of Jesus—I knew it was my own personal angel who had rescued me. No one, not God, not *Santisima Virgin Maria,* not even Rosario Paloma-Bandera, had a prayer of convincing me otherwise.

CHAPTER 38

I had definitely decided to return to Washington, both for recuperation and for business. Then, too, there was obviously a maniac on the loose and, at least for the time being, only a person with a shovel ready to bury himself would stick around for more. The police would do their job, Val would stay on the trail of the missing money (with Bruno and Billy stationed in sight of all three penthouse doors this time), and Sax would check on Hector. I would see Thomas as soon as I got home and let him decide whether to visit Panama or not. My guess was he would make the trip. As Val continually pointed out, there had been just as many opportunities for someone to kill him as me. And each time, to our total bafflement, they had selected yours truly.

It had been hell telling Robyn what happened. I called her after speaking with Rosario, Val punching in the number and turning on the speaker phone for me. I tried to sweeten it, but I knew when she saw me—my nose, my face, and the Michelin Man hands—any glossing over would be to no avail.

At first, all she could do was stare at me. Then a tear slid down her face, then a whole lot more. When all that was over, she gingerly sat on the bed next to me and tried to find a place she could touch that wouldn't hurt.

"There are a couple," I said, with as close to a grin as I could muster, "but I think we'd better leave those for another time."

"You mean the great steed is stabled for the moment?" She also tried to raise a grin but a sob escaped her instead, and then a hiccup.

"The great steed was nearly put to sleep, permanently," I told her. I tried for a light tone but didn't get far. My insides were still roiling and my brain alternated between feelings of relief and residual panic.

"How could—?" She hiccupped. "—someone do this?" Another hiccup. "Your face, what happened to your beautiful face?"

If I'd been able, I would have beamed. I had a beautiful face. Well, I *did* have one.

"It's a long story," I said. She crawled on top of the covers and sat cross-legged. All ears. All eyes. All desirable. A normal person who loved me, who would help to calm the tremors in my mind.

I launched into the story, pausing often to take deep breaths. "Sorry," I said, "that stuff the Voice gave me affected my breathing. It hasn't quite worked its way out of my system."

Robyn listened wordlessly until I was finished.

"It's beyond belief," she said, her eyes wide and moist. "Macabre. Like something out of a horror movie."

"I'm sure I look like something out of a horror movie. I haven't asked for a mirror yet. I'm too afraid of what I'll see."

Robyn made an attempt to cheer me. "All the wounds are fresh," she said. "And superficial. Of course it's dreadful now, but with the cream the doctor gave you and time…"

"Right." My voice was neutral. My "superficial" face, despite the salves, felt, and no doubt looked, like it was on fire.

"In a month or so, we'll be in Aruba or somewhere and all the women will be after your bod."

"I thought I'd grow a beard in the meantime. I can't shave for a while anyway. What do you think??"

"You mean one of those scratchy, ugly things where food always gets caught?"

"Well, since you approve—" I felt a little more light-hearted. Robyn was having a good influence on me. She got up, locked the doors, relieved herself of some clothes. Slid in between the sheets and snuggled up.

"Am I hurting you?"

"Robyn, love." I kissed the top of her head. I hope you never have to find out what hurt really means, I said silently.

She sighed and laid her head against my chest. We stayed like that for a long, long time.

CHAPTER 39

After clearing Customs, I caught a cab, ignored the driver's rude stare, and made a fast call to Val. I had left Panama City four days after the shower scene and arrived to find Washington in the throes of a frigid day. Adding to that unpleasantness, the city's famous charms were hidden under bleak gray skies that promised snow, sleet, freezing rain, or all three—what the local weather people called the "dreaded wintry mix."

I thought about that phrase. My vocabulary had changed since I'd been in Panama. Fear, danger, terror and certainly dread—all those concepts had undergone radical surgery.

So, too, had my understanding of evil.

Although I'd lived to talk about them, the first three rounds in the deadly fight for my life had gone to evil. TKOs, all of them. The fourth and final round, not a Technical but a complete take-down, a knockout, had to go to me.

With every encounter, I was learning more about the man I called the Voice. This was a demon who wanted me fearful, off-balance, looking over my shoulder, not knowing when the next attack would come. I didn't think killing was the primary intent, not yet. Perverted pleasure and making me crumble were. If I had died four nights ago, that would have been fine. Four nights from now would be even better. Until actual death resulted, every chance the Voice could get to inflict pain and terror would make it happy.

I had no idea whether the Voice had expected me to survive the last attack. Considering the odds, probably not. But as to whether it was incandescent with rage and licking its wounds, I doubted it. It would be doing what it did best. It would be planning. And I had already seen how very, very thoroughly and maliciously it could plan.

Hector had imparted something important in the jungle. It was when we were walking toward *Piña Abajo*, trying to be as noiseless as possible. "FARC travels as we do," he had said quietly, audible only to me. "So never ever forget, my friend, we must travel better."

That's the way I felt about the Voice. We were on opposite paths which would cross again at some dangerous undetermined location.

But I planned to reach my destination safely.

And that meant the Voice could not.

CHAPTER 40

Joy's greeting was everything I'd expected—shock, questions, hugs, and tearful concern. She'd been in Washington, operating in the dark, aware of only minimal details, albeit some very disquieting. The stress of it showed.

I promised her all would be revealed shortly, gently peeled myself away, and walked the few steps from her office to mine.

First on my list was Robyn, who'd made me promise to call her when I arrived. It was endearing to be fussed over but it also seemed as though we'd spent most of the time we'd known each other doing just that. One of these days, I hoped we'd settle down to something normal—or at least something that didn't include murder and mayhem.

A moment after I hung up, a middle-aged, well-dressed black man entered the room. He had a few inches on me and the type of build usually found on professional athletes. As most big men do, he walked lightly, but seemed to favor his left side. His face was enormous, wide, and curiously devoid of expression, except for eyes sharp with intelligence and primed to believe nothing without verification. I had met my share of watchful, vigilant FBI agents over the years but something about this one struck me differently. He was like a hunting dog. On point. Ready. And, expressionless or not, having a good time.

"Hi," he said, sticking out a giant cushiony hand. "John Dillinger."

I laughed. Painfully.

"It's one of those ice-breaker things," he grinned, his face pleasantly transformed. "You know how people are about us Fibbies. A little uptight." His voice had a folksy, Southern rhythm to it.

I waved him to a seat. "Call me Pen," I said.

"Ron," he answered.

We studied each other for a moment.

The evening after the attack, Val and I had had a heart-to-heart talk. When we were finished, Val called Joy and asked her to locate a team of investigators for some immediate digging. Criteria: a discreet and efficient firm at the top of its game. Budget: open.

Ron Walters & Associates had descended on the offices of Pen Smith & Associates the next day.

Ron and I chatted briefly, touching on some facts I already knew and others I didn't. For eighteen years, Ron had been with the Bureau, retiring because of injuries suffered in the line of duty (accounting for the left side). After fifteen months' recuperation he started his own business. Now, half a decade later, Ron Walters & Associates employed a slew of ex-agents, lawyers, and assorted other staff, sported a lengthy roster of satisfied clients, and had a big bag of tricks to help out folks like me. There was more, reams of it, in a folder Joy had put on my desk, but for me it all came down to three things: Ron had resources, depth of staff, and the right nose for the hunt. That's all I needed.

"I have a little story to tell you, Ron, as soon as my cousin Thomas arrives." I explained that Thomas was a lawyer who was planning to visit Panama as my legal eyes and ears.

Before I could say more, I heard Thomas in the hall and a second or two later both he and Joy came in, Thomas shedding outerwear and presenting a chilled hand for shaking.

"Walked," he said economically. "Forgot my gloves."

Shorter and thinner than me, Thomas was all edges, with a tense, wiry frame that complemented his tireless personality, and tortoise-shell glasses that gave him a vaguely studious look. The Smith gray-blue eyes and ruddy complexion were in his genes but his forehead was higher, his features sharper than Val's and mine. The only thing soft about Thomas was his hair, rich, wavy brown, movie star hair, something Val had never forgiven him for. Although women found him attractive, his dance card was never quite as full as Val's. But, then, whose was?

After the hellos, we all took our seats and I began the tale, calmly at first, then with an anger that overran my embarrassment at having been helpless prey. As I went on, I told the story rapid-fire, concentrating on facts rather than emotion. At one point, describing the chill of the shower, Joy began shivering. At another, she emitted a single raw sob.

Not unexpectedly, Ron was generally impassive and took extensive notes. Thomas' responses were more visceral, his scribbles often interspersed with vicious little stabs at his legal pad.

At the conclusion there was silence, then Ron cleared his throat and said matter-of-factly, "It's quite an account. Extraordinary, the whole thing. You must feel like cheese that's gone through the grater."

My kind of guy, I thought. He gets it.

"So, the police down there are tearing things apart but you decide to come back up here because you think there might be a connection closer to home."

"Right," I answered. "None of this seems to make sense. The people in Panama had the opportunity but no motive that we've discovered. People here could have had motive but no opportunity. Somewhere, there has to be a link. Otherwise, I don't see how the shooting on the first day could have happened. Plus, the setup with the gun and the spiked bourbon took planning. Just getting into the condominium was a job in itself. Somebody needed time to organize this." I spread my hands in frustration.

"What about the woman who picked you up at the airport? Obviously, she knew where you'd be."

"She and a good chunk of the law firm," I replied. "Everyone involved with the foundations was given a memo with my flight number, time of arrival, the name of my hotel, even my room number. So, yeah," I said bitterly, "she knew, they all knew."

"Bummer," Ron said.

I turned to Thomas. "By the way, just in case you missed it in the story, this particular girl is Val's newest."

Thomas started to open his mouth but I beat him to it.

"Bracelet," I said. "Gold and some kind of stones."

Ron looked from me to Thomas and back again.

"Sorry," I said. "A little family joke at our cousin's expense. Go ahead."

"You were saying the lawyers all knew where you'd be," Ron said. "I think that's where the Panamanian police have to be focusing."

"Maybe," I said. "But unless Marcel had a sidekick, no one else had a motive. Killing me would only shift the assets over to my heirs—Thomas and the rest of my family."

Ron nodded and ran his thumb over his chin. "Regarding those assets, you can be sure the police will be giving all of your companies a close look, too." He looked over at me. "Many people?"

I nodded. "Several hundred employees, maybe more. Everything they do in Panama is people intensive, labor being so cheap."

I moved my weight in the chair and winced. All of a sudden, my aches and pains were back, along with fatigue. The flight had taken most of the day. Though I'd slept some on the plane, my body was worn out.

Ron seemed to pick up on it and nodded. "Well, this is the kind of speculation that's helpful but now that we know what we're looking for we need to crank it into the system. After that, we'll begin eliminating the weaker possibilities and taking a hard look at the more likely folks."

I nodded.

"Good," Ron said, "then let me tell you how it's going to work."

We all sat up a little straighter.

"We start with a database of people connected to you. So far about two thousand names."

I whistled, and, a second later, the skin on my face protesting, wished I hadn't.

"I know," said Ron with angelic blandness. "You include those girlfriends, I'm telling you, the numbers add up."

Everyone in the room laughed. Ron guffawed at his own joke along with the rest of us.

"As you can guess," he said when the laughter died down, "you take ten years of campaigns and staffs and volunteers, it makes for a lot of people. Plus the usual friends and family and acquaintances and doctors and dry cleaners, all those people to kick in. We do a first cut to get rid of anyone who's dead, in prison, was in the hospital when it happened.

"Now, after this, we screen for a criminal background, which will give us an offenders list to work with. We have a whole special routine for those folks. People who don't have any criminal background we'll go at from a different direction. Same thing for anyone with mental health issues. We have a special protocol for them. Now, after we work through the names in the computer, we'll start on phone and personal interviews. We try to keep those reasonable. It can get pretty expensive if we have to interview every other person and his brother. Eventually, though, if someone's there to find, we ought to get a hit."

"Can't ask any more than that," I said.

"One of the most important things we need is for you to give us your personal information. Joy's been real helpful but now we've got to pull a lot of stuff out of you to narrow those names down even more."

"Sure," I said, having expected it, but fighting inertia nonetheless. "How and when do we start?"

"Tomorrow morning," Ron said, "and I'd plan on spending the next couple of days on it. We need you to fill in the gaps—people we don't have, important events we need to know about. Who was screwing who in what campaign…"

Everyone grinned like teenagers.

Ron smiled, wickedly. "Especially you."

Thomas and Joy had the good sense to hold their tongues.

"The meat you can put on those names is gonna make the difference," Ron said. "A lot of it may be a question of how deep your memory is and how fast you can access it." He paused and licked his upper lip, a full yard of it.

"Any idea how long you'll be staying?"

I shrugged and felt the weakness in my body. "A few days, a week. If I find something I need to go back for, well, I'm off."

Joy frowned. Thomas twirled his glasses and looked thoughtful.

Ron observed me closely. "Hard trying to work it from both ends," he said.

I agreed. "It's foreign territory everywhere. Down there, up here. This is the first time I've done this kind of thing."

"Yeah," Ron answered. "Most folks don't even have a first." He stood up from his chair. "Just be prepared. We'll have a lot of questions as we go along. You'd better meet the folks so you'll know who they are when they come calling."

We stopped on that note and Ron took me to see his crew. Like him, they seemed to be solid professionals. I felt good about the whole thing and was mentally sorting through some of the details they'd given me when I rejoined Thomas in my office.

I walked through the door. "Thomas—" I said, and in the next instant, went limp and slumped down on the floor. For the second time in less than a week, I was out cold.

Thomas dropped to his knees and pinched my arm.

"What!?" I barked and a black haze moved away. I struggled to sit up. Thomas simultaneously made two smart moves. He poured me some bourbon and had Joy call a taxi. "You're staying with me," he said.

I gulped down the fortifier, let Thomas haul me into a chair, and a few minutes later didn't resist when he and Joy took my bags and person down to the lobby to wait for the cab. Thomas's house was only a short walk from the office but given Washington's one way streets, Lafayette's circles, and the nation's worst traffic, it took us half an hour to get there. By that time, I was nearly asleep. With Thomas's arm holding me up, I more or less stumbled from the cab, groped my way through the front door and oozed down a flight of stairs to his comfortable game room, our usual hangout. I sat on a soft oversize leather sofa and felt my molecules relax. Thomas ordered pizza and poured more bourbon.

Until the food came, we made small talk. Afterward, I described the foundations, while Thomas listened and made an occasional note. Unlike Val, he didn't rave about the amount of the estate. Instead, he asked questions about Fernandez-Chavira, especially Rodrigo, and the other lawyers I'd been working with. It made sense. Val was the money man, Thomas the lawyer. We also talked about how long I planned to stay. "Until I finish with Ron and his questions," I said. "A few days. A week. Probably not much more." Thomas knit his brows together and twirled his tortoise-shells.

Eventually, Thomas poured another drink and put away the detritus of our meal. I relaxed further into the sofa. There was a spare bedroom down the hall but a combination of the trip, the bourbon, and not being fully recovered from my ordeal in the shower stopped me from going there. Neanderthal man, I reminded myself, slept on the ground in caves. Plenty of people still bunked on straw. So, who was I to disdain a perfectly good sofa? I swung my legs up, made myself comfortable, and reached for my glass. I never made it. Arm extended, fingers reaching, I drifted off to sleep. A deep, untroubled sleep. And a safe one.

When I woke up, I saw that Thomas had covered me with a blanket. The feeling of being physically sand-bagged was mostly gone, and if my nerves were still worn thin by the Voice, at least my body felt rejuvenated. I padded comfortably into the kitchen where Thomas was firing up the coffeemaker, toasting bread, and skimming the paper's headlines.

"You're better," he said, cheer in his voice. Then in the next breath, gloomy as the sky outside the window, "It's sleeting."

"Considering what I've been through," I said good-naturedly, "sleet's the last damn thing I'm concerned about." I moved off down the hall toward the bathroom and a good scrubbing. I flexed my muscles, felt them respond without the tension of the past few days. Sleet, I thought scornfully. I should be so lucky that it would top my worry list.

CHAPTER 41

Ron gave me a minute to grab a cup of coffee and look through my morning mail, then joined me.

"You're looking better," he said, echoing Thomas. He flipped open his notebook and his pen began moving down the page as he unemotionally summarized the team's findings from the data screen conducted the afternoon before.

"Wait a minute," I said, "you mean nearly a third of the people in my database have some kind of record?" Good God, I thought, talk about consorting with criminals.

Ron quickly explained that many were for such offenses as non-payment of child support, DUI, and property disputes. The serious ones, he said, were only about thirty percent of the total and of that maybe half involved violence.

"So, how many people are we talking about?" I asked.

"A hundred that fall into the serious category, fifty with violence," Ron said, and, seeing my face, quickly added, "but most of those will be spouse abuse."

"Ron," I said impatiently, "are there any murderers on the list?"

"Two," he answered, and my mind began racing through campaigns like a movie on rewind, pulling up questionable names and faces from the past.

"One got off on a technicality," he said, "the other plea-bargained to Manslaughter Two, no jail. Here's the material on them both."

He handed me a folder and I nervously glanced inside, prepared to see people who had worked next to me a là Ted Bundy. The next minute, I breathed a sigh of relief. One had been a volunteer, the other a man who serviced computers, neither recognizable. Both had been found guilty of hammering their wives.

"This," Ron said tapping the folder, "isn't really where I expect to come across our suspect. If we get lucky and he or she's committed a crime, having their file will speed things along. But just because someone's tried to murder you doesn't mean they're an habitual killer. In fact, I would say it's highly unlikely. In my opinion, we're looking for someone with a deep-seated grudge against you—either that or an out and out lunatic."

"Those were pretty much my assumptions, too," I answered glumly.

"Theoretically," Ron said, "we could also have a case of mistaken identity. Sometimes, it can be as random as that."

"Oh," I said.

"Or the perpetrator can attribute an event that happened in the past to one individual when it was someone altogether different. Think about overhearing two people talking. You might believe it's Persons A and B having a conversation when in reality it's Persons A and C. So while C is actually the bad guy, you wind up going after B."

"Speaking as a potential B," I said, not happily, "I imagine it's hard to find that kind of suspect?"

"Yeah, but to be fair, these are also one in a million type deals," Ron replied. "They happen, but truthfully they're rare. Still—" He tapped his head. "You always keep that kind of squirrelly stuff in the back of your mind. Just in case."

"Squirrelly stuff," I said tonelessly. Computer keys up the nose fit that description.

"Don't worry yourself over it," Ron said, "whoever's doing this to you has all the signs of being in the grudge category. That's why we need your personal information." He handed me some papers. "Look at this list and make notes of anyone you can think of who's missing." He pulled out a sheet. "Then answer these questions about all the entries."

He put his giant hand on the table. "Now, what we want you to think about, Pen, are anomalies—people who've given you a rough time, or, for whatever reason, didn't seem quite right. Maybe they had peculiar habits or were quarrelsome. Maybe they misunderstood everything other people said to them. Ex-girlfriends—don't be soft on them. They're ex for a reason. People you fired. You may believe they know why you fired them but you'd be surprised how many will say, oh, he just didn't like me. Also real important, think about folks who didn't click with everybody else. The ones who never joined y'all for a drink or a meal, for example. Also people who changed while you knew them. Maybe they started off good-natured and suddenly became sour all the time. We need to identify anyone who had addiction or money troubles, any girl/boy problems you came across, homosexuals, transgenders, really anybody out of the ordinary."

"Gay people?" I asked, surprised.

"Not gay because they're gay," Ron said, "but because in politics that can still be a real problem for them. If you were in the arts, we wouldn't even bother with this question. Remember, were looking for anomalies. People who might have had a problem with the system or the system had a problem with them and somehow they wound up transferring it onto you.

"Every one of those questions is there for a good reason. Try not to make judgments when you answer them. Just provide the information and let us work on the context."

"All right," I said. "I understand."

"Okay, then we'll sit you down with this recorder and let you start. Just say the name of the person from the list and then read off each question and give your answer. Every hour or so, someone will pick up what you've finished and key it into the database."

"A lot of work," I murmured, not thinking just of myself but of the whole team.

"You'll find a rhythm pretty soon," Ron said. "It'll go faster than you think." He clapped me on the shoulder and left me to the task.

Four hours later, I looked up at the clock in surprise. The promised rhythm had developed after all. Nearly a quarter of my list was completed and I was optimistic about the rest. At this rate, I could see finishing by the next day. Ron seemed pleased, too, not just with my pace but with the amount of new information I had generated. I decided to take a break, grab a sandwich, and telephone the folks in Panama.

Val was eager to tell me what he was finding. "Some of these accounts are phenomenal," he said, salivating. "Not only that but working through this process is like taking a PhD in accounting. Marcel was a genius. A little sloppy here and there, but a genius all the same."

"So, you're making progress?"

"A few more kinks to unravel and we'll have our money. And, if I'm right, Hector will be able to fund a million Darien expeditions on what I'll dig up for him."

I found myself grinning. As usual, Val's enthusiasm kick-started his information. "Any idea when it'll be finished?" I asked.

"Assuming," Val said, "I can prove the money in any given account is ours, I could stop right then. The problem is it was obviously pooled. Until I know for sure, we're running the risk that Hector's people will come in and either apportion it or take the whole thing. For sure keep it tied up forever. That's why I've been concentrating on isolating one sizeable account from the others."

"What about Hector's team?" I asked. "Can you tell if they're looking in the same places you are?"

"Not so far. I don't see anything even near us." I could almost hear Val smiling. "But, just in case, as soon as I get account access, I'm going to pull out whatever I find and stick it in a nice safe place."

"And FARC? Any signs of their delicate little fingers out there?"

"I'm sure FARC's fingers are poking in everywhere," Val said somberly. "They set up this game. They know better than anyone how it's played. Ordinarily, I'd have said we didn't have a chance against them. But I've been studying Marcel. Looking at some of his other work, trying to get a line on the way the guy's brain worked. Did you know he was a CPA? Not just a degree in law but in accounting, too. Plus he had street smarts and he was creative. One thing I can tell you for sure, he didn't do anything the conventional way. The guy was simply bloody brilliant."

"Takes one to know one," I said.

Val glossed right over the compliment. Unusual.

"The thing about him, Pen, is that anyone looking would see the money moving so fast and so often it seemed to always be in play. But in reality, he'd created some hidey holes where he could slip funds in to rest while he made it look like all the activity was in another location. Good old-fashioned sleight of hand. These safe spots had some tidy sums in them and, I'm guessing now, but I think every time a packet came out, he'd pare off a small piece before he sent the remainder back into circulation. The key thing is that he had to make sure FARC looked in one direction while he did his skimming somewhere else."

"Hard keeping all those balls in the air," I said.

"Oh yeah," Val allowed. "But, I agree with Rodrigo. I think all the hidey holes are right here, where he knew every square inch of the terrain. If I'm right, Marcel was a greedy-and-a-half bastard. When he decided to make a run for it, I don't think he left anything to chance. I think every nickel went into local accounts."

"Wow," I said.

Val chuckled. "I'm also willing to bet that FARC and all those crooks up the line are going crazy right about now trying to find their money."

We were both silent, contemplating the prospect.

"You know that guy who killed Marcel?" Val asked.

"Hard to forget him," I said, mentally shuddering.

"Well, maybe we should also examine the other side of the coin—the possibility Marcel gave him some of this information before he was dispatched. I know Sax thinks the "minder" guy might have gotten spooked and killed Marcel without thinking. But I keep coming back to the question of why you'd kill a man who knows where hundreds of millions of dollars are hidden unless he's already become expendable."

"In that case, wouldn't you be seeing evidence of someone's fingerprints?"

"That depends on what he told them," Val said. "He could have misdirected them or kept back some information."

A thought, not a nice one, occurred to me. "How many people know you're involved in this?"

"Everybody in the office knows I'm working with the computer guys and the accountants," Val said. "Obviously."

"Stay alert," I said. "Make sure you drive in circles a lot."

"Nobody but you and Rodrigo know I'm any further than the techs. As far as the firm is concerned, we could be doing this the rest of our lives. But the truth is, another week and I ought to know most of the answers. Then, if there are still accounts left to find, someone else can take over. We'll have ours by then. And whether or not Marcel gave somebody the information might even become academic." He sucked in a breath and sighed it out. "Really, Pen, it's an incredible amount of money. And Marcel has left a doozie of a puzzle."

Had I been an accountant, I was certain I would have relished Marcel's puzzle, too. It seemed tailor-made for Val—intrigue, enormous amounts of money, and the whiff of danger to make it even more exciting. Not for the first time, I thanked my lucky stars Val had come to Panama when he did.

I congratulated him again, listened to another burst of enthusiasm, and then turned the conversation to a subject not as important to my pocketbook but much dearer to my heart. My car, I reminded Val. Exactly where might that be hiding?

Not to worry, Val responded, it was presently residing with a friend of a friend (I cringed) who was minding it in his garage.

"He's not driving it, is he?" I asked, in what I knew would be taken for pique—and was.

"Hell no, Pen." Val sounded hurt. "I'd never let anyone touch that car. In fact, I have both sets of keys with me here."

"Both sets are in Panama?"

"Actually, I meant to give you one in case you went back before I did but considering all the other stuff that happened, it was the last thing on my mind."

"Understandable," I told him, "but overnight me a set and then how about getting on the phone and making sure the car is still there. Not that I don't trust a friend of a friend of a cousin…"

"I'll get back to you," Val said.

"I'll be right here."

"Okay."

"Hoping I don't have to sue you."

Val laughed but I think he thought I meant it.

Good.

Friend of a friend of a cousin, my ass.

My next call was to Sax. His first report was about Felipe—still in jeopardy, but improving—then we talked about Hector and what his people could do to help resolve my "little problem."

"I don't think almost getting your head shot off qualifies as a little problem," I protested.

"A manner of speaking," Sax said. "Hector was pissed off that nobody called him right away. It's the fucking bureaucracy they have here. He thought he should have been in the loop, in case this shower thing had something to do with Marcel. I'm also thinking he's feeling bad that he wasn't around to help."

"So, is he helping now?" To me that was vastly more important.

"He's looking at drug traffickers and what he calls FARC-lites. He's also leaning on what's left of the former Panama Defense Force that protected Noriega."

"Could be possibilities in that group," I said optimistically.

"Don't get your hopes up. Hector doesn't really think these folks had anything to do with it. He says the crap in your drink and that weird gun setup aren't their style, but there's always the chance your Voice used some rent-a-thug for part of the dirty. So maybe he'll turn up a connection. Keep your fingers crossed."

"Permanently in that position," I said. "So, what are the police learning?"

"They've been going in a different direction, looking for known criminals who might have crossed paths with your uncle and infiltrated the businesses. They've taken apart Rodrigo's office, which I guess you knew, but they haven't found squat except the business about Marcel. Hector's already running interference on that. From what anybody can tell, Marcel didn't have an accomplice, except FARC, of course."

"Right," I said, thinking that no accomplice meant the perpetrator was dead and the opportunity for additional malfeasance had died with him. On the other hand, the absence of a partner could also mean there was no one else with information about the hidden accounts. That left the burden where it was now—squarely on Val. Of course, the bottom line for me was that none of this had anything to do with the gun shot, the attack with the 2 x 4, or the night of torture in the shower. The news was improving on the money side but just as bogged down as ever on the assaults.

Sax said. "The businesses are next. If the police do anything like what I saw in Rodrigo's office—and remember, he has pull—I think they're in for a big shock."

"I suppose it could be someone at a business," I mused, "but it still seems far-fetched to me."

"Think so?" asked Sax. "We only know about the fraud at the law firm. There could be plenty of it out there on the ground."

"I guess," I said, not keen at the prospect of the businesses being involved. How long would it take to sort *that* out?

I changed the subject. "Speaking of Hector, what would you say his position is on this money thing? You think he's the one calling the shots?"

"Can't answer." Sax said. "From what we saw in the *Darien*, we know he's operational but whether he's usually running a desk rather than a squad, nobody's gonna tell me that. If you ask me, I'd have to say Hector's high up in the command structure. Spends most of his time on strategy, approves operations, gets involved on a field basis only when there's big bucks or a big fish. Now, whether the money wizards are part of his shop or just liaise with him, I don't know."

"Great," I said with no enthusiasm.

"What, you think someone won't play fair with you if they recover the cash first?"

"It's occurred to me. Especially if the documentation turns out to be a little muddy."

"I think you have Panama figured out real good, pal. The one thing in your favor is the deal with Hector but, given what's happened, who can say if he can hold up his end of it? If I were you, I'd try pretty hard to locate the accounts before anyone else does."

"About what I thought," I said, not really dispirited but wishing that something, anything, in this mess would be easy for once. "Well, keep me posted if you come across intel in that area."

"Sure," Sax said. "By the way, there's some news for you courtesy of the police. The ballistics are back on the assault rifle. CAR-15, we knew that. But it looks like you came damn close to messing it up with that water trick of yours. A few more hours, who knows what might have happened."

I knew, and Sax did, too, that I couldn't have kept going that long. I'd been at the limit of my endurance when Rosario found me, and had been living on a thimbleful of hope with a hole in it until the gun was forced away from my head.

"It turns out, there could be one tiny problem when you disable a gun like that," Sax said. "The thing is, you get the ammo wet, that's good. But if the ammo's dry and you stop up the barrel or prevent it from moving the bullets, then the ammo's got nowhere to go. So you pull the trigger, maybe nothing happens, the ammo's too wet. Or..." Sax paused for effect. "...the stock just explodes and, in your case, your hands and knees along with it."

I didn't answer because I couldn't think of anything appropriate to say, not because I was particularly shocked. I knew about guns. I'd used CAR-15's cousin, an M-16. I should have known what Sax had just told me. I was certain I had known at one time. How I could have forgotten…

"Don't sweat it," Sax said, cutting into my thoughts. "There was nothing any of us could do but get you out the way we did. Cutting into that plaster of paris would have been a death sentence. We had to assume the gun could fire. And it did. Dr. Navarro says it was amazing you could think of, much less carry out, any kind of plan, the shape you were in. He also said focusing on it probably kept you alive. So there you have it. Just thought you ought to know."

"Right," I said, sighing. "I'll file it away in case history repeats itself."

"Feeling sorry for ourselves, are we?"

"Yeah, well, you know."

Sax made a noise of acknowledgement and then launched into still more news. As he did, I heard a distinct chuckle.

"This'll make you feel better," he said. "Pen, buddy, you have earned the distinction of being the first man in Panama known to have been date-raped."

"What?"

"Okay, the rape part isn't quite correct but the urine and residue tests show that you were given a date rape drug. Something called GBH on the street. Stands for Gross Bodily Harm. There's a long scientific name." I heard papers rustling. "Gamma-Hydroxybutyric acid. I wrote down the main info. I can send you my notes if you want them."

"I'll take your word for it. Just give me a summary."

"Actually, it's pretty interesting," Sax said. "This GBH occurs naturally all over the place. In our bodies, in your finest

New York strip sirloin, cooked rare of course, and in your accompanying baked potato swimming in sour cream and butter."

"Gross Bodily Harm," I murmured. A name that said it all.

"First of all, it's prescribed to help people sleep. Also for anaesthesia. Which would make sense since part of the time you were out cold. Helps with anxiety. Body-builders use it to promote growth hormones. Not surprising. They'll use any kind of crap. Those are the so-called good things. You hear about this drug, it sounds like oxygen one minute, carbon monoxide the next."

"Let's have the monoxide," I said.

"Okay, it can make you puke your guts out, stop your breathing, drive you crazy—up, down, up, down—dizziness, amnesia, hallucinations, the whole bag. People die from this shit. Currently very popular on the date rape circuit. The molecule has a component of alcohol so it goes nicely with bourbon, thank you very much. Your glass still had residue in it and your cute little Pen decanter probably had enough to kill several people."

"Christ."

"Yeah. It's' a bad one. Navarro said it looked like you ingested a quote substantial but not lethal dose unquote and it caused you to have serious hallucinations. He confirmed you were the one who damn near tore your face off. Skin under your nails was definitely yours. How's it feeling, by the way?"

"Like bark," I said. "But I'm growing a beard so I won't scare the kiddies out on the street."

"I'd go for the plastic surgery," Sax said. "Navarro says it's no big deal and you're like new."

"I'll see when the time comes," I said. "For the moment, this is better than shaving."

"Anyway, there's more on this GBH. As far as euphoria, Navarro said he can't tell about that. There was nothing broken in the condo except your laptop and he says if you'd been euphoric you would've smashed a lot more things, jumped on tables, thrown stuff around. The 'I Am The King' syndrome."

"Why wouldn't I have done that if I hallucinated?"

"I don't get the exact difference but apparently there is one. It's characteristic of these date-rape drugs that they make you suggestible. Probably your Voice told you to do something and, at least partially, you went along with it. Easier, Navarro said, to get people to do that in the hallucinatory stage than when they're flying out the window in euphoria."

I shuddered.

"It was obvious you blew lunch because there was a pile of it on the rug in the living room and the lab confirmed it was yours. According to your own recollection, you went from putting the computer on your lap to sitting in the shower, with no memory in between. Navarro says all this is considered normal."

I used to think normal was a crooked politician who got away with it.

"You felt cold when we got to you. That's another symptom. But Sgt. Caldera says the shower was hot."

"I was freezing at first," I said, "and then I started figuring things out and decided I was in the shower and turned the water on. It seemed like forever but it could only have been a minute or two because I was so cold I would have shivered myself into pulling the trigger if it had been any longer. I kept turning up the temperature as time went on until it stopped the shakes."

"You were lucky that shower was voice-activated," Sax said. "Helluva gadget."

"Uncle Henry," I explained.

"By the way, Navarro's interested in buying a system like that. He wants to know where to get one."

Good lord, I thought, now I'm selling showers.

"There's another thing that squares with this GBH," said Sax. "It can seriously depress your ability to breathe. According to Navarro, a lot of people die because their chest muscles just won't work. They're like gasping fish, a simulated asthma, he said. Navarro doesn't know why this problem was so manageable in your case."

Manageable? Like finding the oxygen particles in an ocean and sucking them out hour after hour while trying not to disturb the sharks. Manageable?

"You can talk to him about it," Sax was saying. "He's decided you have a great constitution and he thinks the drug might not have all the same effects on you as on other people. The medical term is 'idiosyncratic.'"

"Isn't that to do with crazy aunts?" I asked, though I was all for being idiosyncratic if it had kept me alive.

Sax laughed. "I think that's about it for what I wrote down on this GBH drug."

"Well," I said, "I appreciate your filling me in and all."

"Hard to imagine guys wanting to use this on women with the vomit and stuff," Sax said.

"Yeah," I agreed. Wished I knew what the "stuff" was. For a start, why had I made mincemeat out of my face? Dr. Navarro told me I'd probably never know unless I wanted to undergo hypnosis or some sort of regression therapy. I thanked him and said I'd consider it to liven up my retirement years.

Similarly, why had someone crammed two computer keys up my nose? If they had to leave me a message, why not do it the old fashioned way and carve it into my chest with a steak knife?

I thought about this category of "stuff" a lot.

"Oh, there's one more thing that's come out," Sax said. "Or maybe not come out is a better way of putting it. It has to do with how they got into the condo."

"I've been wondering about that myself."

"Keep wondering. It's a big mystery. The police have the sequence down but they can't find any holes in it. You and Val left around nine a.m. with Bruno. Your little white bird"—he meant Rosario—"went out about nine-thirty. She was back in forty-five minutes and stayed until one, when she vamoosed until the next day. You got home at six, left again at seven with Billy, came back about eleven-thirty. Val was gone until the following morning. This is all from what the three of you have reported."

"Sounds about right," I said. "That doesn't mean Hannibal's elephants couldn't have come through almost anytime between seven and eleven-thirty."

"That's the thinking," Sax said. "Plus the afternoon."

"All right. But there was security. Were the guards in on it?"

"Obviously, that's what the police suspected. But their records all came up clean, same with police interviews. That police big shot who was there at the condo—Sanchez—it killed him to find nothing on those guys."

I cast my mind back to the night it had all happened. "When Billy and I came back at eleven-thirty, one of them was nodding off but he rallied after a minute. The other one was nowhere to be seen. Probably taking a piss."

"According to the condominium guards, they were snap-to-it alert the whole time, naturally. They claim they gave everybody a good look-over. I personally don't buy it. There was a party that night. The guards say they inspected all the guests, but there's no real way to tell how they actually handled them."

"Wouldn't have kept a log," I said, knowing they hadn't. No one had ever made me sign in.

"Not instructed to. One item that did strike me was how often their own log shows one or the other of these guys had to leave the desk. Meal breaks, bathroom breaks, walking the perimeter. That would make it hard for the man holding down the fort to get a really good look at those guests, especially if a bunch of them came in together. I can see how they might decide it wasn't any big deal to let all the guests have a free pass. Why would you want to scrutinize people who were obviously going to the party? So the Voice mingles with them and scoots on in."

"Actually, I picked up on some of that, too," I said. "When Billy and I left at seven, one of the guards was on his way out. Again, maybe he was planning on checking the parking lot or walking around the building, but now that I think about it, he could've been headed for the nearest cold one."

"Wouldn't be the first time," Sax opined. "Then, of course, there's the matter of how the Voice managed to get out. Probably exited with some of the party people. The timeframe would fit."

"I don't know," I said in frustration, "where does any of this really get us?"

"Nowhere," Sax said. "The Detective Colombos are stymied, though their money is still on the guards if they can just figure out how they did it. We're turning over everything here but the sand. And still nada. Everyone's hoping like hell Hector comes up with a link or the police get lucky in one of the businesses. Other than that…"

I said good-bye on that pitiful attempt at optimism, thinking ruefully that hope was a luxury I couldn't afford. Now that the people in Panama were stumped, that left Ron and my two thousand closest "friends" to solve the mystery. In Panama they had too few suspects. In Washington, too many. Frustrated, I sipped my coffee, turned back to my list, and began chipping away at the field a little more.

The afternoon concluded differently from the morning. I looked at pages of names, tried to remember what I could, dictated answers into the recorder, but, as the hours wore on, the completed entries took longer and longer to materialize.

"Don't worry," Ron said. "It's tedious work. Hard on the brain. You made great progress this morning when you were fresh. Smart thing is to go home and get rested, start again tomorrow."

I followed Ron's advice and went back to the townhouse, braving the "wintry mix" as I walked. Now that I was feeling better, a five minute walk would beat a twenty minute cab ride any day, even if the weather was nasty.

Thomas was out for the evening, so I watched a TV show, something mindless and forgettable. Visited the bathroom, more to check out my fledgling beard than for bodily functions. Wandered the game room restlessly, looking at the items Thomas had collected.

The centerpiece of the room was a beautiful old billiards table that had once graced the house of a nineteenth century railroad baron and now provided entertainment for Thomas and his friends. Over near the sofa I'd slept on sat a round mahogany table with a mint condition roulette wheel from one of the Bond movies. It didn't get much exercise, except for an occasional turn by Val and a less occasional turn by me. A nineteenth century chemin de fer shoe rested on another table, and, near the door, waiting to greet everyone, was a 1950s-era slot machine from Vegas. Its proceeds went to stock the bar at the far end of the room. Since my favorite game was blackjack, the gadgets interested me mostly as ornaments. My only need was for an honest deck, which could be obtained at any store for a few dollars. Ditto for Uncle Henry, who'd been a take-no-prisoners poker player. His play had been elegantly wrapped but tenacious on the inside. Except for friendly competition with Val and Thomas, mine was casual in all respects.

With nothing better to do, I lost a few quarters to the bandit, spun the roulette wheel, sat down at the poker table. A fresh deck was waiting to be opened. I did the honors, shuffled the cards a few times, then dealt a hand of solitaire, and ignored it.

I was annoyed with myself. I'd spoken to Thomas as though I'd be returning to Panama soon. The words of an idiot. Go back to a place where a madman had tortured me? Where someone's head had exploded? Where the buses were named Red Devils because they killed people?

I thought about it. What was the real difference between being in Panama or Washington? Yes, all the attempts on my life had occurred there but the fact that I was in Thomas' house was testimony to believing there might be danger here as well. That being the case, did it really matter where I landed? After a long moment of consideration, I decided to lump it all and throw my life in with quantum physics and subatomic foam. There were some things I would never understand. How particles, immeasurable to begin with, could be there one second and non-existent the next. How I'd become someone other than myself in only a couple of weeks.

There was nothing to be done for it short of resurrecting Albert Einstein.

Instead, I did the next best thing and called Robyn.

Talking to Robyn was like having a shot of something exhilarating and probably illegal. We made the kind of small talk that lovers indulge in, the sort that makes you hang on every word, no matter how inconsequential. I listened and idly thumbed the playing cards.

"Robyn," I asked suddenly. "What do you know about Uncle Henry and poker?"

The question took both of us by surprise. I couldn't have said why I asked her at that particular moment. Perhaps because I was sitting in a room where so many games had been played. Or because I had glimpsed a possible loose thread that had run through my brief stay in Panama. I had been shot and assaulted outside casinos. I had been picked up, more or less, by a professional gambler. Uncle Henry had been a poker player, a superb one. And he had played in Panama.

Were these actual connections? If so, how had I missed them?

Uncle Henry had played occasionally in the casinos, Robyn answered, but hadn't liked it much. He preferred private games in *Boquete*, the mountain town where *Sophie de las Estrellas* was located.

What did she know about the people he played with? He liked them, she thought. She believed it was a friendly game, high stakes, but mostly congenial.

Did she know who the other players were? Only some first names. An Englishman named Winston. Or maybe the Englishman was Grant and Winston was American. Heinz. Some others. She knew there was a Panamanian but couldn't recall his name.

Was there anything else she could remember?

Only that Henry liked to play at Winston's house. The cook was excellent. Robyn was sorry not to have more information. She had never visited *Boquete* with Uncle Henry, as he used it mostly as a male retreat. It was all right, I assured her. I'd had an idea while sitting at Thomas' poker table. Nothing particularly important.

We talked for a few moments more, I warmed my heart on her words, and we both hung up with reluctance.

CHAPTER 42

The next morning I worked furiously, flashing through names until the sheer volume brought Ron to my office.

"Looks like somebody lit a fire under you," he grinned.

I put the list down. "I just want this finished so we can get on with it."

Ron seemed amused. "We are getting on with it. Interviews start today, among other things." He leaned his bulk against the side of my desk. "Something you're not telling me?"

"There's another possibility," I said. "In Panama." I explained my theory.

"Yeah, there could be something to it," Ron said, "but why not give it to the police?"

"I will if I turn up solid evidence," I answered. "Getting shot close to a casino only makes sense if Uncle Henry was in some kind of trouble because of the poker. Before I get the police involved, I need to make sure I'm not sending them on a wild goose chase."

Ron rubbed the top of his head and looked perturbed. "C'mon Pen, this going after things yourself is for the movies."

"I agree," I said calmly, "but in this case, there's no going after anything. Just playing a few hands of poker and having a little benign chat."

"And if one of them is the guy responsible for all this?"

"I'll sense it," I said. "I'll know."

"You could wind up dead before the police ever get near you."

"I'm going for information, not confrontation."

"That may not be your choice to make," Ron said. "Pen, take it from me, this is a bad idea."

I'd thought the thing out as far as I could, which, frankly speaking, wasn't very far. Nevertheless, I had no intention of backing down. *"Boquete* is only a sidebar, Ron, if it's anything at all. I'm convinced whatever I learn will point back to Panama City. Too much happened there."

"Damn right," Ron interjected. "You want a re-run of that?" He stared at me as though he thought I'd lost my mind. It occurred to me briefly that maybe I had.

"This is deadly serious, man. This is not some amateur sleuth thing. You leave it to the Panama police and me and you work on the list." He slid off the desk and fixed me with an uncompromising eye. "That's the number one thing you can do to help."

I stood up and shot him an icy look. Alpha male challenges had never been my thing but I also wasn't going to my corner like a good little boy.

Ron gave way first, walked over to the window, and kept his back to the room. He put his hands in his pockets and waited a few beats before saying anything. Then, he turned back toward me, slowly. His eyes were troubled, probably a lot like my own.

"Look, we need to be reasonable about this…"

I could sense the heat climbing my face. I didn't feel like being reasonable. I felt like doing something. And not being a clerk poring over names.

"I've been shot," I said, rage unexpectedly roiling up and out of my gut. "Minding my own goddamned business. I've been poisoned. Tortured. Not wearing shit-ass panties on the head crap. Not having my weenie hang out. Honest-to-God fucking torture. You think water-boarding for thirty seconds is bad? Try it for an entire night with an assault rifle propping up your jaw."

The door opened and Joy took a tentative step inside. Ron quietly waved a hand and Joy, ashen-faced, went back out.

I took a deep angry breath and slammed my palm down on the desk. "Some depraved bastard tries to kill me. My face looks like shit. I'm surprised that—that thing didn't make me eat my own vomit…" My breaths were coming hard now. "You don't have any idea what it feels like." I spat the words at Ron.

"Oh, I know all right," Ron said evenly. He stood up and my fists tightened reflexively. But his hands were going for his shirt, pulling it out from his pants, calmly undoing the buttons. He lifted it up and angled his large body toward me so I could see most of his torso.

Befitting a large man, the disfigurement was enormous. A fearsome pattern of ugly pink scars started at the left ribcage, curved around to the back, and messily joined another atrocity that began under his shoulder. There was a shorter scar, jagged and puffy, part of it sickeningly indented. Over the kidney, I saw a round puckered mark the size of a half dollar. The rest of it looked like meat that had been hacked into shreds and pulled back together in a messy alliance, despite the presence of neat tracks that crisscrossed the entire disaster and spoke of a surgeon's efforts to make it all whole again.

The butchery finished me. I sank down in my chair, drained and speechless, all fury gone.

Ron slowly buttoned his shirt and tucked it in.

"See, I do know about it," he said. "It was over six years ago but I remember it all. Yessir, I will never forget a second of that."

I swallowed, still seeing the appalling wounds where some dreadful instrument had plunged in. "How did it happen?"

"Mob hit," Ron answered matter-of-factly. "You might have read about it at the time. We had a tip, I stepped in the middle of it. A newly made guy, all hopped up, shot me in the back and then grabbed his knife and started carving. It took four Brooklyn cops to pull him off and I was almost dead when they did. I lost a kidney, two quarts of blood, was in the operating room eleven hours, intensive care for a week. It was more than a month before I could leave the hospital. When I did, they thought it was some kind of miracle. Nobody, but nobody expected me to live.

"So, I do know what you went through. The details don't really matter, it's being taken to the edge that counts. Most folks never get to that edge." He shook his head. "You and I have to live with it all, the memories…the dreams…"

Neither of us said anything for a long moment.

"I don't have dreams," I finally answered. "Not yet."

Ron regarded me from the chair.

"You just had one, boy," he said. "You just had one."

I regained my wits enough to stumble through an apology. Ron declined it with grace. "You'll get used to it. You'll see the anger coming and walk around the block to head it off. Or find someplace private where you can scream it out. Believe me, this happens to us all. Most of us learn to cope. You will, too."

This happens to us all. I had become part of an "all." There were survivor groups. I had heard of them. Sad little clusters of people whose loved ones had been murdered, women and children who'd been raped, people held hostage, tortured. I didn't want to be part of a group. Now that I had experienced it, I would know what to expect. I would intercept it, knock it down, shout it out of existence. Whatever it took. I had not been to hell and back in Panama just to start an endless replay of it anywhere, anytime. The night dreams might come for awhile and at some point play out. I accepted that. I had endured them after the Army. But I'd never been one for daydreaming my troubles and I damn well wasn't planning to start now.

The shaking rage tamed, I brought up the subject of Panama again. Ron knew exactly why I wanted to go. I could tell him until I was out of words it was to investigate the gambling, but the real motivating force he understood intrinsically. To be where the action was. To help conclude what had been the highest point of drama in my life.

"Hell yes, I understand," he said. "I won't say any more about it. Just don't do anything stupid. Remember those guys in Panama City are putting everything they can into figuring out who did this. We're working our balls off, too. More than likely, one of us will come up with an answer before long. So just be careful and if you find out anything, don't try to be a shit-all hero, let the police know right away."

"Done," I said and Ron stuck out his giant hand. I shook it sincerely and counted myself fortunate I'd gotten away as lightly as I had. The Voice had reached inside me, flicked a switch and just that easily I'd detonated. Providentially, Ron was there to knock some sense into me. The explosion could have occurred anywhere, in front of anyone, set off by who knows what. That it had happened in the privacy of my own office and in front of someone who had experienced it himself was the kind of luck I didn't take for granted.

CHAPTER 43

Thomas was at home that evening, debating whether to accept a new client (securities fraud) or turn it over to one of his associates.

"Give the case away," I said. "I'm going to Panama on Wednesday. Time for you to see what it's all about and help figure out what needs to be done. There's too much money at stake to wait any longer."

Thomas looked at me thoughtfully.

"I don't think anything will happen to you," I said. "Val and I have discussed this ad nauseam and it looks like nobody else attracts this monster's attention, except maybe by accident." I was thinking of Ignacio's murder and the poison spread on both back door handles. With the security team in place and all the protection protocols that were now being run, it was highly unlikely there'd be a repeat of that. As long as Thomas and Val kept their distance from me in public, I was pretty sure they'd be fine.

Thomas made decisions as he did everything else—with alacrity. Moments later, the accused fraudster had a new lawyer and my energetic cousin was figuratively packing his bags for a week in Panama.

I was pleased. Despite the small matter of a murderer out there, somewhere, waiting for me, everything else seemed to be coming together very nicely.

Two days and more names than I ever wanted to see again at one time, Thomas and I were on a plane to Panama. Hearing that I was leaving, Ron's crew had all booked me for face time. I stayed late both nights mining long-forgotten details, trying to force fuzzy remembrances into some kind of clarity. Old girlfriends rematerialized along with memories of joyous nights. Mr. Lee at the laundry counted my shirts with mind-numbing repetition. Candidates smiled and scowled through poll numbers, blunders, media coverage, the tense final reporting on election night. I cheered at victory celebrations. I remonstrated with myself through concession speeches. I answered queries about my cousins and vigorously protested having to do so. I second-guessed people's sexual preferences, bank balances, interest in guns. Who spoke Spanish? Who resented me? Did she have a drinking problem? Did he sleep with another woman? Where did they get their money? What did they do with it? I hope this will help, I said, but left feeling dirty, as though I'd been rooting in someone's underwear drawer.

Regardless of what I'd told Ron, going back to Panama wasn't easy. There's always unease in returning to a place where you've been hurt. You couldn't pay me to go to Iraq again even though I suffered no serious physical wounds there. Nor would I want to revisit Mrs. Garroway's seventh grade class where the beautiful and unattainable Missy Albright had reigned supreme. But to learn whether the poker connection might bear fruit, *Boquete* would have to be broached. I told myself a chance encounter with the Voice was virtually non-existent: Everyone in Panama City believed I was still in Washington, and, in *Boquete*, eight hours from the capital, my appearance would hardly be noteworthy. I owned a farm in the town. It would be normal to visit, equally logical to look up my uncle's poker group. I reminded myself for the hundredth time that I might actually find something that would help in the discovery of the Voice. Surely, my brain said, that should be worth a small trade-off in anxiety.

While I was thinking along these lines, Thomas was focused, naturally, on Fernandez-Chavira, Villaroel and Marroquin, an enterprise, in his mind, that might be anything from incompetent to criminal. At least one employee had already been the latter, he pointed out.

I blustered a bit, curiously defensive about the firm.

"Look," Thomas said, "Rodrigo and group may have done everything they're supposed to. Or, they may have let a few ends slip here and there. Marcel got away with his scam because he falsified documents and no one caught him. Why? Was he paying off the auditors? Was he paying off Rodrigo?"

I protested.

Thomas smiled the deadly smile for which he was known in courtrooms.

"Just how dirty are the waters down there?"

"Covered ground," I replied. It was my turn to tick things off. "The police, the Panamanian equivalent of the FBI,

Hector, who has feelers out everywhere. Not to mention the auditors, insurance companies, and," I said with emphasis, "our very own Val."

"Impressive," Thomas said. "But since the lawyers are holding the pie right now, who's the independent lawyer in that group? I don't see any."

He had me there. "Okay, point taken. What else?"

Thomas launched into some general legal concepts, then shifted to items more specific to us. His thought processes were clear, his preparation seemed excellent. With luck, he might vet the law firm and start on a working legal concept for our business inside a week. In tandem with Val, who was apparently making progress on all fronts.

And what would I accomplish in a week? It had better be pretty damn good, I thought. Endurance, after all, was limited by reality, and survival, as often as not, by luck. I was betting that my new theory was worth the gamble of being in Panama. At the same time, I wasn't deluding myself. If I didn't find a link in *Boquete*, I'd be faced with a daunting choice: leave the country indefinitely and hope the police eventually would apprehend the culprit. Or stay and run the risk of another encounter. The options either way were not appealing.

To leave would invariably damage my fledgling relationship with Robyn, not to mention Uncle Henry's orchard. Without my presence, the police would lose interest in the case. The Voice would stay at large. I would be in limbo.

To stay might be an even more brutal loss.

Love and death. Treachery. Riches. Despair. It sounded like an Italian opera. I laughed ruefully to myself. It definitely had all the ingredients for a great night at the theatre.

All but one.

Iago was still behind the curtain, stubbornly refusing to come out.

The arrival in Panama went smoothly. Val and Thomas left the airport for the condominium. I checked into the airport hotel and the next morning flew to *David*, which lay roughly three hundred miles to the West.

CHAPTER 44

The hamlet of *Boquete* is known as a tourism and retirement spot. My brief exposure showed me an industrious little village where visitors hiked the surrounding summits, rafted whitewater rivers, and screamed their thrills on zip lines in the rainforest. Unfortunately, my own experience there involved excitement of a deadlier sort.

My flight arrived at the coastal city of *David* in mid-afternoon, then I drove another forty-five minutes to reach *Boquete*. The center of the town sat at an altitude of 3,000 feet, surrounded by mountains of various heights, the tallest being the local behemoth, a mostly-dormant volcano known as *Volcan Barú*. Since *Barú* was a scant six miles away, it essentially occupied a seat in everyone's living room.

After receiving some dramatic sign language directions from the fire department, I ascended another thousand feet from the town, give or take a hill or valley, and arrived at my destination, the coffee farm known as *Sophie de las Estrellas*.

Panama City had been big, fast, and sophisticated. The farm was charmingly pastoral. As I pulled in, a flock of parakeets flitted lazily through the trees. Beneath them, brightly garbed Indian women walked by with crimson beans in sacks held infant-like at their waists. The mountains sported acres of tended green, and flowers, in a boisterous jumble of colors, seemed to be everywhere. I took a deep breath and inhaled it all. Until now, I'd never seen a coffee plant, had no knowledge of its cultivation, knew only that coffee was an essential part of campaign life and that I'd already consumed a lifetime's worth. Now I would see where all those midnight cups of fortifier had come from.

Aside from the deed, Uncle Henry had provided no information about *Sophie de las Estrellas*. Lacking a phone number, I had operated on the assumption that any property with a deed would be a going concern. That expectation now satisfied, I ambled around, admiring the view, until I found a man working on some equipment. I gave him my name, and asked for the *jefe*. Moments later, Martín, the broad brown Farm Manager, appeared and welcomed me as though new owners routinely appeared out of the blue. He had someone put my car away and showed me around for a half hour or so, enough to give me the lay of the land. We agreed on an in-depth tour for the following morning, then I was smoothly turned over to a round, sturdy, and likable woman named Señora Acosta, who was the housekeeper for the farm's hacienda. She, too, seemed undaunted that I had suddenly appeared on the doorstep, and cheerfully took me through the house, a generously-sized, but not ostentatious building, with white stucco walls, Spanish-style accents, and comfortable furniture. A man's house, no fuss, no frills. A retreat, as Robyn had said.

As we walked, Señora Acosta's sadness over Uncle Henry's death became apparent. She pointed out his favorite chair, touched a painting he particularly liked. Mentioned *juegos* with his *grupo*, which I took to mean his poker games. She was sorry, she told me in broken English, that he had passed on. I thanked her, registering once again the effect my uncle had had on people here in this small country.

The inside tour concluded, we went to the back of the house where a large terrace came face-to-face with *Volcan Barú*. It was a dramatic view, one not easily forgotten.

The volcano had played hide and seek as I'd driven up from *David*, not looking at all like a demon which had erupted in the time of the *Conquistadores* and buried the hills and canyons down to the sea with ash and flame and scorching lava.

A web article I'd read had explained for tourists the rapture of ascending *Barú's* peak. I'd felt a different kind of emotion viewing the evidence of its handiwork between *David* and *Boquete*. For thirty straight miles, the ground was littered with thousands of round black boulders of all sizes. They sat everywhere—in gardens, at the feet of palm trees, embedded deep in the terrain, loosely rocking to the currents of rivers. Some fields along the way had been cleared, no doubt back-breakingly. Other pieces of land were still pitted, as though the heavens had parted and rained rocks, which it certainly must have seemed to the inhabitants of this place five hundred years ago.

The magazine writer had wanted people to think *Barú* was finished with its nasty business. But a volcano in Chile had recently gone ballistic, and it had been considered extinct. That made it more difficult to pass off *Barú* as a harmless old thing living out its remaining life with moss silently filling its ancient cracks and crevices.

We studied each other for a moment, the colossus and I. It would take courage to live every day with such a titan, to acknowledge its actual potential for harm and death. Before the Voice, I would have said my courage was an open question. Normal life hadn't required it and, even in Iraq, the quality most in demand had been steadfastness, not raw bravado.

I remembered the small native houses I'd passed on the way up to the farm. Their occupants confronted the volcano out of necessity, having no choice but to be courageous as their days advanced in its shadow. For me, necessity had also produced a certain grit. My courage wasn't routinely on display as theirs was but had burst forth in a single night in a cold bare shower stall where I had stubbornly refused to stop living.

Courage, I hoped, wouldn't be fickle. It had come to me from a reservoir deep inside and stood strong. I had to believe it would remain my faithful guardian. I was afraid of the Voice in the same life-preserving way that I would be afraid—and deadly cautious—of any pernicious creature. I wouldn't want to face *Barú* every day. I didn't want to encounter the Voice any time. But however other things might worry me, the question of my courage did not. It had come before. If confronted, I'd summon it again.

I silently bid the volcano goodbye. "Let's go inside," I said to Señora Acosta, and we both turned away, toward the bright and cheerful house.

Señora Acosta unpacked my suitcase, freshened linens, and beamed happily at having someone in the house. She served me a nice dinner, and Martín returned to hand over keys. Shortly afterward they both departed, leaving me to contemplate the farm in my own way.

While the back of the house was all volcano, the front sat on a gentle rise above a narrow plateau, where large wrought iron gates had swung open to greet me, and the words *Sophie de las Estrellas* had jumped to my consciousness and from there to my heart.

My close up view from that side of the house was mostly of a lush garden. Further away, semi-obscured by a grove of banana and orange trees, was a large clearing that contained the farm management offices. Beyond that, more fruit trees and two cement houses where Martín had explained he and Señora Acosta lived with their families. After the houses, the plateau narrowed dramatically and a small path invited exploration. The path was a sham, Martín had warned. The earth there was unstable and, after a few feet, dropped off precipitously, often giving way to landslides that shot down the canyon's side. As a result, no coffee plants grew in that area, and everyone, including Martín's normally adventurous children and dogs, steadfastly avoided it.

Except for that spot, coffee bushes stood in neat rows across every visible slope. The plants were attractive, with glossy leaves and a bright red insignia of ripe berries. Here and there, I caught random flashes of color as pickers deftly culled the crop for the ripest fruit on one bush, then moved on to the next.

More distant, to the North, hidden by one of many mountains, were the guts of the farm, which I would visit tomorrow. There, the berries were received and processed, packaged and shipped. I was surprised when Martín told me a company in far-off Japan bought the entire crop.

I turned from the view and started through the house again. It was not enough merely to stroll through the rooms, I wanted to look deeper. Whatever secrets I uncovered, they were mine now. Based on Uncle Henry's penchant for puzzles, I had high expectations for finding some.

I came first to a bow-fronted drinks cupboard. Even before I rattled the handle, I realized a key was probably needed to open it. Down the hall was a study with a roll-top desk. Not surprisingly, it, too, was locked.

A search for keys in coats and jackets came up empty. I glanced in flower pots, looked in drawers, rattled cans in the kitchen. There were so many places to hide keys if a person were really serious about it. It was when I ran out of likely, and even highly imaginative spots to investigate that I remembered the keys from Uncle Henry's odds and ends box.

Unsure what to make of them, I'd put all four in a plastic bag, tossed the bag in my suitcase, then immediately put it out of my mind. Now, I walked quickly to the bedroom, found the bag in the dresser with my clothes, and carried it back to the study.

The wrought iron key was obviously too large for either lock. Same for the copper with its unusual double-cut shaft. I could tell at a glance the brass would be perfect for the desk. I slotted it in the lock and left it there while I walked back down the hall to the living room and opened the drinks cabinet with the silver key, a tiny emerald winking in my direction.

Uncle Henry had light-heartedly told Robyn these were the keys to his kingdom. I pondered that as I filled a glass with ice and added bourbon. I admired the big wrought iron key, obviously for the heavily built front door. Martín had given me a small steel one, a modern, functional implement for an old-fashioned lock. Uncle Henry's ornamental key was a fit both in size and style. I took the steel one out and left it on a kitchen counter.

That only left the copper. I passed through the house, not particularly surprised but disappointed that I failed to locate a receptive keyhole. Coming after the attacks in Panama City, any new mystery was downright unappealing. I wanted to find the part of the kingdom that belonged to the last key and have done with it.

On the other hand, I knew enough about keys to understand that double-edges often meant extra security, and a hidden site would be part and parcel of the secrecy. I thought about it as I sipped my drink and returned to the study. I could look all night and still not find it or I could wait until tomorrow and ask Señora Acosta, who would probably put her finger on it in ten seconds flat. I opted for the sensible solution, stuck the key in my pants pocket, and turned my attention to the desk.

Although Uncle Henry's riddles had been leading me around by the nose, I sensed that this place would ultimately provide more answers than questions. For a start, owning a farm required paperwork. I was betting the desk would contain it. I also crossed my fingers that there might be information about the poker group.

To my relief, the desk was bulging with goodies—papers, folders and right on top a small note which read: "Poker at Winston's. Fridays, seven p.m." It was followed by that most appreciated of all things, a phone number.

I grabbed a couple of folders and flipped through them on my way into the living room. Although mostly in Spanish, the contents seemed to be normal summaries of activity, the kind any enterprise might produce. I put them aside and sat down, dialed the number on the note, and again crossed my fingers, this time hoping Winston would be home to take my call.

He was, but he didn't come to the phone. Winston was a dog, a black Labrador who'd struck up a special friendship with my uncle. Winston's owner, Grant, was a proper sounding Englishman who had a fit of giggles over Uncle Henry's note. Grant seemed to think it "jolly" that Uncle Henry would refer to "poker at Winston's." It wasn't always, he said chuckling, but for simpatico spirits Henry and Winston, a poker game anywhere else was always a disappointment.

Once he recovered from his amusement, Grant spoke warmly of Uncle Henry. Many sympathies, he said, Henry was a great fellow, it had been a pleasure to know him. He'd been a terrific poker player as well, maybe a little too terrific at times, if I knew what he meant. Yes, I understood exactly, I responded, remembering my own humiliating moments at the hands of my uncle.

The others would be glad to know I was in town, Grant said. Had I settled in satisfactorily? Hard not to with the splendid Señora Acosta to take care of me. Did I play poker? Yes? Naturally, one would expect. There was a game tomorrow night. Perhaps I'd like to sit in? Oh, good. What luck.

Grant dictated directions that were jabberwocky to my ears but would undoubtedly mean something to Martín. I thanked Grant. I would be there tomorrow, I said, and prepared to hang up.

Yes, and, well, by the way, he interjected, not that it made any difference except…it could be…that is, there might be a difference in whether he had to go to the bloody ATM again— half the time they were out of money—such an annoyance— but would I be offended…that is to say, was I the same type of player Henry had been? When Henry was playing, he, Grant, always liked to have a little more money at the games. Just in case, you know.

I laughed inside. No, I said truthfully, breaking the bank was not part of my game. Uncle Henry had been all business about poker. I, on the other hand, was all pleasure. I would enjoy sitting down with the group and simply letting the cards fall according to luck and gravity.

Ah, said Grant, relieved, it was nice to welcome a *sociable* player. So many people took themselves too seriously. He paused. Not Henry. No, no, no he didn't mean Henry. No, Henry was simply a superb player, a natural. Not one of those intense people who stare at you all the time and make the game so nerve-wracking. I obviously was not one of those types. He could tell we would get along very well. Sociable types always did.

Still chucking, I disconnected. I had deliberately soft-pedaled my own ability to play poker. Having grown up with a top-drawer player it would be unusual if none of his talent had rubbed off. But even if I were of Uncle Henry's quality, there was no way I would let Grant and the others see it. As far as the *Boquete* poker group was concerned, Uncle Henry would remain on his pedestal and I would sit well beneath, content to watch and listen and lose as many hands as it took to learn what I wanted to know.

I put the files back in the desk, made myself a snack, read a book, and reveled in leisure. After two satisfactory hours of being involved in someone else's life for a change—Thomas Hoving, hot on the trail of major art forgers—I closed my book, puttered around some more, and finally adjourned to the master bedroom.

I took off my shoes and began to lay them on the closet floor when something caught my eye behind the row of neatly hung shirts. I thrust them to one side, exposing a flat wooden panel the size of a door. There was no obvious means of access, no handle or lock and barely a miniscule gap around the perimeter. That meant the way to open it had to be either electronic or intrinsic. I went back to the desk for a thorough search. No technical devices.

Hmm.

I crossed my fingers that the thing wasn't voice-activated, then started at the top and ran my hands all along the panel, working my way down to the bottom, feeling for any indentation or bump under the surface. My fingertips traced the crack around the board but there were no irregularities or hidden springs. I retrieved a small flashlight from my laptop case and illuminated every inch of the panel. Nothing. Tapped the wall around its perimeter. Nothing. As far as I could see, that left only one possibility. I pressed hard on the upper left hand corner of the panel. Then the upper right. Repeated the action with the remaining corners. Finally, the center. The panel stayed stubbornly in place. I was beginning to run out of spots to push when I decided to try halfway down on the right, about where a knob might be located on a door. I put my hand to the board again and applied pressure with my thumb. Perfectly balanced on its mid-point, the panel swung effortlessly towards me.

Behind it was a metal door with a center keyhole, machined for a double-cut shaft. I'd seen mid-door locks before and knew they secured multiple points on a frame. This was serious protection. I slotted in the copper key, turned, heard dead bolts retracting on all sides, and smoothly pulled the thick metal door open.

I was looking at a well-ordered gun closet with a pump action shotgun, 2 rifles, and three pistols, one a semi-automatic meant to take care of serious problems. I removed the guns one by one and examined them. They'd been cleaned and well-oiled, though not recently. I sighted each one, replaced it in its slot and turned my attention to the drawers below. Magazines, clips, scopes, mounts and various extra gun parts filled half of them; the rest were tidily stocked with ammunition. The whole thing represented a small but self-reliant arsenal, more than adequate for a farm owner who found himself somewhat isolated from town and only occasionally in residence. I wondered if the guns were there in response to an actual threat, perhaps a robbery. Or was there another, more troubling reason?

Whatever Uncle Henry had wanted with them, their find was reassuring. Despite heavy doors and an already functioning alarm system, there is nothing quite like a gun for ultimate protection. If the Voice barreled in through the front door, this time, at least, I could defend myself. And if nothing else, since I had been shot and almost murdered by a rifle, it seemed poetic justice that Uncle Henry had provided me with one of my own.

Despite that, it was a fully loaded revolver that accompanied me to bed that night. I put it under my pillow, thought briefly about the developments of the day, and, feeling the security of the hard metal object next to my head, fell asleep.

CHAPTER 45

The next morning, I called Ron, advising him of the scheduled poker game.

"That didn't take long." His voice registered surprise.

"No," I agreed. "Luck."

"Watch yourself."

"Yeah, of course."

"Still not too late to change your mind."

"We've been over this. Besides…" I described Winston and Grant and was rewarded with a boom of laughter. "Okay, you've convinced me," Ron said good-humoredly. "Just go easy and make sure we can reach you. There's a lot going on up here. Might even have some possibles for you."

"Possibles," I said, swallowing hard.

"Well, we've flagged a few folks," Ron replied, "and we could have some names worth discussing. I'm not saying for sure, you understand. This is all maybe territory."

Possibles…maybe…could have some names. It almost knocked the breath out of me.

"When do you think?" I asked tentatively.

"Oh, any time—today, tomorrow, a few days, when the people in the field finish checking. Try not to think about it.

For now, just go on about your business and if you don't hear from me later today go ahead and enjoy your poker game."

Enjoy my poker game? I credited Winston.

"Okay," I said, taking a deep breath. "You'll let me know right away?"

He would, the minute he knew anything. But in the meantime, I shouldn't expect too much. There could be any number of these "possibles" coming up over the next week or so. It was like a second or third cut. Maybe the pieces would come together on someone and Ron would need to talk to me about them again. Or maybe not. In the end, it might be nothing more than eliminating a candidate from the field. I had to remember, Ron said, this was a sorting process. We sorted until the pieces matched. If something wasn't fitting into the picture, we couldn't reshape it.

"No," I said. "I understand that."

"So just do your thing, don't worry about this, and I'll call if we come across someone you should know about."

"Right," I said.

"And, Pen—"

His voice became less businesslike.

"For what it's worth, I think you're showing a lot of balls. I've seen plenty of folks—professionals—who couldn't have handled this as well as you."

I thought of the vicious mauling Ron had endured and survived. "Coming from you, that's high praise." I was at a loss for anything else to say.

Ron sensed it. He cleared his throat. "Okay, tiger, go get 'em," he said. "We'll talk again soon."

"Will do," I answered, then dialed Sax, hoping for a double dose of good news.

Too much to ask for.

There was little to report except a small improvement in Felipe's condition, welcome but not making up for the lack of headway in other quarters.

"Hang tight," Sax said. "Nobody's giving up."

"Actually, I was thinking about something else, another possibility." I mentioned Ron's group.

"They're looking into things on the Washington end," I explained.

"I didn't know there was a Washington end."

"In case there's some connection," I told him. "You never know."

"Unh, huh," Sax grunted, "well everything helps, I guess."

On the heels of that muscular endorsement, I made my final call to Rodrigo. He was in good spirits, probably because of Val's new information. How was I recovering, he wanted to know. Good as new, I answered. My face was now under a week's growth of beard, general strength had been restored.

And himself? He told me at length about the auditors (praiseworthy), the computer wizards (indefatigable), the police (damnable bastards). Val, I gathered, had confided just enough for Rodrigo to be optimistic about recovering the money, but not enough to build false hopes on.

To be expected, Rodrigo was effusive in his praise of Val, amusingly profane when it came to the local constabulary. The police, once they stopped investigating foolishness (by that I took him to mean Fernandez-Chavira, Villaroel and

Marroquin) and concentrated on real criminals, would quickly snare the villain. Of this he had no doubt. Unfortunately, the police always began with ridiculous assumptions. It had taken several important friends to put them on the right road of thinking. Truly, it had been shocking how they'd intruded into his most private affairs.

I made a sympathetic comment or two and, after a few more minutes, Rodrigo did the verbal equivalent of stretching his body to signal the conversation's end. They missed me at the firm, he said, but everything was in order. I should come back when I felt comfortable and not worry in the meantime. I made all the right noises in response and, at that, we disconnected, and my calls for the day were concluded.

I wandered outside in search of Martín, happy to change gears and go on the tour of the farm I'd been promised. Martín, looking for all the world like a proud father, took me through the *finca's* workings step-by-step, indicating where the property began and ended (mostly over a small mountain in one direction and over some more mountains in another), and explaining the life and times of coffee farming.

I spent the morning learning about the plants, their cultivation, fruiting cycles, and picking. The afternoon was devoted to processing the beans, usually referred to as cherries. Throughout, I was offered diminutive taster's cups of the magical brew, and told over and over again: *El café de Sophie de Las Estrellas es lo mejor de lo mejor.* The coffee of "Sophie of the Stars" is the best of the best. I listened and absorbed and, while I couldn't say that raising coffee was my life-long dream, some parts of it stuck to me very comfortably. I reveled in the freedom of the day and felt no shame in enjoying myself like a kid playing with his newest and finest toy.

Back at the house with some time to kill before heading to "Winston's," I stretched my legs on the terrace and thought about the game. It had sounded harmless enough when I was talking to Grant but I wondered if I hadn't blind-sided myself into a false sense of security. What if Ron were right and one of the players turned out to be the Voice? I'd been entirely dismissive when he suggested it; now I wasn't so sure. I turned the idea over, trying to think it through rationally and unemotionally.

What did I actually know about the group? Being truthful, practically nothing. Robyn described them as "friendly," a word that could mean pretty much anything short of people beating each other up. For all I knew, the polite and pleasant-sounding Grant might just as easily be my antagonist welcoming me into a trap of my own making.

And what had I meant when I boasted to Ron that I would recognize the Voice? Did I honestly expect to hear the unisex-Donald Duck-talking-through-a-bear again? Ridiculous, when I thought about it. On the other hand, the Voice could not be everywhere. It was not hiding under the bushes. Not infiltrating every house. There was no reason to suppose it was in *Boquete* more than in any other place.

I needed to shake off my obsession and refocus on my purpose in coming here. I was looking for information. Any indication that Uncle Henry had run into trouble playing poker. Other games he attended. Most important, someone with a grudge against him who might have transferred the anger to me.

There was absolutely nothing to indicate the game had been infiltrated by a sadistic, murderous monster. My attack of nerves was unfounded. If I sensed something alarming, I could always leave the game, the farm, the town, even the country. Nothing was standing in my way.

I determined to hold fast to this point of view, went to meet Martín, who was driving me, and did my best to leave the heebie-jeebies behind on the terrace.

CHAPTER 46

Grant's house was on another coffee farm in a section of *Boquete* known as *Alto Lino*. We climbed more hills and slithered down deep valleys and found curves in places that shouldn't have had curves. A rocky and pitted side road took us to a tall set of gates and a well-lit drive landed us in front of a large house bordering a forest of coffee.

Winston, fur shining and resplendent in a red bandana, greeted the car with a wag of his tail and solemnly escorted me to the front door to meet the dapper, balding, and cheerfully pink-faced Grant. A second man at the door, Grant's height but thin and pale to Grant's roundness and high color, was introduced as Niles, housemate and partner.

Already at the table were the rest of the group: Allen, a lanky, easy-going American in his late twenties with sandy hair and green eyes; José, a cowboy-booted Panamanian who had lived for many years in Texas and preferred being called Joe; Steve, who greeted me with "G'Day Mate" and a typically broad Australian smile; and Heinz, an elegant gray-haired German gentleman who would have been Uncle Henry's contemporary.

I looked at each man as we were introduced and felt my muscles slacken. None of these people, benign to the extreme, could possibly be the Voice. There was no lion, no lair, no trap after all.

We spent a few minutes in amiable chit-chat, lifted a glass to Uncle Henry, and eventually turned our attention to the affair of poker. Knowing the kind of game it would be—Uncle Henry only played when the stakes made it interesting—I'd come with serious cash. The others were all strong players, even the "sociable" Grant. None were quite at Uncle Henry's level, but all were a good cut above average. No one seemed concerned about the sums on the table. No one sweated unduly.

The cards slapped down. I watched. I listened. I placed bets. I answered various questions. Every now and then, I asked one. Sometimes I made money. Mostly, I lost it.

Looks across the table were shared. Minds were read. "Not really a chip off the old block, is he?" "No, thank God!"

The hours passed enjoyably enough. I picked up on local gossip, learned more about the personalities behind the cards, was given an introduction to all things *Boquete,* and of course, coffee.

About halfway into the evening, we took a break to eat and I pulled out one of the pictures that had been in Uncle Henry's odds and ends box. I handed it to Heinz. "Uncle Henry left that for me."

"Well, there we all are!" Heinz said delightedly. "Imagine Henry having this photo." He adjusted his glasses. "That's me, second from the left."

Steve peered over the German's shoulder.

"I'm this one," Steve said. "Hard to tell."

"So you're the guy with the Oz flag." I laughed. "Never would have known."

"We're next to Winston over here." Niles tapped a black blob on the other side of the photo.

"Let me take a look," Allen said, holding out his hand. A moment later, his voice bore a trace of disappointment: "I'm not in it. Wasn't there that night, I guess." Allen had an attractive and attentive wife who competed with poker night, I was later informed.

"This isn't you on the end?" I said to Joe, squinting a bit at the last person in the picture.

Joe shook his head. "No, they took that before I joined the game. I haven't been here all that long."

"That's Larry," Allen said. "Hasn't been around recently."

"Not as much since he lost the game." Steve grinned. "You know about that," he said to me.

"No." I shook my head. "What game?"

There was a lot of hemming and hawing.

"Oh, c'mon," Steve said to no one in particular, "the guy knew what he was doing. He wanted to do it. Besides, he has more money than God."

"Well," said Grant, "that's true enough. But it was awfully strange. I was just as happy when he stopped playing. Henry seemed to be the only one who understood him. Difficult being put in that position."

"The guy was a rotter," Steve said to me. "Always coming in with a gutful of piss. We have a few during the game, but

Larry…" Steve shook his head. "And his playing. He was an effing maniac."

"He was that all right," said Allen.

"The good part was he usually compensated." Steve again. "He'd drop a few thousand, never notice, go on to the next game, lose big again. Strange, he wasn't a bad player when he had his shit together. If he had a good day, he could effing wipe you out. Didn't happen often, though."

Steve moved away for a minute to get food.

I thought about Larry the rotter. A poker maniac is someone who bets too much, makes unjustifiable raises, bluffs wildly, often loses big, the compensation Steve had referenced. The kind of person who has to be in on the action all the time. I wasn't surprised he'd gone away. Maniacs usually don't last long.

Steve came back munching a delicious-looking beef sandwich.

"And the game?" I prompted.

"Yeah, well, it must be going on a year-and-a-half now, right?"

"About then," Heinz said.

"One night things were really hot. Bodacious pot. Everyone had strong hands. I folded three nines. It wound down to Henry and Larry. And bloody Larry ran out of money. Stupid thing to do. We all know the rules."

"IOUs."

"Right. We run a good tight game," Steve said. "You heard it in the beginning. No markers. You have the dollars with you or you don't play. So that night, Larry was fucked.

But it was weird, he wasn't fucked drunk, he was just fucked. He should have folded and let Henry win, which Henry was going to do anyway. But no, the stupid bloke reached in his pocket and brought out a copy of his goddamn farm papers and Grant here said oh no you can't do that, and Larry said why the hell not, I can sign it right here and it's money, it's a helluva lot more money than what's in the pot. And Henry said, no, he didn't like it either. But we had a couple of other guys sitting in that night, that bloke from Canada, Brad, and an American. They thought it was pretty cool to push the pot like that. Brad, he didn't take to Larry at all. I think he figured if Larry lost we'd seen the last of him. I mean, look, the guy was queer marbles putting up an expensive piece of property like that."

"Henry didn't want any part of it," Allen said directly to me. "He was looking at Larry and telling Larry not to do it and Larry was waving the papers in the air. Everybody was waiting to see what was going to happen."

"So, did the papers go in?" I asked.

"Yeah," Steve answered, "the rotter got his way."

"It was strange," Grant said in his tidy British accent. "There was all this commotion, we were shouting at Larry just to fold, the Canadian was egging Larry on, Henry kept saying no, he wouldn't agree to it. And it went round and round and then, just like that, Larry spoke to Henry, not whispering but as though they were the only two people in the room. Which in a way they were since they were the only ones left in the game. And Larry said 'Henry, please do this for me, I'm so tired.' And then he said, 'Please,' one more time."

"Strange. And Uncle Henry agreed?"

"It took awhile but, yeah, he told Larry, if it's what you want. And then before they started playing again, he made Larry sign a note that he wasn't coerced, wasn't drunk, the usual thing, and Niles and I witnessed it."

"That's when it got really bizarre," Allen said.

"How do you mean?" I asked.

"Well, the game resumed and Larry lost like we all figured he would but it was odd as hell. It turned out Larry had a Dead Man's Hand."

I raised my eyebrows. A Dead Man's Hand consists of two aces and two eights. It gets its name from the hand Wild Bill Hickok was holding when he was shot dead. The significance of it was not lost on me. Larry had been bidding up the game with two pair. He had staked and lost his house on cards of middling quality.

Niles picked up the story. "Henry had a straight flush, ten high, so there was no question he beat Larry fair and square. And Larry never complained about it, I'll give him that."

"Absolutely," said Allen. "He pulled out the papers right away. It was Henry who put his foot down. He wouldn't discuss it anymore and Larry had to agree to see a lawyer in the morning. Larry said okay but he made Henry swear, twice, in front of us all that he would take the property the next day."

"Kangaroos loose in the top paddock," Steve said, tapping his head to murmurs of agreement.

"Where is this farm?" I asked.

Everyone but Winston turned around and looked at me.

"Oh blimey, mate, you really don't know. It's the one you're living in."

Allen took me home and I learned more about Larry. His full name was Larry Jackson and he was in his late forties, an American expat who'd come to Panama from Mexico some years earlier.

"Where is he now?" I asked. "Still in *Boquete?*"

"No," said Allen, "he's moved on. The last I heard Larry found religion and is helping poor people over at the *Frontera.*"

"*Frontera?*"

"Border with Costa Rica. An hour and a half from here. One of those hellhole spots. Larry's down there preaching the gospel to the *Indios.* He'll be back though or he'll go somewhere else. Nobody could stay in that pit forever."

I thought about border towns I had passed through and tended to agree. Still, there were some people who chose to stay. They were usually the ones who made those places the soulless spots they were. It sounded like Larry could go either way.

"How long has he been there?" I asked.

"I don't know exactly," Allen said. "Seems to me I heard it in July or August, three or four months ago, I guess."

I thanked Allen for the ride, went inside and put what was left of my poker money in the gun closet. Like a lot of players, I don't like to drink much during a game so I poured a small bourbon and went out on the terrace where the volcano was illuminated by moonlight. To my disquiet, I noticed an array of lights at its summit. Sensors.

I thought some more about the night's revelations. As Steve described the strange scene with Larry, I'd experienced a stab of apprehension in my gut. Now, I felt it again. I had come to *Boquete* to find an anomaly, a reason someone might have it in for Uncle Henry and, by extension, for me. Larry certainly appeared to fit the bill.

Larry was at the *Frontera*, Allen had said, seeming sure of it. But three to four months are a long time in a place like that. What if he wasn't there at all? What if he was in Panama City? That would cast quite a different light on things. Ron had talked about squirrelly people. The assault on me had been squirrelly. Larry's behavior in the poker game had been squirrelly. Could bitter resentment for having given away his home become murderous intent? Could the demented action of the Voice reflect a change of heart so intense it would result in torture?

According to Steve, Grant, and the others, Larry had handed over the farm unbidden. If Larry wanted to retrieve his property, why not simply buy it back? Surely, Uncle Henry would have agreed to that. And, if he hadn't asked Uncle Henry, why wait several more months, why wait for me?

And why convey the message with computer keys up my nose and an assault rifle to blow out my brains?

Steve said Larry had "kangaroos loose in the top paddock."

Grant thought Uncle Henry understood him.

Allen said he'd gone to minister to the *Indios*.

If Larry was the Voice, he was insane.

I was here in Larry's former house. Had he gone "queer marbles" over it?

Had I walked into the lion's den after all?

If so, how?

No one in Panama knew I was here but Thomas and Val. Everyone else thought I was still in the States.

Larry…the Voice. It made chilling sense.

I went back inside and locked the terrace doors. Fiddled with the alarm, checked the house, visited the alarm again. Drank a sip of bourbon and waited for it to calm my nerves.

Ron had warned me. Tomorrow I would tell him about Larry and take my chewing out like a man. Tonight I was safe enough. No one had seen Larry recently.

Reassuring.

I went to the closet, removed the shotgun.

More reassuring.

Now that I had decided Larry was the Voice, he had to be apprehended. I pulled out my phone and dialed Sax. A lot could be accomplished in his world even at this hour.

Sax answered sleepily but was quickly wide awake.

"Tell me the whole thing," he demanded, and I did.

"You have the paperwork on the farm to back this up?"

I swore at myself and hung up the phone. Five minutes later, I called back. "Okay, here's something that's similar to the deed Uncle Henry left for me at Robyn's. Unfortunately, I gave that one to Rodrigo to be checked out. Hold on, let me see the names…Henry Champion…Henry Champion again…" I flipped pages. "No Larry Jackson, no Jackson at all."

"Then it's a corporation or foundation," Sax said. "Look for those."

I did and found the answer. "What the shit?" I said disbelievingly. "The Portuguese Land Mine Removal Foundation?"

Sax chuckled. "This guy Larry, whoever he really is, has a sense of humor."

"What do you mean, whoever he really is?" I asked.

"Plenty of people use false names when they come to Panama," Sax said. "Almost a requirement for some."

"Oh," I commented tonelessly. If Larry had given a false name, he could have been misleading about other things. Such as being at the *Frontera*.

"Yeah, Panama seems to attract more than its share of con artists and crooks," Sax was saying. "A few years ago, we had a regular run on pedophiles from the States. Fortunately, the police found most of them and sent them back. But generally speaking, this is an easy place to disappear. Yeah, it wouldn't surprise me at all if Larry Jackson isn't someone else altogether."

"He has a lot of money," I said, reiterating what seemed the most important fact.

"All right," Sax said, "so we've got a guy in his forties, you said, rich, name of Jackson, gets drunk one night and—"

"No," I interrupted. "He *didn't* get drunk. That's what made it strange."

"Okay, so he wasn't drunk but he gave away this farm. What's it like, by the way?"

I gave him all the details and he whistled. "Not exactly your forty acres and a mule," he said.

"I saw some of the awards the coffee's won—worldwide awards. Number one a lot. The variety of coffee is called *Geisha*. Very rare. Sells for a hundred and eighty dollars a pound in Japan."

"Christ!" Sax exclaimed.

"I know," I responded. "It makes what Larry did even more bizarre. The main thing, can Hector or whoever you're dealing with on this now do some quiet recon at the *Frontera* and find out if this guy is really there? And if he was in Panama City the night I was booby-trapped?"

"They ought to be able to get a line on him pretty quick," Sax said. "Only a few towns on the *Frontera* are worth sneezing at. If he was in Panama City that night, they'll arrest his ass and have him under the lights in five minutes."

"I don't trust just anyone to go get him," I said. "He's got plenty of money, he's right at the border, we could lose him. I want to be there when they find him."

"One thing at a time," Sax said. "Let me talk to Hector. He owes us one for making that damned trip to the *Darien*. Maybe he has some people on your side of the country who can check out Jackson. Otherwise, the border police can do it. They're a pretty tough bunch, with all the narco traffic that runs through that area."

After that there wasn't much more to say except Sax promised to call as soon as he had information. I should count on it being a few hours, he said, get some sleep while I could in case things began to pop.

I hung up. Lord, I thought, if only things *would* pop.

CHAPTER 47

Thinking I would have no more than an hour or two until Sax's phone call, I didn't plan to sleep. Instead, I propped up the shotgun within easy reach and settled into a chair, again with Thomas Hoving and his master art forgeries. Sometime after a major fraud in Renaissance bronzes, I must have dozed off. It wasn't until seven-thirty the next morning that I woke up, shotgun still in the same position and no call from Sax.

I checked my phone to make sure, wiped the sleep from my eyes, and swapped greetings with Señora Acosta while she poured me a cup of coffee. I hit redial and listened for Sax to answer. Instead, a Spanish female voice disgorged information to ears that might as well have been deaf.

I clicked off the phone, turned back toward the kitchen, punched in the number again and, as the message began replaying, gave the instrument to Señora Acosta.

"Ah," she said brightly, *"no servicio."*

I looked at the phone and felt stirrings of anger. Immovables and unreachables do that to me sometimes.

"How long?" I asked. Señora Acosta shrugged, handing back the phone. "She don't said."

"The problem is here or in Panama City?"

Another shrug.

"Thank you, Señora Acosta," I said and stalked toward the bathroom in barely disguised ill temper. Twenty minutes later, somewhat mollified by a shower and clean clothes, I had a second cup of coffee and optimistically dialed Thomas. The Spanish woman spoke to me again.

I drank more coffee and brooded. It had been nearly eight hours since I'd talked to Sax. Too much time. Larry could be in custody. Larry could be in Costa Rica. Larry could be on his way here. A shitload of variables. Speculation was pointless. I had to reach Sax.

I tried him again. No Spanish lady—the good news. No Sax—the bad. The compromise was his voice mail. "Call me as soon as you get this," I said calmly, stifling my desire to bellow into the instrument.

Thomas was next. Once more, the Spanish lady attempted to strike up a relationship. Fat chance of that. I hung up and called Val. Finally, a human.

"Listen, I have some news," I said.

"Ah, good to hear from you, too," Val answered.

"It's only been since yesterday," I pointed out.

"A little civility never hurts."

"Screw civility. I've found the Voice. "

Val was as astonished to hear the news as I was to deliver it.

"Listen," I said, "the action's down at the border and as soon as I hear from Sax I'm probably off for there."

"First it was the jungle, now the border. Hell, you just can't get enough of the Indiana Jones shit, can you?" Val asked.

"It's a chance to nail the sonofabitch. You think I'd miss that?"

"No, I guess not," Val said resignedly. "But, I'm coming to *Boquete.*"

"And why would that be?"

"I'm coming."

"Val—"

"We all know no one's interested in me. You go nail Larry and I'll have a little R&R. The mountains sound like fun."

I sighed. "All right. You stay here at the farm. If something happens to me, you can sort out the mess. But, no screwing around and trying to come with me to the border. We need at least one of us alive to manage those businesses."

Val didn't think that was funny but he agreed to the plan. We spent a few minutes talking about the logistics, then disconnected.

I tried Sax again and took pleasure in hanging up on the Spanish lady.

Señora Acosta served me breakfast and put on a fresh pot of coffee, one hundred eighty dollar-a-pound brew that might have tasted like every penny of it if I'd paid attention. Instead I drank the coffee the way I ate the meal, gulping it down and avoiding all taste buds on the way. It could have been dishwater for all I cared. I was about to catch the Voice.

CHAPTER 48

The last hour of the morning was given over to some of the folders left by Uncle Henry. Hard going, since I stopped to try Sax about every fifteen minutes, and cursed the rest of the time. I paced the living room, wandered down to the farm office, even ventured near the unstable precipice. Eventually, I went to the bedroom, threw some things into an overnight bag and stashed it in the main hall.

After that, I camped out on the terrace, looking up at the volcano. At one point I tried communicating, but found it withdrawn, ringed with clouds at the peak, flat and static on its slopes. Definitely not in the mood for a chat. Well, talk to me or not, I'm staying on the terrace, I informed it. There was nothing quite like having one killer fill my view while another filled my mind.

No matter how I looked at it, the problem remained the same. Larry was the killer. I was sure of that. But I didn't know where he was at the *Frontera*. I needed Hector to do the recon and Sax to give it to me. Until then, I was stymied.

Sometime during the morning, I restored the shotgun to its rack and removed the pistol. For awhile, I left it on top of Thomas Hoving, but, as I began to move around, it joined me, tucked at my waist. Señora Acosta crossed my path a time or two but if she thought it was odd, she gave no sign of it. Around twelve-thirty, the phone rang. Even though I was used to the ring-tone—the finale of Tchaikovsky's "1812 Overture," complete with cannons—it startled me. I leapt on it and excitedly pushed buttons, after several attempts, even the right one.

It was Val letting me know he was at the airport, he'd talked to Thomas, and the rental car in David was reserved.

I got off the phone, dialed Sax again, and listened to the Spanish lady, who at that instant became my most detested enemy.

Señora Acosta served lunch and was disappointed when I left it largely untasted.

"My stomach," I told her. Partial truth at least.

That had not been the thing to say.

I soon found myself bombarded with powders, pills, even a heating pad.

Poor Señora Acosta, I thought in a calm moment. She was lucky enough to have a rational, courteous fellow like Uncle Henry for several years, now she had me, on the way to becoming a nervous wreck.

I smiled at her wanly and accepted a powdered remedy.

By one o'clock I was seriously pissed off. Had Señora Acosta looked toward the terrace she would have seen me pacing back and forth, constantly checking the phone, responding to the results with disgust.

Finally, determined to do something worthwhile, I returned the pistol to the gun case and sat down with Uncle Henry's papers. They weren't particularly interesting and too many were in Spanish, but at least I was keeping myself busy. After half an hour, I came across a folder labeled "Pen," which seemed to contain miscellaneous items that were more personal in nature than the other folders.

One file detailed retirement plans for Martín, Señora Acosta, and Rosario. A second contained an envelope with a key for a local safety box. A note said it held gold coins and emeralds from Colombia. My eyebrows rose at that.

I flipped through the rest of the folder's contents, wondering what else I'd come across. Suddenly, I stopped, stunned.

One piece of paper was blank except for two sentences written across it.

Two sentences that changed everything. That explained so much. Yet suddenly explained nothing.

I stared at the paper, grabbed my car keys and left the house.

CHAPTER 49

The map I'd hurriedly asked Martín to draw showed my destination about forty minutes down the mountain and another hour westward on the Pan-American. It was the border town of *Paso Rocosas*, a grimy little strip of cantinas, shops, and open-sided markets, all overlaid with Reggae music and a distinctive, unpleasant smell.

As I drove, I thought about the implications of what I'd just learned, thought some more about last night's poker game, about the *finca* named after my mother, about the Voice that had spoken to me on a cold, terrifying night. I tried, without success, to tie it all together in a package that didn't have any sharp edges poking out. Unfortunately, I was now almost certain that wasn't going to happen. As much as I didn't want to accept it, it looked like there were two packages, not one.

I parked the car and tried Sax one last time. When there was no answer, I got out and was immediately besieged by a gang of urchins selling and begging, mostly trying to slip tiny, nimble fingers around my wallet. Knowing that if I didn't shrug them off they'd be like locusts, I regretfully ignored them and walked down the first street I came to.

It wasn't long before that street ran into another. I concentrated on finding the landmarks Sax had given me. There was the store called "Texas." A right just afterwards…around another corner…looking for a tin house with a corrugated roof anciently painted half red, half blue. There was no parking on these streets and no street signs. Forget about house numbers.

A barefoot, bare-chested young boy had followed me when the others had given up. He chattered at my side, asking questions I couldn't understand, gesturing toward places I didn't want to see. I kept my eyes open for the house but many were made of metal and most of the roofs were at least partially red.

Near the end of a dank cross-street, I found an unbelievably tiny hut, sandwiched between two others that made the wretched building I was seeking seem positively palatial.

I stopped and looked at it.

"Papa Lah-ree," the child said and pointed.

"Gringo?" I asked.

He nodded. I dug in my pocket for change to give him, crooked my finger, and motioned for him to follow.

The door was open except for a flap of fabric. I rapped on the tin siding and a man, medium height, decently shaved, tanned but otherwise of light complexion and with eyes and thinning gray hair that matched, pulled aside the curtain and stood in the doorway.

"Papa Lah-ree!" the child exclaimed and turned the chatter in the man's direction.

"Tell him if he'll hang around and show me how to get back I'll give him some more money," I said.

The man spoke to the boy, who nodded enthusiastically, moved himself away from the door, and squatted in the street.

"Give him a dollar when you leave and he'll think he's died and gone to heaven," the man said. He looked at me and expelled breath smelling faintly of last night's drinks.

"You'd better come in."

CHAPTER 50

I entered a neat interior with a tamped-down earth floor and bars on the sole window. The furniture consisted of a neatly made-up bed, two plastic chairs, and a tiny round plastic table tilting on three legs. On one wall there was a sink. Behind a curtain, there was presumably a toilet, though I had also noticed on my walk through town the presence of a communal outhouse.

On the wall perpendicular to the sink stood a single-ring gas burner with a cylinder of propane beneath it and a metal coffee pot on top. Two nearly black bananas and a large, half-full bottle of good scotch sat next to the burner. A colorful picture of Jesus, arms outstretched, completed the scene. There was no evidence of electricity that I could see.

My host and I looked at each other for a minute, then he waved me to a chair.

"I had a visit from the police this morning," he said. "I told them I haven't been out of this place in the last three months. Strange as it might sound, I'm the nearest thing the people here have to a priest. They keep pretty close tabs on me."

I nodded. "Sorry for that. I figured it wasn't you as soon as I saw Uncle Henry's note. Although that poker game had me going for a while."

"Whatever I might be…" He didn't finish. "Drink?"

"A little too early for me. You go ahead."

"Coffee, then?"

"Thanks, I'll take some."

A clean-looking mug, some sugar— "sorry, no cream, no fridge, as you see—" and a half full plastic glass made their appearance on the wobbly table.

"Hold on," he said, "forgot to do this first." He went over to a second curtain, opened it to reveal a tiny closet, and brought out a nice-looking suitcase to stand in for the table's missing leg.

"*Salud,*" he said, picking up his cup and taking a swig.

I drank my coffee.

He cupped his hands around his glass and looked at me. His face was thin, he had wrinkles around the eyes, and the tan couldn't hide the pink sheen of the heavy-duty drinker. His eyes were curiously dog-like, without the sadness that dogs so often convey. They were eyes that said: You came to see me. Well, here I am.

"I figured you'd come one day," he said. "Sorry about Henry. I heard he passed on."

"A few months ago. Leukemia."

"Rotten stuff."

"At the funeral, the doctor told me the adult kind isn't so bad. Not really painful or anything."

"That's good."

We both took another swallow of our drinks.

"Do you want to tell me about it?" I asked.

"I guess that depends on what you want to know," he said. "There's a helluva lot I never want to tell." He made a grimace, sighed, and pulled out a cigarette.

"I've been in this shit-hole about twice as long as Henry's been in the ground, I guess. Do you know there are people here in *Paso Rocosas* who live on fifty cents a day? I didn't know that when I came here. I had some romantic notion that I would blow into town and save all the starving kids and dogs and help all the mamas and papas. Shit, you could put the whole Catholic Church, along with the Pope, in this town and you still couldn't make a dent in it. Too many people who like what they do here. It's God's truth. Some people don't know how to be anything but miserable and others don't know how to be anything but crooked."

"So you're thinking of moving back to *Boquete*?"

"Nah, Panama City, maybe, or Belize for a few months. I might even stay here, who knows?" He took a puff from his cigarette and looked at me. This time the dog eyes had a tinge of sadness. "I'm tired."

"I'm not sure I understand," I said. "I know you're John Lawrence Jackson."

"Junior."

"Junior. I know Uncle Henry found you in *Boquete.*"

"In *Boquete*?! In Paris, Amsterdam, Milan, Acapulco. Wherever I went, he found me."

"Now I really don't get it," I said.

Larry looked at me for a long moment.

"It started when I graduated from college. I had a big trust fund from my grandmother. Still do, amazingly enough. I came into it when I was twenty-two. So I did what every twenty-two year-old kid would do, I went to Paris. Found a little place on the Left Bank. Everything was cool. I could've stayed there forever. Then I hear this guy's been showing up around the neighborhood, asking questions about me. I was scared shitless. I had no idea who he was or why he was interested in me. I thought maybe the police, for drugs, you know. Well, I waited for something else to happen but nothing ever did. The guy went away and, when my lease was up, I did, too. I decided to go to Amsterdam. I'd heard about the sex, grass anytime, any drugs, really. Nice open city. My kind of place.

"So, everything was good. I was doing more weed than booze for a change. And one day, same damn thing happens. This time, it's two Dutch guys, thugs, one of my neighbors says, and they're asking questions about me. Do you know this man? You know where he spends his time? Does he have a girlfriend? That kind of crap. And all the people are looking at me sideways like I did something wrong. But just like in France, nothing else happened. Except that these guys were toughs and they got people upset. The Dutch are like that, even in Amsterdam. The French really don't give a damn but the Dutch are different. So, I was afraid, you know? And one day I quietly got my shit together, didn't tell anybody what I was going to do, and just bolted.

"I always figured I'd go to Italy sometime so I hopped a flight to Milan and I liked it and decided to stay there a while.

But this time, I didn't rent anything long-term. I moved around a lot, stayed in different hotels and a nice hostel or two. And I was there a while, maybe close to a year, and feeling pretty good about things when it happened again. Some guy, Italian, starts asking around at my hotel about me.

"So at first, you know, I got good and drunk and I had a girlfriend and I told her about it and after that she didn't want to see me anymore. So, what else do you do? I got pissed. And I thought, okay, I don't know who you are, but I'm going any damn place I want to go and you're not going to get in my face.

"And I did for a while. But everywhere I went eventually there'd be someone who'd find me and they always made sure I knew they'd found me, they asked those questions and it got on my nerves. It was like I was never alone. Even if they weren't watching me every minute, it felt like they were.

"So about, I don't know, maybe six years ago, it changed. There weren't these guys showing up and asking questions anymore, there was only one man, the same man, and he'd go right up to my hotel or apartment building and he'd ask for me and when the receptionist said I wasn't in, he'd leave an envelope. And the note inside always said: 'Compliments of Henry.' That's all. No questions like before. Just fucking 'Compliments of Henry.'"

"So you think these other men and this Henry were what? From the same—I don't know, organization or something?" I'd thought I'd understood but apparently not.

"You've been reading too many novels," he said. "It was never anyone but Henry Champion and some local people he hired to check up on me. Once your aunt died and I guess he could move around a little more, he did it himself."

I sat quietly for a moment and forced myself to sip the coffee.

"I thought you met by chance in *Boquete*," I said slowly.

Larry emitted a harsh laugh. "There was no such thing as chance with your uncle. Wherever I went, he found me. That was his plan. For as long as he lived, he wanted me in his sights."

"In his sights," I echoed, vaguely beginning to understand.

"It was his form of punishment. The only one, he said, that was open to him."

"He *talked* to you about it?"

"Oh, we talked a lot. I told him everything. Almost, anyway. You know, I was only seventeen when it happened. The papers were full of it. A lot of people thought it was wrong that I hadn't been prosecuted but I was a kid and my dad hired a good lawyer. He told my parents to get me out of town so they sent me to my grandmother in California. He said that way I wouldn't be accessible to the media and the whole thing would die down faster."

I hardened inwardly, remembering the reporters and news cameras that had relentlessly tracked my every move.

"I can't feel sorry for you," I said.

He looked startled. "No."

"I began using the name Larry instead of John but that didn't fool Henry for long. He found me anyway and after a bunch of countries I wound up here." He waved. "In Panama, in *Boquete*, and I decided to stay. Bought some property. Became a regular citizen. Henry, he became some kind of magnate." He laughed. "I guess he figured I was here for the long haul so he might as well be, too."

"So, when did you and Henry meet up?"

"I met Henry face-to-face at a poker game. He arranged it, probably. We started talking, he dropped a hint here and there, and it wasn't long before I figured it out. At first, I was really, really angry. But, then, we started talking." He shrugged. "He wanted to listen as much as I wanted to talk.

"Look, I'm a drunk, I admit it. I've been to a gazillion fuck-all programs and I'm still a drunk. I just wanted some peace in my life, a place where I could retreat for awhile."

The word "retreat" stung. Was that why Uncle Henry had called *Boquete* his retreat?

"You named the farm."

"Yeah, I did."

"And you lost the game deliberately. Why?"

This time he paused. "I was tired of feeling guilty. I'd been a kid, for Christ's sake. I didn't mean to kill your parents. But I did and I've paid the price every day, every single fucking day."

The pink/tan skin now showed a tinge of red. There was a slight whine in Larry's voice. "You don't know what it's like," he said.

I thought about walking out the door. I only stayed because I had come to get the story and it wasn't complete yet.

"I lost because I lost," Larry said and I knew he wasn't talking only about cards. "Henry had beaten me. He understood what kind of person I am. He knew that if no one reminded me of the accident, I'd stick it in a corner out of the way and rationalize it."

You just did a minute ago, you bastard, I said to myself.

"So he made me remember. And after a while it didn't matter if Henry was there or not. I remembered anyway. Every day.

"I even remembered you, Pen, because Henry talked about you."

It was too much. My face showed it, I suppose.

"Oh yeah, Henry was a genius at torture." He laughed bitterly. "In another time, he'd have invented the rack. In this one, he just used it."

I wasn't falling for the self-pity. I'd been on the receiving end of enough evil and self-centeredness to last a lifetime. This man killed my parents but never sent as much as a postcard expressing remorse. It was only because of Uncle Henry— deep and heroic in ways I could not have imagined—that this miserable specimen across from me could even accept his responsibility.

"So you tried to bribe him with the *finca*," I said.

Larry hung his head. "I tried to *reconcile* with him, to show him through the name I gave the farm. I tried to *end* it. It wasn't a bribe."

His eyes were moist. In his own way, he was pleading with me to understand.

I understood all right.

"And did he end it?"

"Yeah." An intake of breath. "He did. He ended it completely. The only thing—" He let the air out and drank from his glass and did not go on.

"The only thing what?" I asked.

It took him a long time to answer. He put his head between his hands, got up from the table, and poured himself some more scotch. He walked over to the small bed and sat down, head bent.

"I *am* trying," he said. "I help the people here. I do try to be more than I was."

His face showed the fatigue of a man worn down by that most brutal of all battles—the fight against himself.

I looked at him hard for the first time. He was seventeen when the accident took place. Only nine years older than I was. So much pain caused by one so young. So little understanding of it, even now as a man.

"What else did Uncle Henry say?" I asked.

"It was finished for Henry. He kept his word. After we transferred the *finca*, I had a sense of peace like I couldn't remember having before. I never saw Henry again except at poker, and I pretty much stopped that after a year or so. Not that he ever took advantage of the games to say or do anything. He was a gentleman about the whole situation." Larry laughed ruefully. "Oh, but he was tough, your uncle. He was steel where it counted."

"Then what was the only thing?" I asked.

He glanced at me and shook his head. "You."

"*Me?*"

I looked at Larry.

Then I got it.

The King is dead. Long live the King.

I stood up.

"Uncle Henry gave you enough for both of us," I said. "Stay here or go somewhere else. I don't care. You won't see me again."

I could see the muscles on his face relax. It had been an insult from me. It was a benediction to him.

I walked out of the hut and found my urchin aimlessly kicking stones.

I whistled at him and was led back to my car. I reached in my pocket and, knowing it was in the despised *gringo* fashion but not caring, took out twenty dollars, which I surreptitiously wrapped into a tiny packet. I placed it in his hand and got in the car. By the time he'd opened it up, I'd already pulled out of the place and headed for *Boquete*.

CHAPTER 51

I arrived back at the farm at four, just in time to see Señora Acosta before she left for the day. At five, Val was on the phone again.

"Made it," he announced. "We're here in *Boquete* at the *bomberos*." *Bomberos* being the Fire Department.

I must have misunderstood. "We?"

"Maria and I," he said cheerfully. "I decided to surprise you and bring her with me. We also have another surprise for you." Even for Val, he sounded inordinately cheerful.

It was about fifteen minutes from the bomberos to *Sophie de las Estrellas,* assuming Val didn't go off in some strange direction, which he'd been known to do. I went out to tell Martín there would be visitors, then settled down in the living room to wait.

I was thinking again about the Voice when my phone rang, followed an instant later by a knock on the front door.

"Hello," I said. It was Ron on the other end. "Sorry," I told him, "not a good time."

Ron's voice came through the phone, emphatic and urgent.

My hand touched the doorknob.

He spoke again.

There was a second knock.

"I'll call you back," I said numbly and opened the door.

Val was on the stoop, a vibrant and sparkling Maria on one arm, Robyn on the other, the lop-sided grin more mischievous than usual.

"Surprise number two!" she said, throwing open her arms. She moved a step in my direction, wrapped herself around me and nuzzled my neck in a way that normally would have had my knees weak.

I kissed her back, my mind racing. "Go on in the living room," I said to Val and Maria, motioning in that direction, trying to recover my composure. "I'll bring some drinks."

I enfolded Robyn's hand in mine and led her down the hall to another passageway that ended in the kitchen and butler's pantry.

"Rum and tonic for Maria," Val called. "You know what I like."

"Stay here a minute," I said to Robyn, when we reached the kitchen. "I'll be right back." I walked down another hall and headed toward my bedroom, my thoughts in turmoil. When I returned, Robyn was filling a glass with ice. She looked at me, then her glance fell to the gun I held in my hand. Her eyes widened and her lips parted. "I'm sorry to frighten you," I said. "Any chance you know how to use one of these?"

She shook her head, her eyes wildly scanning the room. "Come on now, love," I said. "I'm not going to shoot you." I took the glass and set it carefully on the counter. My smile was genuine but, given the circumstances, probably not very reassuring. I took her ice-cold hands in mine and rubbed them gently. Not much help. Mine were as cold as hers. And mine were trembling.

"Something very bad has happened," I said. "I don't have the time to go into it now. You just need to believe in me and do what I tell you. All right?"

She nodded, her face taut.

"Now, listen carefully," I said, my tone as soothing as my own apprehension would allow me to make it. "Stay in here." I led her to the kitchen table and pulled out a chair. I smoothed back the bangs off her face. "Don't go anywhere, no matter what you hear. Remember when we were in the ocean? Remember, I asked you to trust me when I took you underwater?"

She nodded, her eyes bigger and bluer than I had ever seen them.

"Trust me and we'll come through this, I promise. Now, I'm going to leave you for a few minutes but I'll be back. If anything happens and you're afraid for your safety—"

Fear played across her face. "You go straight out that back door and you run as fast as you can to the first house you see, the house down the slope and straight ahead. Señora Acosta is there. She'll take care of you. Understand?"

Robyn was rigid.

I kissed the top of her head and looked deeply in her eyes. I had never felt more like taking her in my arms—or less able to. "I love you," I said, and left her.

CHAPTER 52

I walked from the kitchen to the butler's pantry and through a French door out to the long terrace that ran the length of the house. Noiselessly, I moved past groupings of furniture, a large outdoor barbeque pit, and up to the area, just off the living room, where I had spent much of the day.

"Great house," Val was saying, as I opened a set of French doors and noiselessly stepped inside the living room. Val's and Maria's backs were to me.

I gripped the pistol in my hand.

"Turn around, both of you."

They both turned, perplexed, and saw the gun.

"Val, step away from Maria." The gun was pointed directly at his head.

Val looked at me, mouth gaping. Maria was to his right, his hand resting lightly on her shoulder. His pale eyes were almost white.

I kept the gun aimed at him. "Now, Val, take a step to the left. Go on." I was harsher this time. "Do it!"

Val gulped. "Pen, this is me. This is Val. I don't know what—"

"Shut up, Val. Move to the left this minute or I'll shoot."

Val gulped again. "Ah, Pen, m-my left or yours?"

I motioned angrily with the gun. Val quickly moved one step.

"Not enough."

"You did say one…"

"Move your butt." I gestured toward a chair. Val slowly advanced in its direction.

"Sit." Val sat.

"Don't move."

"Pen." It was a plaintive sound.

"Val, do what I tell you. Don't get up. Understand?"

Val nodded weakly.

"Pen? What …?" Robyn's shaky voice came from somewhere behind me.

Val began to rise.

I waved the gun at him.

"I told you to stay in the kitchen," I said to Robyn.

"Why do you have a gun pointed at Val?" Her voice mirrored my own emotions. Anger, frustration, incredulity. Most of all sadness.

As hard as this was already, I knew the next step was going to be a ball breaker.

Before I realized what she was doing, Robyn was headed for Val. I grabbed her with my free hand and spun her down into a chair.

"That hurts!" she blurted out, her eyes throwing sparks.

"It'll hurt a lot more if you don't pay attention to what I'm telling you. This isn't about you, Robyn. Now, stay where you are and don't interfere in what you don't understand."

Robyn looked at me, disbelieving—and furious. So be it. I'd have to make it up to her later. In the meantime, there were lives to be saved—mine among them.

"Val," I said, keeping the gun on him. "We've been friends a long time, almost as long as we've been cousins. We made a blood oath when we were six, pledged our allegiance to each other, remember?"

Val gulped and took a deep, stuttering breath. "Friends…friends forever."

"So, no matter what, friend, I mean it when I tell you not to move. And you know I mean it."

Val gulped again and nodded.

I took a deep breath. My heart was pounding.

"On the other hand," I swung the pistol around and pointed it at Maria. "I would dearly love for *you* to move."

Robyn emitted a horrified cry. Val gasped and gripped the chair arms.

"Val…" I grunted, warning him.

Maria's expression, cool as always toward me, hadn't changed. Except for her eyes. If ever there was hatred, I was looking at it.

"Val," I said, "how are you?" A shitty question to ask your cousin who's just been at the point of your gun.

"One to ten scale…barely a one. What in hell do you think you're *doing?*" Val's tone was hot but it cut like ice.

There was no way except to say it. So much for cushioning the blow, preserving dignity, and all that. My needs came first this time. My own self-preservation.

"Maria is—" I shook my head. My lips were compressed so hard I wasn't sure I could get the words out. "Maria is the person who tried to kill me, Val. Maria is the Voice."

Val stared at me.

His face cracked.

"I'm sorry," I said. "And for aiming the gun at you. I had to think of a way to get you away from her. She could be armed."

I should have amended that. The Voice *was* armed—with dagger-like eyes and a cunning mind, if nothing else.

"If there'd been another way, Val, believe me, I would have done it. Ron called just when you were at the door. Bad timing. And, love," I said to Robyn, "I'm so sorry you had to be part of this."

"You can't be serious?!" Val suddenly interjected. "You said it was someone named *Larry*. You said Sax and Hector were checking him out. *Maria? For God's sake!*" His eyes showed disbelief and rage.

"Maybe Maria should explain," I replied, conscious of my cousin's pain, but also his ability to go off like a rocket if he decided his true love was being unfairly accused. I had not one volatile person to keep under control, but two. Add Robyn in there and I could only hope to keep it all together.

"Go ahead, Maria, tell Val. Why don't you start with doping me and then explain how you rigged the gun to blow my head off?" For Val's sake, I tried to sound dispassionate. Impossible.

"Don't use that tone of voice with her," Val said. He stood up, fists tight.

"Val, if I have to shoot you to make you sit down, I will." Did I actually hear Robyn snicker? It was a crazy day, now I was hearing crazy things. On the other hand, hysteria manifested itself in many different ways. I needed to hurry before the whole thing collapsed like a house of cards.

Reluctantly, Val dropped back into the chair.

"Now, let's hear from Maria," I said, looking directly at her.

"You should have died. You deserved to die," Maria said coldly, and momentarily, I was back in the bathroom, experiencing the viciousness of the Voice all over again.

"But why?" Val's cry was a wail. He started to leave his chair.

I waved him back with my free hand.

Maria shifted her weight and I tapped the gun. "You know about guns, Maria. Don't make me demonstrate that I know, too."

"Oh, God, Pen, oh God." Robyn choked on the words. "Are you sure? The Voice? How can—? It was a man. It *had* to be a man."

Maria laughed, a thin, hard sound.

"You killed my sister," she spat at me. "You tortured and killed her."

"Now that's ridiculous," Val interjected, rising again.

"Do I have to tie you up?" I asked.

He slid back down.

"What does she mean, Pen? Maria, Pen couldn't, he *couldn't* torture anybody." Robyn got up and moved toward

Maria, hands outstretched, her head swiveling between Maria and me.

"Stop!" I shouted. "For God's sake, Robyn, don't go any closer. This woman is a cold-blooded murderer. She's the one who killed Ignacio and attacked me."

Robyn halted mid-stride.

"Don't believe him," Maria said. "He murdered my sister."

Both Val and Robyn looked at me with bewilderment. I was lucky Maria's accusations hadn't caught me off guard. Ron had already sketched out the horrible story.

"I didn't do anything like that," I said. "Your sister and I went out together a few times. That was it."

As I spoke, Maria's face hardened and her skin turned an ugly mottled crimson. "You promised to marry her. You left her. You refused her emails, her calls, you wouldn't answer your door…"

I looked at her, tired now, wishing the whole thing were over.

"She was devastated! You—you abandoned her. You made her feel dirty, pathetic."

Val sat with a horrified look on his face. "What are you talking about? Who is your sister? How does Pen know her?"

The question was addressed to Maria but I answered. "I knew Maria's sister briefly, about a year ago."

"No! It was not briefly. *Months*." The words were hurled at me.

I spoke as calmly as I could, knowing what lay behind her outburst. "I saw your sister during the last two months of a campaign. Val, you know what that's like for me. Depending on the election, I might have a few hours here or there or no free time at all. No matter what, the last month, I'm all business. So, Maria, I might have gone out with your sister, let's say, four times, she might have stopped by headquarters once or twice, that's all.

"*No!*"

"Yes," I said. "You see, we have log books on campaigns, very extensive records of where people are. The log books say I was out of town for most of that election. I just didn't have the opportunity to see your sister any more than I did."

"*You're lying! You cocksucker sonofabitch!*"

"I'm sorry, Maria, you have to accept it. We had a few dates and when the election was over, we said goodbye and I left town. The relationship, if you can even call it that, was over.

"You never answered her! She *tried…*"

"I explained I was going on vacation. She knew she couldn't reach me."

"She killed herself because of you, you *bastard*," Maria hissed, so venomously her face contorted. Val sat up in his chair like he had a cow prod up his ass. The outside of the well-groomed, attractive woman had turned into the convulsed, hate-filled person she was inside.

"No," I said, "I'm truly sorry about what happened to her. But it wasn't because of anything I led her to believe. I liked her. I was honest with her—even if she wasn't with herself."

"She put...a rifle between her legs... she taped it under her jaw...there was a bottle of valium. The last thing she did...she *glued* her fingers to the trigger. *Glued.* Can you even imagine...?"

Actually, I could.

"The doctor said she...then she passed out...and...and the gun went off."

Val's face was thunderstruck. Robyn looked as though she might be sick.

"It was a terrible way to die. No one should die like that, least of all a nice girl like your sister. You have my deep sympathy for that." I spoke slowly. "But it was not my doing. It was not even because of me. I have an investigator in Washington. He spoke with your mother. Your mother knows the truth."

"My *mother.*" The word was a condemnation. "My mother would say anything. She never cared that my sister was dying inside. She listened to the stupid doctors. This psychosis, that psychosis. It was all SHIT. *You* were the reason. *You* made her die. So you deserve to die. You *will* die. I'll kill you. I'll make you hate every second you live and afterwards I'll kill you."

I stole a glance at Val. He was paralyzed with incredulity. Robyn was motionless, her face beginning and ending with horrified eyes.

"You understand?" I said to Val quietly, hoping his feelings would cave in the face of reason. The worst thing would be if Val thought he could intervene and somehow save Maria. He was visibly struggling, sitting in the chair, arms hugging his torso, his body pulled in on itself. For protection, I thought.

"And us?" Val asked Maria, his face screwed up in pain.

She turned her head. The look she gave him was scorching and contemptuous. She never opened her mouth.

I had hated the Voice every second since that night in the shower, but I hated her even more for what she had just done to Val. I knew her corrupted soul. Val did not. I'd thought deeply about the Voice and what kind of depravity it took for a person to do what Maria had done to me. She was tormented, yes, but still capable of extraordinarily cold and rational planning. She'd used the death of her sister to exact retribution where none was deserved. Other people would have empathized with her sister's situation, would have seen the tragedy of her inappropriate attachment to me, and would have rightfully viewed her appalling death as the act of a severely disturbed person. Maria, on the other hand, had chosen to brandish it as a sword of vengeance for an act not even committed.

I, at least, had been given a few minutes to prepare. Val didn't have that luxury. He'd been in love with Maria when he walked in the door. What right did I have to expect him to abandon those feelings in a matter of minutes? I looked at my cousin—humiliated, rejected, despairing—and wondered if I could ever make amends.

As it turned out, I had too little faith in him.

He slowly rose from the chair, arms unfolding, body straightening. This time, something in his demeanor made me refrain from motioning him back. For a long moment he stood without moving, his eyes unfocused. Then he sighed, looked into the face of the twisted, evil, grievously flawed human being before him, and said: "I want my bracelet back."

At first, I thought I hadn't heard him right and, for one brittle moment, feared I would break into laughter. Then it came to me. I had never understood Val's glittering presents, given out like so much candy. Here in front of me, I saw the reality. Val was one of those rare men who actually falls in love as often as he lusts. His present to Maria was no small token, it was a mark of deep affection. And, in one devastating, truth-telling look at Val, she had declared herself unworthy of it.

Before I realized what was happening, Maria unbuckled the bracelet and began to throw it at him.

"Stop!" I said, leveling the gun.

Maria jerked her hand and launched the object head-on at me. With no time for thought, I ducked reflexively. When my head came back up Maria was holding a small pistol, moving it back and forth between Val and Robyn.

"Don't do anything," I told them. "You're not her real target. She's only interested in me. Isn't that right, Maria?"

Val looked properly terrified. Robyn was paralyzed.

"Now," Maria said to me, "if you don't do what I say, I will shoot them."

She pointed the gun at Val's heart.

I stared at her, wondering how far she would take it, trying to think of a way to get her to aim the gun at me. Maria's lack of emotional attachment to my cousin notwithstanding, did that mean she'd be willing to murder him? I was afraid the answer was "Yes." And Robyn...I couldn't even let myself think about that.

"Drop the gun on the floor," Maria said. "Kick it toward me."

I held it pointed down and opened my mouth to negotiate for the two lives most precious to me.

"Maria—"

My cell phone rang. The cannons fired.

I lunged for Maria.

Her hand contracted and pressed the trigger.

Slowly, Val fell to the floor.

"Val," I shouted, as Maria, all in a single smooth action, ran toward Robyn, and put the gun to her head.

Everything stopped.

"Maria, you don't want to do anything foolish," I said. As though shooting Val had showed stellar judgment.

She grabbed Robyn's arm and pulled her around.

"Robyn—" I said.

A second later, the two women disappeared out the door.

CHAPTER 53

"Holy Christ!" Val gasped. "She shot me. I've been hit!"

Blood was cascading down the front of his shirt. I yanked it open and saw a red hole below the collarbone, in his upper chest. I grabbed an afghan off the arm of a sofa and pressed it hard against the injury.

"You'll be fine," I said, terrified for him and frantic for Robyn. "It's just a flesh wound." Not exactly true but I'd tell a thousand lies if they helped keep Val alive until a doctor came.

Just then Martín appeared in the room. "Señor Pen—a gunshot—"

He saw Val and stopped, his eyes growing wide.

"Martín, come over here," I said urgently. I moved away as the farm manager took over pressing the wound. "Keep the pressure on. Don't stop. I'll get Señora Acosta to call an ambulance and then come help you." I looked at Val. "I have to find Robyn, Val."

"God, Pen, go," Val said shakily. "I'll be okay."

"Car keys?"

"Pocket."

"Good," I replied, "at least Maria doesn't have that way to escape." I put my hand on his good shoulder. "Just hang in there. The ambulance will be here soon."

A second later, I was in front of the house, looking around wildly. The coffee plants stood like an impenetrable legion of fat green soldiers, occupying virtually every surface, offering perfect concealment. Jesus, I thought, they could be anywhere. Val could die while I was looking for them. Robyn could die. They both—I couldn't let myself think those thoughts. Val would be all right, I'd find Robyn. We'd all come out of this unscathed.

First, I had to get Señora Acosta to call the ambulance. I raced toward the two employee houses.

Señora Acosta was on her doorstep, calling to a pair of boys who were edging toward the end of the plateau. They were Martín's children, both in their early teens, usually a daring age. Now, their faces were stricken and they were yelling nonstop at Señora Acosta, frantically waving their hands.

I ran faster, sensing the bad news. The gate was closed. There were only two other ways out—through the maze of closely-planted coffee or on the small trail at the end of the plateau. To someone not knowing the instability of the ground, the latter would appear an inviting path.

"They go," Señora Acosta said in horror. "Joachim and Paulo scream the earth there no good, but, Señor Pen, the woman with the gun no listen, she pull the other woman, they go, and then we hear the rocks is falling down."

"Doctor," I uttered in shock. "Call a doctor. My *primo*. He's been shot."

Señora Acosta's eyes bulged. She punched in the doctor's number. A rapid conversation ensued in Spanish. "He coming, *ambulancia*, *policia*, all coming."

I walked to the edge of the path.

"Señor Pen! You no can go there!" She moved toward me.

"Is there another way to reach this part of the mountainside?"

"The bottom," she answered, "and is difficult. The women no is down all the way, no is possible. The rocks they move. You hear? No stop."

I held my breath and heard the reverberation of stones caroming off each other.

I shut my mind to the horror. The only thing that mattered was to find Robyn and take her away to safety. I hadn't heard another gunshot, which was obviously good. Now if only she'd been able to avoid the rocks and somehow hold on, maybe I could reach her. I started to make my way down when I realized I'd left my gun in the house. Shit. I turned and sprinted back to the house, the sound of a boulder oppressively thumping its way down the side of the mountain following me all the way back.

CHAPTER 54

Val was sitting up, his skin alabaster, everything sloppy wet red. I grabbed some towels out of a bathroom and tossed them to Martín, then found a jacket in the hall closet and put it over Val's shoulders.

"The doctor's on his way," I said.

"You thought…it was a flesh wound," Val panted.

"The flesh *is* wounded," I said, trying to lift his spirits any way I could. "I didn't say a bullet wasn't in there."

Val started to smile but wound up nodding, his head flopping over to one side. "Cold," he chattered. Blood loss, I thought. We have to get the doctor now. The last thing I wanted was another makeshift stitch-up job.

I darted into the nearest bedroom, grabbed some blankets, and draped them around Val's shoulders. His lips were turning blue and his face was pinched. I had my industrial pain pills with me but they took time to work. I went to the liquor cabinet instead, grabbed a bottle, and poured a stiff measure of bourbon. I fed Val sips until he'd swallowed the equivalent of a large gulp.

"Shit," he said. I interpreted that as a positive sign. The chattering subsided and a little color rouged his cheeks.

"Yeah, I agree."

"Robyn?" His pained eyes fixed on mine.

"Disappeared with Maria," I said. "Into the canyon."

"Are…they…are they…?"

I walked over, picked up my gun from the floor, and stuck it in my pocket. "I don't know. They went off a place at the end of the plateau that's prone to landslides." I looked at Val's drawn face. "I'm sorry, Val, I have to go after them. You're in good hands—" I nodded at Martín. "—and I'll be back as soon as I can."

"Go…stop her," Val groaned, and whether the groan was out of physical or mental anguish, or more likely, both, I couldn't tell. The trembling started again so I gave Martín the bourbon and Señora Acosta arrived at that moment with more towels and bandages.

"Doctor, *policia*, *ambulancia* soon," she said to me. She eased Val to the floor, put a pillow below his head, and made soft cooing noises. As I left, she was replacing the bloody shirt with a makeshift bandage, patting Val's forehead with a moist cloth, and smoothing back his precious hair.

CHAPTER 55

Martín and Señora Acosta had not exaggerated. The path went almost straight down and was an ordeal of loose soil, jagged rocks, and smooth boulders, plus an occasional outcropping of grass. Here and there trees grew up, mostly thin, unhealthy looking saplings.

I couldn't see Robyn and Maria, which left me no choice but to start descending—fast. I took a first step and felt pebbles skate away, then went into a full-fledged skid. After a few feet, I gained control and gingerly lowered myself to a sitting position. I carefully turned around so I was on my stomach, prepared to body slalom.

From here on out, everything was in contact with the ground—my head, hands, forearms, elbows, torso, knees and feet. Each one could be used to speed up or slow down momentum. At first I skidded with almost every new foothold, then I got a feel for the soil and rode out several small slides. Periodically, I glanced over my shoulder to look down. No Robyn. No Voice.

My skin was on fire, not just in the places that had already been wounded but plenty of new ones as well. My chest and arms took the brunt. Every now and then my face scraped the surface, lighting me up in pain.

As I moved, small rocks broke loose under my feet and crumbled in my hands. I didn't want to think of them striking a helpless Robyn below, but, if I were to rescue her there was no other choice. Either I went down or Robyn would die.

I scuffled with the landscape inch by inch, and, within a couple of minutes came on a ledge, about three yards wide and projecting a couple of yards into space. It seemed remarkably solid, given the looseness of the surrounding soil, but I didn't want to get fooled. I scrabbled sideways above the ledge and to its end, and began descending from there. It was then that I could see them. Maria was lying crosswise on her stomach about fifteen yards down from the ledge, one arm coiled around a rock, her legs splayed, knees bent. She was holding on with every muscle in her body—except one. The muscle that pointed her gun straight at Robyn.

Robyn was another eight feet beneath her, both hands wrapped around the base of a small, spindly tree. Her knuckles were white. She looked at me with shattered eyes.

"Don't come any closer," Maria said, turning her head upwards toward me. "I *will* shoot her."

The soil beneath my hands suddenly pulverized and I skidded down a few feet, braking with hands, feet, elbows, whatever I could use to get a purchase on the slope. Finally, I came to a halt.

Maria turned the gun on me.

"That's fine, Maria," I said, my voice shaking. "Let Robyn go and you've got me instead. That's what you've wanted all along."

Maria looked at me for a moment, then down at Robyn.

I was doing a quick calculus in my head. I had the gun in my pocket. Close but no prize. Maria would see me going for it as soon as I tried to bring it out. I'd also put the safety on. Good for shimmying down a mountain, lousy for getting the drop on someone.

Another few feet down and over to my right there was a rock about the size of a grapefruit. It looked like it was loose, on the margin of letting go and plummeting down. I shifted my weight to my right foot and hand and moved laterally. A rain of pebbles shot down the slope. Maria swung her head back at me. I tried to look terrified, which wasn't difficult.

Robyn shifted her eyes to the rock. She understood.

"I can't—I can't hold on much longer," she said. Maria whipped her head around. "Shut up."

A rock under her foot slid away and slammed into the side of Robyn's head. Robyn reflexively jerked and her eyes momentarily squeezed shut. A small whimper escaped her lips.

I tamped down on my anger, tensed my muscles and moved another few inches to my right.

Robyn spoke again. "I'm afraid, Maria. I don't want to die. Please help me." She began to weep.

Maria kept her eyes on Robyn.

I moved a foot this time. The rock was almost within reach.

Maria started to turn.

Robyn screamed.

I pressed my body to the slope as close as I could and strained the final inches to reach the rock. My fingers touched its surface. I willed the pebbles beneath my feet to stay intact. One last reach and I had my fingers around it.

Robyn screamed again.

I threw the rock with all my might.

Maria turned toward me, her mouth wide open, her eyes disbelieving. The rock caught her full in the face, its momentum enough to force her head away from the slope. One hand scraped at the soil, fingers clutching at pebbles on the move. The other hand tightened on the gun.

I shot her.

She tumbled over once, kicking up the rocks in her way, the gun coming loose from her hand. She fell toward Robyn, a jumble of limbs, and Robyn stretched out one hand to grab her.

"No!" I shouted. "She'll take you with her."

Maria's hand passed within a whisper of Robyn's and then she was gone, racing down the cliff to a cacophony of sounds from the rocks that trailed in her wake.

Robyn looked up at me. Her face reflected the horror of the past few seconds, yet her eyes were clear. Good girl. Her crocodile tears might just have saved her life.

Now I had to see about getting us back to safe ground. I was sure that Martín and the police would organize a search and rescue effort, I just didn't know how fast they could pull it together. The sun was going down rapidly. Even if we could avoid slipping away until help reached us, there would be the chill of the tropical mountains. Perhaps even the *Bajareque*, the misty rain that moves over the Continental Divide from the North. People could die from exposure, I'd read, in *Boquete's* highest elevations. The night also brought slithery things—poisonous toads and above all, snakes. The "Two-Step," so named because its victims supposedly take only two steps before falling down dead. The Pit Viper, bright, beautiful, green, and deadly. The jungle animals, too. Big, stealthy cats, wild tusked pigs. While they couldn't inflict the same level of pain, even monkeys at night would be terrifying. And the insects—scorpions, tarantulas, swarming lethal ants. I had no idea what creatures inhabited a canyon like this one at night—and I damned sure didn't want to find out.

I knew that trying to reach Robyn was liable to get us both killed. That meant I had to go up, grab a rope if Martín and the police had thrown one over, or scramble all the way to the top, if they hadn't. I was sure that Robyn would be terrified of being left alone, but the sooner I could start the climb, the more likely it was that we could get out of this mess before dark. I had to hope Robyn would understand. She did even more than that, encouraging me to go quickly, her sapphire eyes showing steel and determination.

Climbing up was harder than coming down had been. Reliable handholds were scarce to none, and no sooner would I think I had one than it would slip away in a shamble of dust and stones. After half an hour of wrenching my body upwards inch by frustrating inch, I was only back to the ledge I'd passed on the way down, with scores of holes in my clothes and bleeding scrapes underneath them to show for it. The ledge barred Robyn from seeing me so I gave her a shoutout every now and then to let her know I was still on mission. I was just getting ready to give her another one when a rope snaked down.

It was only a matter of minutes before I had it tied around me and I was slithering down the slope to Robyn. She was exactly where I had left her, hands throttling the plucky little tree that was keeping her alive. *My* tree she called it, as I grabbed her, put my arms around her, and took her away from it forever.

CHAPTER 56

By the time we were hauled up and had made our way back to the house, the ambulance had already taken Val down the mountain to *Chiriqui* Hospital in *David*. Robyn and I wanted to leave for *David* right away but the *Policia National*, who had participated in our rescue, had other ideas. There had been a gun battle. Someone had been killed. Procedures had to be followed.

Meantime, questions ate me up. Was Val all right? Had the surgeon extracted the bullet? Stopped the hemorrhaging? Robyn and I clung to each other until finally the police politely escorted us into the back of their squad car and barreled us down the mountain.

Val had been out of the operating room for some time when we arrived, the bullet consigned to history, his chest stitched. The surgeon came out and gave a brief, stern assessment. Val had been inordinately lucky. An inch or so south and he would have bled to death. They would keep him in the ICU for a day, perhaps two, mostly for precautionary reasons. A few more days after that and he could go home.

My relief was enormous, almost disabling.

Robyn and I both had our share of scrapes and bruises, which the doctor offered to clean up. More of the walking wounded, I thought as I watched him work. Would it never end?

While the doctor attended Robyn, I finally had a moment to take in what had happened. It's the end of the Voice, I told myself. The end of the fear. But at a cost. A terrible cost.

I squirmed mentally, guilt creeping in. If it weren't for me, Val wouldn't have come to Panama and met Maria. He would be smitten with a nice girl at home, someone warm and loving who would enjoy her baubles. In place of that, he'd given his heart to a callous woman who was coldly prepared to kill him even though he adored her.

Hard not to feel blameworthy for that. And there was more. I had worried about Val's safety in Panama City but blithely looked past it when he announced he was coming to *Boquete*. It didn't matter that I hadn't known Maria was the Voice or that she would come with him. I should have urged him to take the same precautions I had. At least to travel with one of the bodyguards. Just a simple suggestion from me and his life would never have been in jeopardy.

Yes, I thought, there was plenty of guilt for Pen Smith, enough to keep me replaying every decision for hours on end. I could have sat there all day, lost to absorbing regret, except that more important matters needed my attention. For one thing, Thomas and the family had to be notified. Other people would also be waiting for information only I could give them.

I reached for the phone, glanced at the display, and burst out in disbelieving laughter.

Robyn looked at me.

"It's all right." I smiled faintly. After all the futile hours trying to reach Sax, all the frustration and aggravation, his—*his* was the call that had startled Maria into firing the gun. I shook my head at the irony. But for Sax, Val would not have been shot, at least not then, and Maria would not have fled and plunged to her death. On the other side of it, Sax's phone call probably prevented a double, or even triple, murder. Incongruity was brimming over in all directions. I wondered if any of us would ever get to the point of being able to appreciate it.

The doctor finished up with Robyn. I called Thomas. After a few moments of intense agitation on his part, I cut it short. Val was doing fine, I told him. We'd be back in Panama City by the end of the week. Get the condo ready, I said. Have Rosario stock the fridge with champagne and some beautiful girls to pour it. Robyn poked me. For Val, I said. She grinned.

CHAPTER 57

In due course, Maria was officially declared dead, although her body was never located.

"The *Indios* know how to navigate some of these slide areas," said Sax, who'd joined us in *Boquete*. "She might turn up yet. Of course, given what we've seen of the site, it'll probably just be bones if they do find something. Here in Panama, bodies get eaten fast."

For my own part, it had become academic. I didn't worry at all about Maria crawling back from the dead. I believed in gravity and the fragility of the human body when a ton of rocks descends on it.

After a day and a half with us, Sax was headed for Costa Rica and a new client. A stolen car ring. Smuggling. Boring after this, he said. Before he left, I apologized for putting him onto Larry Jackson.

"Hey," Sax said, "I thought he was it, too. Shit, who'd ever have thought a *woman* for a crime like this…?"

"Speaking of a woman…" I told Sax about my attempts to reach him by phone. It turned out I wasn't the only one cursing the Spanish lady. Sax had tried to reach me to report on the result of the police interview with Larry. He had called me perhaps as many times as I had called him, and with the same level of frustration. We shared a wry laugh over that and I waved him off to his car smuggling, knowing we would probably see each other again before too long. There were some people you kept in contact with and others you didn't. It was always good to be honest about the difference between the two.

The next several days passed quickly. Robyn and I visited Val every morning. His hospital room was filled with flowers and chocolates. More than once I caught a nurse perched comfortably on the side of his bed. I ceased worrying about his recuperation and, after a week, he was well enough for us to return to Panama City.

After we got back, I told many parts of the story to many different people. Val and Thomas already knew most of it. I filled them in on the rest. After getting over his shock at what had happened, Rodrigo was incredibly relieved at Val's recovery, but sad for Maria and what he rightfully termed her "madness."

I heaped praise and gratitude on Ron and left him with a standing invitation to enjoy Panama at my expense.

Joy, I kept the worst from, though like Ron, she already knew much about the Voice and would learn the grim details sooner or later. But she was a sensitive woman, and too many people had already been damaged in this saga. At bottom, Joy was simply satisfied that life was more or less back to normal. Many things were still up in the air but, thank God, there would still be plenty of time to talk about the future.

For the three days that were left of Thomas' visit, Val, Thomas, Robyn and I made a practice of adjourning to the condominium's terrace in the evenings, spirits accompanying us. All three of them were fascinated by Uncle Henry's unique quest, as I was then and remain today.

"I don't understand how he tracked Larry overseas," Val said. "It must have been difficult. And expensive."

"I don't think so," Thomas replied. "We use investigators in our cases all the time, sometimes for years. You take a firm like Ron's, it's one thing for them to do an intensive job like tracking down the Voice, another to be hired for a task that's basically deadline free and relies mostly on in-country guys having good connections. I imagine Uncle Henry was able to get it done fairly reasonably."

"Still pretty amazing," Val said.

"To think, all those years we—you, Pen—never knew any of it," Thomas said.

"Uncle Henry definitely played a lone hand," I replied. "It was a lot like a poker game, a few strong cards, a really good bluff, keeping the other player in the game whether he wanted to be there or not. Take the guys in Europe. They never did anything except ask a few questions, but Larry turned his gut inside out over them. Uncle Henry read Larry perfectly. He didn't just have a dead man's hand that one night—that's been his whole life. All Uncle Henry did was what any good poker player would do. He used Larry against Larry."

Talking about Uncle Henry and Larry had been a good place to begin our conversations. Dealing with the Voice was harder. All of us tried to soothe Val, whose involvement with

Maria was deeper than he'd let on to any of us. The word was never actually spoken but, improbable as it seemed, it was clear he'd been hoping to marry her.

Thomas was especially confused, as we all were, about Maria's life before Fernandez-Chavira. There were a lot of questions that still bounced around unanswered. Ron was the one who provided much of the information; the police, who continued to dig, supplied the rest.

Maria's sister, Carolyn, the woman whom I had known briefly, was actually a half-sister. The father of both girls had divorced Carolyn's mother, moved to Panama to work for the Canal Authority, and married a local woman, who bore Maria. The father was an expert in using small arms in a jungle environment. He was known for taking his baby daughter to the firing range and introducing her to firearms almost from infancy. Ron had located a quite amazing photo of four-year old Maria and her father annihilating Coke cans.

As to Uncle Henry's choice of Fernandez-Chavira and Maria's job with the firm, that appeared to be a legitimate but devastating coincidence. There was no way to tell what galvanized Maria into action and whether she would have sought me out had I never gone to Panama. It was clear, however, that proximity to Uncle Henry gave her a unique opportunity and that she capitalized on it.

There were several other open questions. How Maria had eluded the guards and gained access to the condominium was a big one. In the end, the answer was simple, revealed once the police buckled down and grilled the guards again.

The key to it all had been the party. Val was with Maria at her apartment when I called that evening to tell him I would be having dinner with Alberto. In perfect innocence, Val repeated the conversation to Maria, who knew it meant the condominium would be empty, that being Rosario's afternoon and night off. She also was aware that Rosario normally didn't return until very early the following morning.

Maria had all the ingredients she needed at hand; it was a chance too good to pass up.

As the police reconstructed it, she first doped Val with ordinary sleeping pills found later in her bathroom cabinet. Val was astonished, then reflective. "I admit I felt a little hung-over the next morning," he said. "I remember thinking it was odd because I'd only had a glass or two of wine with dinner. But I forgot all about it when I got to the condo and saw what had happened to you."

Maria knew from Val that I was due to meet Alberto at seven. Her phone records showed she'd called the condominium shortly afterwards, probably to verify it was empty.

The police surmised that she waited in the parking lot until she saw a group of people approaching the building, and entered with them. Establishing through further questioning that the guards hadn't been quite as vigilant as they first maintained, the party had given Maria a cloak of invisibility she otherwise wouldn't have had. While this was an element of luck in her favor, for the resourceful Maria, if one thing hadn't worked to her advantage, another surely would have.

The police guessed that, once in the elevator, Maria had made some excuse for not getting out when the party guests did—a forgotten item in her car, perhaps. Then it was a simple matter to take the elevator to the condominium floor, and slip inside using Val's keys.

Getting the gun in was also simple. The CAR 15 is known for portability. Broken down, it's easily concealed. Maria had been to the condo often enough to know that purses and packages were not searched.

As far as Maria's affection for Val, it was easy to view cynically and assume it was all a ruse aimed at getting closer to me. It was true that she had disdained him, pointed the gun at him, and ultimately shot him. What none of us could know was whether that had been a giant bluff and she'd actually wounded him by accident. Although I believed in my heart that eventually she would have killed us both—and Robyn as well—there was no way to prove it. Val had a special charm with women that was undeniable and I couldn't swear that Maria had not legitimately been attracted to him, even while pursuing her own menacing agenda.

The day before Thomas' departure, another mystery was put to rest: The foundation's funds had been located and everyone at the law firm had been formally cleared of all charges. Fernandez-Chavira immediately underwent a cataclysmic mood change and Val became Rodrigo's newest best friend.

Tracing the enormous amounts of drug money had taken manpower. Besides Val, the computer wizards and accountants had made a contribution, while Hector's anti-narcotics task force, which had first discovered the cash movements, had located another share of the pie. Needless to say, there were a lot of happy people in Panama, though not, I suspected, where FARC lived.

I watched the fallout from these discoveries and thought about the tremendous human costs I had witnessed. Maria, twisted, tortured, and at the end crushed by forces greater than her own evil nature. Val, physically wounded and emotionally scarred as well. Felipe, more than once teetering on the edge of survival, now thankfully recovering. Marcel, blown apart by greed. Dr. Navarro, Sgt. Caldera, Sax. Three brave people in a deadly shower. Rosario, my angel. Larry, the man who had killed my parents. Robyn, my love.

And what of myself? I could bring a smile to the surface and I had stopped the habits of carrying a gun to bed and pushing furniture in front of the door. Nonetheless, something more fundamental had changed. I had shot and probably killed a woman, something impossible to carry lightly. I was no longer Pen Smith, defined by the won-lost columns of politics or the egos of Washington, DC. What I had become was not as sharp-edged as the person I had left behind. Not as certain of myself in many ways, more assured in other, perhaps more important, ones. There were plenty of gray areas I would need to examine. Such exploration, I knew, would not happen overnight. It could only be accomplished by deep withdrawals of that most precious of all commodities and one that I nearly lost in entirety—time.

EPILOGUE

A week later found me going home for Christmas. I would be coming back after the New Year, primed to take another crack at the orchard, more than ready for what would lie ahead with Robyn.

Val was going with me. He was collecting our baggage and would be waiting, along with Rodrigo's car and driver, at the condominium. As soon as I appeared, we would head for the airport.

I was busy retracing my steps, my back to nine thousand miles of Pacific Ocean, striding toward a place where I had come close to being killed and where I had begun an adventure I could never have dreamed of.

I entered a crosswalk and exited it under my own steam. I mounted the stairs at a bound, not even thinking that it had taken two strong men to drag me up them before. I easily crossed an expanse of concrete terrace and headed for an outdoor café where I had last sat in great pain and puzzlement.

My friend was there waiting for me. I had already explained on the phone that the person who'd shot me had been found and, unfortunately, had suffered a fatal accident while trying to escape. Now, under an umbrella, watching the traffic go by and enjoying a cup of Panamanian coffee, I told him more, mostly about Marcel, a little bit about Maria. I didn't share the nightmare scenario of the Voice, having concluded it was a private burden not to be inflicted on any more people.

Enriqué shook his head and pushed his thick black hair off his face.

"A woman," he said. "I never would have believed it."

"It's been hard for everyone to swallow," I told him, "but she was a crack shot, she knew this city cold, and she had a lot of freedom of movement at Fernandez-Chavira. The police have the rental receipts for the silver SUV and she confessed in front of three witnesses. There's a lot more and when you add it all up, it fits."

He nodded. "I suppose you'll be returning to the States," he said after a moment, and I wondered if I was imagining a tinge of regret in his voice. After all, how many people have a chance to play James Bond together—for real?

"Only for a short vacation," I said, "and after that I'll be back with my family to organize my uncle's companies and see what we can make of them."

"Ah," he said and sat back in his chair. "Well, I think that calls for a toast." He raised his coffee cup, smiling.

I returned the smile. "Maybe we should toast with something a little more appropriate to the occasion," I said, and hailed the waitress. I ordered champagne and she returned a few moments later with a nice bottle and two glasses.

She opened the sparkling stuff and poured and Enriqué held up his glass and opened his mouth to make a toast.

I beat him to it.

"To Enriqué Soong, without whom I would not be here today."

Enriqué grinned foolishly and watched me drink to his health.

"And," I said, raising my glass again, "to the new *Paitilla* branch of Soong & Rivera."

Enriqué looked confused.

I reached inside my jacket, pulled out several pieces of paper that Val and Thomas had put together with Rodrigo, and handed them over. Enriqué read the first page and gaped at me.

"There is no value I can put on what you did for me," I said. "But I'd like you to have this anyway, to say thank you."

"But this is—this is—"

"The agreement between Soong & Rivera and *La Fundación de hoy y del mañana*. And the second page is the sale of the foundation's entire interest in Soong & Rivera to you."

Enriqué had gone from being perplexed to looking concerned. "But how? It's really not something…" He ran his hand through his hair and began again. "I don't know where to start. This wasn't in our plans…our budget, that is…and how did you…?"

"My cousin, Val, came across it when he was working through the files at Fernandez-Chavira, back when he was tracing Marcel's activities."

"My company was part of—?" He was intently reading the second page.

"My uncle operated in mysterious ways. The people who capitalized your company were actually part of a group Uncle Henry formed. In essence, he was your partner."

Enriqué looked up.

"You have to pay me, you know. It says so right there. So hand me the dollar and let's drink some champagne."

Enriqué, eyes wide, beginning to believe, dug in his pocket for a one dollar bill. I accepted it solemnly.

I looked toward the great bay of Panama and the ocean beyond it.

"A toast," I said, "to *Del Aquí*...the Here and the Now, represented by Panama's *almost* biggest tour agency, Soong & Rivera. And to *El Más Allá*...the Great Hereafter. Uncle Henry, wherever you are, *Saludos* and God bless."

We both raised our glasses, bubbles rose into the air, and the froth of binding friendship cascaded down our throats.

ACKNOWLEDGEMENTS

Special thanks to Herta and Harley Bernbach for reading, reading, and reading; Margo Carey, Melissa Price, and Michelle Clark, my invaluable Sisters in Crime critique group, for the same; Bob and Aurora Crusoe for their proficiency in Spanish, knowledge of Panama, and help with firearms; Ellie Simon for her excellent suggestions; Alicia McGuigan for proofreading; Fran Hogan for her poker expertise; and Jeanne Saussy and Lehman Franklin for their kindness and support throughout the development of this book.

Thanks also must go to the following for providing details about the *Darien Gap*: www.panamanews.com; www.panamaguide.com; http://dg.travelnow.com *("Yaviza-- The End of the Road")*; Andrew Beatty (Reuters); Anne Stanton of www.northernexpress.com ("Panama Connection"); http://www.american.edu/TED/ice/darien.htm; Alex Sanchez of the Council on Hemispheric Affairs, www.coha.org ("Tiny Panama Roars"); The Center for International Policy; outsideonline.com; roaming.wordpress.com; Scott Doggett, LA Times; Marie-Helene Verney; Isabel Castro, La Prensa; www.outbackofbeyond.com; Moon Handbooks Panama; and www.hernanarauz.com

For anyone interested in learning the basics of rock-climbing, I can heartily recommend http://www.abc-of-rockclimbing.com, and for those who have not yet discovered the unique world of "trekking," I would like to thank and recommend Karl Bushby of Goliath Expedition (http://goliath.mail2web.com) for his unique on-line diary, with drawings. Pen's jungle suit was liberally based on one Mr. Bushby designed and used to successfully cross the *Darien Gap*.

The Thomas Hoving book which Pen so enjoyed is titled: "False Impressions: The Hunt for Big-Time Art Fakes."

Although all of the above contributed mightily to the preparation of this book, any and all errors remain solely the author's.

--Britt Vasarhelyi

12/3/2022
$14.95
AMAZON

Made in the USA
Monee, IL
30 December 2021